Donna Baker was born in Hampshire just before the outbreak of war, and is the youngest of four children. She has had a variety of jobs ranging from civil servant to matron in a girls' school. She began writing articles for magazines in 1973, moved on to short stories and has since written a number of romantic novels under a pseudonym. She is married and has two children and one step-daughter, and now lives in the Lake District where, she feels, the beautiful views and tempting walks present a constant threat to her writing.

Crystal

The Glassmakers Saga

Donna Baker

Riverside Books
Fairview Farm
Littley Green
Essex CM3 1BU

ISBN 1 904154 47 6

Printed and bound in the United Kingdom

Contents

To all my friends at Swanwick

Acknowledgements

The information on glass and the Black Country which I have used for this book, comes from many sources, the major of which include the following:

The firm of Stuart Crystal, of Wordsley, and especially Christine Golledge and the guides; Mr Jack Haden, who gave me much information and whose notes on Stourbridge in the 19th century were especially useful; Harold Parsons, whose books *Portrait of the Black Country* and *A Thousand Events in the 19th Century Black Country* were invaluable; a number of other books, most prominent of which were *The Labour Aristocracy Revisited*, by Takao Matsumura, *From Broad Glass to Cut Crystal*, by D R Guttery, *Victorian Glass*, by Geoffrey Wills, *English Glass*, by W A Thorpe, *19th Century British Glass*, by Hugh Wakefield, and *A History of Glassmaking* by R W Douglas and S Frank.

I would also like to thank my friends Eileen Jackson and Mary Pemble and my husband Peter, all of whom have given me both encouragement and practical help.

Crystal

The Glassmakers Saga

Chapter One

The Master of Henzel's died as the clocks struck three into the raw darkness of a November afternoon in 1844. And as she felt the power drain from the hand that had controlled her life, Christina came into her own.

Not that she was at all aware of it. Indeed, as she stared down at the twisted face, cullet-grey against the pillow, she was conscious only of a rising anger that threatened all her taut control, gripping her heart with a white heat that could be blazing from one of the family's own furnaces, tearing its way from her throat to burst from her lips in bitter denial.

'*No!*'

At her shoulder, she was vaguely aware of Doctor Thorpe, stepping forward to lean over the still figure in the bed. She watched him feel the dead man's chest, touch his lips and then – impossibly, intolerably – pass his hand down Joshua Henzel's face, closing the glaring eyes.

'No!' she cried again, tightening both her hands around her father's massive fingers, gripping them as though she could pump her own life back into the silent heart, will the receding spirit to return. 'No! He can't die, he can't! I won't let him!'

The doctor turned to her, his kindly face full of concern, which only served to anger her the more. 'I'm afraid there is nothing we can do,' he said gently. 'Your father is dead, my dear, and you will have to accept it.' He laid his hand gently on her shoulder, but to Christina his touch was cold, the touch of death, and she twisted violently away from it, her hair, loosened during her long vigil, flying in a chestnut cloud around her shoulders. 'Go to your room and rest,' he advised her. 'I will arrange for your maid to bring you some tea.'

1

'*Tea*?' To Christina, the suggestion was almost obscene. Tea, while her father's body still cooled on his bed? Tea, when her whole world had been taken by one corner and shaken as a maid would shake a tablecloth? 'I want to stay with him,' she said, and took up again the hand that she had dropped when the doctor touched her.

'My dear Christina, you can't, there are things to be done –'

'But not immediately.' The green-gold eyes she lifted were bright but dry, and not for the first time the doctor recognised the likeness to her father. Not in body – Christina, fully-grown now at twenty, was still barely a third the size of Joshua Henzel – but in a certain indomitability, in a certain look. And the brilliant glance that met his so squarely and commandingly, was Joshua's through and through, and as impossible to resist.

'Not immediately,' she repeated, her voice softened now, yet still with a thread of steel running through its tone. 'I want to stay with my father, Doctor Thorpe, alone, for a little while. I want to say my own goodbyes.'

He inclined his head. The idea of leaving a young girl alone in a room with death was not appealing to him, but he could not refuse her this.

'I'll notify the rest of the family,' he said quietly and, with another small bow, turned and left the room.

Christina's eyes turned towards the corner of the room where one other watcher had kept her and the doctor company for almost all of the past forty-eight hours.

'You too, Ruth,' she said, more gently than she had spoken to Doctor Thorpe. 'Leave me alone now. Go down to the kitchen, and ask Mrs Jenner to make you some broth; tell her I said you were to have it. And tell them that I am not to be disturbed for half an hour.'

The little maid came out of her shadowy corner, skirting the bed timidly, but reluctant to go.

'Are you sure you'll be all right, miss?' she whispered, her voice dry with grief and weariness. 'I don't hardly like to leave you here with – with . . .'

2

'Go and have some soup, Ruth,' Christina repeated, and her voice shook with the effort of remaining calm. 'Come to me after half an hour.' And the maid, with one final, scared glance towards the big bed, slipped like a shadow through the door.

Christina remained quite still for a moment, staring down at the body of her father; he didn't look dead at all. He looked fearsome enough, his face, already distorted from the stroke that had felled him two days ago, twisted afresh from that last dreadful spasm. But he was still her father and Christina, alone of all who knew him, had never feared him. She was not going to begin now.

'Why did you have to die?' she asked him, gazing down at the closed eyes, the ashen face. And then, her tone louder, throbbing with a bitter, angry despair, '*Why*? Why did you have to die *now*?'

Ever since early childhood, Christina had known she was her father's favourite. Always, when he came storming through the nursery door, she had been first to run to him, ahead even of her brother Frederic, thrusting her way into his arms while her elder sister, Alice, hung back timidly by their nurse's knee and Adela stared from her cot. Third of the large family, she seemed always to have been aware of him – much more than she was of her mother, the frail invalid who had lived in a shady room, to be visited for just a few moments each day, and that only when she was strong enough.

But Joshua, a swarthy giant of a man with a voice that could shake the house and send the dogs scuttling for cover, Joshua had been Christina's world. He was part of her earliest memories. He had been there when they lived in the country, near her grandparents' home, when she and Frederic had been allowed to run wild in the garden and the woods, to make mud pies and dam the trickling stream. In the mornings, she had run down in her night-gown to lift her face for his goodbye kiss; in the evenings she had swung on the gate, stubbornly refusing to go indoors until his carriage had arrived and she had been once more enveloped in his bear-hugging arms.

Leaving that house in the country and coming closer to the smoke of Wordsley, thickened by that of neighbouring Amblecote and Stourbridge, would have been more painful for Christina if it had not been for the fact that her father would not have to travel so far to the glasshouse, so that she could see more of him. And any lingering regrets she might have had, for the woods, the fields and the streams, were soon forgotten in the intoxication of discovering the world that Joshua inhabited during those hours when he was away from home.

The glasshouse! Even now, the very word sent a thrill of excitement pulsing through her veins. She remembered how Frederic had come back from his own first visit to the huge red-brick cones, glowing with enthusiasm, passing it on to her. From that moment, her one consuming desire had been to see it too, and to become a part of the world they knew. But winning the right to go into the glasshouse had come only after a long, hard fight. Even Joshua had shaken his head, laughing that great laugh of his, telling her that it was impossible, that she was a lady and the glasshouse was no place for a lady. Persistence, cajoling, all the wiles she had learned to use so successfully, none of them had been of any use, and Christina had almost despaired.

It was sheer impudence that had eventually won the day. Impudence and daring, and even now, in the first throes of her grief, Christina could smile at the recollection of Frederic's fearful doubts when she had insisted, and his relief when Joshua, inevitably discovering them, had simply flung back his head, roared with laughter and capitulated.

'Dressing in your brother's clothes!' he'd exclaimed, his voice loud enough to shatter the entire output of the factory. 'Why, you little minx!' Lips twitching, he'd

4

surveyed the two of them, caught before they'd even reached the glasshouse doors. And then, to Christina's delight, had shrugged his shoulders. 'Well, if it matters so much to you, you'd better finish the job. Come along, the pair of you. Frederic, you can show your sister what it is she apparently longs to see. Show her what buys those clothes, and all the other gewgaws and trinkets around the house.' And he had taken them both on a long and comprehensive tour of the three cones that formed the factory, explaining the entire process of glassmaking and returning them afterwards to a shocked Aunt Susan and wide-eyed Alice and Adela. Perhaps he thought that this one visit would satisfy his headstrong daughter, who would then return to the nursery, to her sewing and her dolls.

But for Christina, that first visit had been like the first taste of an addictive drug. She could not sleep that night for reliving the entire experience, seeing again the hot, dark glasshouse, populated by half-naked men who moved in muscular ballet across the shadowy floor, skin bronzed by the fiery glow of the furnaces. Lifting glowing, red-tipped spears, they had stabbed Christina's heart with an excitement from which it had never recovered. And even now, years later, she could not enter the glass-cone without a throb of that same violent delight.

She had had to fight for the right to return to the glasshouse, and if her father had failed to support her she might have lost that fight. Her Aunt Susan, who had come to the Henzel house to look after the family when Joshua's wife first took to her bed after Thomas's birth, and then stayed on after her death, had been shocked at the very idea, had tried to forbid all such visits. But Christina's obstinate determination, allied with her father's amused compliance, had beaten her.

'You'll spoil the girl, Joshua,' Christina had heard her aunt expostulate time and again. 'She'll never learn to be a lady while you treat her like a boy – taking her to that dirty glasshouse, letting her mix with all those men. Why, I've never heard of such a thing, a young girl like Christina, going into a factory, it's most unsuitable. And it will do her a great deal of harm.'

'Harm?' Joshua's shaggy brows bristled. 'How's that, Sue?'

'Why, she simply won't be fit to appear in society, that's how.' Susan, usually so submissive, had faced her brother with unusual boldness. 'Everyone will think her queer – an eccentric. What lady will invite Christina into her drawing room, knowing that as like as not she comes straight from the glasshouse? And as for marriage –'

'Do you mean to tell me that Christina will have difficulty in finding a husband?' Joshua demanded. 'With her looks? The child's a beauty already; small, I'll grant you, but a lot of men like the petite figure. And with that hair of hers – Titian, isn't that what they call it? – and those great green eyes and the way she has of using them, why, I'll not gamble on any man's ability to withstand her once she's grown.' And he laughed, filling the big drawing room with the reverberations of his amusement. 'No, sister, the problem will lie in finding a man fit to marry Christina, not the other way about. And it's a problem neither of us is in any hurry to solve,' he added, forestalling Susan's inevitable complaint that Christina ought to have a husband by now, that at nineteen, almost twenty, she was in danger of being left on the shelf. 'Christina doesn't have the starry-eyed view of marriage that you and her sisters seem to enjoy. She sees well enough that for her it would be little more than a trap, a comfortable, scented little cage. And she's right, too, dammit!' He snorted and felt in his pockets.

'Really, Joshua! A trap, a cage, what nonsense you talk. And you fill Christina's head with it, too. You'll do her no favours, you know. She'll never settle down with these silly ideas of yours to plague her.'

'And I wouldn't want her to. My Christina, sitting at

6

home all day sipping tea and gossiping with a lot of feather-brained women! It would be a waste – a tragedy.'

'The truth is,' Susan said with some shrewdness, 'that you don't want her to marry because you don't want to lose her yourself.'

At this, Joshua's laugh shook the house. 'Well said, sister! You may well be right. But no – where is that damned pipe? – I'll have no objection to her marrying when the right man comes along, whoever he may be, and he'll need to be someone very special to warrant her. Mark this, the man who does wed her will be a man who can appreciate having a wife who understands the value of his work.' He rose and searched the cluttered mantelpiece. 'He'll thank me then for the way I've brought up my daughter, and so will she.'

'I'm surprised you don't allow her to learn to blow glass herself, and make her own wedding bowl,' Susan said acidly, and again Joshua's laughter made the shimmering drops of the chandelier tremble.

'That's not a bad idea, not a bad idea at all! Don't worry so much, sister,' he said, patting her shoulder with a hand large enough to span a dinner-plate. 'Christina will be a fine young lady, as fine as you could wish; she has a natural quality, a bearing she's inherited from my dear Margaret. But she'll also have a head on her shoulders that isn't filled with nonsense. I understand her better than you do, and I know that if she doesn't have the opportunity to learn, to do something with her life, then things could go ill with her. And I'll brook no interference.' His tone changed suddenly and Susan flinched, her uncharacteristic courage wilting under his glare like a spring flower out too early. 'You'll leave me to bring up this daughter as I think fit,' he said implacably. 'You had your way with Alice, and you may do the same with Adela, should you think it best. But Christina, you leave to me.'

He left the room and Susan stared after him, unaware

that Christina herself, drifting with apparent idleness about the landing outside, had heard every word. And also heard the muttered remarks that her aunt made as soon as Joshua was out of earshot.

'Such nonsense! Joshua should know better. There will be nothing but trouble to come of it and then he'll blame –' She came to the drawing-room door and caught sight of her niece by the window, apparently absorbed in watching the clouds fly past in the wind. 'Christina! What are you doing there, child? Have you nothing to do? No work for Miss Crossley, no embroidery, no mending?'

Christina turned. She had no dislike for her aunt, only an impatience for the authority she commanded. But as Joshua had come through the door he too had seen his daughter lurking there and given her a wink that had made her want to giggle, and she knew that the days of her aunt's authority over her were numbered.

As for the authority of Miss Crossley – that never had amounted to much. The governess, joining the family when Frederic was only five, had found herself with less and less control over the headstrong second daughter of Joshua Henzel. With Alice and Adela, both docile and content to recite the alphabet, chant their tables or sit peacefully with their sewing, she had had no trouble at all. But with Christina, flying through her lessons and then fidgeting impatiently in her seat, there had been constant battles.

'Christina, please!' she would remonstrate. 'Young ladies do not twist about in their seats and stare out of the window at the gardener's boy. Attend to your lessons – have you finished those sums I set you?'

'Yes. Hours ago.' Christina would wrench her eyes away from the window with difficulty. It wasn't the gardener's boy she was interested in, but what he was doing; the freedom he had to be out in the fresh air, digging, planting, weeding. All the things that Christina's restless body longed to be doing rather than be cooped up

8

in the stuffy schoolroom with her sisters and little Harry. 'If they're right, can I go outside?' she pleaded, holding up her slate.

Miss Crossley would agree, confident that the sums she had set Christina were far too hard for the child to have got right – but to her chagrin, as often as not, right they would be, and Christina would leap up with delighted disregard for the inkpot on her desk and go flying from the room, to be seen minutes later racing across the grass in the most unladylike way, pursued by the gardener's boy whose rake she had snatched from his hand . . . Miss Crossley, defeated again, would sigh and wonder what was to become of her difficult charge, though she had to admit that it was much more peaceful in the schoolroom without Christina's presence. And when the time came to test the children, and demonstrate how much they had learned, Christina never let her down.

Christina turned and met her aunt's accusing eyes with a dimpling smile.

'I'm going out,' she answered pertly, lifting her skirts to run down the stairs. 'I'm going to the glasshouse with Papa. So I can't do any schoolwork, or embroidery, can I!'

And she had gone, scampering to join her father in the hall below, leaping into the carriage with him and her brother Frederic, leaving the house behind to go to the looming, sooty cones where her heart belonged.

And now, standing in the gathering darkness of the cavernous bedroom, with the shadows of death encroaching upon her soul, Christina dragged together all the shreds of her courage and faced the fact that her father was dead. Dead, as her brother Frederic was also dead – the two who had mattered most to her in all the world.

She was alone now, for none of the rest of her family were as close to her. There was nobody now to understand her, nobody to support her in her battle against the trappings and restrictions of 'being a lady'. Nobody now to stand beside her and fight.

The hand she held was chilling against her palm. Was it her imagination, or was it already beginning to stiffen? Christina lifted it to her lips, then laid it back, gently, on the counterpane. She stepped back, keeping her eyes on the pale distorted face.

Her anger had died a little, transmuted into a fierce determination. Joshua had taught her well, by example and by rote. He had urged her to be strong, and now was the moment when she needed that strength, when she could call on it and know that it was there.

The walls of the house had begun to close in around her, a prison of propriety. With a sudden violent gesture, Christina flung out her arms as though pushing them away.

'I won't let them beat me, Papa,' she said aloud, her voice steady with resolve. 'I'll go on as you taught me. I *won't* become a nothing – a doll. I swear it.'

But even as she turned away, hearing the timid knock on the door that signified that Ruth had come back, her heart shook a little within her. For with her father dead, who knew what would happen next? To the glasshouse – or to her?

Chapter Two

The funeral was held five days later, at the yellow-bricked church of Holy Trinity, with a bitter wind scouring the graveyard and sulky, black-bellied clouds hanging like a bruise in the sky.

The church was filled. Joshua Henzel had been an important man in Wordsley; one of the leading glassmakers, keeping himself obdurately separate from the rest of his family, determined to make his way alone even in these difficult times. He had talked to Christina many times of his desire to see Henzel's outstrip the larger company. 'Henzel's was the original house hereabouts,' he would say, gazing with grim satisfaction at the great beehive shapes of the cones. 'Once they take this damned excise off, we'll be able to expand, make lead crystal our prime market. We'll not need any Henzel cousins then, Christina my love. We'll stand alone, head and shoulders above the lot of them.'

And Christina, green eyes afire, would nod her agreement and tighten her slender hand on the iron muscle of her father's arm. If only she were a man! If only she could, as her brother had, make the glasshouse her life, go with her father every day to oversee the production of the glass, make new designs, find new markets. As much as possible she had done so, taking every opportunity to accompany him to the glasshouse, learning every stage of the making of the glittering substance that fascinated her with its strength and its fragility.

'You're as good as a son to me, Christina,' her father had told her, and she'd felt her eyes mist, knowing that he was thinking of Frederic, his first-born, the son who should have followed him into the business. But Frederic was dead, struck down by the cholera when everyone had thought the epidemics over, and of the rest of his children, Alice, Adela, Harry and poor, damaged Thomas, only Christina showed any interest in the glasshouse that provided all their living. And Christina was a girl – destined for the marriage she didn't want, for the drawing room and the boudoir . . .

Watching the deep black crepe of her aunt's heavy mourning dress sway ahead of her to the front pew, Christina felt a surge of bitter fear. Until now, her father had been her champion, laughing at her aunt's disapproval, teaching her all she wanted to know, treating her as the son he had lost. But now . . . now that he was gone?

Would Aunt Susan have been left with complete control over Christina and the rest of Joshua's children? Would the glasshouse pass to the other side of the family, the cousins who had coveted it for years, and should that be so, would they do exactly as Joshua had always believed, appropriate all the exciting, innovative artistic side of glassmaking for which Henzel's was famous, using the skills and knowledge which Joshua had so carefully amassed, to enhance their own reputation? Leaving only the mundane, everyday glassware which would do little more than provide a living for Christina and her family. The Henzel cousins had never managed to scale the heights of artistic fashion over which Joshua, with his unerring eye for beauty, his instinct for fine design, had reigned for so long. Their success lay in the production of sheet and crown glass for windows, together with a small amount of more ordinary ware; table glass for great houses, yes, but not of that sparkling, rich quality which would be brought out for a royal visit. Christina knew that their envious eyes had fallen more than once on Joshua's own craftsmen: men like William Compson and his son Joseph, Jack Haden, the Scriven brothers, Jem Husselbee. All trained glassmakers whose skill amounted to artistry, any one of whom could walk into any glasshouse and be as welcome as excise-free lead. Men who could lift the Henzel cousins from the status of solid manufacturers to brilliant innovators.

Her eyes dull with fatigue, heavy with the weeping she had allowed herself only in the privacy of her bedroom, Christina lifted her face and looked around at the family who surrounded her. Her aunt, pale and erect; her father's cousins, big and solemn, with their fluttering wives, their stiff-backed sons; her elder sister, Alice, with John, the aristocratic but inarticulate husband she had married only a year ago; Adela, three years younger and impatient to be out of the schoolroom; Harry, allowed a sad holiday from school for the funeral, white and looking as apprehensive of the future as she felt herself.

Sharply, Christina was reminded that her father's death affected other lives than hers, and she felt a momentary shame for the self-centredness of grief. She knew just what it was that Harry feared; a change in his life that was wholly unwelcome. And the others, were they afraid, too, of what the future might bring? Or were they already making plans – plans that she knew nothing of, yet might bring changes to her own life that were as unwelcome as they were unknown?

They were all dimmed by the heavy veil she wore, yet in that moment Christina saw them with piercing nightmare clarity. Not as her family, not as those close and dear to her, whom she loved, but as looming, threatening figures that closed about her. As jailers, menacing her freedom, her very life. A protective, suffocating web that fastened her with the implacable strength of a spider's silk, wound around its struggling victim.

The family filed into the pews, knelt, sat back on the hard, narrow seats. The coffin stood before them, at the head of the aisle, draped in sombre black. Christina took one quick glance, then kept her eyes fixed on her prayer-book.

She would be thankful when this most public ordeal was over. Until now, she had managed to keep her grief private, refusing to indulge in the open weeping of her aunts and sisters. Stony-faced, bitter, she had concealed her pain at their covert accusations that she felt nothing, was unaffected by her father's sudden death. If only they knew of the beast which lurked within her, alert for the least unguarded moment, ready to rip at her composure with talons as cruel as a tiger's claws. But she could not let them know; dared not reveal her precarious state, knowing that to do so would somehow put her in their power. And she had to stand alone.

Without looking round, Christina knew that the church was filled now, with family, friends, with the other industrialists of the town – ironmasters, coal-mine owners, the men who produced chains, nails and bricks as well as rival glassmakers. And with the men who worked in Joshua's own glasshouse; men who had known him since he was a boy, men who were second or third generation glassmakers, many of them descended – just as were the Henzels themselves – from the original Lorraine and Huguenot families who had first brought the skills of glassmaking to England. Some of these families still had ties with their French counterparts, keeping in touch with them just as Joshua had done all his life.

Six of the most talented gaffers, those men who worked their own 'chairs' or teams of glassmakers, were bearers. And as they came forward to lift the coffin on to their powerful shoulders, Christina raised her eyes, unable to keep her head decorously bent while her father left her to take his final grim journey. The men were dressed in their Sunday black, the stiff, uncomfortable suits they wore for church. To Christina, who had seen them in their own world, moving in and out of the shadows like bare-chested demons, they looked unnatural, out of their accustomed element. Their faces, scrubbed clean of the smoky grime which was a part of their normal surroundings, had the dull, greyish pallor that came from working long hours indoors.

Except for one. He was the last to pass Christina, bearing the end of the heavy coffin on his broad shoulder. He walked more easily than the others, as if the weight were of little account. He was dark, as dark as her father had been, but his skin was clear and freshly-coloured, his eyes a deep, fathomless mahogany. They caught Christina's glance and narrowed slightly.

Christina felt her breath jerk in an involuntary gasp. She knew this man, had seen him often in the factory, had spoken to him about the glass he was making. He had been a friend of her brother Frederic's, teaching him the ways of glass when Frederic had been little more than a clumsy visitor to the glasshouse, on holiday from school. She knew that he must have grieved with everyone else when Frederic had died. Yet he was not like everyone else. He spoke to her civilly enough, but she was always half-aware of an undercurrent in his tone, something that ran counter to his respectful words. Something that set up an uncomfortable tingle in her body, a desire to react in some reckless, violent fashion she could not identify. And he knew it. Always, he looked at her in just that way; directly, almost arrogantly, with a question in those disturbing eyes, a question he seemed to think she could answer – *would* answer.

Impatiently, Christina turned her head away. It was nonsense, this strange discomfort Joe Compson could arouse in her. After all, she really knew nothing about him – only that he was one of the best gaffers in the shop, young, talented, a master glassblower already. Beyond that, there was nothing for her to know. Between Christina Henzel and a glassblower there was a gulf too wide to be bridged. The man was over-arrogant and conceited enough to think he could look boldly at his master's daughter.

Still aware of his glance as the coffin was borne slowly

15

past, Christina felt her colour rise, her heart quicken. And then he was gone, and she realised with dismay that her father had passed by and that she had spent those last few seconds thinking, not of him at all, but of a mere employee in his factory. A man who was nothing – could never be anything – to her, yet who had succeeded in distracting her thoughts at one of the most significant moments of her life.

With a swift tilt of her head, she identified the emotion she felt as anger, the searing, white-hot flash of fury she had experienced at the moment of her father's death. An anger compounded of grief and loss and bewilderment, and a burning determination not to be overcome by it. In the past days, Christina had learned to welcome the pain it brought. It was something she could fight against; something that kept the drowning tears at bay and enabled her to hold her head high. Fiercely, welcoming it now, she bit her lips. The tears, so dangerously close to her eyes, receded, and she breathed again. But it had been an unpleasant moment, and she knew that she had come close to giving way.

And all because of Joe Compson. If her control had snapped at that crucial moment, just as her father's coffin passed her on its way to the grave, it would have been due entirely to the insolence of a gaffer's glance. And he would have been witness to her tears. She determined that he would regret this moment.

The solemn music of the organ filled the church now and the family turned to follow the coffin, the men to go with it to the graveside, the women to return home in their carriages. Christina walked thankfully beside her sisters, relieved that it was over at last, that there remained only the funeral meats to be eaten and then the reading of her father's will. That, of course, would not concern her, except in the possible size of her dowry. What would happen to the family home and the glasshouse was the business of the men of the family – her father's cousins and, ultimately, her younger brother Harry.

Christina came to the door of the church and stood for a

moment in the raw air, feeling the sly wind pull at her veil. From the hill on which the church stood, she could look down at the swarming streets of the town, see the smoke belching from the factory chimneys to merge with the cloud that hung above, threatening snow.

Once, and not so many years ago, so her father had told her, Wordsley had been a small, pretty Staffordshire village, clustered about the little hill on which she stood now. A girl standing here then would have looked down upon farmland, would have lifted her eyes to see Amblecote on its neighbouring hill and, just over the border in Worcestershire, the market-town of Stourbridge with its three fairs a year providing a day out for the whole district.

But there had been great changes since those days. A tremendous surge of energy had swept through the land, an 'industrial revolution', Miss Crossley had once called it. It had started on the farms, where an increased population had produced a demand for more food. Someone had invented machinery to assist in the increased production: machines for sowing, hoeing and ploughing; then there had been a need for better transport, to bring the food to the towns; with the sudden rise in cotton manufacturing in the towns of the north, machines had been invented to speed up the production; factories were built to make the machines; coal-mines sunk to provide fuel for the factories – and so it had gone on. Miss Crossley's lessons had been, Christina knew, much simplified. But they served to explain to a manufacturer's children why the pretty village their father and grandparents spoke of had become a densely-populated cluster of tightly-packed streets. Why, because of the coal that was needed to fire the furnaces, and the fireclay that was used to make the furnace-pots, the area around Stourbridge had been recognised by their Lorrainer forebears as being ideal for glassmaking; why so many other industries – nail- and chain-making, brickyards, ironworks

17

and forges – had grown up around the first glasshouses and turned a rural area into a smoke-darkened clutter of cones and chimneys.

Down there, amongst the crowded buildings, was the glasshouse that had been more her home than her aunt's fussy drawing room. Even as she gazed, she knew that men were working there in their rhythmic dance, passing from chair to furnace, swinging the long irons with their bulbous tips of molten glass, blowing the orange-hot spheres into the graceful shapes of bowl, jug and vase that had made Henzel's famous. Calling to each other, bawling for ale, cheering when someone carelessly dropped an iron to send bubbles of liquid fire rolling over the floor . . . Was she no longer to be any part of this? She stared down at the red-brick cones, her blood quickening as she imagined herself back in there, surrounded by the noise, the heat, the grime – and vitally, vibrantly alive as she never was at home.

Unconsciously, she lifted a hand to sweep back her sombre veil, to clear her vision of the obscuring nets. Unaware of her aunt's censorious clucks, her sisters' gasps, she clenched her fists and stood proud, arching her body like a ship's figurehead, leaning towards the smoky town beneath. Somehow, she vowed, she would remain a part of that world and nothing, nobody, should stop her. The glasshouse would remain her life, as it had always been, whatever she had to do to ensure it.

'. . . and that,' Henry Ambrose said slowly, glancing up at the silent family over his thin-rimmed spectacles, 'is the substance of Joshua Henzel's last Will and Testament.'

The silence continued for a few moments, as if everyone in the room were too stunned to speak. Christina sat with bent head, not daring to look up in case her exultation showed too clearly upon her face. Not that she was at all worried about the effect of it upon her relations, even though she knew that it could only inflame their fury, adding fire to the storm that must surely break at any moment. But until it did, she felt a desire to keep her delight entirely to herself, just for a few brief moments.

Christina had been as surprised as anyone when the family lawyer announced that she must attend the reading of the will, together with the male Henzels. Apart from Aunt Susan, who was there too as a beneficiary, there were no women present. Alice, as the eldest of Joshua's children still living, was represented by her husband John. Adela, only seventeen, had taken it for granted that she would not be expected at the ceremony of the reading. Even young Harry, nominally head of the family on his father's death, had been told that his interests would be taken care of until he reached mature years. And nobody had expected that Christina would attend. 'I'm afraid it's necessary,' Ambrose had insisted, his pale eyes magnified by their lenses. And Christina, aware of the cousins' disapproval, had followed her aunt into the library and taken her place at the end of the long table that had been brought in especially for the occasion. She had sat silent throughout the reading, listening to the long list of bequests to servants, to distant members of the family, to a few friends. These dealt with, Henry Ambrose had turned to the major dispositions, and at once the tension had increased. Still Christina had made no sound. Her eyes, dark as jade in her pale face, turned from one cousin to the other, watching as each responded in characteristic fashion to the various bequests: Cousin Harold, his big oblong of a face wooden with displeasure; Alfred, the most like Joshua, brows and lips twitching with thoughts he would not reveal; Samuel, his sharp, ferrety eyes already snapping with calculation.

'It's a joke!' Cousin Harold said at last. 'One of Joshua's jokes. I suppose he thought to frighten us all before the real will was read. A joke in poor taste, if I may say so.'

'Joshua wasn't known for practical jokes,' Reuben

pointed out, and Christina glanced at him, sitting so quietly on the other side of her aunt that she had almost forgotten his presence.

'There is no question of a joke of any kind.' Henry Ambrose's tone was affronted. 'The will was, to my certain knowledge, considered very carefully, and it was drawn up with the meticulous care that we give to all our clients' affairs.' He paused, and Christina knew that he was indicating deep offence at the idea that he might have been a party to such a 'joke'.

'But it can't be taken seriously!' Alfred exploded. 'Leaving the entire glassworks – everything – to a woman, to a mere girl, a child!' His slightly protuberant brown eyes settled on Christina, staring at her as if he'd never seen her before. 'What of Harry? Surely *he* is Joshua's natural successor. Young, I know, but he strikes me as a sensible enough lad: intelligent, respectful, perfectly able to run the glasshouse when the time comes. And meanwhile –'

'Meanwhile, who better to assist and advise him than us, his father's cousins, already experienced in glass with our own business, and on the spot to manage his affairs until he comes of age.' Samuel's sharp eyes snapped as he spoke. 'What is he now, fifteen, sixteen? Time enough –'

'Time enough to take Henzel's over completely,' Christina cut in. 'Time enough to make any changes you desire. What kind of business would Harry inherit in five years' time, I wonder? But as it happens, the question does not arise. Harry doesn't want the glasshouse. We had a long talk yesterday evening and he told me that the possibility of inheriting the glasshouse was his greatest fear.'

The cousins stared at her. Harold shrugged impatiently.

'That's just foolish talk! The boy's not old enough to know his own mind. Not want the glasshouse, indeed! And what *does* he want to do, pray?'

Christina felt a flood of relief that Harry had already

20

spoken to her. She remembered the tense anxiety in his voice, the fervour burning in his eyes as he poured out his ambitions. Too young to know his own mind? He should be here now, so that they could see and hear him as she had seen and heard him last night.

He had already seen the threat the cousins presented. For if he'd cared to pursue the matter of the will, any court in the land would have handed over the inheritance to him. And then it followed, as the night the day, that the elder Henzels would be appointed to safeguard it for him until he was old enough to take it over for himself. And that was exactly what he dreaded.

'I want to be an engineer, Chrissie. I want to follow Stephenson, Telford, Brunel. I want to build bridges, railways and tunnels.' His face alight, he had turned to her, gripping her hands tightly in his. 'I'd like to work with Brunel himself. He's the finest engineer of the century, Chrissie, do you know that? Do you know what he's done – the Thames Tunnel, the Great Western Railway, the Avon Bridges? That's the sort of man I'd like to become, travelling all over the country, surveying the land, taking on challenges like the Box Tunnel. Mapping out new railways – for there will be more, Chrissie, a great network of them all over the country. And I want to be there, helping to build them.'

Railways! Christina's own imagination caught fire from his, thinking of Henzel glass, speeding by train to distant parts of the country, trains that ran on lines Harry had planned. Excitement lit her own eyes as she gazed at her brother, and then died away when she remembered that until the will was read no one knew what would happen to Henzel's. But nothing could dim the light in Harry's eyes, or dull the throb in his voice.

Remembering this gave her confidence as she faced the ring of faces around the library table; and it gave her a triumphant pleasure too, to be able to answer them so boldly.

21

'Harry knows quite well what he wants to do. And Papa knew too, and approved. Harry intends to become an engineer; he wants to work with Mr Brunel – Mr Isambard Kingdom Brunel.' What a fine ring that name had! Mentally, she thanked Sir Marc for naming his son so imposingly. 'Harry believes that engineers are vital to the development of our country and I agree with him and shall do all I can to help him.'

There was no denying the effect of her words. The faces were blank with astonishment. They turned to each other and then stared back at Christina. Alfred was the first to recover.

'An engineer!' Even he could not speak the words with any real disparagement. No industrialist in these times could deny the positive contributions that engineers were making to the prosperity of the country. For achievements that ranged from developing new machinery to designing great ships and railways, men like Brunel, Stephenson and Telford had earned the respect of every man. 'Well, I would be the last man to deny the worthiness of such an ambition. But –'

'But in this case,' Samuel interrupted smoothly, 'would we be wise to place too much reliance on it? Harry is young, boys change –'

'It's what he has always wanted,' Christina said. 'And Papa knew it. That's why he didn't leave the glasshouse to Harry.'

'But again, he never expected to die so soon.' Samuel's tone was as reasonable as ever. 'Doubtless, he thought that Harry would have gone through all his training, completed an apprenticeship perhaps or attended university, become a fully-fledged engineer, before the question of inheritance ever arose. As it is –'

'As it is, the boy will have to forget his dreams,' Harold declared. 'He must be brought to see sense. There is a family business to be run, and glassmaking surely can't be so very different from engineering. We can see that the

22

business carries on until he's ready, it will only be a few years now, and then –'

Christina drew a deep breath. Could nothing convince these men? They were all talking now, agreeing with each other, explaining just how it could be done. She tried to speak but they ignored her. Suddenly enraged, she jumped to her feet and banged sharply on the table.

'No!' she cried strongly into the astounded silence, her clear voice in sharp contrast with the harsh tones of the cousins. 'No. Harry will *not* have to forget his ambitions. Papa knew of them and approved, and so do I. I intend to give him every chance. I shall start by approaching Mr Brunel at the first opportunity. Harry *shall* become an engineer, and the name Henzel will one day be as well known in engineering as it is in glass.' She challenged them with her eyes, snapping green fire around the table.

There was a brief silence. The cousins seemed to be lost for words. Again, Alfred recovered first.

'That's all very well, but circumstances have changed.' He spoke with irritated impatience. 'Look, let's get this business settled, I've my own glasshouse to get back to in Newcastle. I agree with Harold, Harry must forget his dreams. I cannot imagine what Joshua was about in allowing them – *encouraging* them, it seems – when he knew there was no other son to follow him.' Like everyone else, he didn't even bother to mention Thomas, alone in his nursery at the top of the house; had probably forgotten all about him. He shot a quick glance around the table from under black brows, drawn together like an iron bar. 'If you ask me,' he burst out, 'Joshua must have been suffering from some kind of brainstorm. The stroke was simply its final manifestation, it's quite clear. The will must be contested on the grounds of insanity.'

Insanity! Christina felt a fury of indignation. She opened her mouth, but was forestalled by the solicitor. He spoke quietly, his voice as dry as ever, but she could sense the controlled anger behind his precise words.

23

'Mr Henzel was in full possession of his senses when we discussed this will. It was quite clearly his wish that Miss Christina should inherit the management of the glasshouse. And Harry is very adequately provided for – he has the old family house in the country, shares in the business and a substantial sum in trust so that when he comes of age he will be able to set up in whatever business he chooses. The entire document was drawn up and dated some time ago – eighteen months, to be exact – and I think you would have difficulty in proving that he had been anything but sane in the interim.'

'Eighteen months ago. That's when Frederic died.' Alfred gave a swift glance of triumph around the table. 'Would any of you say that Joshua was entirely sane at that time?'

The others looked doubtful. 'He was certainly beside himself with grief,' Harold offered dubiously. 'But –'

'And can one be "beside oneself with grief" and still entirely sane?' Alfred demanded. 'At the loss of an eldest son, well-grown, intelligent, capable, destined to follow one's footsteps into the family business? Ask yourselves – Samuel, Reuben, Harold – would any of you be truly sane after such a blow? Would you even *expect* anything you said, or wrote, at such a time, to be taken seriously . . . eighteen months later?' He paused, his eyes travelling round the table, intent on his brothers' faces, passing over Christina as if she were still of no account. 'Ask yourselves,' he repeated softly.

There was a short silence. Christina's heart was thudding in her breast. Her father insane? Joshua Henzel, the giant of Wordsley, whose presence caused strong men to quail, who could not walk down a street without turning every head and quickening every heart, insane? She saw a dawning of hope on the faces of her companions, heard a murmur of agreement that had nothing to do with truth or justice, and again she leapt to her feet, ignoring her aunt's faint protest.

24

'No!' It seemed she was forever having to shout her objections with that word. 'No, it's not true! My father was as sane as any man here, and Mr Ambrose will bear me out in that. His will stands, it must stand. There is no reason to contest it, none at all except your own greed.' She stared proudly round the table, knowing that she was alienating these men, yet strangely exhilarated by the knowledge. It was as if her father were there, at her elbow, approving, encouraging, roaring out that great, full-bellied laugh yet able still to intimidate all except her with his terrifying ferocity. 'You want Henzel's,' she continued, her voice quiet now that she had their attention. 'I know that. Father knew it. And he swore that you would never have it. If Frederic had lived, you would never have had the chance. Well, Frederic did not live –' They would never know what pain it cost her to say those words, 'but I do, and I have inherited, as fairly and legally as any man. There will be no contesting my father's will.' Her voice rose again, ringing through the silent room. 'He knew exactly what he was doing when he drew it up. Hasn't he been training me for this moment; even before Frederic died, wasn't he taking me to the glasshouse with him, letting me watch the men, teaching me all he knew? Didn't he do all in his power to ensure that I should be fit to run the business?'

She paused, watching the faces that stared up at her. There was no doubt as to the reactions of her unwilling listeners. Her aunt was almost in tears of mortification, her face red with distress. The cousins were barely troubling to conceal their anger and shock at being addressed in such a manner by a mere girl; their sons – Harold's wooden-faced Edgar and thin, dark James, Samuel's younger boy, Rupert – were looking embarrassed and uncomfortable. Only Jeremy remained cool. As Christina's glance rested on him, he looked up and caught her eye. And as she found her gaze momentarily held by his, she was conscious of an odd sensation somewhere low inside her; a sensation that disturbed and faintly alarmed her.

'Do you seriously expect us to believe that you think yourself capable of running the glasshouse?' Alfred asked, a sneer in his voice.

'I do. And why not? My father taught me a great deal.'

'He didn't teach you manners,' someone muttered, and there was a general laugh.

Christina felt her face flame. She trembled suddenly with the effort of controlling her temper, and gripped the edge of the table. There might be a time for letting that control go, for releasing her fury, but it was not now, not in response to a cheap gibe.

'I know you all think my father was wrong to take me with him to the glasshouse,' she said, relieved to find that her voice retained its steadiness. 'But he and I understood one another. He knew that I needed something more than simply sitting at home. Some women do,' she said, raising her voice against their exasperated mutterings. 'There *are* women who work, who do things, it isn't unheard of. I must have something to do with my life.'

'You'll have plenty when you're married,' Harold told her curtly, and at his words the same thought struck everyone at the table simultaneously. Christina, still standing there, saw their faces change, saw them glance at each other and then away. Unwillingly, she let her eyes follow the direction of their glances. But now Jeremy had his head bent, staring at the table.

'Aye, that's another thing,' Samuel said slowly. 'Marriage. What happens to the business when she marries, Ambrose?'

For the first time, the lawyer looked directly at Christina, but his eyes were concealed by the light which flashed on his glasses. She could not tell whether he might be indicating his support of her father's will, or his dislike of so unconventional a document. Nor was there any hint in the unemotional tones of his paper-dry voice.

26

'Mr Henzel went into this matter with me most carefully,' he said. 'He was anxious that Miss Christina should retain full control of the glasshouse, even after marriage. I was forced to point out to him that this went against the letter of the law, and he finally agreed.'

'So on marriage, ownership would pass to her husband!' Again, the cousins looked at each other, but before they could begin to weigh up the implications, Henry Ambrose held up a thin hand.

'Not entirely. In such an event, Mr Henzel has laid down certain conditions. Firstly, that the name of the company would remain as it is today. Secondly, that Miss Henzel should retain fifty-one per cent of the shares on marriage.'

A gasp ran round the table. Fifty-one per cent of the shares! So Christina would retain control of the company, in a voting capacity, even though all her income must be, in law, her husband's.

'And now,' Christina said, her voice trembling a little, 'do you still maintain my father was insane?'

Harold moved impatiently. 'Still? I think this confirms it! I never heard anything like it, leaving a slip of a girl with the power to take an old-established family firm to perdition! Why, if I had my way –'

'But you don't, do you.' Christina's voice was dangerously sweet and she exulted secretly at the consternation on the faces of the men who sat staring up at her. To be able to cause such dismay in men who had never considered her even worthy of their notice beyond an occasional pat on the head or patronising word when they came upon her on a visit to her father's glasshouse! Her eyes glittered and she lifted her chin, a wilful smile tugging at her lips. 'You don't have your way,' she repeated coolly, meeting Harold's eye with a directness that brought a dull colour to his already florid cheeks. 'Not as far as Henzel's is concerned. From now on, it's *my* way that counts there. Don't let anyone be in doubt of that. I shall run the glasshouse as my father wished me to, and in the way he would have wished. After all,' she added, 'the idea of a woman in charge is not so very unusual. We have a queen on the throne, and she is only three years older than I.'

There was a brief silence, as if the brothers were nonplussed, and for a moment Christina thought she had won. But then Reuben, the quiet one, spoke, and they all turned to look at him.

'But consider, Christina, my dear,' he said, and his voice was mild and reasonable. 'Consider this. Your father died untimely. He could not have expected – nobody could have expected – that he should take a stroke and go so suddenly. He was still a comparatively young man. Of course he thought you would be fit to undertake all the responsibilities of the glass factory – of course he intended that you should do so, if it were your wish. But so soon?' He had everyone's attention now, and Christina, listening unwillingly, saw that their faces were clearing, as if Reuben's words carried some undercurrent of meaning that brought them new hope. 'Don't you think that when he made his will he was looking forward many years – ten, fifteen, twenty? When you would be a mature woman, experienced in all the ways of the business, fully able to judge, able to take over from him at any moment? Don't you think that it was an eventuality far in the future that he had in mind?'

He paused, his pale eyes on Christina's face. She hesitated, unable to refute his logic. Of course her father hadn't expected to die so soon! To her fury, tears pricked at her eyes. Reuben was waiting for an answer. Mutely, reluctantly, she nodded.

'Then would it not be wise, my dear, to accept a little help now?' he went on softly, persuasively. 'Even our dear young queen has her advisers, after all. That's all we are suggesting. To allow us to advise you, guide you, just at first, until you are sure of your own way. Of course you are capable of running the factory! We each of us must admit that, mustn't we, brothers?' He glanced round the table, pale eyes resting on each man in turn until, as reluctantly as Christina, they inclined their heads. 'But, just at first, is it not possible that you might welcome a little support?' He was watching her again, his gaze as mild as his voice, yet with an intentness that brought her a twinge of discomfort. She flinched and bit her lip. What was it about Reuben that always made her feel like this? As if he were harbouring secret thoughts that couldn't be told? Thoughts that slithered in his mind like snakes, or worms . . .

Impatiently, Christina shook herself. Such fancies were for silly, simpering maidens like her sister Adela, not for someone like herself, strong and capable, with more insight into a man's world than was enjoyed by most matrons twice her age! Reuben was no different from the rest of her cousins – a man who had until today barely noticed her presence, and had now been forced to recognise her as someone to be reckoned with. And yet, was still doing his best to demean her. There might be logic in what he said – Christina would consider that later – but if there were any help needed in this task bequeathed her by her father, she would do the asking herself. In her own time. In her own way.

'Thank you,' she said steadily, her voice clear. 'You may well be right. I shall know that better when I have looked fully into the affairs of the business. And now . . .' She glanced along the table towards Henry Ambrose. 'If there is nothing else in my father's will . . ?'

'Nothing else,' the lawyer answered, and Christina bowed her head.

'Then I thank you for coming here today, Mr Ambrose, and, gentlemen, I thank you too for your attendance.' She watched, remaining quite still, as their faces suffused with colour, their jaws tightened, and they turned to each other with baffled displeasure. Then she glanced at her aunt,

29

who had sat throughout with a bewildered face and trembling lips. 'Come, Aunt Susan.'

Slowly, the two women made their way to the double doors that led out to the landing. As they reached them, Christina turned her head to look back. The cousins were leaning across the table, all talking at once in their eagerness to be heard. Henry Ambrose was gathering his papers together, his expression cold and withdrawn. Only Jeremy was standing; a little apart from the rest, his slender figure detached, his stance thoughtful. As Christina looked back, he raised his head and their eyes met. Something flashed between them, something too brief, too quickly over, to put a name to. For a bare second, Christina hesitated. And then she turned away and followed her aunt out of the library.

She closed the doors behind her and leaned against the wall, feeling suddenly drained.

Chapter Three

Christina opened the inner door of the glass cone and stood for a moment, as she always did, on the threshold.

It took a moment or two for her eyes to become accustomed to the smoky dimness of the circular chamber, lit only by the red glow from the mouths of the pots that gaped with fiery jaws all around the great domed furnace. Above her, the brick walls, dark with soot, tapered a hundred feet or more to the round disc of sky that was all the natural light the cone admitted. Though it was seldom that the sky could be seen for the smoke that poured forth, sometimes eddying back in a strong wind, or turned to steaming soot by the rain that lashed against its scorching heat.

Christina never lost the excitement of that first moment as she passed from one world to another; from the ordinary, everyday world of the street outside into this magic realm. She never tired of watching the process of glassmaking, seeing the men weaving between the shadows with practised ease. The glow was steady, its heat kept constant by the teasers stoking its fires below, each man blackened with dust from the great piles of coal they constantly dragged from the canal outside and along the narrow brick passage, to shovel into the hungry maw of the furnace. Up here, the eyes of the gatherers were white against raddled skin as they passed through the smouldering light. Like demons, she thought, toiling in the furnaces of hell.

Only the booth of the duty-gatherer, just inside the inner door, struck a discordant note, and Christina could not help casting a glance of disdain at the man within. Thomas Pritchard might, for all she knew, be a decent, honourable, even pleasant man to know outside the glasshouse. But, like her father and cousins, neither she nor any of the glassmakers were ever likely to find out, for duty-gatherers were universally hated for the work they did: stationed inside every glasshouse to weigh and tax every piece of glass made, with the extra tax on lead glass being almost twice as high as that on ordinary bottle-glass.

'The government's crippling the glass trade,' Joshua Henzel had railed, over and over again. 'How can we produce fine flint crystal with this – this extortion going on? And to have those creatures stationed there in their sentry-boxes, so that we have to ask permission to enter our own premises, why, it's nothing but a damned humiliation. No wonder the glasshouse boys harry and taunt them, they hate them as much as we do. I'd like to do a bit of harrying myself, and that's the truth of it!'

'Do you suppose they'll ever be taken away, Papa?' Christina would ask. 'After all, the tax has been imposed for nearly a hundred years now –'

Joshua snorted. 'And looks like going on for another hundred, at this rate! That Royal Commission in, when was it? thirty-three, it actually made some sense out of the whole mad business. Pointed out that with this excise on, there'd never be proper research into new methods of production. Made it quite clear that we were losing trade to foreigners – d'you know there's more glass imported into this country than ever before, and none of it as fine as the stuff we could produce if we were allowed? And what's been done about their recommendations? Nothing!' He flung himself into a chair and shook out the pages of the *County Express*, his moustaches quivering with rage.

There was talk now that the excise was to be removed at last, and if it were Christina supposed that Thomas Pritchard and his ilk would leave the glasshouses and go to other government work. What that would be, she neither knew nor cared. She only knew that every glassmaker in the Stourbridge area would be thankful to see them go.

Christina lifted her skirts a little to keep them clear of the littered floor. The noise of the cone battered at her eardrums: the clang of iron pipes as gatherers hurried to the furnaces to collect red-hot 'metal'; the clatter of boots on the stone-flagged floor; the shouts and bawls of the men at each other and at the boys scampering between them to fetch ale, cloths, whatever the men demanded, all echoing around the great cavernous dome, yet all dulled by the steady roar of the furnaces as they were fed from below.

Slowly, she moved forward to the edge of the working area, standing quietly in the shadows to watch the men on the nearest chair. The gaffer here was Jem Husselbee, one of her father's older glassmakers, a third-generation man at Henzel's: his father had worked with Christina's own grandfather, Roger Henzel, and his grandfather with the man who had first started the glasshouse, old Joshua himself, a legend in the glassmaking history of Wordsley. Like many of the other working glassmakers, the Husselbee family took pride in their long association with Henzel's. A pride that had kept them with the firm even through its bad times; a pride that would, Christina hoped fervently, keep them loyal through the years to come. She was under no illusion that the men who had worked so loyally for her father would find it easy to accept her own authority. The welcome they had given her as their master's daughter, visiting the glasshouse with him, was quite a different matter from the feeling they would have for her as their mistress.

Jem Husselbee saw her and nodded. He handed the glass jug he had just completed to the servitor to be taken to the man who would attach its handle.

'Good of you to come to see us, Miss Christina.' He paused to wipe a grimy hand across his sweat-shining face. 'Us needs a bit of interest from the fam'ly, like. Though Master Jeremy's been in a time or two, but that in't the same as the real fam'ly.'

'I haven't been able to come before, Jem.' Christina didn't tell him that her aunt had been vociferously disapproving of this morning's visit. 'There's been a great deal to attend to.'

'Ah, that's right. Bad job all round.' Husselbee waited as his gatherer went to the furnace and inserted a long iron, withdrawing it a moment later with the glowing bulb of molten glass on the end. 'Still, we're keeping busy, that's t' main thing. Metal's looking grand too.'

Christina smiled. 'That's good, Jem. We need to keep up the work.' He was right, she thought, watching as the metal was brought to him on its iron and he took it, swinging it easily to prevent the glass losing shape, and then seating himself in the crude wooden chair that his father had made years ago, to roll the iron expertly across the broad arms. Keeping busy; keeping the work going. Those were the main things, the important things.

He had just finished shaping a wineglass which, still too hot to touch with the bare hands, had been placed into the *lehr*: the long tunnel which led through the outer wall of the cone, its moving floor wound slowly out by a man whose job it was to sit at the far end turning a handle, so that the glass inside could gradually cool. The glass wasn't safe yet, it could still crack or craze in the cooling, or be damaged in the hands of the engraver. But this, Christina knew, wouldn't worry Jem Husselbee. The glass blown, his job was complete.

She moved on, pausing here and there at the other chairs, speaking to the men in the quiet yet penetrating tone she had learned to cultivate in the incessant commotion. It had been Joshua's policy to keep in touch with all his workmen by these small tours. A word here, a nod there; an enquiry after a sick wife or an ailing child; condolences after a death, it was all part of what had brought him the men's loyalty, the respect that kept them working for him even when harsh excise laws had threatened their jobs. And Christina had accompanied him frequently enough that she should feel at ease now, walking around the glasshouse without him at her side, even though she missed his giant presence almost intolerably. So why *didn't* she feel at ease? Why this strange tension in the air, this consciousness of eyes that followed her as she walked, yet never met her gaze directly? She had almost completed her circuit. There was only one chair left unvisited, one gaffer she had not spoken to. Christina hesitated. She had been here long enough, she argued silently. Mr Honeyborne would be waiting in the office; there were figures to be gone into, and she had promised to talk also to the general overseer, Charles Turner. It was unfair to expect him to carry the entire burden of the factory without some discussion with the new owner . . .

'You've come to see us, then, Miss Christina.'

Christina started and felt herself blushing. The voice, deep and rough, held a note of irony that told her its owner knew exactly what had been going through her mind. He had seen that she was about to leave, without stopping at his chair, and he wasn't going to let her get away with it. Her momentary hesitation had betrayed her.

Reluctantly, Christina turned her head and looked at what she had been trying so hard not to see – the gleaming bare chest and shoulders of this giant of a man, dark hair falling in thick curls over his swarthy face, the glow of the furnace turning his sweat-shining torso to the bronze of a magnificent statue.

Joseph Compson. The man who had caught her eye as he bore her father's coffin from the church to the grave. Once again, Christina felt her colour rise, her heart quicken. She had determined that she would not approach him, would not give him the opportunity to favour her again with that insolent stare. Hadn't she promised herself that he would regret that, the way he had distracted her from her thoughts at the very moment when her father was passing from her life for ever? Yet even as she formed the thought, her steps were taking her in his direction. Joe's brief comment had been enough to make it impossible for her to leave the cone without pausing by his chair, without exchanging with him the courtesy of conversation that she had extended to all the other gaffers. And now, as if ironically aware that he had virtually compelled her to remain, he turned casually away to begin work on a new wineglass. Teaching me my place, she thought furiously, and felt again a flash of the bewildered anger he always managed to arouse in her.

The gatherer had returned to the furnace and thrust his iron into the molten glass. With a dexterous spin, he drew off a fiery bulb and approached the chair again, bringing another long blowing-iron with its gob of molten metal glowing on the end. Christina watched as the long iron was swung with expert skill so that the red-hot bulb lengthened and changed shape until it was ready for blowing. He brought it to the servitor, who rolled it back and forth on the marver, to make sure that its shape was even before he dipped the glass into a sizzling bucket of water, raised the iron to his lips and began to blow.

Christina stood a little behind Joe, watching as the glowing mass took shape, grew, thinned, became almost transparent on the end of the iron. She looked at the men, grouped in their little team which took its name from the crude, sturdy 'chair': the wooden seat with broad arms and stocky legs which was central to the glassmaking process. She knew that Joe himself had, like every glassmaker, started by making his own tools and building his own chair. In this way, the chair and tools were made to reflect and add to his own efficiency. An efficiency that in some glassmakers – and she had to admit Joseph Compson was one of these – went on to become artistry; even genius. The marver, too, had been made by Joe – a small wooden bench on which each glass was shaped before the blowing began. And although the servitor blew most of the small pieces of glass being made by this particular chair, Christina knew that when larger bowls or vessels were made Joe would do it himself, his great chest thrusting air into the raw glass with effortless ease, the power of his lungs almost miraculously matched by the delicacy of his control.

Now the glass was ready for him and he swung into action, seating himself in the chair, working quickly to form the stem and foot from the small molten lumps brought to him next. Christina watched, spellbound, aware that this was the moment when any gaffer, however fine, might occasionally allow the glass to sag and lose shape. But Joe's hand was steady. Within moments, he had the foot formed and the solid rod of a punty-iron fixed to its centre. Now he could discard the blowing-iron and work even more efficiently, using the tools he had made as an apprentice: the willow-stem pucellas for shaping, the battledore for flattening, the shears for slicing off the ragged surplus from the rim. Before Christina's eyes another of the elegantly-shaped wineglasses for which Henzel's was famous was formed. As soon as it was done, the taker-in snapped off the punty-iron and placed the glass in the *lehr* beside its fellows.

The whole process had taken no more than a few moments. Christina let out the breath she had been holding and Joseph Compson turned back to her.

'Morning, Miss Christina,' he said, civilly enough, as if he had not already spoken to her.

'Good morning, Joe.' Christina was aware that she would have called most of the men by their surnames. But, like the Husselbees and a few of the other working glassmakers, the Compsons were different. Old William – Joe's father – and his father before him, had both been gaffers in Henzel's glassworks, and Joe had been Frederic's special friend, helping him with his first attempt at glassblowing. Frederic had often, laughingly, told Christina how startled he had been to find the iron – so easily handled by the older boy – become heavy, cumbersome, almost hostile in his inexperienced hands. Humiliatingly aware of his father's amusement, he had been grateful for Joseph's calm intervention, the strong hands closing over his own as the iron swung wildly to and fro, taming and controlling it so that the liquid glass began to turn from a shapeless mass of molten fire to a recognisable object.

Perhaps it was the fact that Joe Compson and her brother had become friends that made him stare at her in that over-familiar way, Christina thought, meeting Joe's bold dark eyes with a haughty look. She wondered if Frederic had talked about her to Joe, as he'd told her about the gaffer's son; knowing that few opportunities to swing the iron and blow the glass would come Frederic's way. 'It would have been an intrusion, you see, sis – they'd have lost wages over the time I took,' and the two boys would take the chance at baggin-time; while Will Compson and the rest of the chair were eating, they would try their hands at making 'friggers'; glass toys, animals, fruits, anything their imaginations evoked. Christina still possessed a stumpy-legged glass pony which Frederic had blown and given her; it stood on the mantelpiece in her bedroom. But most of their efforts went back as cullet to be melted down again.

'You're doing some good work, Joe,' she remarked, inclining her head towards the wineglasses. 'Those will be beautiful when they're engraved.'

'Aye, if the engravers don't smash 'em.' The reply came automatically, part of a traditional jealousy. Each craftsman, whether he was a blower, engraver or polisher, liked to think he was the most important. Though no one, Christina thought, could really gainsay the gaffer's claim; without him and the men on his chair to blow and shape the glass, there would be nothing for the others to work on. And it was the gaffer and his chair who were closest to the master-glassmaker. The engravers worked alone, in their own small workshops – often no more than a garden

38

shed or backhouse – and were not a part of the glasshouse itself. Joe Compson, like many of the glassblowers, believed that the shape of the glass was its most important characteristic. There were even times when Christina thought he would have liked the glass to go out entirely uncut and undecorated. And when she saw the beauty of a new shape, the curves of a jug or the slender elegance of a decanter, blown by Joe, she almost agreed with him.

'I'd like it better if we could do more flint work though,' Joe went on, wiping the pouring sweat from his skin. 'There's naught like lead for putting heart into a bit of glass. You can feel the weight of it on t' iron, seems to bring life to it, somehow. An' when the piece is made you can see t' difference.'

He glanced with disgust at the sodden rag in his hand and threw it away, looking round impatiently for his ale. 'Where the hell's that boy – begging your pardon, Miss Christina, but those lads get lazier by the minute . . . crawl about like old grannies going to fetch water, and then expect to become skilled workers in five minutes. Towd that one only this morning, it were three year before I were even allowed to touch an iron, let alone try blowing. But it's watter off a duck's back.'

As he spoke, the inner door opened and the boy – no older than Thomas, at home – came scuttling through it, clasping a brown jug and almost colliding with a gatherer. Christina winced, imagining the effect if that red-hot, molten glass were to touch the child's skin. But accidents like that were few; the gatherers were adept at avoiding each other and too intent on their work, and the money earned from it, to take any risks. The boy was cursed and kicked as he passed, without any of it apparently disturbing the rhythmic movement as the iron was swung into the hands of the waiting footmakers, and the ale was handed to Joe with barely a drop spilt.

'Well, if they take off the excise as we hope, we'll be able to go much more into flint production.' Christina watched as Joe tipped the jug to his lips and drank deeply. This was what her aunt and cousins' wives disapproved so strongly, this coming into the glasshouse alone, talking with the men. She felt more at ease with Joe Compson now; once that first moment of meeting was over, the challenge of the dark eyes met and answered, they were able to talk comfortably together. But she was always aware that the link between them – her brother Frederic – must not be taken advantage of, that Joe must be kept in his place. She had a feeling that he would be only too willing to step outside it, and then . . . Her mind turned quickly away.

'If that happens, you'd have the chance to work full-time on flint glass,' she added, and caught the gleam of scepticism in Joe's eyes.

Joe drained his jug of ale and wiped his mouth with the back of a dirt-ingrained hand. His gatherer was already at the glory-hole, waiting to bring another gob of metal, and the rest of the chair were ready to take their parts with Joe at their head. Nobody could afford to let the work lapse for more than a few minutes; Joe had a quota of wineglasses to make before he went off shift and any less than that number would mean a loss of wages for them all.

But to her surprise, Joe did not move. He gestured to the gatherer, a brief shake of his head that indicated that he was not yet ready for the iron. He stood quite still by his chair, massive hands thrust against his hips, as if he were waiting.

Slowly, the cone fell silent. Other men stopped working. They glanced at each other, then moved nearer to Joe, gathering in a half-circle behind him. The clatter of irons ceased; only the roar of the furnace, so commonplace that it went unnoticed, sounded in the echoing dome.

Christina found herself confronting a ring of smoke-blackened faces. For a moment, she was frighteningly conscious of her small stature and the fact that she was alone. Then she reminded herself sharply that these were men she had known all her life, and took a small, positive step forward.

'I assume you have good reason for stopping work,' she said, her voice cool. 'Is there something you wish to say to me? Something that cannot wait?' Concerned though her father might have been for his men, he would never have allowed liberties, and neither could she. She directed her gaze at Joe, seeing him, as the men clearly did, as their natural leader and spokesman. 'Joe?'

Joe came forward. He stood close – closer than he need, she thought, too close for comfort, and knew that he was as aware of it as she. He was challenging her with those dark, insolent eyes, daring her to stay where she was, expecting her to step back, literally give ground.

Well, it seemed that Joe Compson had a few lessons to learn. Christina stood firm.

'Is this your doing, Joe?' She indicated the silent circle of men. 'Are you leading a strike already?'

'It's no strike, Miss Christina.' His voice had a deep roughness, paradoxically overlaid with gentleness: velvet made with tiny fibres of iron. 'Us only wants to know where we stand. There's rumours about Henzel's: some say you're tekkin' over, some says Master Harry, some thinks we're to be part of Henzel Brothers. We just wants to know the truth of it all. And who do we look to, a boy still at school or –'

'Or a wench in frills and furbelows,' Christina finished for him, and cast an amused glance downwards at her plain black dress. 'Yes, Joe, I understand what you must be thinking. But you have nothing to worry about, any of you. I am in charge of the glasshouse now. My father left everything here to me, knowing that I would carry on just as he taught me, and that's what I intend to do.'

There was a brief, stunned silence.

Then Joe Compson laughed. '*You* run the glasshouse, Miss Christina? It'll never work!'

'And why not?'

'Why, because it's man's work, that's why. Petticoat government in a glassworks! What do any woman know about running a factory?'

'But I'm not *any woman*, Joe.' Christina raised her eyes to his and felt a spark leap between them at her words. Hurriedly, she went on. 'Remember, I've been coming here with my father since I was a child. I've watched you all at work. I've sat in the office for hours and listened while he talked with Mr Honeyborne and Mr Turner. I've even taken part in their discussions.' She swept her eyes proudly round the watching, listening faces. 'I know exactly how my father wanted his glasshouse to develop. With your help, I can carry on just as before. We all can. And not only that –' her voice took on an eager note, rising echoingly, commandingly, through the vaulted spaces '–as soon as we're rid of this excise I have plans for new glass: crystal such as you've never made before; coloured glass – blue, ruby, deep jade green. Don't you see, we're on the threshold of wonderful times. Together, we can make Henzel's the best glasshouse in Stourbridge, the best in the land!' She paused, allowing the echoes to soar, reverberate and finally fade, and then added quietly, 'I know this can be done – but only if we work together.'

There was a hush. The men shifted a little, glancing first at each other and then at Joe.

'Fine words,' he said at last. 'But can you make them deeds, Miss Christina?'

'Can *you*?' she asked, and threw the challenge back into his eyes. Their glances met, clashed, locked. Christina felt a strange thrill vibrate through her whole body, trembling even to the tips of her fingers, the points of her toes. She lifted her head proudly and felt the muscles tighten at her jaw.

'I reckon we can, at that,' Joe said slowly. 'I reckon it's only fair to give you a chance, Miss Christina.' He swung round on the others, his voice suddenly fierce. 'Well? Is

42

that right? Do we work along of Miss Christina? Let's let her see what we think!'

And the cone echoed again, this time with a cheer so massive that it threatened to set the sooty bricks a-tremble. Grimy faces split with grins, voices broke into a chatter of relief and Christina, her eyes misted, knew that it was a relief she whole-heartedly shared.

Joe Compson turned back to her.

'Reckon that's all right then, Miss Christina,' he said. 'The lads are behind you. Us'll work for you, same as we worked for your pa, an' hope as the place does as well for you as it did for him. And now we'd best be getting back to work.'

He nodded curtly and the men dispersed, hurrying back to their own chairs to work even harder in an effort to make up their quota. Christina stepped back out of the way, to watch the work proceed as if nothing had happened. But she remained wary. Something told her that to congratulate herself on victory would be unwise. The men – and Joe Compson in particular – would continue to need very careful handling.

But for today, at least, all was well and she could watch the process of glassmaking which, as it never failed to do, once more enthralled her.

She never knew quite what she loved most about this. Perhaps it was the constant, unhurried movement; the skill of the servitor, allowing exactly the right amount of metal to accumulate on the end of the iron as he held it in the pot, withdrawing it and swinging it rhythmically to allow it to cool and lengthen; the rolling of the metal before it was shaped, the blowing down the hollow iron to swell and shape it. All done with no apparent hurry, yet so swiftly that, almost before the watcher knew it, a wineglass or tumbler had been detached from the iron which was then thrown like a spear to the bit-gatherer, to be returned to the hot shoe beside the pot for re-heating.

Glass and the love of it had been in Christina's blood for as long as she could remember. With her father, she had shared a fascination for the beauty that could range from a minute glass made with the delicacy of spun sugar to the drama of a great chandelier; and make you catch your breath with wonder that it could be created by man. And she was equally held by the act of creation itself, by the place where their living was wrought from the shining, red-hot mixture of sand and alkali. From that first, illicit visit she had been thrilled by the cavernous glasshouse, its blood-red shadows peopled by great looming giants, muscles shining with sweat and reddened by the glow of the furnace, moving with purposeful grace – like the Greeks Miss Crossley had told her about, who had taken part in ancient games, throwing the javelin, competing with spears.

That feeling still came back to her on each visit, even though she knew now that the men were no different, outside the glasshouse, from any other workmen. She had seen them in the narrow streets on her way home, lounging on corners, drifting into the public houses. And at her father's funeral, stiff and self-conscious in their Sunday suits, silent in their mourning for the man they had revered.

Christina felt a sudden twinge of panic. Could they, in spite of that heartwarming cheer, ever feel the same respect for her, a woman?

Restlessly, she turned back to the door and, under the cold eye of the duty-gatherer, paused and looked back. Joseph Compson had finished yet another wineglass and stood waiting for the next iron to be brought to him. As she watched, he glanced up and their eyes met across the shifting red light.

Joe Compson. A man with glass in his blood, as surely as it was in hers. Was he really for her – or against her? As she tilted her head once more, answering again the challenge in his eyes, Christina knew that Joe Compson was going to be important. He had already proved that where he led, others would follow.

Today, he seemed ready to co-operate with her. But tomorrow. . . ?

Joe thrust his way out of the cone into the evening air. It was still hung with smoke, as it always was, but in the darkness he scarcely noticed it. The thirst that dried his mouth and burned his throat was too powerful to be worsened by the acridity of the Wordsley air, and all he was concerned with was to get into the tavern and slake it with good strong ale.

'The Glassblower' stood close to the works and beside the canal that brought so many of the raw materials needed by the various industries in the town: forges, potteries, brickmakers, nail and chain makers as well as the glasshouses. All had either sprung up or expanded during the past few years as England's prosperity had increased. And the expansion had been faster than had ever been known before. With the invention of machines, production of many of these things had increased. They had been sold abroad, to the new colonies as well as the old countries. Manufacturers were making huge profits, and using much of the money to expand even further, employing more and more workers who flooded in from the countryside, where life was harder than ever now that machines had begun to take over so much agricultural work. New workers, all needing homes to live in, food to eat, clothes to wear . . . and so it went on, work making work, new factories, houses, public buildings being built every day.

'There weren't none of these streets when your mother and me got wed,' William Compson would say, staring out over the narrow, tightly-packed terraces, teeming with the men, women and children who laboured in the factories or at home to earn a living. 'It's all grown up in a few years. Took 'em all by surprise, I reckon. Well, somebody's done theirselves a good turn out of it, that's for certain. Only wish 'twas me.' He spat and turned away, still a powerful man and capable of turning out as fine a piece of glass as any gaffer in the Black Country.

But Joe thought he had detected signs lately of his father tiring. A sag in the shoulders when he thought no one was watching him, a hand rubbed across his eyes . . . And shouldn't he be tired? Joe would ask himself then, angrily. After working near forty years, since a lad of nine, running for ale and getting a clip over the ear when his gaffer thought him too slow in coming?

Joe remembered his own impatience with the boy who had brought his ale, remembered too his own childhood twelve, thirteen years ago. Six hours on and six off, turn and turn about, the same as the men. Stumbling into the glasshouse still half asleep before it was light of a morning, getting cuffed out of the way of the gatherers, scuttling here and there at everyone's behest, learning to be nimble to avoid catching a gob of red-hot glass on his flesh. Conscious all the time of the gnawing hunger in his belly that would not be relieved until baggin-time, when his father would toss him some scraps of bread and cheese and he would be allowed to rest for a few minutes on a pile of old sacking in a corner. But never for long. He wasn't there on holiday, he was told, and soon enough the men would be up and working again, shouting for ale, for rags to wipe the sweat from their eyes, for this, for that, until his head reeled. Until at midday when the shift ended, all he could think of was his bed, a haven until six in the evening when it all began again.

Well, everyone had to go through it and there was no virtue in being soft. He was grown now and a gaffer himself, with skills he could match with William's. Skills, he was determined, that would soon be known throughout the Black Country.

Joe pushed open the tavern door and the warm, fetid air gushed out at him, smelling of beer and sweat and oil from the lamps. A thick haze of smoke hung over the crowded room, rising from the many pipes that had been lit as soon as work was over. He felt in the pocket of his rough jacket for his own, then remembered he had no tobacco. Well, whoever owned the place now that Joshua Henzel was dead, would be glad enough to sell him some. He wondered if Miss Christina owned the tavern now as well as the glasshouse, and he felt a spurt of anger. It was one of Joe's resentments, having to buy ale and tobacco from his employer.

'The Glassblower Tavern' had been built when Joshua Henzel first expanded his glassworks and started to lay out the narrow streets, pulling down the scattered cottages to build rows of back-to-backs – houses with three or four tiny rooms that would be expected to take a family of ten or twelve children. It was a good home for a working man. In nearby Stourbridge, some of the streets were even more crowded. The poorer labourers there lived in damp, chilly courtyards surrounded by crowded buildings which would house sixty or seventy people, sharing one privy between them all and with one standpipe for water, turned on for just an hour or two each day. And that fit for nothing more than washing the floor. For cooking or washing, most people were forced to buy from the carriers, at a cost of several pence a week – and washing, as often as not, went by the board.

And at almost every corner either a public house or a shop, and you were expected to patronise those built by your own employer. Well, you had to have shops and pubs, Joe knew that, but it irked him just the same. Because when you came down to it, however you spent the money you earned, whether in rent, food or drink, it all went straight back where it came from – into your employer's pocket. Made you feel as if you'd never really had it. Made you feel *owned* – and that was the feeling Joe Compson hated most of all.

As Joe swallowed his pint, a gust of laughter shook the

dingy walls. Someone slapped his back and as Joe turned he heard the name 'Christina Henzel' and a fresh burst of laughter. He stopped.

'What was that?'

'Christina Henzel,' the other man repeated, and Joe recognised one of the servitors at the Richardson glassworks. 'Spent long enough talking to you, Joe, by all accounts. Think she fancies you, eh, lads?'

Joe ignored the banter. 'What about her? What were you saying?'

'Why, you wor there. Weren't she tellin' how she've inherited the works from her old dad? Tekkin' over – mistress of Henzel's. What do yer think o' that, then?' The speaker shook with laughter. 'Workin' for wimmin – that's what comes of hevin' a queen on the throne! We'll be cookin' our own dinners next.'

The others joined in, delighted by the new joke. 'Ah, and gettin' our own water . . .' 'Lookin' after our own childer', and, most hilarious of all, 'Hevin' our own childer!' . . . The idea was received with roars of laughter and calls for more beer, and the men carried the comparisons into obscenity, ignoring the serving-women who scurried between them, pitchers filled with ale.

Joe listened without comment. There were glassmakers from most of the rival glasshouses there, all enjoying what seemed to be a huge joke. Miss Christina, in charge of Henzel's! That little piece, nobbut bigger than an ale-boy for all she could look so haughty when she'd a mind, running a glasshouse! She'd been in and out of the place for years, of course, following the old man, but in charge? They shook their heads. Someone must have got it wrong somewhere.

Joe found he didn't want to join in the laughter. He drained his tankard and then shoved his way out, some fresh tobacco in his pocket. He never drank much in the tavern. He preferred to go back to the terraced house he shared with his parents and several brothers and sisters, getting something to eat from the hot pie shop on the way perhaps, sluice off a bit under the yard tap if it was on, and then meet Maggie Haden up on the hill before catching a few hours' sleep and starting work again on the midnight turn.

Tonight, however, Maggie was waiting for him at the corner of the street under the flickering gas lamp, and he stopped, letting his dark eyes rove over her, knowing that the slow, assessing way he did it made her shiver with delight. It was almost as if he was touching her, he thought, his gaze lingering on the breasts that showed white under the fold of her shawl, and he felt a quickening of excitement deep in his loins.

'What are you doing here, Mag?' he asked brusquely. It would never do to let her know he was already wanting her, already imagining himself on Dob Hill with her in his arms, generous and warm against his body . . . 'Don't tell us you've lost your job. Don't they want you any more?'

Maggie Haden looked up at him. She was small and rounded, with full breasts like oranges, and as sweet. Her lips were full too, a moist, inviting red, and she always held them as if she were expecting to be kissed. Her eyes, the colour of the cobalt which was used to make blue glass, were dancing and merry.

'And what if I have?' she asked him now, head tilted provocatively. 'What would you do about it, Joe Compson? Tek me in and make an honest woman of me?' She burst out laughing at his expression. 'No, there's no risk of that, Joe, you needn't look so worried. I've gone on a different shift, that's all. Working nights now, eight till eight, so if you want any little jaunts up the hill you'll have to get me back in good time, see?'

'Night shift? Why's that?' Joe was already working out what it would mean, having to get Maggie back to Richardson's glasshouse, where she worked as a packer, for eight o'clock. 'It dunna give us much time,' he grumbled, and Maggie laughed again and came close.

49

'What sort of man are you anyway, Joe, that you need more than two hours for it?' she murmured, and he could feel her soft shape under the old wool dress she wore. 'You can eat later, if that's what you're worrying about. Anyway, we've no time for arguing – I was let off early today so that I could start the new shift tonight, and it's half-past six now by t' church clock. So are we going or not?'

She was moving gently against him and his senses reeled as she'd known they would. Joe looked down at her, catching the gleam of her teasing eyes in the shadows. There were times when he hated her for what she could do to him, for the weakness that invaded his body whenever she pleased to give him a glance. It gave her a power over him, something no man had, other than Joshua Henzel, who held his life in his hands simply because he employed him. But Joshua was dead – Joe himself had helped to lower the old man's coffin into the grave. It was Christina Henzel he belonged to now.

The thought brought an odd twist to his stomach. Belong to that proud little thing – he, Joe Compson, on his way to becoming the best gaffer Henzel's had ever known? Belong to *any* woman? His belly hardened at the very idea. Being owned by old Joshua was bad enough, but he'd accepted that, it was part of life and you had to take it. But owned by Christina, who ought to be thinking of marriage and children . . . He recalled the spark in Christina's green eyes as their glances had clashed, felt his stomach twist again and jerked his attention violently back to Maggie.

Maggie Haden was no haughty glassmaster's daughter with ideas above her place. No, Maggie was a real woman, warm flesh and blood, honest and straightforward. Liking the difference between men and women as much as he did, ready to make the most of it. Generous, satisfying, ripe for the picking.

Joe held her tight against him, feeling the shape of her

50

melt softly to merge with his own hard muscle. His stomach lurched and his loins, already spread with heat, throbbed painfully. He slid his hand round Maggie's back and under her arm and gave her breast a squeeze, rewarded by a small gasp and a flicker of desire in her blue eyes. He grinned down at her, feeling himself a man again and in command.

'O' course we're going!' he said roughly, and turning away from the street corner, keeping his hold on her. 'And you want to watch yourself, Maggie Haden. Two hours! I've been tekkin' me time up to now – and tonight's the night I'll prove it.'

Maggie giggled and squirmed against him as he led her through the dark streets to the hill that rose above the village. He moved quickly, feeling relief in the action, but his body was burning now with a slow, scorching heat and he found it difficult to be patient until they reached the bushes that dotted the hillside. His blood was racing and he wanted to behave freely, naturally, like the dogs that copulated in the streets, throwing Maggie down and possessing her without regard for passers-by! His fingers tightened round her wrist and she gave a little cry, but when he looked down at her again he saw that her eyes were hot and shining, and knew that she was as avid as he. Feeling the heat increase and the slow throbbing that was so exciting begin to intensify, he quickened his pace. There was a place just up the hill, easily found even in the dark, a hollow surrounded by hawthorns; it was their place, the spot where they had first lain together . . . He dragged Maggie along, ignoring her pleas to go slower. She didn't mean them anyway.

'Two hours?' he muttered into her hair half an hour later, when they lay panting and assuaged on the rough tussocky grass. 'I reckon that's boy's time don't you, Maggie?' He moved his hand masterfully over her breast, freed now from her bodice, and squeezed it, pinching the nipple between his finger and thumb. He was still lying

51

half across her, her softness like a pillow beneath him, and she moved under him, pushing him off.

'I can't breathe,' she complained, and lay looking up at him, eyes heavy-lidded now, smiling the secret smile that all women wore when sated. 'Yer too heavy, Joe – and too rough. There's some nights when I wonder if I'm goin' to be able to walk down t' hill.'

'But you always do, don't you? And you always manage to walk back up it next night. Anyway, you know you like it that way.' He moved his hand down her body, settling his fingers comfortably in the moist warmth between her thighs and working them against her so that she writhed and whimpered. 'Shall I kiss it better?'

'Get off!' She pulled at his hand, but not hard enough to remove it. 'Give us a bit of time, Joe, do. You've only just finished the once.' But she twisted closer to him and let her legs fall apart again, her own hand sliding down to tangle in thick, curly hair. 'I bet you can't anyway,' she murmured tauntingly. 'Not so soon. And I've only got a while now – if I'm late for shift I'll lose money, you know that.'

'You won't be late.' He felt the heat flood through him again and tightened his grip on her. 'We've plenty of time to enjoy ourselves,' he muttered, laying his mouth against hers and feeling a surge of triumph as her lips opened beneath his. 'Come on, Maggie – one more for luck, eh?'

He pushed her skirts aside and straddled her, rising on his knees to stare down at her, rejoicing in his domination. What of her power now, as she lay beneath him, vanquished, eyes closing and then fluttering open again, flinching and moaning with each aggressive thrust? What of his so-called weakness which could become this strength, this victory declared night after night on a dusty hill over the smoky town?

Joe lifted his head and stared up at the sky, lit with a sullen red glow from the furnaces that belched smoke day and night. Through the haze, he caught a brief glimpse of the moon, riding high, tinged with colour like a globe of red-hot glass on the end of a blowing-iron. He saw a few stars, faint and shifting, and as the pressure inside him increased he felt himself soaring amongst them, free, untrammelled, unowned by anyone. And then the night exploded and he knew himself to be a king.

Chapter Four

As soon as she decently could, rather sooner, in her Aunt Susan's disapproving view, Christina began to make herself known in every quarter of her new domain.

Thanks to her father and to her own insatiable curiosity, she was already familiar with a good deal of it. But there was a difference, she discovered, between simply standing by watching and being in control herself. It made demands on her that she didn't expect; sharpened her brain in a way that she found stimulating and enjoyable.

'These are the wages ledgers, I see,' she remarked one day in the small back office where Mr Honeyborne worked. She hauled a large volume, two feet by one and weighing several pounds, on to the desk and opened it at random. 'Yes, I see, all the men are recorded here. Scriven – twenty shillings a week; Cartwright – seven shillings and sixpence; Rockes – twenty-eight shillings. Cartwright – who is he?'

'One of the footmakers,' John Honeyborne replied. 'The redheaded one, works on George Rockes's chair.'

'Oh yes, I know.' She replaced the volume. 'Show me the sales ledgers, please.'

Honeyborne lifted down another heavy ledger. 'This shows our sales over the past quarter, Miss Christina. As you see, we're supplying several large shops in London, as well as our usual customers: Lord Chester, Sir Ranulf, Mr Danby . . . And if I may say so, the catalogue which you illustrated yourself has done very well. We've had a good many enquiries for it, and several orders resulting.'

Christina smiled. She had enjoyed making the drawings for the new catalogue, and it had been her idea to embellish their price lists with tiny pictures too. It had given her a feeling of belonging to the glasshouse, working for it, long before her father had died and she had found herself in charge.

'And the advertisements in the *London Illustrated News*?' she asked, for she had been the first to see the possibilities of using the new picture paper when it began publication only two years ago. 'Are they having effect?'

'Very good effect,' Honeyborne confirmed. 'We've acquired a good many new customers through its columns. Many of them overseas – families who have gone out to the colonies or to America. Yes, I think we may say that sales are looking very promising, and largely due to your own suggestions.'

'Well, that's all very good.' Christina ran her eye down the neat, flowing script of the pages. 'Yes. I see we're supplying a little to France as well. The Thietry house has bought some – do you think they intend to copy us?'

'They may do, but how are we to prevent them?' Honeyborne shrugged. 'After all, one cannot stop people buying our glass. And your father was always friendly with the Thietrys – he never sought to hide his methods from them.'

'No. And we might benefit from their expertise too . . .' Christina slapped the great book shut. 'This is all very reassuring, Mr Honeyborne, but I'm sure you will agree with me that we must not rest on our laurels. Good trade can become bad trade overnight if care isn't taken always to remain in the forefront of development. Henzel's must not be allowed to fall behind now.'

'Of course not. But I don't really see –'

'New glass, Mr Honeyborne! Fine lead crystal, as soon as we are able. And coloured glass – I want to try ruby and a particular green. We should start experimenting now, so as to be ready to go into production as soon as the excise is removed. And engraving; we have fine shapes, but I feel they are being spoiled by poor cutting and engraving. We need to think of new methods. The Bohemians are fine engravers, Mr Honeyborne, and so are the French and Germans. We should be looking to them for lessons.' She moved to the window, looking out into the long room where the ledger clerks sat working on their high stools. 'There are other things I would like to try too, cameo incrustation, for example. Or enamelling. Silvering – oh, there's so much, so much!' Her hands clasped at her waist, she swung round, eyes on fire. 'Don't you feel that we are standing at the threshold of a great era in glassmaking, Mr Honeyborne? A tremendous surge of power and prosperity? Don't you feel that we need only the tiniest thrust to send us all soaring into spheres we've never dared dream of? Glass – it's so wonderful. And we're so – *fortunate* to be making it!'

John Honeyborne stared at her. He had been working for glassmakers for over thirty years. For all that time, he had been coming to the glassworks every day, shutting himself into his musty office and surrounding himself with the big, heavy ledgers. He had seen the glass being made, he had watched it being engraved and cut, and he had seen it go out of the showroom, packed carefully in straw, its gleaming surface wrapped in soft rags to prevent damage. He had a few pieces at home: a set of wineglasses, a tumbler or two, a few friggers. But he had never before seen it as Christina saw it. Never felt that thrill of excitement that now transmitted itself from her to him. Never known his heart to leap, as it did now, at the thought of more and different glass to be made.

'Yes,' he said slowly. 'I do feel that, Miss Christina. And I do think we're fortunate to be making it.'

It was a feeling that had come late to him. But he knew that it was a sensation that would be with him now and for ever.

Others, however, were less impressed by Christina's zeal.

'The kitchen! You went into the kitchen?' Susan Henzel pursed her lips with exasperation. 'Christina, what will you do next? Haven't I always told you –'

'That no real lady ever sets foot into her kitchen. I know. But then, I'm not a lady, am I.' There was an excitement in saying it, a daring feeling that reminded her of the time she had worn Frederic's clothes to make that first excursion into the glasshouse. 'You've told me that often enough, too, Aunt Susan. No lady would have dreamed of entering a glasshouse either – at least, unless it were on some special occasion, with the men wearing their Sunday clothes and all the clutter swept from the floor.' Christina smiled. 'I've done that, gone in and out as if I were a man myself, yes, and seen the glassmakers working half-naked, and taken it as calmly as if they were my own brothers!' She took no notice at all of her aunt's horrified gasp. 'And what harm came of it? None, unless you think inheriting the family business can be considered harm!'

'That, certainly, is a matter for conjecture,' her aunt retorted acidly. 'But there is little I can say about *that* – unfortunately. However, as regards the kitchen –'

But the kitchen, once forbidden territory, had become part of Christina's domain too. And she was determined that no part of her new kingdom should remain a mystery to her.

She thought again of what she had seen there, from the moment she had opened the green baize door and passed through into the passage and down the cold stone stairs. No one had noticed her at first. She stood just inside the kitchen door, her green eyes moving about the dim cave of a room, taking everything in.

It was much bigger than she had expected – as big as the grand dining room which was Aunt Susan's pride and joy with its highly-polished furniture and glowing silver. But with size, the resemblance ended. The dining room was quiet and comfortable, the sounds of footsteps muffled by rich carpet, the darkness lit by the flames of the coal fire and tiny points of light from the candelabra standing on the table and the sideboard. It shone with cleanliness, the air scented by flowers and perfume. Here in the kitchen, the scene was very different. It took Christina a few moments even to see. Although there was a large window giving on to the basement area, it was barely three feet from the area wall and only a gloomy dullness indicated that it was daylight outside. Oil lamps flickered in corners and on the big central table to assist the faltering light, but even so it was so dark that she wondered how anyone could work at all.

Slowly, she moved across the stone-flagged floor, feeling the cold strike up through her thin indoor shoes, and the short, stout woman at the table glanced up and saw her.

'Well, as I live and breathe. . ! Miss Christina! What in the world brings thee down to the kitchen, miss?'

Christina frowned a little. Mrs Jenner had been cook-housckeeper for a good many years and had known all the children since they were small. And there had been a time, before Aunt Susan had decided that they must be 'ladies and gentlemen', when Christina and her brothers and sisters had run in and out of the kitchen at will, begging titbits from Mrs Jenner. But that had been when they lived at the old house, where everything was smaller and closer and somehow more companionable. When Joshua had built Henzel Court and they had moved in, all that had changed.

'I imagined you had heard,' she said. 'My father left everything to me. I am mistress here now, and I wish to see the kitchens.'

'See the kitchens?' Mrs Jenner pursed her lips. She looked as disapproving as Aunt Susan. 'Is there something not to your liking then, miss?'

'No, of course not.' Christina glanced around the room, her eyes slowly becoming accustomed to the dimness now. Along one wall stood the big range, a coal fire glowing in the centre between the two ovens. A large dresser occupied another wall, its shelves stacked with everyday china and glass. Under the window was a low sink, with a small, thin girl bent over it vigorously scrubbing at pots and pans. She had given Christina one scared glance and gone back to her work, scouring frenziedly as if she expected to be dismissed at any moment for extreme idleness.

'There's nothing wrong at all,' Christina said reassuringly. 'I simply wanted to see where you all worked. Our food just arrives in the dining room, and I realised that I had no idea how. Perhaps you'd like to show me.'

Mrs Jenner cast a harassed glance at the kitchen clock, ticking loudly on the mantelpiece. 'To be sure, miss, if you say so, but Miss Henzel did say that luncheon would be wanted prompt at one, and there's mutton to boil and a pudding to be made, as well as all the vegetables. But if you say you're mistress here now –'

'I am. But I don't want to interfere with my aunt's arrangements, and I certainly don't want to interrupt your work.' Christina smiled at the cook, unaware that the softening of her eyes and mouth took the woman straight back to the days when the young Henzels had been in and out of her kitchen as if they were her own family. 'Perhaps if I could just sit here for a while and watch you . . . ? Don't take any notice of me. I just want to get to know you all.'

'"Get to know us," indeed!' Mrs Jenner exclaimed later when she was recounting the story to the other servants over their tea. 'As if we were friends called in for morning sherry and such! And that's just what her did. Sat there, easy as you please, watching while me and Daisy got the luncheon things on. I hardly knew where to put meself, and that's honest. I mean, to have the mistress watching everything you do – though it's hard to think of Miss Christina as the mistress, I must say.'

'I don't know that I agree with you there,' the butler said judiciously, spreading jam on a thick slice of bread that was still warm from the oven. 'I've always thought there was more to Miss Christina than met the eye. Got a lot of her dad in her, and that's a fact. And he always had to be in charge.'

'Well, that's true enough, Mr Parker, I know. But there's a deal of difference atween old Mr Henzel and Miss Christina. She's just a bit of a girl, when all's said and done, and while Miss Henzel's still in the house I can't help looking to she for my orders.'

'And I daresay that's where they'll be coming from for a good while yet,' Mr Parker said comfortably. 'Miss Christina's just a little girl playing at house, and when the novelty's worn off she'll be only too glad to go back to her dances and plays and having a good time, before she gets wed and settles down. It's bound to go to her head a bit, being left everything that way, but once she realises the responsibility that goes with it all she'll be happy to hand over the reins. I should carry on just as always, Mrs Jenner, and don't take too much notice. She won't be coming down here again.'

'Wish she would,' Daisy said, passing her cup for more tea. 'I 'adn't never seen her afore. I thought her were right pretty. And them clothes! Wish I was you, Ruth, seein' into all them upstairs rooms and touching them pretty things an' all. I wonder if I could ever get to be a lady's maid.'

'Not much chance of that if you can't even clean a pot proper,' Mrs Jenner told her sharply. 'Some of those saucepans were dirtier when you finished than when you started. And there's still some to be done from luncheon, so you'd better finish your tea quick and get on with it, I'll be wanting them again for dinner. Lady's maid!' she added when the scullery maid had gulped down her tea and scurried back to her sink. 'About as much chance of becoming a lady's maid as a sweep's boy, that girl has. And you're not much better, Ruth.' She rounded on the girl who had stayed silent so far, sitting between the parlour maid, Rose, and Robert, the footman. 'I thought you were supposed to be doing nursery tea today?'

'Yes, but Nurse wants tomorrow off instead of today so I had to change.' Ruth's voice was soft; she rarely raised it much above a whisper, which irritated Mrs Jenner but made her a favourite in the nursery, where Thomas was always distressed by raised or harsh voices.

'So you'm at a loose end, then?'

Ruth spoke hastily, seeing the gleam in the cook's eye. 'Not really, Mrs Jenner. I have to go and help Miss Adela wash her hair, and there's some mending to do, Miss Christina caught her dress at the glasshouse and tore it badly. And then –'

'Tore her dress at the glasshouse!' Mrs Jenner had stopped listening. She turned back to the butler, as stout as herself, steadily eating his way through the new bread and home-made jam. 'I really don't know what the world's coming to, Mr Parker! When little chits of girls like Miss Christina are put in charge of great factories meant only for men to work in – and them some of the roughest men in the Black Country – well, words fail me, they really do. What Mr Henzel must have been thinking of . . . !'

'I'll tell you what he was thinking of.' Mr Parker wiped his mouth delicately and leaned forward. 'He was thinking of her marrying that young Mr Jeremy; combining the two family firms. Stands to reason, don't it. I mean, a girl like that, barely twenty years old, controlling a great house and a factory besides . . . ! No. He meant it all to work out just like I've told you. Miss Christina married to Mr Jeremy so that he can take charge of the glasshouse, and Miss Henzel left here to look after the house and the rest of the family.' He paused and took a long drink of tea. 'That'll be the way of it, you mark my words. In a year's time, we'll be looking back at this and laughing. And there'll be no more talk of petticoat government at the glasshouse, and no more having the mistress sitting at your kitchen table, watching everything you do. Just a flash in the pan – that's all it is, a flash in the pan.'

'I expect you'm right, Mr Parker,' Mrs Jenner said comfortably, and lifted the big brown teapot to refill his cup.

In the drawing room, however, things were not so comfortable, and Christina was aware that her aunt was really angry. Her foray into the kitchen seemed to have struck a very tender nerve.

'I am at a loss to understand you, Christina,' she was saying now. 'You seem to believe that this inheritance has made you all-powerful, that nobody else can be trusted to do even the simple tasks they have been carrying out for years.' Her mouth trembled a little with self-pity and her voice took on the martyred tone Christina had heard all too often during her aunt's altercations with Joshua. 'I cannot think, Christina, that you have any cause for complaint in the way that I have managed your father's home – yes, and brought up his children too, since before your poor mother died. I have always tried to do my best for you, for your mother's sake, and your father's, though little thanks I ever got from him. And this latest madness – leaving you the entire property – I have to say that I am inclined to agree with my cousins. Joshua must have suffered some kind of brainstorm. It can happen, I believe, that a man is quite mad yet appear perfectly normal. Not that Joshua was ever quite like other men – ever –'

'Ever normal?' Christina's eyes flashed danger. 'Be very careful, Aunt Susan.'

The older woman looked at her, seeing the small, tense face, the rigidly-held body. Her voice softened.

'Christina, I know this is a difficult time for you. I know how much your father meant to you. But surely you must see, it simply isn't practical to behave as you're doing now. Visiting the glasshouse every day, trying to understand the work your father did, endeavouring to run the household here. You're not prepared for any of it.' She moved towards her niece, touching the fine wool of the sleeve that hid the thinness of the arm beneath. 'Why

63

must you try to take it all on yourself? There are plenty of us willing to help you. I've run the house for years now, why not let me continue to do so? And the glasshouse –'

'Yes?' The word came out sharply, a ragged indication of the stress within.

'Wouldn't it be sensible to allow my cousins to help you with the glasshouse? They are all only too willing, Samuel, Alfred, Harold. Even Reuben. And –' her aunt paused '– there's Jeremy, too. He's very fond of you, Christina.'

Restlessly, Christina turned away. She moved across to the window, looking out over the garden to the smoke of the town. The tips of the three red-brick glass-cones were just visible. Her father had taken pride in the view of those cones; he had sited the house with care, felling trees that might obscure it, so that he could stand at any of the windows on this side and see the tawny, sloping walls.

The cones were nearly fifty years old now, built at the turn of the century. The new system had made the manufacture of glass a great deal more efficient than the old way; not only did the great cone, often a hundred feet high or more, act as the furnace chimney and create a powerful updraught that kept the fires at white heat, but the space between the furnace itself and the outside wall provided a very convenient working area. Up to twelve pots could be housed in that central furnace, each with a chair of men working at it, and arches at the sides for the annealing tunnel and stores. There were cones all over the glassmaking area of the Black Country now. But Henzel's were the only ones visible from the house and Christina felt again the surge of pride that she knew her father had also experienced whenever he looked out at the sooty red tips.

Let the cousins take over Henzel's? For that was what her aunt was suggesting. Her instincts rebelled, as they had from the moment of first hearing her father's wishes read out by Henry Ambrose. But Jeremy? That was something she would have to think about. Meanwhile . . .

She turned away from the window, facing her aunt across the darkening room.

'I'm sure you're right, Aunt Susan. About the house, I mean. I have no real wish to become a housekeeper, and I think, in a little while, that I will be very happy to leave such matters to you. But –' she glanced around the drawing room, indicating the furniture, the carpets and curtains, with a small, delicate hand '– don't you see, if all this is now my responsibility, I must know just what it all means. Until now, it has just been my home, I've never taken much notice of it all. Now, suddenly, it's mine and I find myself looking at things as if I've never seen them before.'

Susan stared at her, trying to understand. 'But, Christina, why trouble yourself with such things as the *kitchen*? Even I seldom go there – it's Mrs Jenner's business what happens there. It's not simply that it isn't seemly, Christina, you could cause real offence to the servants by going into their quarters, particularly unannounced. And really, did it serve any useful purpose to sit at the kitchen table and watch the luncheon being prepared?'

'Yes, I believe it did.' Christina was still walking about the room, her hands clasped together. 'Aunt Susan, have you any idea what conditions the servants work in, down there? It's dark, for a start, hardly any light comes through the window, with that gloomy wall right outside. And it's cold underfoot, even though the range fires are lit early each morning. In summer, it must be unbearably hot. And the scullery, it's almost pitch dark in there and there's a little girl, Daisy, they call her, who does nothing but *scrub*. She scrubs pots and pans, she scrubs the kitchen floor, she scrubs the range and when she's done all that she scrubs pots and pans again. A child, she can't be more than nine years old, and she never sees daylight. I asked Mrs Jenner and she told me that the girl goes out only one afternoon a month, to church, and she has to go straight there and straight back, and speak to no one on the way.'

'And quite right too,' Susan said tersely. 'Christina, you're making far too much of this. I know the child you mean and she's a good twelve years old, although I admit she's small for her age. What would she want with time off? She has no family to visit – she came to us from the workhouse. The other servants are her family, and very fortunate she is to have such a good place. Why, in time she should become a kitchen maid, she could even rise to be a cook one day. Someone has to do the work, Christina – unless you wish to take that over too!'

Christina flinched away from the unaccustomed sarcasm, but she was too occupied to think of a reply, her mind still busy with the image of the white-faced child who had spent the whole morning bent over the low sink.

'It seems such hard work for such a small girl,' she said. 'I think we should employ another scullery maid.'

'Another scullery maid! And then a second kitchen maid, no doubt, to help Jane, and perhaps two or three more footmen and a second butler!' Having once tasted the power of sarcasm, Susan found it coming more easily to her tongue. 'Christina, you are making the mistake of thinking of the servants as if they were like us. They are not. They are different: stronger, accustomed to hard work and long hours. And indeed, what would they do with the extra time that all these additional servants would give them? Most of them cannot read, you know. They have no letters to write, no calls to pay. The younger ones would be restless, bored, wanting time off – and what would *that* lead to? And the older ones would be unhappy without their work. No.' Susan rose from her chair, smoothing down her skirts. 'You must take my advice on this matter and leave matters below stairs just as they are. And let me oversee the household affairs, just as I always have.'

* * *

Harry was in the nursery when Christina found him. He was playing with Thomas, before the fire, helping to pack the wooden animals back into their Noah's Ark.

'Elephant,' Thomas said, picking the creature up by its trunk. 'Horse, camel?' A look of doubt crossed his face and he glanced at Harry for confirmation.

'No, that's a zebra. This is a camel.' Harry placed the two camels side by side at the foot of the ramp and Thomas chuckled and walked them up into the Ark. 'That's right, Tommy. Now you put the rest in yourself.'

'He always gets mixed up between the camel and the zebra,' Christina observed. 'I can't think why, they're not a bit alike.'

'You can't tell what goes on in his head.' Harry helped the stubby fingers to close the door. 'Now they're all safe from the flood, aren't they, Tom? Come out and play again tomorrow, eh?'

'Play again tomorrow.' Thomas grinned at his brother and sister, and Christina caught him to her and hugged him. There was something very endearing about Thomas, the youngest of the family and doomed never to be more than a child. She looked at the flattened face, the slanting eyes and rounded ears, wondering why he had been born like this, his mind always groping for understanding, never quite able to develop the skills that had come so easily to the rest of them, growing slowly and unsteadily where his brothers and sisters had raced ahead. Mongolian Idiocy, they called it, this condition for which there was apparently no cure. And Christina could remember the arguments that had taken place when it was first realised, when Thomas was about a year old, eleven years ago now. She herself had been only nine and not supposed to know what the adults were talking about, but that had been before they moved to the big house and gossip had, as always, filtered through to the kitchen and the nursery.

'Doctor says he'll have to be put away,' Mrs Jenner

had said, shaking her head over the pastry she was rolling. 'Never grow up properly, babies like that. Never right. It seems a shame, for he's a dear little baby in spite of everything, but it's not fair to keep him here, getting used to the family and all, when everyone knows he'll end up in an asylum.'

'I'm not so sure.' Parker had come down to the kitchen for a silver tray to carry Joshua's lunchtime sherry up to him. 'The master says he won't have it. There's quite a ding-dong going on up there about it, this very minute. With the mistress still so poorly and Miss Henzel taking charge – she's all for sending him away at once, but the master won't agree. He's getting into a real temper about it.'

'Won't agree? You mean he's going to keep Master Thomas here?'

Christina, hidden under the table with a piece of gingerbread, had pricked up her ears.

'That's what it looks like,' Parker said, giving the tray a polish.

'But how? I've seen children like that before – they had one at my last place. Sent him away straight off, they did, and carried on as if he'd never bin born. And what else could they do? He was never more than an idiot and he died when he was no more than ten years old – a happy release it was, too.'

Died at ten years old? Christina felt the smart of tears behind her eyelids.

'Well, the master says if Master Thomas is going to die young he might as well stay at home and have a bit of comfort meanwhile. And if he's going to live longer and still be like a child, he can stay in the nursery – it's to be kept for him as long as he needs it.'

'Kept in the nursery? Well, I never did!' Mrs Jenner slapped the pastry on top of a big pie-dish. 'You never know what the master will take it into his head to do next. What will people say?'

'The master doesn't care what anyone thinks of him, and that's the truth of it.' Parker went towards the door. 'If he means to keep Master Thomas at home, that's what he'll do. Mark my words.'

And that was exactly what Joshua had done. Thomas had been as much a part of the family as any of the other children. Always there, in the nursery, learning slowly to walk, to talk in his odd, slightly slurred voice, to play a few simple games. They had taken him on picnics, helped him with the dissected pictures which he loved, played endlessly with his Noah's Ark and farm, for Thomas loved animals. And they had been rewarded by a love and an adoring affection that drew them all to the nursery whenever they had the chance.

Of course, the cousins had never approved. A permanent child, in a nursery that would never change, it was a matter of shame to them and their wives. A sign of some weakness in Joshua or Margaret, that could bring forth an idiot. He should be sent to an institution, they said over and over again. An asylum for the simple and the mad.

'People like that aren't quite human,' Christina had heard one of them tell her father. 'They're not to be trusted – like wild animals. Oh, endearing enough now, while he's small, I grant you, but one day he'll turn nasty. He'll be dangerous then. One of these nights you'll wake up to find your house in flames or your daughters murdered in their beds, and then perhaps you may regret your foolishness.'

But Joshua, first laughing off their cautions, had at last grown angry and threatened to close his doors to his cousins unless they went about their own business and left him to do the same. He had refused to send Thomas away, to be treated as a lunatic and visited like a sideshow on Sundays by those who thought the spectacle of the unhappy inmates an entertaining one. And he had kept the child at home, where Tommy's sunny temper and enduring happiness had warmed the whole family.

'Do you remember when we were all together, before we started to grow up?' Harry said as Nurse came to take Thomas for his bath. 'Not so much Alice – she always seemed to be grown up! – but you and I and Frederic and Adela. We had some happy times with our games and our picnics. It was never quite the same after we came to this house.'

'Frederic went to King Edward's,' Christina said, thinking of the loneliness that had assailed her without the elder brother she followed everywhere. 'And Miss Crossley seemed stricter, somehow. And now, Frederic's gone and you are at the Grammar School. And Alice is married and there are only Adela and I left at home. And Tommy, of course,' she added quickly, but they both knew that Thomas would never leave the nursery. 'And without Papa everything is different.'

'Yes.' Harry frowned at his boots. 'Christina, I want to talk to you.'

'Talk away,' she said, smiling, but he shook his head and she saw that his face was unusually serious.

'Not here. Let's go out.' He glanced impatiently at the darkening sky. 'Let's walk in the garden, up the hill, anything. I feel crowded indoors, Chrissie. There are too many people about.' He uncoiled his long body from the fireside chair and stretched. Christina wondered if he was ever going to stop growing. He seemed taller with each month, and even seemed to have grown during the few days since their father's death. But he was nothing like Joshua. Fair-haired, blue-eyed and slender, he took after their mother, Margaret, and there was sometimes about him an air of the same delicacy.

In less than five minutes Christina had fetched a cloak and Harry a jacket. They tiptoed down the stairs, aware that the family would be taking tea in the drawing room, and slipped unseen out of the side door.

70

'I expected to see that young maid – Ruth, is it? – in the nursery today,' Harry remarked as they went out into the cold air. 'But Nurse says she wants tomorrow off instead, so Ruth agreed to change.'

'I like Ruth,' Christina said thoughtfully. 'She's very good with Thomas, and I don't mind having her around me. I've been thinking of making her my personal maid – she could still help in the nursery – and engaging another girl to help Adela and do the kitchen work Ruth does now. We really don't have enough servants, Harry.'

'Don't we? I haven't noticed anything wrong.'

'Oh, there isn't anything *wrong*, not in the sense that they don't do the work. But they have to work so hard! I saw Rose the other evening, struggling up the stairs with more coal for the drawing room fire and she looked so tired. It can't be right.'

'Well, you can do as you please about that now.' Harry was obviously not very interested in the problem of servants. 'But I do think it's a good idea to make Ruth your personal maid.' They had passed the lawns now and were walking down the path that led to the little wood. Harry slapped at the trees with his stick and fell silent.

'What was it you wanted to say to me, Harry?' Christina prompted. 'Was it about pocket money? I haven't access to Papa's accounts yet, but Mr Ambrose says that I can apply to him for anything we need. If there's anything you –'

'Pocket money?' Harry stopped and stared. 'I hadn't even thought of that! No, it's not money.' He frowned and shook his head. 'It's our whole future, Chrissie. You seem to think it all so simple. But I can see what it will be. The cousins will wear you down, sis. They never liked Papa's unconventional ways, and this is the worst thing he's ever done, as far as they're concerned. They won't rest until they've got their way.'

71

'And what is their way? They want to own the glasshouse themselves, combine it with their own firm. It's impossible, without my consent.' Christina spoke proudly, but Harry shook his head.

'It won't be easy for you, Chrissie. Even with their support, it would be hard for you to make your way in a man's world, and there's no world more a man's than glassmaking. Without it, I don't think you can manage. And that's what they're hoping. And then they'll look to me.'

'To you?'

'Yes.' He stopped, catching at her arm, his voice taking on an urgency that startled her. 'Christina, they all know how stubborn you are. You're just like Papa – neither of you would ever give in. The cousins know that you'll try to run Henzel's yourself, whatever the difficulties. They believe that you'll fail, and that when you fail, you'll turn to me to help you. Because I am your brother – the only one you could turn to without admitting defeat.' His voice shook. 'I don't want to go into the glass industry, Chrissie. You know I have other plans, but I'm afraid that now Papa's gone, I'll never be able to carry them out.'

They had reached the end of the little wood and Christina stopped by the wicket gate that led into the field beyond, and turned to search her brother's expression in the shadowy twilight. His hands were gripping the little gate, the knuckles gleaming white. A lump rose into her throat, blocking her words, and she shook her head, momentarily mute. Then she reached forward and took Harry's hands in her own slender fingers.

'Harry, you know I wouldn't stop you doing anything you wanted to do. How could I? I –'

He interrupted her, his voice ragged, cracking a little. 'How could you? Chrissie, don't you realise you have power over us all now? Me, Adela, Tommy, Ruth, Mrs Jenner, Parker, all the other servants. Even Aunt Susan.

We all depend on you.' His blue eyes burned and he shook her hands, trying to force understanding into her. 'It wasn't just the glasshouse Father left you in his will,' he said intensely. 'It was the whole family.'

Chapter Five

Ruth Compson pulled her shawl closer around her shoulders as she hurried between the pools of thick yellow light cast by the gas lamps on the uneven pavements. In a few moments she would be turning away from the light, plunging into the maze of unlit backstreets where only the flickering of a candle or oil lamp in a window might show the way. But Ruth was not likely to lose herself; she had grown up in these teeming alleys.

William Compson had been one of the first of Henzel's gaffers to be allocated a house of his own in the new streets built during one of the glasshouse's periods of expansion. It was no more than any of the others, just two rooms downstairs and two up, with an outside privy. But an entire house to one family was a luxury to which few of the glasshouse workers could aspire, and it was a measure of Joshua Henzel's regard for his best gaffers that he was so generous.

It had been crowded enough, at times. William and his wife Sal had brought up eight surviving children there; four had died, either at birth or in infancy. But Ruth could not remember a time when all eight had lived there together – by the time she had been old enough to take notice, her sisters Ann and Sarah had been out at service, and in the time since she herself had left home, little Willy had been born. All the same, there had seldom been less than five of them sharing the small rooms, together with their parents. And, always, there had been Joe.

Ruth sometimes wondered why Joe had stayed at home for so long. He must be twenty-seven years old now, an age when most men were married and starting their own family. But Joe showed no signs of giving up his single life, and neither did his parents appear to want him to go. He remained in the small terraced house, contributing enough from his wage to make life considerably more comfortable in the crowded house than in most of the others. Like other men, he had his interests – his whippet, the occasional prize-fight or bull-baiting, his night classes at the Mechanics' Institute and, Ruth knew, he had his women. Perhaps Joe was wiser than others of his generation. Or perhaps he simply hadn't found the woman he wanted to settle down with.

But that, Ruth thought as she turned the last corner and saw the light of the oil lamp that was her mother's pride and joy, was just romantic nonsense. The kind of nonsense that Joe himself would say had been the inevitable result of working in a big house such as Henzel's.

The front door was unlatched as usual and she pushed through the dark, narrow passage, past the seldom-used parlour with its religious tracts on the painted walls, its tiled fireplace and rag rug, pride of place given to the organ that William played for an hour each Sunday evening. It had never occurred to either of her parents that this room could be used for living in – as a bedroom for some of the children who shared one of the upstairs rooms with Joe, or even for Joe himself. A parlour, closed off from the rest of the house and entered only on Sundays, was essential for a respectable working family who occupied their own house.

In any case, everyone preferred the kitchen into which Ruth now stepped. With a fire always burning in the polished black range, it was warm and cosy. And there was nearly always a smell of cooking, either from the Dutch oven standing on its stride in front of the fire, or from the bread oven, or occasionally, when either Joe or William had brought in extra money, from the meat jack which twisted a joint slowly before the heat, its spring taking nearly an hour to unwind. Ruth could remember clearly when it was her job to sit there, constantly basting the precious meat to prevent it from drying out.

There was no meat to baste this afternoon, but her mother had just taken a fresh loaf from the bread oven and slapped it on the table that stood in the middle of the room, where it was immediately surrounded by the smallest of the children, who gazed at it with wide, hungry eyes.

'Now you leave that alone,' Sal ordered them, brushing them back from the table as if they were flies. 'That's for your father's supper. Mebbe there'll be a bit left over for you, and mebbe there won't. There's still a crust from yesterday's loaf, and that's to be eaten first.'

Ruth's father had already left for work. He worked alternately with Joe, Joe's hours being from midnight until six in the morning, and again from twelve noon until six in the evening. He would pass his father in the door as the shifts changed; they were only at home together at the weekends, Saturday until Tuesday, when the glasshouses were silent as new pots were brought to full temperature and fresh batches mixed and melted.

These hours made Sal's life as difficult as that of most of the other glassmakers' wives. There was never a moment when one or other of her men was not either just going to, or coming from work, wanting meals, or sleeping. It meant that work for her, outside the home, was impossible. A few wives did manage to work. The wives of footmakers, generally younger and always less well-paid, were forced to. They worked as packers, like Maggie Haden, or did jobs at home – dressmaking, washing, even nailmaking in outhouses. Even then, Ruth knew, they found it difficult to make ends meet. Sometimes one would open up a shop, often in the damp, crowded cellar which was her home, and you would pass old boots and shoes laid out on the pavement for sale.

Gaffers like William and Joe were well-off by comparison

and their families well-fed. But even they couldn't afford to eat as Ruth did in the Henzel household.

The children groaned, cast the loaf a last, longing look, and then went back to their occupations. The girls were making a peg rug from old clothes torn into shreds, using a wooden peg, cut into two and shaped for the task. Willy was frowning over a pair of scissors and some old sheets of the *County Express*, folding and cutting it to make patterns, which were then painted to decorate the edges of the dresser shelves.

Sal and Ruth sat down in the two easy chairs, one on each side of the range. It still felt strange to Ruth to be sitting there, in her father's chair instead of on the floor or one of the wooden chairs that stood pushed under the table. As if leaving home and going into service had raised her to the status of visitor. It made her feel slightly uneasy, as if she had become distanced from her family; no longer part of the warm, integral whole but outside, on the edges, like someone looking in wistfully through a window.

'So 'ow bin things up at the house?' Sal asked, picking up her work. She too was making a rug, but she was using a steel podger instead of a peg, her fingers moving rapidly as she pushed it in and out. 'Settlin' down? Young Miss Christina given up her wild ideas?'

'No, an' I don't see her giving them up neither. She's set on running the whole place herself, and she won't listen to none of them other Henzels. She were in the glasshouse again today, settin' 'em all by the ears. Not that it'll last, Mr Parker says. He reckons it's just a flash in the pan – says she'll be tiring of it soon, like a kid with a new toy.'

'And what does he think'll happen to the glasshouse then?'

It was no idle question. Since the conditions of Joshua's will had become general knowledge, every man in the glasshouse, and thus every woman or child whose livelihood depended on it, had been asking it. What would happen to the glasshouse and would Christina continue to manage it? Few of them believed it likely. The most widely-held view was that it would pass to the Henzel cousins. But this was of little comfort to the men who had worked under Joshua.

'Aye, Joshua Henzel were a hard man,' Joe said later when he came in from his latest bout with Maggie Haden on Dob Hill. 'But he had some good points. You allus knew where you were with him, and he was allus fair. And he didn't mind you trying summat new, neither. He knew it was the man as blows the glass as knows what can be done wi' it.' He rubbed his hands together and held them out to the glowing coals. 'By, it's cold out there tonight.'

'And you don't think the other Henzels'll be so good to work for?' Sal asked, still busy with her rug.

Joe snorted. 'Them! They don't know what glass is for! Turnin' out their bottles by the dozen – they 'ouldn't know fine glass if it hit them on the nose. And sheet glass for winders, where's the skill in that, blowin' a plain roll and slittin' it open to roll flat like a woman mekkin' pies! Not that crown glass is any better, spinnin' an iron round like a woman trundlin' a floor mop, and finishing up with something you can't even see through.' He jerked his head at the windows, the vision through them obscured by the round 'bull's eye' that resulted from this method of manufacture. 'As for lead – when we gets it back in any amount worth working on – well, they won't know what they've got and that's the truth on't. No, it'll be a sad day for Henzel's if the others gets their hands on the glasshouse. I won't be staying there, for one!'

'You won't?' Ruth looked at her brother. Nearly twelve years younger than he, she had never been especially close to him, seeing him more as another father, a great, gruff being with rough and casual authority over her, than as a brother. It was only since she had left home to go into service that they had found a common link in the Henzel family.

'You'd rather work under Miss Christina than the Henzel cousins?' she asked now.

Joe looked exasperated.

'We've said so, haven't we, but what sort of a choice is that to give a man?' he demanded, lifting the tankard of ale Willy had just brought in from the tavern. 'Petticoat government or flat glass for windows – for that's what Harold and Samuel will have us mekkin', mark my words. After the kind o' work we've been turnin' out, and with the other houses goin' over to flint any time, I'll have none of it, none of it, I tell you!'

'You mean you'd go to another glasshouse? Leave Henzel's?' There was a note of incredulity in her voice, and Sal dropped her work in her lap to stare at her son. 'But Compsons have worked along of Henzels as long as there's bin glass. D'you really mean to say you'd do that, Joe?'

Joe shrugged irritably.

'I never said anything. I just said I'll have none of flat glass, and if that's what it comes to –'

'You wouldn't think of settin' up on yer own?' Sal's tone held dread and Joe gave a snort of derision.

'A crib? Me? Don't talk so far back, our Ma! I've got a bit more pride than that, I hope. I wonder you can even think on't – me, workin' in a back shed, on some rubbishy fire, meltin' down cullet that's been scraped up in the streets! I suppose you'll be thinkin' to send young Willy out to pick up broken bottles for me next, like those gyppos from Mud City.' He gave the women a withering glance. 'Look, forget I ever said anythin'. All I said was, I 'ouldn't go into flat glass, if that's what Henzel's comes to. Me and the men have agreed to give Miss Christina a chance. We'll just have to wait an' see, and hope them other Henzels don't get control.'

'But even they couldn't want *you* to make flat glass,' Ruth said, dismay showing through her quiet voice. 'Not you and me dad. You're artists.'

'And who says that?' he demanded, so abruptly that she flinched and stammered.

'Why, Miss Christina, of course. And Mr Joshua. They both said so. They think – Mr Joshua thought – the world of you, Joe. You couldn't leave the glasshouse, not now when Miss Christina needs –'

'Needs *me*?' He flashed her a look from his dark eyes that made her cringe back even further in her chair. 'Dunna make me laugh, Ruthie! She's never said that.'

'No, she hasn't. But you know she needs *all* the men to work together, to prove she *can* run the business. I've heard her say that, many a time, she's said it to me herself.' Ruth looked at her mother and brother, her eyes shining suddenly. 'Ma, I forgot – I meant to tell you but then Joe came in and it went right out of my mind – Miss Christina's made me her personal maid! What do you think of that?'

'Her personal maid?' Sal echoed. 'You mean lookin' after her clothes and such?'

'And doin' her hair and goin' with her when she wants to go out, and all,' Ruth confirmed. 'And I won't have to do no more kitchen work – I'm to help Nurse with Master Thomas when she wants, that's all, and that's just because he likes me, Miss Christina said. Otherwise I'm to work only for her. In't that something like?'

'Well, it is. Our Ruthie a lady's maid.' Sal shook her head. 'You've done right well since you went up there to work, Ruth. I'm proud of you, and that's a fact. What do you say, Joe?'

'Aye.' He nodded slowly and glanced at her sideways. 'Reckon you'll be too good for the likes of us, sis.'

'Don't be daft, our Joe,' she said, her pale face flushing. 'This is home, you're my family. We're all close here, not like –' she stopped, flushing again.

'Not like up at the house, is that what you're sayin'?' Joe was watching her intently. 'Don't reckon there's much family feelin' there, now that the old man's gone; only

Miss Christina and her auntie, and that poor little idiot kid. Dunno what they do with all them big rooms and only the few of them to rattle around in 'em.'

'There's more than that,' Ruth protested. 'There's Miss Adela, you've forgot her. And Master Harry. And Mrs Jenner and Mr Parker and Rose and Daisy and Nurse. And Robert the footman, and the boots – oh, and there'll be another girl soon, Miss Christina says they'll need more help in the kitchen now I'm to be moved up, so that'll be another one, and then there's old Mr Crook, the gardener and his boys, and Jake who looks after the horses and –'

'All them folk to look after a handful of people,' Joe marvelled. 'I dunno how you manage here, our Ma, with no servants to wait on you. Of course, not having them big gardens and half a dozen horses to worry about must help, but still –'

'Still, I could do with an extra pair of hands now and then,' Sal said tartly. 'Especially on washday, with the water to be pumped up from the rainwater butt, and the copper to be lit and all the mangling to be done. But that's life, innit? You has your kids and you struggles to bring 'em up and just when they'm getting useful you has to send 'em off to do some other body's bidding. Anyway, our Ruth, you'd best be getting back now, you've been here hard on your hour and if I know that Miss Henzel, she'll be looking at the clock by now. Or has Miss Christina took over seeing to the servants as well?'

'She thought of it,' Ruth said, getting to her feet and holding her hands to the range for one last warm. 'But Miss Henzel didn't like it, and Miss Christina says it's better for her to do it. Running the glasshouse's enough for her, she says. There's plenty to be thinking about there. And there's the family, Master Harry and Miss Adela, she's responsible for them too now, she says, and –'

'Seems to me Miss Christina says plenty to you, seein' as you've only just been made up to personal maid,' Sal observed dryly.

'Well, so she does. She talks to me a lot.' Ruth pulled her shawl back around her shoulders. 'It's my belief she's lonely, got no one she can really talk to, on'y me. I mean, she can't say much to her auntie. Owd Miss Henzel don't like her going in and out of the glasshouse as it is. And Miss Adela's only interested in her clothes and gew-gaws, and Master Harry's at school all day and studying in the evening as well. So who else is there for the poor lass? Anyway, I got to go now.' She bent to kiss her mother's cheek. 'See you next week, Ma, 'night, Joe.'

'Here, I'll see you back.' Joe stood up and stretched his muscular body. 'Don't like you walkin' back through all them dark streets on your own. Too many queer characters about these days.'

Ruth stared at her brother, open-mouthed. Joe had never offered to escort her before, and she half-thought that he was making fun of her. But already he had pulled his heavy boots back on to his feet, thrust his arms into the sleeves of his jacket and wound a scarf around his neck.

'No need to look so pop-eyed,' he remarked, catching her expression. 'I suppose I've a right to see my sister back to her place, especially now she's a lady's maid.'

'I suppose you just wanted an excuse to come out and see one of your fancy-pieces,' she said once they were outside. 'Maggie Haden, she's the latest, in't she?'

'Maggie's at work, and she's not my fancy-piece, and if she were, 'tis nowt of your business.' Joseph tucked her hand into his arm, guiding her over the rough ragstones that paved the street and past an evil-smelling pile of rubbish. 'So you think Miss Christina's finding the glasshouse a bit of a burden, do you?'

'Oh, so that's why you wanted to come.' But there was a smile in Ruth's voice. Joe was as anxious as anyone to know the future, after all. 'No, I never said that. I on'y said she don't want to be bothered with the house and the kitchen an' all. She means to run the factory just as her dad did, and good luck to her. But it depends on you, Joe – you and the rest of the men there.'

'And how d'you make that out?'

Joe's voice was defensive, but Ruth didn't notice it. She spoke slowly, thoughtfully, as they picked their way through the littered alleys towards the gaslit main street.

'Well, it stands to reason, don't it? Henzel's depends on your work. If you all slack off now, don't produce so much or such good glass, just because you're not sure what's goin' to happen, well, things'll get worse, won't they? And folk'll say it's Miss Christina's fault, because she's a woman and should never have been left the glasshouse, and because she wouldn't hand over to Mr Samuel and Mr Harold and that lot. And then she'll find it harder to manage and the men will start to leave and get jobs in other glasshouses, so it'll go on, goin' from bad to worse. But if you and the others keep your word and makes up your minds that Henzel's *will* go on – an' be just as good as in owd Joshua's day – well, I don't see how she can go wrong.'

Ruth stopped. It had been a long speech for her, and she wondered in some panic whether this brother of hers, so much older and so experienced – and an expert glassmaker to boot – would think her impertinent for talking to him so. But Joe said nothing for a few moments; it was as if he were considering her words with some care.

'See, it's like this, Ruthie,' he said at last, and she had the feeling that he was explaining not so much to her as to himself. 'The kind of glass I make, well, that's good, good glass, or I wouldn't be bothered with it, but it in't all I can do. I've never done half the things I want to, not yet. I've got ideas in my head, Ruthie, ideas for really fine crystal glass, bowls and goblets and chalices such as have never been seen before. I've only been waiting for this damned excise to be taken off, and now there's talk of it happenin' at last and owd Joshua has to go and die before we can get usselves started on it. I mean, it's never fair, that, is it. He'd have let me try, I know he would – he was all for mekkin' something new, owd Joshua Henzel, he wasn't one of these cautious Johnnies who waited to see which way the wind blew before he'd put to sea . . . Ruth, when we can use as much lead as we like in glass again without heving to hev it weighed and measured every time we move, we'll be able to mek more than the wineglasses and such that we've been mekkin' for years, we'll be able to experiment, find better mixes, try new shapes. We'll go ahead like a steam train and leave all the other houses standing. Miss Christina's spoken to us, told us she wants to try new things, but has she got the guts to do it, that's what I asks meself?'

'But Miss Christina *has* – I'm sure of it!' Ruth cried. 'She loves glass just as her father did, and she's as tough as him when she's a mind. You've heard her, Joe, she talks to you in the glasshouse, don't she? But do you tell her what you want to do, same as you've towd me?'

Joe shook his head. 'I dunno, girl. It in't never like that between me and Miss Christina. I don't see how it could be. But now you're goin' to be her maid, mebbe you can talk to her.' They reached the big iron gate Joe had spoken of and stopped beside it. 'Does she know you're my sister, Ruthie?'

'I don't know. I've never said so. Probably she don't – 'twas her auntie that took me on, and I don't suppose she ever towd her – if she knowed herself. Why should she? Why, Joe? Do it matter?'

'No, I don't reckon so.' He looked at her for a moment, as if to say something else, then changed his mind. 'Go on in, Ruth, and mebbe we'll see you next week, eh? An' don't get too many airs and graces now you're a lady's maid – you're still our Ruthie, see, and don't you forget it!'

Ruth put out her tongue at him, giggled and slipped in through the gate and along the short drive. Joe stood a moment looking through the dusty trees at the lighted squares of the windows, behind one of which Christina was presumably to be found, and then he turned away and walked slowly back through the mist-laden yellow light that fell in sodden patches over the mud-slimed pavements.

He found it hard to explain to himself just how he felt about Christina Henzel. Away from her, it was easy enough, or had been until recently. She had been simply Joshua Henzel's daughter, playing at being a glassmaker, coming in with her papa to watch the men at work, her cat's eyes big and wondering as they roamed about the vaulted spaces of the tapering cone. Joe had found it easy enough to relate to her then; to slip her the occasional frigger, blown specially for her during baggin-time, to take her aside and let her watch him blow a tiny bowl or vase for her to put a flower into. He had enjoyed her breathless thanks, her admiration. And, as the child had grown and become, lately, a woman, he had enjoyed seeing those same eyes – the eyes of a tiger now, sparked with hints that both excited and disturbed him – move with sudden awakening over his gleaming bare chest, travel almost guiltily across his muscular shoulders, down to his sturdy thighs.

He'd looked at her too, in much the same way, though more surreptitiously – old Joshua would not have tolerated any impertinence even from one of his finest gaffers. But Joe had seen enough to know that Christina Henzel was what he termed a very tasty little morsel. She hadn't got the voluptuous allure of Maggie Haden, it was true, but, by God, she had something – something with those buds of breasts and that tiny waist, so small he knew that if he tried he could have spanned it easily with his two hands.

But he was never likely to get the chance, was he! She was now his employer, and between him and Christina Henzel there stretched a gulf as wide as the Atlantic – as far as from here to America. And it was this awareness that caused him to feel awkward and tongue-tied whenever she came near him, so that his only defence was in an arrogant insolence that concealed his real feelings, yet left him feeling angry and resentful because he seemed unable to control his own behaviour. Why *shouldn't* he behave as easily with a chit like Miss Christina as he could with any other wench? Why couldn't he?

If she *were* any other wench, he mused angrily as he strode through the clattering streets, he would know just what to do. Woo her, and win her, and make her his. And then there'd be an end to it. An end to the soft words and sultry glances that kept him awake at night; an end to the vision of a small, slender body that even came between him and Maggie Haden's more generous attractions.

His woman. If there were any justice in this world, Christina Henzel would be his woman, possessed, tamed and then forgotten. If there were any justice.

But there wasn't. Not for the likes of him.

With Joshua Henzel only six weeks in his grave, Christmas was necessarily kept quietly. Only the nearest cousins came for Christmas dinner, Alfred remaining in Newcastle. Alice and John were there, of course, although John was restless all the day, wanting only to be back in his beloved Warwickshire in time for the Boxing Day Meet; to this end, he and Alice left before supper on Christmas Day. And Harold and his family, together with Reuben, departing also, only Samuel, Lavinia and their two sons were left to keep the family company for the rest of the evening.

'I think,' Jeremy observed in an amused drawl, when he and Christina found themselves alone in the library that evening, 'that Cousin Susan felt we should be chaperoned.'

Christina was sitting on a low stool by the fire, thankful for the respite from family chatter, the others having remained in the drawing room to play cards. She shrugged impatiently, but kept her gaze on the flames, unwilling to admit that Jeremy's presence did in fact cause her a slight uneasiness.

'What nonsense,' she said in a low voice. 'As if we hadn't known each other since we were children.'

'Nonsense indeed,' Jeremy agreed cheerfully. 'And fortunately, her sick headache prevents her from carrying out the task herself. Not that I'm not very sorry for her,' he added quickly. 'Poor Cousin Susan's headaches must be a sore trial to her. But if she has to have them . . .'

'They might as well benefit the rest of us,' Christina supplied with a flash of mischief. 'Isn't that what you wanted to say?' She glanced at him over her shoulder, unaware of the provocative gleam in her eyes.

Jeremy stared at her for a moment, then smiled. 'You read my mind, cousin,' he said equably. 'And I cannot deny that everything certainly has turned out to *my* benefit. And I hope to yours as well.'

Christina turned back quickly to the fire. 'I don't think I understand what you mean.'

'Why, simply that it's given us the chance to be alone together. To talk. There's been so little opportunity in the past few weeks, and there's so much I want to say to you.'

His voice was low, pleasantly musical. Christina thought that it would be very easy simply to listen to the sound of it, without taking in the meaning of his words. But that, she thought with some alarm, could be dangerous. Knowing Jeremy from childhood, she knew also that he said very little that was without meaning – and that the meaning wasn't invariably what it at first appeared.

The library was very quiet, lit only by the soft glow of the oil-lamp and the murmuring flames of the fire. Outside, the air was still, the wind that had torn the hillside for the past few days now muted. It had turned colder; there was talk of snow.

'What do you want to say?' she asked quietly, half-afraid of the answer.

Jeremy did not answer immediately. Instead, he moved closer, coming to sit on the chaise longue so that Christina was almost at his knee. It was a position of some intimacy, yet she could not move away without appearing ungracious. He was, after all, her cousin – or, more correctly, her second cousin – whom she had known all her life, his home a bare three miles away on the far side of Stourbridge. With his younger brother Rupert, he had been in and out of Henzel Court ever since the family moved in; his parents too had been frequent visitors, strong though the rivalry had been between Joshua and his cousins. So there was really no reason why Christina and Jeremy should not share the fireside, which after all was all that his closeness amounted to.

'I wanted to tell you how much I admire you,' he said softly, and she jumped. 'Don't misunderstand me, Christina. I don't wish to embarrass you in any way. I am talking simply about the glasshouse and the way you have shouldered your burden without complaint, the way you –'

'The glasshouse is no burden,' she answered sharply, wondering why she felt a twinge of disappointment. 'I am glad that Papa left it to me.'

'I know. I didn't mean a burden in that sense. But it's a heavy responsibility, doubly so because you're a woman, and a very young one. Not many girls would have had the courage to accept it, even loving the business as much as you do. Not against the opposition you've had to face – will continue to face. It takes courage, Christina, a great deal of courage. That's what I admire in you.' He paused and added softly, 'One of the qualities I admire in you . . .'

Christina kept her face to the fire. Her cheeks were burning now and she wished that she had had the forethought to place the Berlinwork fire-screen handy, to shield her from the flames. But to turn away from the heat would bring her in even closer proximity to Jeremy.

He seemed to read her mind. 'Don't fear me, Christina. I've told you, I don't want to embarrass or upset you. Can we not talk, as cousins – as friends?'

Now she did turn and look into his eyes. They were clear and blue, expressing no more than an open friendliness which comforted and disarmed her. She smiled and, impulsively, put her hand into his.

'Of course we can, Jeremy. To tell you the truth, I've needed someone to talk to. Someone who won't try to persuade me –' She hesitated.

'Persuade you to hand over the glasshouse, lock, stock and barrel, to my father and his brothers?' Jeremy's grin was both wry and humorous. 'Christina, my sweet, did you ever really believe that I agreed with them in that?'

'Not really, perhaps,' she said slowly. 'But, you never said, you never even hinted –'

'How could I? With all the family crowding around us?' His eyes, so like those of his aristocratic mother, widened. 'It wasn't that I didn't want to, Christina. I longed to come to your defence, to range myself beside you, to stand against them all as you did so courageously. But I could do nothing – nothing except try to tell you with my eyes what my voice longed to say. I thought – I hoped you understood.'

Christina was silent, remembering the moments when she had caught Jeremy's eye across the room, trying to remember just what meaning she had read into his glance. Had she seen then that he was on her side, that he was only awaiting his chance? Perhaps she had . . . It was certain that there had been something; some moment of communication between them. With the memory came another. The shifting eyes and sidelong glances of the older men when someone mentioned marriage. And of Jeremy gazing at the table. As if detaching himself from the rest of the company? Or . . ?

'I had to remain silent until I could speak with you alone,' he continued. 'And until now, that moment never came. But now, with Cousin Susan safely confined to bed and the rest of them busy with their cards, now, at last, we have time to talk together. It's what you've wanted too, isn't it, Christina?'

Almost mesmerised by the intensity of his gaze, she whispered, 'Yes.'

He was possessed of both her hands now, their slender fingers entirely encompassed by his warm strength. He had his mother's hands too, she noticed, long and narrow, tapering gracefully to smoothly-manicured nails. They weren't the hard, work-roughened hands that her father had had until the day he died, hands that knew glass with a greater intimacy than simply filling it with wine. But Samuel had never expected his son to learn all the ways of glassmaking, and his mother Lavinia would have been horrified at the very idea. It was in the administration of the rival business that Jeremy made his mark. In the fining down of expenses, the increasing of profits; in the finding of new markets in which to sell glass; the contact with other newly-prosperous manufacturers who wished to buy glass for their own homes.

The two sides of the family had been rivals for two full generations now – ever since old Roger Henzel, Christina's grandfather, had quarrelled with his brother Timothy and split the original firm into two. What the quarrel had been about, nobody was quite sure, but since the two businesses now concentrated on different types of glass, with only a slight overlap, it was generally assumed that glass had been the cause of their dispute. And indeed, what else was there for glassmakers to quarrel over? And it was certain that Timothy's sons, Alfred, Harold and Samuel, had always cast covetous eyes on Joshua's success with fine table glass. Of Reuben, the fourth son, Christina had never been quite sure. He drew a good income from the family business, she knew. But apart from that, nobody seemed sure of Reuben.

And now, perhaps the traditional jealousy burned in Jeremy's heart. Was he truly as friendly as he seemed, or was there some of Reuben's deviousness in that open smile? Joshua had said more than once that it was Jeremy's acumen, together with his easy charm and aristocratic yet friendly good looks, that posed the greatest threat to Henzel's.

Christina looked at him. Even as she longed for the comfort of someone to talk to, to confide in, she wondered just why Jeremy should offer her his friendship. Could she really trust him? He was, after all, Samuel's son. And her father had never trusted any of his cousins . . .

Again, Jeremy seemed to understand what she was thinking. 'You're wondering why I say these things to you, Christina. You're not quite sure of me, are you – no, don't trouble to deny it. After all, why should you be? Our families have always been rivals. And my father and uncles have made no secret of their desire to take over Henzel's. Why should you believe me to be any different?' His grip tightened on her hands and he drew her almost imperceptibly closer. 'I can only ask that you try. Give me a few minutes, half an hour perhaps, to talk to you, to convince you that I am your friend, that I want to see you succeed, and that I shall stand by you in all your endeavours and give you whatever help I can to see that you *do* succeed.'

He paused, his eyes searching hers, and Christina was once more struck by their intense colour and transparency. She held their gaze and felt that surely there could be no duplicity here, only an honest desire for understanding. Jeremy meant what he said; he was her friend – and, God knew, she needed a friend.

'Tell me what you want to say,' she said again, softly.

Jeremy leaned back on the chaise longue, loosening his hold on her hands. He kept one clasped lightly between his fingers, gently stroking it almost absently as he spoke, and he looked away from her face and into the fire.

'You've had a difficult time, these past few weeks,' he said thoughtfully. 'Losing your father so suddenly, when you and he had been so close. And only a year and a half since poor Frederic's death.'

Christina bowed her head. Reference to Frederic had seemed even more painful since Joshua had died. It was as if her sensibilities had been sharpened all over again, so that any grief left unexpressed had come to the surface, demanding its place in her mourning. She kept her eyes on Jeremy's caressing fingers and waited.

'I feel our family has been less supportive than it might have been,' he went on. 'You needed comfort and consolation in your loss. Instead, everyone has looked upon it as wholly gain, and a gain that might almost be thought a personal insult to the rest of them. And they have treated you as if it is all your fault.'

'I don't think Aunt Susan –' Christina began fairly, but he silenced her with a slight movement of his free hand and a little laugh.

'Cousin Susan doesn't have a malicious bone in her body. All her disapproval has been just that – disapproval. Because it isn't seemly, it isn't ladylike, it's unsuitable, you don't have to tell me what Cousin Susan has said. On the other hand, I would guess that she hasn't really been of much comfort to you. Has she? Or a source of strength?'

'Not really,' Christina admitted. 'But Papa was her brother, she's had her own grief –'

'I'll allow that. We won't blame her for it. But that doesn't help you, does it?' He paused. 'And my own father and his brothers – they have been of no help whatsoever, have they? Not even their wives – my own mother included. Nobody has offered you a shoulder to cry on.'

Christina stirred uneasily. Jeremy's words, his soft, velvety tones, could so easily move her to self-pity. But she had set her face against that from the start, aided by the anger that had torn at her night and day. Was she to give in to it now?

'I don't wish to cry. I think it is better to work. There was work to be done, and Papa trusted me to do it. I didn't need any shoulders to lean on.'

'Are you sure?' he asked softly, and her control wavered. She shook her head, not trusting herself to speak, and Jeremy leaned forward again, his head close to hers.

'Christina, it's just this quality in you that I admire so much. And I've wanted to help you – all the time, when my father and uncles have been pressing you to give up the factory, to allow them to manage its affairs for you, even to hand it over to Harry –'

'That's out of the question,' she broke in. 'As I explained before, Harry doesn't want it.'

Jeremy clasped his hands warmly around hers again. 'I know there's no question of Harry being forced to take over,' he said now, his long fingers moving gently against her palms. 'I believe you're right about that. He'd make an excellent master, I'm sure, he has a steadiness and air of commonsense that would enable him to make a success of anything he undertook, but if it's an engineer he wants to be, then I believe it should be allowed. You are entirely capable of taking on the trust your father bequeathed to you.'

'You are the only one who thinks so, then,' she murmured.

Jeremy shook his head. 'Not at all. The men who work for you believe in you too. I've been into the glasshouse, Christina – I beg your pardon if that offends you, and I shall never do so again without your permission – but I wanted to find out for myself just what the attitude was there. And I was heartened by it. They respect you. They may be a little cautious at first – and who could blame them? – but if you prove to be the woman I think you are, the woman *they* think you are, then they'll take you to their hearts and work for you as perhaps they never even worked for your father.'

Christina felt her eyes mist again, but the tears that hung there were not of self-pity now. She bit her lips, shaking her head a little, and Jeremy placed one finger under her chin and lifted her face.

'Look at me, Christina,' he said gently. 'Never mind the tears. I know what they mean. Tell me that you will always look on me as your friend.'

'My . . . friend?' she breathed, and he nodded.

'A friend is what you need most just now. You must forgive me for not speaking before. You realise that I am still, at present, under my own father's authority. Even, to some extent, my uncles'. But one day, when I am free, independent, able to make my own way . . . then I can speak and act as I wish. Meanwhile, let's meet and talk whenever we may, Christina, and you shall share your troubles with me. Does that suit you?'

'Yes, it does,' she said simply. Jeremy's words had shown her just how lonely she had been, how friendless she felt herself. Of all her family, there was only Harry – and he had come but lately into her mind, he was younger than she and at school for most of the time. And the rest were, she saw now, too absorbed in their own lives to concern themselves with hers. Alice, away in Warwickshire, was busy becoming as aristocratic as her husband, in setting new fashions as fast as they came from London. Adela thought of nothing but clothes and Aunt Susan was making what amounted to an occupation of her disapproval.

'We are to be friends, then?' Jeremy persisted softly, and Christina nodded.

'We will be friends.'

1845

Chapter Six

Christina was watching the pot-setting. It was something she never tired of seeing. A dramatic and dangerous procedure, needing as many as ten men working in close co-operation and using all the power of their rippling muscles. With the furnace laid bare, the heat was at its most intense and not infrequently one of the boys, unaccustomed to it as yet, would faint and fall towards the white-hot maw. When this happened, rescue needed to be swift – anyone who fell into the mouth of the pot itself would certainly be burned beyond saving, and even the floor in front of the furnace was at that moment almost red-hot and spattered with molten glass. But there was no time for compassion, the staggering body would be thrust aside, kicked roughly out of the way, while the hard, heavy work went on.

The pots were set inside the domed furnace, their mouths gaping holes of glowing heat, and the metal, a mixture of sand, potash and cullet, was melted in them for gathering and blowing. They were made locally of the fireclay which was found all around the area and when a new one was to be set it was heated in a pot-arch beforehand, to bring it up to the temperature of the main furnace. At Henzel's, as at most of the other glasshouses, this was usually done on Friday, so as to give the pot time to heat thoroughly and the new metal to melt before work started again on the following Tuesday.

Today, Joe was in charge of the team working on the pots, and down below, in the dark, airless caves and passages that ran beneath the cone and led out to the banks of the canal, the teasers were waiting to stoke up the furnace as soon as the new pot was in position, to prevent too much loss of heat.

Christina stood at a safe distance. She was holding a piece of heavily-smoked glass, for when the pot came out of the furnace it was dazzlingly white-hot and her father had never allowed her to look directly at it.

'Your eyes are too tender,' he would say, giving her the smoked glass. 'The heat and brilliance would damge them.'

'But what about the men's eyes? They don't use smoked glass.' And she would look anxiously towards the group of glassmakers clustered around the furnace, their faces reddened by the glow and shining with perspiration.

'How could they, unless we had special spectacles made? Anyway, they're different. They're used to it. You're too sensitive, my dear.' But his own eyes would soften as he looked at her, and his great hand was gentle on her shoulder.

One of the takers-in was standing at the furnace now, ladling great gobs of fiery metal into a huge wheeled cauldron filled with water. Clouds of steam rose into the air, and where the metal spilled over the sides it hardened immediately into long trails and splinters of glass. When he had finished, he wheeled it away and left it in a safe place to cool down, when it would be broken up and put back into the metal mixture as cullet.

Christina felt the familiar tightening around her breasts and stomach as the team, led by Joe, moved forward and began to break away the firebricks that held the old pot in place. They worked quickly, jabbing their long iron chisels at the mortar between the bricks, forcing them loose and levering them out on to the floor. It was hard work, occasionally made even more difficult if a pot had cracked so that molten glass had oozed out and fused the pot to the floor. It could also be dangerous for the teasers, down below, for if more glass seeped out at this stage it could fall into the fire, or even on to the men themselves, causing serious burns. Christina had once heard of a pot cracking so badly that its full load of metal had poured out and killed a teaser who was at that moment stoking the fire. But accidents like this were rare; the men were all well aware of the danger and took care accordingly.

The firebricks were all out now and the pot stood revealed, with the intense heat of the furnace scorching around it. Christina raised her smoked glass hastily. The scene immediately became darker, almost black, with the white shape of the pot now an unearthly luminous green and the men nothing more than shadows moving in and out. She saw them bring the twelve-foot-long iron pot-wagon, which she had once likened to an elongated wheelbarrow, and take up their positions, each man laying hard, work-roughened hands on the spot which would give him most leverage. Together, they thrust its pointed ends underneath the old pot and forced it further into the furnace, lifting it, still heavy with its residue of metal too deep to be ladled out. There was a moment's pause. Joe, at the head of the team, shaded his eyes to stare into the searing eye of the fire, and then gave the signal.

'Now!'

The team heaved together. Out came the pot, glowing with the ferocity of a wayward sun. Christina stepped back quickly, startled yet again by the force of the heat it brought with it. With grunts forced from their lungs by the weight and bulk of their burden, the men dragged the pot-wagon back from the furnace and turned it towards the main doors. Both the inner and the outer ones were open now, the danger of a draught cooling the furnace less than that of keeping the pot too long inside the cone. With a steady rush, aiming the cumbersome vehicle straight for the opening, they pushed it across the stone-flagged floor and out into the grey afternoon. Christina heard the ringing crash as the pot was overturned on to a bare patch of earth and left to cool before it could be smashed and removed. The entire procedure had taken less than twenty minutes.

Now the new pot, glowing with its own heat, would be brought from the pot-arch and installed to do its own three months of duty. But as the men came back in from the cool of the April afternoon outside, Christina saw another figure follow them in.

'Jeremy.'

He came towards her. There was a tense excitement in his figure, a glow in his blue eyes, that she hadn't seen before. She watched him curiously, her own excitement rising, and from the corner of her eye saw Joseph Compson, his dark eyes fixed on them both.

'What is it?'

Jeremy waved a newspaper at her. It was crumpled, as though he had given it one glance and then swept it up with both hands to hurry to the glasshouse. Christina's breath quickened. Surely there was only one piece of news . . .

'Jeremy, tell me, have they – after all this time, have they really –'

'They've taken the excise off glass.' His voice was thick with excitement. 'After a hundred years of taxation, extortion, a hundred years of crippling the trade, they've taken it off. All of it.' He flung a triumphant glance towards the duty-gatherer, standing guard in his booth at the door. 'We can say goodbye to them, Christina, Pritchard and his like, we can show them the door and put something *useful* in their place.' His face was alight as he moved out of the way to allow the men to pass with the new pot, fresh and glowing from the pot-arch. 'What do you say to that, Christina, my love?' And he put both his hands on her waist and whirled her about.

'Jeremy!' Half-laughing, half-embarrassed, Christina protested and he released her immediately. She looked about her, thankful for the heat of the furnace which could be blamed for the warm colour in her face. But her own pleasure was as great as Jeremy's and she put her hands on his arms, smiling up at him.

'It's wonderful news. It's what we've been waiting for. We can go into full production on lead crystal now, concentrate on it as Papa always wanted to do. Nothing can stop Henzel's now.' Her face shone, green eyes sparkling. 'We shall produce the finest lead crystal this country has ever seen. Imagine the difference it's going to make.' She moved away from him, her hands clasped in front of her, pacing the floor almost unseeingly as she looked into the future. 'No more weighing of every single item made, no more paying tax on glass that will only be cut away by the engraver, or on flawed pieces that will be returned as cullet so that duty is extorted over and over again on the same metal . . . We'll save both money and time. Our glasshouses will be our own again, with no government spies forever watching.'

Turning, she caught sight of Thomas Pritchard, staring sullenly from his box, and had an impish desire to thumb her nose at him, as rough street-boys did when they wanted to show scorn. 'Don't worry, Mr Pritchard,' she called gaily. 'I'm sure Her Majesty's Government will find you another comfortable post somewhere – weighing mothers' milk, perhaps, before the baby begins to suck!'

Pritchard looked down his nose and did not deign to answer. But Joe Compson, leaving the men to build in the pot with new firebricks and fresh cement, came over to her, wiping his hands slowly on an old rag.

'Do I hear right, Miss Christina?' he asked. 'Hev they takkin' off the excise? Are we to mek good flint glass again?'

Christina turned to him, her face jubilant. 'Yes, Joe, we are. As soon as – as – Jeremy, when does this become effective?'

'From the fifth of April,' he said quietly, and her eyes widened.

103

'Then it's already happened! We can begin straightaway. And Mr Pritchard will have to refund any tax he's collected between then and now!' She wheeled back to Joe. 'Joseph, we must celebrate! Tomorrow – no, not tomorrow, it's Saturday – Tuesday, when you start work again, you must make something special. Some large, beautiful piece that will show our customers just what Henzel's can achieve. A – oh, what shall it be? A jug, a decanter, a bowl, something that will look really impressive.'

Joe looked back at her, his dark eyes moving slowly over the animated face, flushed with warmth and excitement.

'I'll put my mind to it, Miss Christina. A large showpiece. But not next week. We've not enough flint in the pots for that. It'll have to wait until we're set up for production, like. And I'll draw summat out – summat special, like you say – and show it to you beforehand.'

'Yes, that's wonderful, Joe. And you're quite right about the lead – we'll have to start straightaway on changing the mixture. Tell the batch mixers not to start on the new mix until I've looked at Papa's old recipes. Or would it be better to wait a week or two, until we're sure of our materials?' She stood thinking for a moment, then shook her head decisively. 'No, we'll begin at once. After all, flint is nothing new to us, we've been making small amounts all the time. Now, we'll just be able to make more. The pots you've changed today can be filled with a good lead batch, and you can start on some wineglasses next week, so that we can see how it turns out. And then you can make the piece the week after that.' She smiled up into the dark, grimy face.

'That would be fine, miss,' Joe said, and the darkness of his face was lit by the whiteness of his smile.

Christina stood quite still. She felt breathless suddenly, as if an invisible hammer had struck her full in the chest. Her lips parted, but she had no words, even if she could have spoken. Her eyes remained fixed on his, drowning in their smouldering depths.

Jeremy touched her arm, and when he spoke his voice was tight. 'Come outside, Christina. It's too noisy to talk in here.'

Christina turned her head, looking at him blankly for a moment, then relaxed and laughed.

'Of course! What am I thinking of? There's so much to discuss, to decide. Plans to make.' She gave Joe a brief, brilliant smile. 'See to the new batch, then, Joe, and I'll come in next week to look at the wineglasses. A good shape, with a twist in the stem, please, and then we'll decide whether to produce it as a regular line.' Her nod was as brief as her smile, and then, her arm linked in Jeremy's, she was gone, leaving Joe looking after her, his expression unreadable.

A taker-in, young and nervous, approached and asked him if he was satisfied with the newly-installed pot.

'Satisfied?' Joe barked. 'Of course I'm not satisfied! I ent even looked at it yet, hev I? All that chatter about wineglasses and the like . . .' He marched over to the furnace and glowered at the newly-set pot. 'It dunna look straight to me,' he grumbled. 'There's a crooked brick in the corner, there. Here, give me the chisel –' And as he hacked and thrust at the firebricks with the long iron tool, it was as if he were stabbing a mortal enemy to an agonising death, and the men around him glanced at each other and moved uneasily away.

Dinner that night began as the lightest-hearted meal Christina could remember since her father had died. Jeremy had been easily persuaded to join them, and their excitement over the news of the excise infected the others.

'So you really think this will make a difference to glass-making?' Aunt Susan had been accustomed to hearing shop talk from Joshua and was always willing to encourage

Jeremy. In fact, her inclination to treat him as if he were head of the glasshouse frequently annoyed Christina.

'It certainly will, Cousin Susan.' Jeremy spoke easily, his blue eyes smiling around them all. 'I imagine every glassmaker in the land – certainly in Stourbridge and Wordsley – is at this moment making plans for expansion. You'll have plenty of competition, Christina,' he added with a twinkle.

'Then we'll be ahead of it,' she returned staunchly. 'I intend to make Henzel's the best and most famous glasshouse in the land. And now that we're free to work flint glass, there's no reason why we shouldn't be. We have the finest workmen in the district.'

'I imagine you mean the Compsons,' Jeremy said, and Christina gave him a sharp glance.

'Of course I do. Amongst others. William has always been one of our best men. And Joe is outstripping him. He's an artist – very nearly a genius.'

'Oh come, that's a little strong, don't you think?' Jeremy spoke pleasantly, but there was a slight edge to his voice. 'Joe Compson's a fine glassmaker, I'll grant you that, but he's no better than a hundred others. Why, in your own foundry, there's Jem Husselbee, Jack Scriven, a dozen more.' He paused, and then added, 'I think you should be careful with Joe Compson, Christina. He's the kind of man who could give you trouble.'

Her breast tightened. 'Trouble?'

'Yes. He's a great deal too independent for my taste, Christina. I've seen the way he looks at you – he's not the man to take kindly to a woman's rule. He's a member of the Flint Glassmakers' Friendly Society, isn't he?'

'Yes, I think he is.' The Flint Glassmakers' Friendly Society had been formed the previous year, a descendant of an earlier society which had existed between the workmen to help each other in times of need. Nobody had minded that; but the new Society modelled itself on the lines of the new trade unions. 'But Joe would never –'

106

'Joe would do exactly what he felt would be of most benefit to Joe,' Jeremy said firmly. 'Don't allow yourself to imagine anything else, Christina. He may be a third or even fourth generation glassmaker with Henzel's, but that won't stop him from rebelling against you if rebellion suits him. These so-called trade unions – they're a sinister development. They bring trouble: strikes and lockouts. They mark the end of loyalty.'

'Not in glassmaking,' Christina said. 'Glassmakers are different.'

'Glassmakers are men,' he countered, with a smile that did not quite reach his eyes. 'And Joe Compson more than most, I suspect.'

There was a small silence.

'I don't think I understand what you mean,' Christina said tightly.

Jeremy glanced around the table at Aunt Susan, whose face was bearing the ugly flush it so often displayed these days; at Adela, wide-eyed, every curl carefully arranged, and at Harry, who was looking bored with the turn of conversation but still ready to leap to his sister's defence should she need it.

'I apologise,' Jeremy said smoothly. 'It is not a subject for the dinner table with ladies present. I should not have mentioned it.'

'Indeed you should!' Christina was beginning to feel angry. The euphoria with which the meal had begun was evaporating quickly, and she blamed her cousin for introducing a discordant note. 'The glasshouse is mine, Jeremy, and Joe Compson one of my best workmen. If you have anything to say about him, please say it – and if Aunt Susan and Adela don't wish to hear, they are welcome to leave the room.'

'Christina!' Susan Henzel protested, but Christina flung her a quelling glance.

'Well?' she demanded imperiously.

Jeremy smiled. 'You misread me, my love,' he said

easily. 'I have nothing to say about Compson, or indeed about any of your other workmen. Only one thing, if you must have it –' He paused and Christina thumped her fist on the table in exactly the way her father would have done.

'Jeremy! Please!'

He sighed and shrugged. 'Very well. And if you don't like it, remember that you demanded to know. I've seen a good deal of Joseph Compson in the past few months. I've been in and out of the cones frequently – at your invitation. I've seen him when he is working: I've seen him when you are there, and when you are not. And I have to tell you that he is different when he is aware of your presence.'

'Different?' Christina felt her cheeks grow warm, and she lifted her head.

'Different.' Jeremy paused deliberately. 'His manner towards you is . . . impertinent. I think I need say no more.'

Christina returned his look. She knew that her aunt was bridling with shock and dismay, that Adela was stifling nervous giggles, that Harry was now sharply attentive. She tightened her lips.

'I think you could say a great deal more, Cousin Jeremy,' she said coldly. 'But I agree it's probably better that you don't. As for myself, I can only say that Joe Compson has never been in the slightest degree impertinent. He's a fine workman – an artist – and yes, he has a certain independence of spirit that I believe goes with an artistic nature. I respect that. I respect *him*.' She glanced around the table and rose to her feet. 'I'm sure you are ready for your port, Jeremy, and Harry would enjoy a glass with you. Aunt Susan, Adela . . .' She moved towards the door without looking back and, with a wavering glance at Jeremy, her aunt followed her. Adela, dimpling and tossing her curls, went too, and Jeremy watched their departure with a rueful look on his face.

But there was speculation in his glance too. Christina had hidden her reaction well; but reaction there had certainly been, when he had mentioned Joe Compson and his familiar behaviour. There was a sensitivity there that spoke of more than an employer's natural awareness of a particular workman's value. It was a sensitivity that, having once noticed it, Jeremy meant to watch.

Christina went to her room that night feeling disturbed and unhappy. It was the first time she and Jeremy had disagreed – indeed, they had come perilously close to a quarrel. And over what? Nothing more than an over-familiar workman in the glasshouse. A man who could never be more to her than an employee and no more valuable than any other. Restlessly, she paced the room, and then moved to the window and drew aside the curtain, staring out into the night. The darkness was lit by the smoky red glow that hung over the whole area, from Kingswinford to Brierley Hill. Glasshouses, iron foundries, smelting works, all added their acrid sunset to the raw night air. It was only by walking or driving right away, leaving the cramped streets for the fields and woods that lay around them, that you could experience the sensation of breathing fresh air. For a moment she thought half-longingly of her childhood home, and the freedom to roam that she had enjoyed then.

What was Jeremy doing now? Probably, he was back at home on the other side of Stourbridge, comfortably ensconced in front of his parents' fire, sharing a whisky with his father and discussing the events of the day, the problems encountered in their own glasshouse. They would be exchanging views on new lines, deciding whether to discontinue old ones. And without doubt they would be doing what every glass manufacturer in the country must be doing at this moment – celebrating the news of the excise repeal, drinking to their long-awaited triumph over the tax that had held back the industry's development for so long.

If only her father had been here to celebrate with them –

with her. Christina laid her forehead against the window and felt the familiar bitter yearning for his presence, the comfort of his arm, heavy on her shoulders, the vibrating roar of his laughter. The house was unnaturally quiet without him, and there was no one to whom she could turn. But that wasn't fair. Jeremy had done his best to fill the gap in her life. It wasn't his fault that it was a gap too large for any normal man to fill. And now, feeling miserably cold and lonely from their near-quarrel, Christina would have given much for him to return. And her thoughts turned then to the man who had been the cause of her dispute with Jeremy.

Jeremy had been quite right in saying that Joe Compson was over-familiar. She could not understand why she had been so annoyed. Hadn't the man even managed to upset her at her father's funeral, with his bold looks? He had been allowed far too much freedom in his manner towards her. It would stop at once. And tomorrow, she would make her peace with Jeremy and they would forget their quarrel and celebrate the good news that had come today, without any dissension to mar their pleasure.

Jeremy was suffering no such soul-searching. As Christina had imagined, he was stretched out comfortably in front of the fire in his father's library, a glass of whisky in one hand and smoke wreathing from the cigar he held in the other. His father and Uncle Reuben watched him.

'She's still determined then,' Samuel said.

'On running the glasshouse herself?' Jeremy shrugged. 'As far as Christina's concerned, there's no question. The glasshouse is hers and it stays hers. I am allowed in on sufferance only, as a friend, someone to talk to and discuss things with. Interference would not be countenanced.'

'You can give advice, though? When asked.'

'*If* asked,' Jeremy said wryly. 'Well, perhaps I'm being a little unfair there. Christina does ask my advice, very

110

charmingly, but as a colleague only, not because she admits in any way that I might know better than she does. And she reserves the right not to take my advice.'

His father shifted irritably in the big, leather-covered armchair. 'We don't seem to be getting anywhere at all with this business,' he grumbled. 'One of the best glasshouses in the area, which should by rights belong to the family, and left in the hands of this obstinate girl. I still say Joshua must have been insane. There are kinds of madness that don't show themselves until it's too late. And there's the idiot child, Thomas, as evidence. Another lawyer –'

'Would be out to line his own pockets,' Reuben interrupted smoothly. 'And Christina wouldn't give in easily – as you say, she's stubborn, as stubborn as her father. She would fight us every inch of the way, right into the courts. In the end, there would be nothing left for anyone – except the lawyers. We can't afford a costly battle, Samuel, especially not just now. With the excise off, we need all our capital for research, for increased production, for the expansion that's been held back for so long. Lawsuits are a luxury.'

Samuel grunted. 'You're right, of course. But it's galling to see that chit holding herself equal to us . . . And we need that glasshouse. Those cones, with all their equipment, the men she has, the contacts, with all that added to our assets, all our troubles would be in the past. We all know the problems the glass trade has had to face in the past few years – decades. God knows how Joshua managed to survive as he did, and not only survive but expand as well. And now we're on the brink of a golden age, we need extra capital, extra facilities. We need Henzel's.' He turned back to Jeremy. 'It all depends on you. You're the only one she seems inclined to trust – to confide in.'

'Because I'm nearer her age, and because I don't attempt to interfere. She'll talk to me, yes. But trust –

I'm not sure of that.' Jeremy watched his smoke rise slowly towards the ceiling. 'She doesn't forget who I am, or what was said after Joshua's death.'

'Trust doesn't always come easily,' Reuben remarked. 'It takes time and patience to achieve, and even then it's easily lost. You must not rush it, Jeremy.'

Jeremy glanced at his uncle. The expression in the pale, sliding eyes was enigmatic.

'Christina has nobody else to confide in,' Reuben said. 'Harry may try to help, but he's too absorbed in his own life. And he's young and inexperienced, of no use where the glasshouse is concerned. She needs someone. A man. I cannot think of anyone she can turn to other than yourself.'

Jeremy gave a short laugh. 'Unless she looks to the glasshouse!'

'The glasshouse?' Samuel said sharply. 'Why, who is there at the glasshouse?'

'Nobody of consequence. But one of the glassblowers could cause trouble. He and Christina are on far too friendly terms. And he's the sort of man –' Jeremy stopped abruptly, frowning. 'Well, I daresay there's nothing in it. And I've warned her, though she took my warning ill.'

'You mean she *talks* to this man? Discusses things with him? A *glassblower*?' Samuel sat up in his chair, his moustaches bristling indignantly. 'Are you sure you're not making too much of this, Jeremy? Even Christina –'

'Christina is a law unto herself. She was when we were children, and even more so now. But I agree, even she could not seriously consider a workman worthy of her notice. In fact, I'm not even sure she likes this man at all, only that there seems to be some feeling between them. It could as easily be dislike as anything else.'

'Then you must make sure that is what it is,' Reuben said, and again held Jeremy's eyes.

The door opened and Jeremy's mother came in. As

usual, she was dressed in the height of fashion, her neckline low and her skirts rustling as she moved. She came over to the fire and smiled at the three men.

'Still here, and still talking business! It's easy to see you have no wife, Reuben – and if you were here often you would soon draw Samuel back into bachelor ways! I'm not sure I can allow it.' Her eyes moved to Jeremy. 'You're looking tired, my love. You work too hard, this constant dancing attendance on Christina is too much for you. Why can't the girl admit the task is too much for her, and employ an adviser, or better still, give in and make the business over to us? She'll have to in the end, so why not now and have done with it?'

'Because she doesn't agree that she'll have to in the end, Lavinia, my dear,' Reuben drawled. 'In fact, if I understand that young lady aright, she won't agree to *having* to do anything. That's why I say we must act with extreme patience. And since Jeremy is the only one of us who can do anything active in the matter, the rest of us must contain ourselves as best we can and leave it to him.'

'And what do you suggest Jeremy does?' Lavinia arranged herself gracefully on the sofa. 'Marry the girl?'

There was a momentary silence.

'I can think of worse solutions,' Reuben said mildly. 'And few better. But that really depends on Jeremy, doesn't it? Does he *wish* to marry Christina?'

The three of them turned their eyes upon Jeremy. But he said nothing. He merely drew deeply on his cigar, then blew out a puff of smoke and smiled at them through it.

'Marry Christina?' he said at last, as if the idea had never before occurred to him. 'Well, now, that's quite an idea. Marry Christina . . . It would certainly make life interesting.'

'And any husband worthy of the name,' Reuben suggested with a sidelong glance at Lavinia, 'should be

113

able to deal with the little matter of those fifty-one per cent of shares.'

'Oh yes,' Jeremy agreed with another deep inhalation of cigar-smoke. 'I think I could promise that there would be no problem there.' His eyes glinted. 'Yes. Marriage to Christina could be very interesting indeed . . .'

Chapter Seven

Joe and Maggie were as pleased as anyone to see the light April evenings. It wasn't dark now until gone seven; and although this made concealment more difficult when they were on Dob Hill, it was pleasant to lie together under a soft blue sky, savouring the gentle warmth of the air on their bodies instead of shivering with cold after hasty love.

All the same, there was an uneasiness between them these days. Joe was aware of it as a dissatisfaction within him, though he couldn't – or didn't want to – say what that dissatisfaction was. And Maggie was increasingly petulant.

'What bist thee thinkin' of, Joe?' she murmured, snuggling close to him. 'You seem miles away. In't you interested no more?'

'Didn't I just show you I was?' he muttered, pretending not to notice her straying hand. 'Let it rest, Mag. A man's weary after a day's work.'

'Is that so? He never used to be.' She raised herself up and looked down at him, her red lips pouting. 'Mebbe it's workin' for women that's so tirin'. Does she ask too much of yer, Joe? Is that it?'

'You're talkin' nonsense, woman. Let it rest, I said.'

'Oh, I've heard things about your Miss Christina Henzel,' Maggie said tauntingly, ignoring Joe's darkening flush of anger. 'Always round the glasshouse, and in and out of one cone in particular, so they say. Is it you her's interested in, then, Joe, does her like to watch you, half-naked there? Well, and mebbe I don't blame her at that, she'll never find as good in her own class, that's for sure. But I thought young leddies were above all that sort of thing – lookin' at men's bodies. Mebbe her'd like to be

115

up here on the hill with you instead of me. D'you think that's what her's thinkin' of, Joe, when her watches you blow the glass?'

'I said, leave it, Maggie,' Joe snarled. 'I won't listen to you talkin' like that about Miss Christina. She's a fine young woman – a *clean* woman – and I won't hear no dirty talk about her, so shut your trap!'

Maggie bridled and opened her eyes wide at him, her head on one side, mouth pouting.

'So that's the way the wind blows, is it! We mustna speak ill of Miss Christina. Miss Christina is as pure as the driven snow and no dirty talk must sully her delicate ears. It wouldn't be that you fancy her yourself, would it, Joe Compson? It wouldn't be that *you'd* like to be up here on the hill with her too. Maggie Haden's not good enough for you now, is that it? Too common, I daresay. No fine clothes and pretty speech to beguile you with.' Her tone changed from mockery to anger as she spoke, and she began to scramble to her feet. 'Well, why don't you invite her up here one afternoon after work, and see what happens? Mebbe you'd both get a big surprise!'

'For God's sake, woman!' Joe reared up and grabbed her, dragging her down on top of his broad, muscular body. 'I told you not to talk rubbish. Fancy Miss Christina! I've got better things to do. And you've got better things to do than get yourself worked up into a state about her. Like this . . . and this . . .'

His hard mouth took hers with a ferocity that made her cry out against his lips, and his hands were rough on her body as he twisted her underneath him. A rush of excitement strained her against him, fuelled by an angry determination to prove to him that no other woman could satisfy him as she could. The violence of her response brought an answering savagery erupting from his body, his fingers tightening cruelly, his mouth attacking her flesh so that she knew she would carry the bruises tomorrow, and rejoiced in the knowledge. With tongue, lips, teeth and

116

nails, she nuzzled and bit and tore, knowing that whatever marks he laid on her would be borne on him too. And she felt the surge of primitive heat that told her he knew it and welcomed it as much as she.

Within seconds they were thrusting together with a frenzy that had little to do with love. The sky wheeled above them; the first swallows dived and soared in their search for insects; and for a while the smoke and clatter of the factories below the hill faded as pleasure took their place.

But when it was over and they lay panting in each other's arms, their senses cooling under the darkening sky, they both felt a dawning sourness, an instinctive and disturbing repugnance for what had happened. There had been more than a measure of desperation in that frantic coupling, and it left uneasiness rather than satisfaction.

For the first time, a touch of real fear entered Maggie's heart as she faced the possibility that she could lose Joe. And Joe, his thoughts turning away from the woman in his arms, found Christina's face in his mind, her tawny hair loose as he had seen it when she was a child; her ice-green eyes bright and challenging. He groaned aloud and tightened his hold on the compliant body. But the picture would not fade.

Now that the duty-gatherers had gone, there was a completely different atmosphere in the glasshouse. As soon as the news had been announced, the dour-faced men had packed up their papers and the hated weighing-machines and departed. The booths from which they had watched the comings and goings of the glasshouse were left empty, only an odd scrap of paper fluttering to the floor to denote that they were ever there.

'Tek it out!' the cry went up in every cone. 'Get rid of the bloody things! Burn 'em!'

With a yell of delight, the apprentices rushed forward and ripped up the booths, tearing the flimsy constructions

117

from the stone floor and smashing them to pieces before carrying the wreckage out through the double doors to the blackened space where the old pots were thrown to cool. The splintered wood was flung down, and at once another crowd of apprentices arrived from the second cone, and then the third. In less than ten minutes, the three booths were nothing more than a heap of firewood, raising flames of triumph towards the sky.

'That's what we should've done years since,' one of the blowers remarked to Joe in tones of satisfaction. 'Aye, an' the bastards that lived inside 'em. Parasites on hard-workin' men, that's all they wor.'

Joe grunted agreement. But no one had time to stand and admire the fire, mingling its smoke with that of the furnaces. Each chair had a quota to fulfil, and time was money. The younger men, mostly footmakers and servitors, and the takers-in who received the smallest share of the weekly wage, were no less anxious than the glassblowers themselves to return to work, and within a short time they were all back in their positions. But there was a distinctly lighter feeling in the air, and when one man began to sing, the others soon joined in until the entire cone was echoing with song.

> 'Full twenty years and more are passed,
> Since I left Brummagem,
> But I sct out for home at last,
> To good old Brummagem.'

'No, lads, not that! Let's give 'em this to remember us by!' Joe shouted, and as the men paused and listened expectantly, he began to sing, punching the savage words from his throat.

> 'My name it is Sam Hall, Samuel Hall,
> My name it is Sam Hall, Samuel Hall,
> My name it is Sam Hall, and I hates you one and all,
> You're a gang of muckers all, damn your eyes!'

There was a roar of approval from the rest of the men, and they all joined in the well-known song of a murderer on his way to the gallows, relishing the idea that it was somehow the duty-gatherer whose lot it had been to harry their daily lives who was now going up Harrow Hill to the gallows at Tyburn in the hangman's cart. Each curse was sung with ferocious glee as the criminal's progress was related from his own lips, and when they came to the final lines:

'This is my funeral knell, and I'll see you all in hell
And I hope you frizzles well, damn your eyes!'

There was a roar of approval that almost lifted the cone from its foundations.

'Right, lads, that's enough. Back to work.' The overseer had been as amused as anyone by the aptness of Joe's song, and aware that the men needed to let off steam – an expression he'd recently gleaned from the new jargon of the railways – but he was equally aware of the quota that needed to be filled. The blowers would have to work extra hard this morning to make up for their minutes of amusement.

Joe went back to work with a will, but his mind was more on Christina than the wineglasses he was making that morning. She had spoken to him more than once on what they would be able to do once the excise was lifted, and he knew that she was eager for expansion and to make the name of Henzel's famous wherever glass was bought. Only yesterday, she had talked of a special piece of glass, something that could be shown with pride to customers. A piece that she would treasure down the years as a symbol of her reign over the family firm.

Reign . . . His mind stopped at that thought. Yes, Christina was like a queen, like Queen Victoria herself: both thrust to power as young girls, both women in a man's world. Both small, strong-willed, indomitable, rising to the challenge . . . And that was what he liked about her, he thought suddenly. She wouldn't give in. She was determined to be mistress of this factory – mistress of Henzel's – and nothing, nobody was going to stop her.

Well then, if she wanted her special piece of glass he was the one to make it for her. It would be made to his own design, blown to the shape he decreed, and presented to her by himself. No one else, other than the men on his chair, should have any hand in it.

Joe took the blowing-iron from his servitor and brought it to his lips, aware of the power of his lungs and the delicacy, the precision of the control he had over them. The smallest, daintiest scent-bottle – the largest, grandest punch-bowl – all came as easily to him. But the new piece, to celebrate the long-awaited freedom to make fine lead crystal, that should be something to tax even his powers. If not, it wouldn't be the piece he and Miss Christina wanted.

As he blew the wineglass, almost without knowing, and sat in his chair to finish it, Joe felt a strange bond within him. A bond between himself and the girl who held his livelihood in her small, slender hands. The bond was of many strands: Henzel's, the glass he was to make, glass itself as a product and a way of life – a way of expressing his own ideals of shape and beauty. And there were other strands, ones that he knew could only complicate his life; perhaps in ways he had never dreamed of. Life was simpler, he reflected, with a woman like Maggie Haden, who wanted nothing but the delights of his body and the unspoken promise of ordinary, settled life in the terraced streets of the town. But he had conquered Maggie; the challenge was no longer there. With a woman like Christina Henzel, there would always be challenge. But Christina Henzel was beyond his reach.

'There's a person to see you, Miss Christina.'

Christina and her aunt looked up sharply. Rose's voice was prim and tight, indicating severe disapproval of whomever had called, so late in the evening. And 'person' denoted someone of the lower orders, someone the haughty parlour maid would consider unfit to come calling anyway.

'A person? Do you mean a lady or a gentleman?' Christina asked, and was aware of Harry and Adela lifting their heads from their game of chequers. Rose looked down her nose.

'I couldn't say he's either of those, miss. In fact, I believe he said he was one of the men from the factory.' Clearly, whoever had had the temerity to come to Henzel Court did not, in Rose's view, warrant even the briefest attention. 'He said his name was Compson, or some such,' she added reluctantly.

'Compson? Joe?' Christina came to her feet. 'Whatever can he be doing here?'

'Christina! Where are you going? You surely don't intend *seeing* this – this person?'

'But of course, Aunt Susan. That's why he's here. He must have some reason for coming – it would be discourteous not to discover what it is. Besides, I want to know!'

'But a workman . . . The impertinence of it!'

'I don't think you can say that, Aunt Susan. Not until we know why he's come. And we won't find that out unless I see him.' Christina turned to the parlour maid. 'Where have you put him?'

Rose glanced quickly at Susan Henzel, as if sure of approval from that quarter at least. 'Why, I haven't let him in at all, miss. I didn't think you'd want – I wouldn't even have come to tell you, only he refused to go away.'

'Wouldn't have told me?' Christina's eyes flashed. 'Let's make this quite clear, Rose. If anyone comes to see me – *anyone*, you understand – you tell me at once. Do you hear? It is not for you to decide what I shall or shan't know, nor whom I shall see. Now, go and let Joseph Compson in, and show him into the library. I shall join

121

him in a few minutes.' She raised a small hand to stay her aunt's demur. 'Joe is one of my best glassblowers, Aunt Susan, an artist in his own right. If he has come to see me, it's for some good reason and I intend to hear him.'

Susan Henzel sighed and let her own hand drop. 'Very well. But I shall come with you. No –' this time it was she who stopped Christina's protests '– it would be most unsuitable for you to see him alone. I insist that you have a chaperone. I still have *some* responsibility towards you,' she added with a quiet dignity that left Christina silent.

Harry came to her rescue. 'Don't you disturb yourself, aunt,' he said, getting up from the table where he sat with Adela. 'You must be tired. Stay here by the fire, with Adela. I can go with Christina. I may even be able to be of some help. This man must have come on glasshouse business, after all.'

Christina gave her brother a grateful look. Seeing Joe Compson here, in her own home, was going to be uncomfortable enough, but with Aunt Susan present it could have been intolerable. And she had a feeling that Susan Henzel's palpable disapproval might have daunted even the sturdy Joe. But Harry's quiet young presence would disturb neither of them, and might even ease the awkwardness of the situation.

Why had Joe come? Her heart, which had jerked painfully when Rose had told her who was at the door, began to thump. Seeing him in the glasshouse was one thing; for although neither of them ever forgot that it was she who owned everything about them – even down to the willow-stick pucellas that he used for shaping the glass – he was on his own home ground, where he was confident and at ease. By coming here, he had stepped out of his own surroundings, and she half-feared the change it might make. Since her argument with Jeremy, she had been determined to keep Joe at a distance, and she hoped she could now maintain that coolness. She tried to compose herself as she entered the library, but her heart beat all the harder.

Joseph Compson was standing in front of the fire. He looked massive and she realised with a painful catch in her throat how much she had missed the sheer size of her father, missed his bulk hiding the flames as Joe's did now – and as Jeremy's slender figure never did. Like Joshua, Joe seemed to fill the room with his presence. The air quivered with his vitality, as it had so often vibrated to the roar of Joshua's laughter or sudden quick temper. Even the fact that the glassblower was dressed in the sober black of his Sunday suit, where Joshua would have worn a much more flamboyant style of costume, could not destroy the resemblance.

Joseph Compson might be out of his normal sphere, here in the space and luxury of her father's library, but he was certainly not daunted by his surroundings. He had too much confidence in his own worth, and in himself as Joe Compson, glassblower, to allow that.

Slowly, followed by Harry, Christina came into the room. She stood before him, looking up at the powerful figure, wondering why he looked so much bigger here than he did in the glasshouse. And, with a touch of indignation that was distinctly helpful, why she should feel as if she had been called into his presence, rather than the other way about. Once again, Joe Compson had managed somehow to disconcert her, and once again the realisation was swiftly replaced by a spurt of resentful anger.

'Well, Joe,' she said crisply, 'this is something of a surprise. I take it you've good reason for coming here tonight.'

'I think I have, Miss Christina.' To her annoyance, he wasn't in the least discomposed by her coolness. 'I wanted to see you about summat special.'

'Something that could not have been discussed in the glasshouse? It *is* to do with the glasshouse?'

'That's right, miss. It's about that special piece you want

– the flint, to show what we can do. I've been workin' on it at home. Mekkin' patterns and such – designs. I wanted to show you, quiet-like. That's why I came. I couldn't ask you at work, you'll understand that, miss, I'm sure.'

Christina did understand. It would have been impossible for Joe to suggest such a visit in the glass-cone, with the other workmen around to hear every word. And although he could have given her his designs there, she could appreciate his wish to show them to her himself, where they would not be interrupted.

'Let me see your ideas, then, Joe,' she said, and the three of them moved over to the library table. Rose had already placed a lamp there and it cast a soft glow over the mellow surface. The glow reflected upwards too, on to their faces; Christina's creamily luminous, Harry's ruddily fair and Joe's almost the rich colour of the mahogany itself.

'This is what I've brought, Miss Christina,' he said, feeling in his pocket and producing a few sheets of thin paper. He placed them on the table, smoothing them carefully, and Christina saw that they were sheets torn from an exercise book, rough-surfaced and scribbled over in an uncertain hand. She frowned at them, trying to make out any pattern in the scrawls, and then realised what she was looking at.

'Oh, I see. You've cut out the patterns. Like dissected drawings – see, Harry? This is a goblet, and this a bowl, and here's a ewer. But they're small pieces, Joseph – I had in mind something large and impressive.'

'They *are* large, Miss Christina.' Joe took one of the shapes from her hand and held it up. 'This bowl, I reckoned to mek it a good eighteen inch across – hold a deal of punch, that would, at one of your fine parties. And this piece in't no goblet, it's a chalice. Stand a foot high, that would, and weigh a tidy few pound too. I thought you'd want summat to stand out, like. There's a few others here too, miss, but I can do some other designs if you want,' he finished in an uncharacteristically humble tone.

'No, no, these are wonderful.' Christina stood at the table, turning over the flimsy sheets. 'The bowl, that would look very fine, I think. A magnificent piece. But the ewer has the more graceful shape – it shows off your artistry better. And this piece – the epergne – I think it would be a good symbol for the new Henzel's. But no, on the whole –' she fingered again the pattern that had first caught her eye, and gazed at it, her green eyes half-closed as she tried to visualise what it would look like as a piece of glass, glinting and shimmering in the lamplight '– on the whole, I think this is the piece I like the best. It has such a strong, yet elegant shape. Such a pretty curve. And you could make a special stem – a spiral twist, perhaps, or some bubbles to decorate it further. Yes . . . that's my favourite. The chalice.' She laid the pattern down gently and turned to smile at Joe, her resolve beaten by excitement. 'The Compson Chalice. Doesn't that have a fine ring to it?'

Joe blinked as if someone had suddenly shone a bright light in his eyes. He cleared his throat, pushed back his dark curls and said gruffly, 'The Compson Chalice. That has a ring as fine as the crystal itself will sound when 'tis struck.'

'What do you think of it, Harry?' Christina turned to her brother.

'I like it. It's a strong shape, as you say, but it will look delicate as well in crystal. Will you have it engraved?'

Christina slanted a look of amusement at Joe. 'I think our glassblower would prefer not. You have little fondness for the engraver's art, have you, Joe?'

'If you can call it art – smothering a good honest shape with so much decoration and prickled cutting a man can hardly tell what it is, let alone pick it up and use it. Why, I've seen good glasses turned out of our glasshouse and come back from the engraver's shop no better than hedgehogs!' He glanced at the patterns lying spread out on the table. 'Well, I've done what you asked, Miss Christina. I've made up a few patterns and it's for you to choose what to do with 'em. Throw 'em out if they don' please you, but if you want me to blow the pieces I will, an' do my best at the job. An' if you want to get 'em engraved after –' he shrugged, as if the matter were of no importance whatsover to him, '– why, 'tis your glass and for you to decide. Nothing to do with me, once the glass goes to the *lehr*.'

'Of course it's to do with you, Joe,' Christina said warmly. 'If you make as good a job of those as you make of your everyday work, I shall want to give you all due credit for them. Yes, make them all and let's see which is best when you've done. And if you like, I'll make you a promise.' She stood straight, her slender body erect, head thrown back to look up at him. 'Whichever piece I choose to be the symbol of Henzel's, I promise not to have it engraved. You're right; to show the beauty of fine rock crystal, only a good shape is necessary. We can engrave other pieces, indeed, we must, for the public demand is for engraved glass and we're all of us here to earn our living. But that piece shall stand unadorned as an example of the glassblower's art.'

Joe coughed again, and when he spoke, his voice was still gruff. 'Like I said, Miss Christina, that's for you to decide. I'll leave the patterns here, shall I? You might want to look at 'em again.'

'Yes, do. Though I'm sure I shan't change my mind.' She turned as the door opened and Rose looked in. 'It's quite all right, Rose. Mr Compson is just going. And you may tell my aunt that Harry has looked after me perfectly.' She smiled at Joe. 'I'm glad you came, Joe. Please don't be afraid to come again, if you should ever need to. I think we may discuss designs again. You seem to have as much talent for them as for your blowing. All right, Rose, you may show Mr Compson out now.'

She ignored the parlour maid's outraged face, well able to imagine the shocked recounting of the story later, below stairs. 'And she called him *Mr Compson* – imagine – and him no more than a common glassmaker! And told him to call again – any time he pleased! Really, I don't know what the world's coming to – what her aunt would have said to hear her, heaven only knows!' With a straight back, as cool and imperial as the young Queen Victoria, indifferent to the girl's scandalised expression, Christina moved to the door and rustled out, followed once more by her brother.

Rose gave Joe a severe look.

'You heard Miss Christina,' she said. 'You can go now.' She watched suspiciously as he gathered up his cap, and looked at him as if she would have liked to search him. 'I just 'opes you haven't upset the young mistress, coming here like this.'

Joe half-closed his eyes and gave her an impudent look. 'Me? Upset her? Now do I look the sort of cove to go around upsettin' young women? I don't upset you, do I?'

'Indeed you don't!' Rose retorted sharply, but her colour had deepened and Joe chuckled as he passed her into the hallway. She let him out through the front door with no further comment; but she took longer than necessary to close it behind him, standing on the top step, silhouetted against the light, for several moments as he strode whistling down the drive.

Joe felt unexpectedly cheerful as he swung away down the street. It had cost him a good deal of thought before he had decided to approach Christina at home. All too easily, he knew, she could have been offended and angered by his presumption, and ordered him away without even glancing at his patterns. But he had counted on the strange bond he felt between them, that strand that drew them together even when that other element in their relationship – the barrier of class and employment – was at its highest. And he'd counted too on Christina's curiosity and her often deliberate flouting of convention.

And he'd been right. She'd over-ridden that haughty piece of a parlour maid – he grinned in the darkness at the thought of Rose's haughtiness melting into submission under his hands, if ever he got the chance – and she'd only brought the young lad, Harry, into the library with her, instead of the dragon of an aunt whom he'd expected. Plainly, Christina Henzel was mistress in her own home as well as at the glasshouse.

Mind, she hadn't liked it at first, seeing him there – thought he was making free with her, taking advantage, he didn't doubt. And there'd been that spark of arrogance in her too, as if every time they met she had to put him in his place, remind him that she was his superior – never knowing, he thought with a grin, that it was just that touch of half-frightened haughtiness that was what he liked best about her and made him want even more fiercely to sweep her up and carry her away somewhere quiet and dark where they could be just a man and a woman with no pretence.

For a moment, Joe allowed his mind to toy with the images it conjured up. Then he dismissed them impatiently. Only fools allowed themselves to dream. He'd made the patterns and she'd liked them, that was all that mattered. As soon as the new pots were filled with good flint metal from the mixtures that were being made now, he would be able to set to and make the pieces. And that would be an end to it, as far as he was concerned. Except that, from now on, he hoped to be acknowledged as the leading glassblower at Henzel's, the one who made all their best lines, the one who could demand the best men in his chair and the highest wage.

Maybe then he'd think about what seemed to be bothering Maggie Haden lately. Marriage. He'd held it off long enough, content, as he'd thought she was, to take their pleasure without responsibility. And he wasn't over-keen on the idea now. But everyone came to it sooner or later. And there wasn't any other woman he could fancy as much. Not one he could have, at any rate.

Chapter Eight

'This is the one,' Christina announced excitedly.

For weeks, she and the men had been experimenting with old recipes and new ideas to find the most effective proportions of lead to use in their mixtures. Now it seemed that their hard work had brought about the desired result. She took the finished bowl and held it to the light, turning it this way and that so that the glow from the furnace glimmered hot and red within it. 'See how it reflects the light.' She walked with it towards the double doors and out into the sunshine. 'Yes . . .' she breathed in delight, her fingers caressing the gleaming surface. 'Yes, this is what will make Henzel's famous. Nobody else is making crystal of this quality – this brilliance.' She turned to Joe, her face alight, and gave him back the bowl. 'That's the metal you'll use for the Chalice. And I want to be here when you make it.'

Joe stood looking down at her and she returned his gaze steadily, aware as always of the challenge lying somewhere deep in his eyes. Almost unconsciously, she lifted her chin. Her own eyes widened a little, dark as rain-wet grass, and her lips parted slightly, showing teeth that were fine and white, while the tip of her tongue just touched her upper lip.

'I assume this will be convenient for you, Joe?' she said with cool irony, and the dark head nodded with a con-sidering slowness that brought a flash of annoyance to her eyes.

'Ah, I reckon that'll suit, miss,' he answered gravely. 'I'll reckon to mek the Chalice – say next Tuesday, after-noon turn, if you'd like to be about then.'

'I'll be here.' The ice in her eyes melted to a smile. No

doubt he would have made more than one piece of the pattern they'd agreed on before Tuesday, for Christina was aware that Joe Compson wouldn't be satisfied with a single attempt, even though he was craftsman enough to achieve a perfectly acceptable article every time. For this, as for any other special item, he would want perfection – which meant a selection of pieces to choose from, with nothing that most people could see to choose between any. The rest would be smashed and returned to the mix as cullet. There was to be only one Compson Chalice.

With Ruth at her side, Christina made her way back to the house.

'Did you hear that, Ruth? Joe's making the Chalice next Tuesday.' She gave a small skip. 'We'll make a special occasion of it, just as Papa used to do. All the family there, and a party afterwards. And I'll arrange for all the men to be given a special issue of ale in "The Glassblowers".'

'That's a good idea, Miss Christina. It's a long time since we did anything like that. I remember me dad tellin' me of some of the times . . . And our Joe's to mek the new piece. Me mam'll be right proud.'

'She shall come too,' Christina said impulsively. 'And any of the rest of your family who can do so too. Run home this evening, Ruth, and tell them. And you, of course, you must be there. Why, our families are quite closely connected! Your father and mine knew and respected each other – you're my maid – and Joe –' She stopped suddenly.

'And Joe works for you, just as me dad does. But it's always been like that in glass, hevn't it, miss? Families workin' together. Me grandad, he worked at Henzel's too. And I daresay when Joe gets wed, his children will come along as well. You hev to be bred up to it, after all.'

'Yes, that's what they say, isn't it.' Christina walked for a few steps in silence, then went on more briskly, 'Well, this party – let's see, who will be there? Aunt Susan, she'll

132

come for a special occasion, and it will do her good to go into the glasshouse for once. Adela, of course, and Harry if his schoolmaster will give him a half-holiday. And I wonder if Alice and John might come over from Warwickshire . . . Jeremy, I couldn't leave him out, even though I don't think he likes the idea of the Chalice. And I suppose I must invite his mother and father. And that means Cousin Harold and Cousin Ada too . . . and Cousin Reuben,' she added even more reluctantly. 'And, do you know, I believe I'll bring Thomas as well! He's never been to the glasshouse and he'd love it. And there'll be plenty of people to look after him. Nurse can come too, and you'll help give an eye to him, won't you, Ruth?'

'Why, of course I will, miss.' But Ruth's tone was clearly doubtful. 'Only I wonder what your aunt will say.'

'What she always says, of course – *really Christina!*' Christina mimicked her aunt's shocked tones perfectly, and both girls laughed. 'But there really isn't any reason why Thomas shouldn't have an outing too. Papa never wanted him to be locked away, and neither do I. He isn't an idiot, Ruth, whatever people may say, he's a dear, loving little boy and he does enjoy the things he can understand. And he'll love to see Joe blowing glass; he'll talk about it for months to come. Look how he remembers things like Christmas and birthday parties.'

'And games, he never forgets a game.' Ruth paused, then added, 'He thinks the world of you, Miss Christina. And of Master Harry.'

'Harry's very good to him. I believe he goes to the nursery quite often to see Tommy.'

'Yes, he does. He – he has tea with us quite a lot. I think he likes it there, after school and that.' For a moment, Ruth seemed about to say more, but after a brief hesitation all she said was, 'Don't Mr Jeremy like the design for the Chalice?'

Christina made a rueful face. 'I don't see how anyone could *not* like it, Ruth. But no – he did not seem pleased with it. He would have liked me to accept his own designs, I think.' She remembered Jeremy's reaction when she had rejected the patterns he brought her, and knew that she was considerably understating the case. Jeremy had been more than displeased – he had been bitterly resentful.

'You really mean you prefer the – the childish scrawls of an illiterate workman to *my* designs?' he demanded, thrusting the two examples under her nose: Joe's painstakingly cut from rough paper already used for exercises at the Mechanics' Institute which he attended in the evenings, Jeremy's neatly executed on fine parchment. 'Christina, this infatuation of yours has gone too far.'

'Infatuation? I don't know what you mean. Joe has simply brought me some designs that I like and wish to use. There is no more to it than that. And he isn't illiterate,' she added.

'No more to it than that?' he sneered. 'Perhaps you may forgive me for doubting that, Christina. It seems to me that there is a great deal more to it – but we've discussed this before, to no avail.'

'We have indeed,' she said coldly. 'And I would rather not discuss it again . . . I thank you for bringing me your designs, Jeremy, but I have to say that I prefer Joe's. And it does seem more fitting that Henzel's new symbol should be designed by one of my own men. Surely you can see that.'

Jeremy looked at her, and Christina could still feel the shock of the bitter venom in his glance. She watched him gather up his drawings, his face tight, lips compressed, and although he said no more, she knew that the humiliation of being passed over in favour of a glassblower was not something he would easily forget. Or forgive.

But on their next meeting, it seemed that she had been wrong about that, for Jeremy was his usual self, good-tempered, tender, slightly teasing, and she had comforted herself by thinking that, after all, it didn't really matter.

'I suppose Mr Jeremy will get his designs made up in his father's factory anyway,' Ruth observed now. 'They're going to expand their table-glass side, so I've heard.'

'Yes, that's true. Of course he will. And it seems only natural that he should keep his best designs for his own glasshouse. I would be surprised if those he offered me were the only ones he had drawn.'

'Or the best,' Ruth said shrewdly, and Christina laughed, feeling a relief from the discomfort that had been nagging at her.

'Are we maligning my cousin, do you suppose? Or simply being what Harry would called realistic? Ruth, it *is* good to have you to talk to. There's no one else I can speak to like this, saying whatever comes into my head, and know that it will be understood. And, more important, go no further. You're better than a sister to me, Ruth.'

Ruth blushed deeply. 'It's only because you're so good to me, Miss Christina,' she muttered at length. 'And because – well, because I'm right fond of you. But as to being like a sister –'

Christina considered her gravely. Her words had been impulsively spoken, but there was nevertheless a good deal of truth in them. She could talk to Ruth as she could never have done to either of her own sisters. There was a closeness between them that was surely more than that of mistress and maid. 'I mean it, Ruth,' she said quietly, 'I'd like to think that you could feel the same. That we could be as sisters.'

Ruth's usually pale face was as pink as a pearl, her soft brown eyes bright. Briefly, Christina thought of the timid girl who had been with her in Joshua's death chamber and saw how Ruth had matured and blossomed during the ensuing months. Why, she's really pretty, Christina thought with surprise.

'Sisters!' Ruth said, with a sudden, nervous giggle. 'Oh, miss, the things you say! And what our Joe'd say I can't think – mebbe he'd want to be your brother, too!' And she stifled her giggles with her hand, as if afraid she had said too much.

Christina smiled. But she was disturbed, all the same. Joe her brother? It was true that he was much more like Joshua than Harry was – even more than Frederic had been. But that was simply because Joseph Compson and Joshua Henzel were the same kind of man: big, aggressive, thrusting.

And the feelings that she had towards Joe, darkly confused as they were, were quite different from any she had ever had for any of her brothers.

The special party to visit the glasshouse and see Joseph Compson blow the Chalice was arranged, though not without some difficulty. Aunt Susan made no objection; she had been to the cone with Joshua on occasions like this, when a special piece of glass was made. The last time had been just before the young queen's Coronation, when Joe's father had made a set of fine wineglasses as a wedding present from Henzel's. They hadn't stayed to watch the whole process, of course, just the first few glasses, and then they had gone home to one of Mrs Jenner's best suppers.

'But we had sufficient time to prepare for it then,' Susan said plaintively when Christina told her. 'We knew in good time, we could plan and arrange the menu. How can all that be done in five days, one of them Sunday? Poor Mrs Jenner will be at her wits' end.'

'She'll love it,' Christina said confidently. 'It's a long time since we had a real celebration here.' Her voice faltered a little as she realised why it was a long time; even Christmas had had to be quiet, coming so soon after her father's death, and her own twenty-first birthday party, a month ago, had been similarly restrained, just a simple dinner. 'It's not a big party, after all,' she went on persuasively. 'Just family. And it needn't be too elaborate. Some cold meats, perhaps, a few trifles and some tarts. I'm sure Mrs Jenner will manage.'

'And there's Alice, too,' Susan grumbled, changing the direction of her argument. 'It's hardly fair to give her such short notice. How can she and John come over from Warwickshire without upsetting their own arrangements?'

'They may not have any. And if they have, well, it's a pity but there will be no great harm done if they can't be here.' Christina looked at her aunt. 'Please realise, Aunt Susan, that this really *is* a special occasion, but its importance is wholly in the glasshouse. We must begin to produce fine lead crystal as soon as possible if we're to take our rightful place in the market, and this party is as much to convince the men themselves of its importance as to give Alice and John and ourselves a special supper. If they see that we think it's worth celebrating, they'll take all the more pride and pleasure in it themselves. And that means better work. So we'll arrange our party for next Tuesday, and we shall all wear our best clothes for it and show the men just how proud and pleased we are by what they're doing. Now, will you see to the house arrangements? Or shall I call Mrs Jenner and speak to her myself?'

'No, no, I'll do that since you're so determined.' Susan spoke grumblingly, but Christina knew that she had won and let the matter rest there. She went upstairs, more concerned for what she ought to wear than for what they might eat.

Clothes had never taken up many of Christina's thoughts. As a child, she had been happiest in a brown holland overall, scrambling round the garden with Frederic, climbing trees and building dams under his direction. And later, as she grew up, she had been too engrossed with the glasshouse to spend time as her sisters did with fashion plates and magazines like *World of*

Fashion or *The Lady's Newspaper*. However, for such an occasion as this, her own first real appearance as the new owner of Henzel's, which was bound to attract a certain amount of interest, she was aware that she ought to give her observers no possible cause for complaint. And a lack of femininity was just the kind of fault they would pounce on.

Mrs Biddle, the dressmaker, had come as usual in the spring with her three girls, all of them stitching away in the basement room by the kitchen, set aside for them to work in. She had made clothes for all the women in the household: summer gowns for Aunt Susan, Christina and Adela, a new uniform for Rose and stuff dresses and aprons for the rest of the female servants. Christina had suffered her attentions with impatience, wanting only to get back to her increasingly absorbing work. But now she opened the wardrobe door and gazed at the dresses hanging inside.

'The green silk, do you think, Ruth?' she asked doubtfully. 'I like the velvet ribbon round the sleeve and skirt. Or the dark blue challis, with the muslin collar? I'm not sure . . .'

'They both suit you, miss.' Ruth had been longing to see her mistress in either of the gowns and, like Susan Henzel, wished that Christina would pay more attention to her appearance. 'The green matches your eyes,' she added shyly.

Christina took the dress from the rail and held it against herself, moving over to the long mirror. The colour of the glacé silk changed as she walked, looking now light and now dark, the glimmering green of dappled sunlight slanting through quivering leaves on to a rippling stream. It did indeed match her eyes. She stared at her reflection, fascinated by the way the colour lit up the pearly luminescence of her face and brought the glow of autumn beech to her tawny hair. Absently, she raised a hand and undid some of the pins that held her exuberant waves firmly pinned back out of her way; and shook her head with sudden, surprised vigour as the curls sprang up like released prisoners and tumbled around her shoulders.

'Do you think Aunt Susan will think this suitable to wear to the glasshouse?' she asked, dubiously, and then laughed. 'Of course she won't! I don't myself. It makes me look –' She paused, unable to find a word for the reflection that both disturbed and excited her. 'I think the blue, after all, it's less noticeable.' She took the blue dress, with its inset of lace and its demure puffed sleeves, and gazed critically at it. 'Yes, I think that would be better,' she said, and replaced it. 'Though I do like the green . . .' Again, she held it against herself.

The door opened suddenly and she whirled, the shimmering skirt flying out around her and settling in a fall of graceful folds.

'Harry! What are you about, bursting in like this?'

'Sorry, sis, I just wanted to show you this. Look!' He waved a copy of the *Wolverhampton Chronicle* under her nose. 'They're launching the new railway – the South Staffordshire. There's been a meeting in Walsall, at the George Hotel.' He read the report out loud. 'And there's been an Act of Parliament passed to construct a line from Oxford to Dudley, going through Worcester. That'll be part of the Great Western Railway – Brunel's line!' He lowered the paper and gazed at the two girls, his face shining. 'Isn't that splendid? Don't you realise how it will benefit us all? You'll be able to send goods by rail – we can even go to London, if we want to, just for a *day*. And . . . What on earth are you doing with that dress, Chrissie?'

Christina smiled at his enthusiasm, but she knew he was right. A railway *would* make a considerable difference to the marketing of their glass, enabling them to send orders all over the country far faster and more efficiently than by carriage or canal. Perhaps it would even make a difference to manufacturers, if railways would carry the raw materials to them.

'But will the railway come to Stourbridge?' she asked, handing the gown to Ruth to hang up. She turned to her brother, eyes glowing. 'Imagine if we could be the first to transport glass by rail – to London, for instance! Orders given this week, despatched next . . . With the mails so efficient now, we could outstrip all our rivals on delivery time alone. When will we have the railway here, Harry?'

'I'm not sure about that. Perhaps not at once. I'll have to look at the map. But in any case, it'll be a lot nearer than it is now. And it *will* come, Chrissie. It must. This whole area is one of the most important manufacturing areas in the country now, and it must be given the railways to serve it.' His eyes followed Ruth as she replaced the dres in the wardrobe, and he added half-shyly, 'That's an awfully pretty dress, sis.'

'I was thinking of wearing it next Tuesday, but I've decided on this blue one instead. We're having a special celebration, Harry – our first piece of lead crystal. Joe's going to make the Chalice then.' Harry needed no explanation of that, the whole family had heard of little but the Chalice ever since the idea had first been suggested. 'You're to come too, Harry, to see it made – we'll arrange a half-holiday for you – and we're having a party afterwards. All the family are coming, even Thomas. We might even have a daguerreotype done, what do you think?'

'A grand idea, if everyone can sit still long enough! How do you think Tommy will manage?'

'Well, we might leave Thomas out of that. But I do think Joe ought to be in it.' Christina swung round to Ruth, her flying hair a bronze halo round her head. 'Don't you, Ruth?'

'Joe? Our Joe? Oh, miss, I don't think he'd – I mean, he wouldn't be dressed right and –'

'He could change at the glasshouse, after he's made the Chalice. Of course he should be in it! We wouldn't have the Chalice without him. He designed it, he's making it –

he *must* be in it.' Swiftly, Christina crossed to her bureau and took out the scrap of paper on which Joe had originally drawn the Chalice. 'There, Harry, you saw his design, do you know what that is? It's a page from the book Joe had at the Institute – the book he learned to write and do his sums in. He cut it up to make a pattern for the Chalice. Don't you think that's wonderful?' She gazed down, marvelling again at the flimsy, rough crudeness of the paper, in such vivid contrast to the delicacy of the pattern, so carefully drawn and cut out with old kitchen scissors. Harry took it from her and Ruth drew near him and looked at it too.

'That's from the Institute, all right,' she said. 'But Joe learned to read and write at the old dame school. Owd Mrs Scriven's, down Beauty Bank way. We all went there – me and Joe and the others, till she took sick with the cholera and died. Then me mam wouldn't let us go down that way no more. She said it were unhealthy.'

'And so it is,' Harry said with sudden vigour. 'Beauty Bank – how ever did it get such a name? Nearly a mile of dwelling-houses, and not a proper drain in the whole length – just one long open gutter to carry all the filth. And not a well amongst them all that supplies water fit to drink – they have to buy every drop from the carrier. Precious little beauty there!'

'That in't the only place like that,' Ruth said. 'There's plenty more as bad and worse. Us on'y went there because she was a good teacher and me dad wanted us to have a good education, like, afore us went to work. None of the dames round Wordsley were so good as old Mother Scriven.'

'Well, she did a good job with you and Joe,' Christina observed as Harry handed back the pattern. 'Although I believe Joe would have been an artist whatever happened. He has talent – sensitivity to beauty . . . I think you have it too, Ruth.'

Ruth turned scarlet. 'Oh, I don't think so, Miss

Christina,' she protested, her face hidden as she busied herself with the dresses that hung in the big wardrobe. 'I mean, I like pretty things and that – but nobody could call me clever, not like our Joe.'

'You've embarrassed her,' Harry murmured to Christina, his blue eyes dancing. 'Poor girl, it's not fair.'

'Nonsense. Ruth and I are like sisters. She's only embarrassed because you're here.' Christina smiled at her brother, thinking how much closer they had grown of late. 'I'm glad about the railway, Harry. How soon do you think they'll begin work?'

'Almost at once, I hope. It will take time, of course, and a deal of labour – I suppose that means more Irishmen coming over. I don't suppose we'll have a railway working in less than a year – perhaps longer. So the sooner they start, the better.' He paced restlessly about the room, slapping his leg with the rolled-up newspaper. 'I wish I were old enough to leave school and begin work. Everything interesting will have been done before my chance comes!'

'Have patience, Harry,' counselled Christina, who was learning the same painful lesson. 'You need your education if you're to be as good an engineer as Brunel – and that's what you want, isn't it?'

'Just to work with him would be enough,' Harry grumbled. 'All right, sis, don't worry, I'll stick to my books. Thank goodness we've a good science master at King Edward's. And talking of books, I must go, I've some studying to do before morning.'

'Then go and do it.'

Adela was the only one of the family to be uncomplicatedly pleased about the party.

'I'll be able to wear my new red silk!' she exclaimed. 'But do I have to go to that dirty glasshouse first, Christina? I mean, wouldn't it be better if I just stayed at home and helped Rose arrange the table? There will be flowers

142

to do, and someone must make sure the silver is properly polished, and –'

'Parker will see to all that. And yes, you do have to come to the glasshouse first. That's the whole point of it, to watch Joe make the Chalice. And I want to have a daguerreotype made of us all, with Joe in it too. So –'

'With *Compson* in it?' Jeremy, who had listened so far without comment to Christina's plans, interrupted swiftly. 'Christina, you can't mean that. He would look entirely out of place.'

'On the contrary, I think he will be very much *in* place,' she retorted. 'And of course he must be in it. He designed the Chalice and he will be making it. The picture would be incomplete without him. And after all, Mr Turner and Mr Honeyborne will be there, so why not Joe?'

Jeremy said no more, but the tightening of his lips warned her that there would be more discussion later. She sighed a little, wondering if there were any way of escaping it and knowing there was not; it was an accepted practice now for her and Jeremy to be left alone in the library when he had stayed for dinner. To talk over the business was the unspoken excuse, and indeed that was often what they did, but she knew that Aunt Susan expected something more from these evening tête-à-têtes. She knew that she was right about this evening as soon as coffee had been poured and Parker withdrawn.

'Don't you think,' Jeremy began, lifting his cup elegantly to his lips, 'that you're in danger of assigning rather too much importance to this glassblower of yours – this Compson?'

'In what way?' Christina spoke guardedly, well aware of Jeremy's meaning but determined not to give him an ounce of help.

'Christina, you know perfectly well in what way!' Clearly, Jeremy was in no mood for circumlocution. 'I've told you about this before. You've been making a great deal too much of him lately. Stopping to talk to him every time you visit the glass-cone – something which, in my opinion, you do far too frequently anyway – taking him into your confidence. Allowing him to come here with his childish bits of paper. Accepting what he is pleased to call a design – a scrawl that anyone could have made. Making a special occasion of this new piece being blown, and then, to cap it all, including him in a daguerreotype of the whole family! Why, you might as well let the whole chair crowd into the picture, right down to the taker-in, and have done with it! I'm warning you again, Christina, you're giving this man an entirely false sense of his own importance, and it will only lead to trouble.'

'Jeremy, please. I know what I'm doing. And Joe *is* important. He's the best glassblower we have. He has immense talent. And I don't see why it shouldn't be acknowledged.'

'Talent!' Jeremy laughed scornfully. 'Any blower could do what he does, Christina. There's no such thing as talent. It's simply a matter of controlling the breath, in knowing how to shape a mass of raw metal.'

'Just as playing the flute or the oboe is a matter of controlling the breath?' she asked coldly, and felt a lump of misery begin to form inside her. Why, when all Jeremy had ever done was try to help her, did they seem increasingly at odds with each other? And always over Joe! 'Please, Jeremy,' she said forcefully, 'let's not argue about this. I simply want a celebration, and something to remind us all of this day – the day when Henzel's began to produce the finest lead crystal in the country. It's going to be important to us all.'

'Not in the same way,' he reminded her. 'You seem to forget, Christina, that we are still rivals.'

Christina was silent. She had indeed forgotten that Jeremy might not take such delight in her own success, the success that she envisaged for Henzel's. That all the time she planned for such success, she was also inevitably planning his own failure. She bit her lip and went to him, laying her hand on his sleeve.

'I'm sorry, Jeremy. You've been of such help to me that I

do forget that. And I wish it were not so. But I want so much to carry out Papa's wishes – to make Henzel's the most famous of all glassmakers. Can you blame me for that?'

His blue eyes softened. 'I don't blame you at all, little cousin. And don't worry about the rest of us. We *can* look after ourselves, even when faced with such charming competition. Have your little celebration next Tuesday, yes, and include Compson in it if you must. I'll say no more on the matter.'

He spoke loftily, humouring her, and she repressed a flash of irritation and looked up at him, thinking how handsome he was, and how elegantly different from the swarthy, rugged Joe. 'And will you come to a dinner I'm planning the week after?' she asked. 'When the Chalice is ready to be shown?'

'Another family celebration?' he asked, but she shook her head.

'No, a business dinner. It's time I entertained more,' she went on with determination. 'I ought to be meeting the other manufacturers in the area. Ironmasters, coal-mine owners, all the people Papa knew. I should be able to talk with them as he did, see them on an equal footing, or they'll never accept me as one of them.'

'One of them!' Jeremy laughed. 'Christina, you'll never be "one of them". You're a woman – a young woman. How can you expect men like Rob Pennyfield and John Fenton to take a young girl like yourself seriously in matters of business?' He smiled indulgently. 'I'll come, by all means, to speak for you if you need me, but you mustn't try to talk business with them yourself, they'll be at best embarrassed and at worst deeply offended.'

'Indeed?' Christina said coldly. 'And why should that be? I thought you understood –'

'I do. I understand very well, my dear sweet little cousin. You run the glasshouse admirably and so far all has gone well. But that's because your workmen and your more senior employees like Honeyborne and Turner know and love you as they knew and loved your father. I'm sure they respect you too, for the gallant way in which you've carried on. But as for talking with other businessmen – no, you must forget that, my dear. Forget it and leave it to me. I'll deal with all those problems for you.'

'But I don't want you to. And, as you've just pointed out to me, we are rivals.'

Jeremy smiled and touched her chin with his finger. 'Don't worry about that, Christina. We're friends, too, aren't we? More than friends, I had begun to hope.'

His finger holding her chin so that her face was tilted towards him, he bent his head and laid his lips gently on hers.

For a moment, Christina stood still, too surprised to move. Jeremy had kissed her before, of course, the brief touch of lips on cheek, to wish her a happy birthday or Christmas, to greet her on meeting or parting. But this kiss was quite different. A searching, questioning kiss, with lips parted, stroking hers with a lingering tenderness that brought a swift shock to her body, low in her stomach, and a tingling to her limbs. She felt a movement in her throat but could not turn her head away, and after a moment, Jeremy released her and stepped back a little.

'Well?' he asked softly. 'Are we friends?'

Christina stared up at him. Her knees were unaccountably weak, her heart fluttering. She wanted him to kiss her again, so that she could confirm those odd, disturbing sensations she had experienced while his lips were on hers – but at the same time, she feared his apparent control over her body. Why should he be able to exert such an effect on her? And what kind of power did it give him? With an effort, she pulled herself together.

'Friends?' she repeated coolly. 'I didn't know our friendship was in question. I merely invited you to a small business dinner I intend to give. As a guest,' she said with some emphasis. 'I intend, as I've already said, to meet these men on an equal footing.'

'And just how do you propose to make them accept you – as an equal?' Jeremy's good humour was fading now, and there was a betraying sneer in his voice to which Christina reacted with sharpness.

'By doing as I've said. Meeting them and talking with them. Entertaining them to dinner here, and not withdrawing with the ladies afterwards. By talking business *with* them, so that they can see for themselves that I am not just an empty-headed female, playing at running Henzel's. It will take time, I know.' She spoke ruefully, her restless, impatient nature unwilling to be fettered by the conventions that needed patience to overcome. 'But I'll do it, Jeremy. I'll *make* them take me seriously.'

'Yes, and how?' Jeremy's irritation had now gone beyond his control and he stepped back again and let his eyes move over her with a rapid assessment that was as insulting as it was hurtful. 'By denying all the natural feminine virtues,' he mocked her. 'By pretending you're a man! Already, you're beginning to resemble one. You despise feminine clothes – dressing in those plain gowns, with no ornaments, not even a scrap of velvet or lace. And your hair, so tightly scraped back, all its beauty spoiled. You're making yourself look old, don't you realise that – old and plain. What are you trying to do, Christina? What are you afraid of? That some man will realise you're a woman after all and want to marry you, taking away that precious independence you're so fond of?' He turned away from her, as if in contempt, then whipped back. 'Well, never fear, sweet cousin. If the way you responded to my kisses just now is any guide, no man will want to go further than that. Your valued independence will remain inviolate, just as you will yourself!'

Christina stared at him. She raised a trembling hand to her hair and found the pins that held it back – to keep it tidy, she'd told herself, in the glasshouse. With a quick

147

movement, she released them, letting her hair spring out as it had done while she was trying the dresses in her room, cascading in a warm autumnal fall to the neckline of the plain dress she wore – again, at first because it was more practical for the glasshouse and then because she felt it gave her appearance more authority. Didn't Jeremy understand that she looked too young, too feminine, to command respect? 'Is that any better?' she demanded haughtily and stood before him, the flash of burning emerald in her widened eyes, her full red lips parted to show small white teeth.

She heard the intake of Jeremy's breath. With a quick, firm step, he took her in his arms, and she arched against him to look steadily up into his bemused face. With a deliberate movement, she placed her hands on each side of his head to bring it down to hers. And then, no longer certain of who had begun the embrace, she was being crushed against his lean body, her softness pressed ruthlessly against the hardness of male bones and muscle. This time, it was she who offered the kiss, less gentle now, and as he took her lips she found herself responding to his rough demands with a surge of emotion that transmitted itself through lips, hands and body, astonishing her and bringing a murmur of satisfaction from Jeremy's throat. He held her away from him, his eyes moving over her with an interest she had never seen in them before, and then he drew her against him again, folding his arms about her with lazy confidence.

'You see?' he murmured against her mouth. 'Being a real woman isn't so bad after all, is it?'

His lips were on hers again and Christina could not answer, even if she had been able to find words in the whirl of emotion that was pounding through her blood. But a moment later, before any more could be said, they were simultaneously conscious of steps outside the door. They had barely sprung apart when it opened.

'I'm sorry, Miss Christina, if you were busy.' Ruth,

innocently apologetic, stood just inside the room, hands folded decorously in front of her. 'Your aunt sent me to ask if you'd be coming back to the drawing room – Miss Adela wants to practise her new song and she needs you to play the pianoforte. She said not to worry if you and Mr Jeremy were talking business,' she added.

Christina had been moving away from Jeremy before Ruth had begun to speak, and now she turned and smiled brightly, not looking at her cousin.

'It's all right, Ruth. Mr Jeremy was just leaving, weren't you, Jeremy?' She didn't look directly at him, afraid that her eyes would complete the betrayal of her body. After what had just happened, she would be quite unable to behave naturally with him in the drawing room. 'I'd like very much to accompany Adela. I'll come along at once.' She nodded briefly in Jeremy's direction. Her poise was returning, her heartbeat steadying and it would do him good to wonder whether or not she was offended. She waited until he had collected his hat and coat and departed, and then turned to Ruth, her eyes sparkling and her colour high.

'Put the blue dress away, Ruth, and take out the green one instead and make sure it's ready. I've decided to wear that one on Tuesday, instead. I think it is *entirely* suitable!'

Christina's appearance on the following Tuesday afternoon had an effect on almost everyone present.

Aunt Susan was, predictably, shocked.

'You don't really intend to appear like that, Christina! Why, you look – you look –' As so often happened when her thoughts were too shocking to put into words, she floundered, using widened eyes, raised brows and fluttering hands to convey her meaning.

Surprisingly, Alice came to Christina's defence. She and John, grumbling at the short notice, had nevertheless come from Warwickshire, arriving just in time for luncheon.

'I think Christina looks very nice,' she said. 'Those little ringlets falling in front of the cap soften her face, and the curls behind are most fashionable. The shape of the dress shows up her figure, which is really very lovely, and the colour suits her exactly. I always knew you could look better if you chose to exert yourself,' she added, addressing Christina herself for the first time.

'Yes, well, all that may be true,' Susan said in a dissatisfied tone. 'Taken separately, each item is perfectly innocuous. It's only when they are all together – on Christina – that they begin to look . . .' Again, the only words which came to mind were ones she did not care to speak aloud, and Christina caught Alice's eye and smiled impishly.

She knew exactly what her aunt meant. She had been startled herself by the reflection her mirror showed her, and had almost decided, after all, to wear the more decorous blue. But Jeremy's words still stung. Afraid to be a woman – how dared he say such a thing! Tossing her head, she looked again at the image in the glass and allowed a smile of surprised delight to curve her lips. Yes, she did look different – bolder, more vivid, more alive. More, in fact, herself. As if she had been hiding the real Christina under all those plain, dull gowns worn for practicality and had slowly been becoming like the image that they presented: plain, dull, practical. She twisted and turned in front of the mirror, letting the skirt float out around her, shimmering now sea-green, now the dark, mysterious shadow of deep forest. Am I plain and practical? Or am I really this exotic creature, all flashing colour and fire?

The door opened and Adela whisked in, a cloud of white muslin and blue bows. She had been impatient when Aunt Susan insisted on this dress, declaring that it was too childish for her, that she wanted something more grown-up, more fashionable. But now she had it on, she looked pretty, her hair still in loose, fair curls that swirled softly about her small face, her blue eyes alight with

150

excitement. Not that she was excited about the glassblowing, Christina knew that. It was the idea of a party that thrilled Adela, the chance to wear a pretty dress and take a few hours off from her lessons.

'There! Do I look nice?' She moved to the mirror, pouting at her reflection. 'Aunt Susan insisted I wear this – but it doesn't look too bad, does it?' From the artless way in which she asked the question it was apparent that she knew just how well the dress suited her. 'Anyway, it doesn't really matter, since it's only family.'

'You look very pretty, 'Del, and you know it quite well.' Christina allowed herself to be pushed aside from the mirror. 'And we'd better go down now, everyone will be ready. I don't want to be late at the glasshouse.'

'Do I *have* to come?' Adela pleaded. 'It's so dirty and noisy there, and all those horrid men looking at me, they make me feel quite embarrassed. It's all right for you, Christina, you don't care what anyone thinks of you, but I'm sensitive, Aunt Susan's always saying so.'

Christina looked at her. Was that really how she appeared to her sister – to everyone else? Insensitive, not caring what anyone thought of her. She felt a pang, similar to the one that had stabbed her when Jeremy accused her of being un-womanly, afraid of men. Was she really like that, hard and unfeminine? How would she normally have answered Adela now? With a curt, yes, of course you must come? Or with a gentleness that she was alarmed to find came less easily?

'Please come, 'Del. It really is a special occasion for me – and for all of us, if the new crystal is successful. And it will make the party all the nicer if you're there.'

Perhaps she had overdone it. But the startled glance Adela gave her confirmed her fears – that she really was growing hard, that people were now expecting it of her. And I'm not like that at all! she wanted to cry out. I have feelings too, and they're just as easily hurt. And I need help and comfort, just as the rest of you do. I just don't know who can give it to me.

For a heart-shaking moment, as she followed her sister

151

down the stairs, she longed desperately for her father. Or for someone who was made in his mould. Being strong was all very well, most of the time. But there were moments when you needed someone stronger, to lean on.

Aunt Susan and Alice were not the only ones who noticed the difference in Christina. Everyone else – except Adela, who was too absorbed in herself to notice anything at all – saw it too and reacted, in their different ways.

Samuel glanced at her, blinked and took a second look that was almost suspicious. His wife Lavinia, who had never approved of Christina anyway, raised her lorgnette and pursed her lips; perhaps her thoughts were the same as Aunt Susan's, shocking and unmentionable. Her thin, aristocratic nose flared slightly, like that of a thoroughbred horse on being offered a titbit it considered beneath its dignity, and she moved, very slightly, away.

Reuben's shifting eyes stilled for a moment and narrowed, remaining on her as if in sudden thought. His inspection threatened to rock her precarious poise and she glanced quickly away, resenting the discomfort he caused in her. She met instead the astonished stare of her blustering Cousin Harold and his wife, meek and submissive Ada.

'Good heavens, Christina, what *have* you done to yourself?' Harold demanded loudly. 'Is that paint you've got on your face?'

'No, indeed.' She lifted her head and felt the tiny ringlets brush her cheeks. 'I've nothing on my face at all.'

'Well, something's different about you.' He took out a pair of spectacles and put them on, staring at her more closely. 'Hmm. Well, if you say so, but I'd swear you'd done something, wouldn't you, Ada my dear?'

'Christina does have unusual colouring, dearest,' Ada ventured timidly, and he snorted.

'Something more than natural colouring there! Sure you haven't been using any of these chemists' stuffs; arsenic, belladonna, whatever it is you women slap on your faces? Do you no good, you know, no good at all.'

'I don't use anything, uncle. I think it's just the colour of my dress, or perhaps the new way Ruth's done my hair.'

'Well, if you say so.' He turned away, clearly unwilling to believe her, and Jeremy took his place.

It was his reaction that Christina had anticipated most. She faced him and lifted her chin, daring him to laugh at her – though why he should, she couldn't tell. She saw his blue eyes settle on her face, the pupils widening slightly; saw them move over her hair, down to her shoulders, sloping gently into the neckline of the shimmering green dress. She watched his glance go further, comprehensively taking in her whole appearance, the shape of the bodice tightly enclosing her firm breasts, narrowing to the pointed waist before billowing out into a swirl of foaming silk.

Jeremy bowed slightly, his eyes tender and mocking.

'It seems I owe you an apology, little cousin,' he said.

'I'm sure I don't know what you mean,' she answered lightly, keeping her eyes lowered to hide the gleam of triumph, and turned towards the door. 'Unless it's for almost being late. Shall we go now, if everyone's here? I know they'll be waiting for us at the glasshouse.'

'And we mustn't keep Mr Compson waiting, must we,' Jeremy commented as he held his arm for her to take. Christina gave him a sharp glance, but his expression was bland. 'Do I take it that you've stopped other production this afternoon?'

'Until the Chalice is made, yes. There would be far too many people around for the other chairs to continue working.'

'And no doubt you've agreed to pay the men for lost time.'

'Naturally,' Christina said a little stiffly as they went out-side. Jeremy smiled and bent nearer.

'You look delicious, little cousin. I hardly recognised you.'

'Not so much of a compliment after all,' she retorted, unable to resist an impulsive, upward glance through her long, smoky lashes. 'Am I usually so dull, then?'

Jeremy laughed. 'Dull? Never! Only a little – hidden, sometimes. And it seems a shame to cover a beautiful flower with dead leaves, don't you agree?' He smiled again at her colouring cheeks. 'There, now I've made you blush. If Uncle Harold should see you now, he'd be convinced it was rose petals you were using to stain your cheeks. But I know it's all natural, don't I.'

Christina said nothing. She turned her face away, glad of the large sun-bonnet that Aunt Susan had, at the last moment, begged her to wear. There was something in Jeremy's tone – an implied intimacy – that disturbed her. Something that hinted at a change in their relationship, an increasing closeness that she wasn't sure she wanted. And yet, she realised she'd encouraged this by accepting his friendship, by making him her confidant, asking his advice.

Friendship, yes. But more than that . . ? Christina was aware that her aunt had other hopes for this relationship, that Jeremy's parents would welcome a closer attachment between the two families, but she knew too that their hopes were centred around the two glassmaking firms rather than any personal consideration. Marriage between herself and Jeremy would settle the matter of Joshua's will very satis-factorily indeed. Christina knew she was attracted to Jeremy, had found his kisses exciting, sending a tingling sensation through her body. But she wasn't certain she was yet ready for any more, for marriage, to put herself in his control. She shivered and hoped nobody had noticed her confusion.

Joe was waiting beside his chair when the party arrived at

the cone, filing through the double doors and forming a group around the glowing furnace. Around him were his team, each one, like Joe, wearing clean working clothes and with hair brushed severely back. In the background were the members of the other chairs and the members of Joe's family who had come to see the new glass being made.

Christina looked at them with interest. His father, William, she knew already, of course. And that thin, pale-faced woman must be his mother, giving Ruth that funny little half-smile of embarrassment. And those children his two small sisters and little Willy. How small and white-faced they looked, yet Ruth had told her that the family was well-off compared with many others.

But that other – the dark young woman with the eyes that flashed and the ripe bosom that showed so much above her low neckline – surely she was not one of Joe's family? Christina stared at her, noting the clothes that were shabby and yet somehow gaudy, the dirty, coloured shawl flung carelessly round plump shoulders, the tumbling curls that looked as if fingers rather than a brush kept what little order there was . . . And then the girl's eyes met hers with an insolent stare, and Christina, conscious of a mounting antipathy, knew somehow that it must be Joe's woman. Abruptly, she turned away and caught Joe watching her.

Their glances met and locked together. Joe's eyes, dark and compelling, held Christina's with an arrogant power that jolted her heart. How long she stood, frozen by that one spearing glance, the roaring of the furnace dulled by the pounding of her heart, she didn't know, but a cough from Aunt Susan brought her back to reality. Conscious now of a waiting silence beneath the clatter of the glasshouse, she tore her eyes away and fought to compose herself. 'Please begin, Joe. Make the Chalice.'

But Joe had other ideas. They'd come to see a show and to his mind one Chalice, however impressive, wasn't

155

enough. He nodded at the taker-in and settled himself to begin. Now they would see some fine glass-blowing. He was gratified that Christina had brought the other Henzels; he knew that they had no man in their cones to touch him.

He began, with the golden metal brought to him by his apprentice, to make friggers. It was seldom that he did this officially, as it were; but although Christina had not asked him to do it, he knew with one glance at her delighted face that he was doing exactly the right thing. He gradually relaxed, feeling his built-up tension begin to ebb.

Joe had not been looking forward to this afternoon. Making the Chalice, to his own design, was a task he knew he could carry out with satisfaction both to his young employer and to himself. Making it in front of a crowd didn't bother him; he was accustomed to being watched, and confident enough not to be distracted. But there was something about this particular crowd, about this particular piece, that made it a little too special, somehow. Made it matter more than it should. And the fact that Maggie was there, as well as Christina, made it worse. He wouldn't have asked Maggie, not if she hadn't been there when Ruth had come with the message . . . He forced himself back to the matter in hand.

Joe shaped the cooling metal, blowing it gently to create a bubble of sunshine, swinging to extend and alter it, using the pucellas to give it a curve here, a flattened surface there. He could feel the small crowd watching, intrigued, waiting for the final shape; he heard their long-drawn out sigh when it finally appeared as a magnificent swan, wings spread, neck stretched out, even the beak opened as if the bird were standing upright in the threatening posture Joe had seen on the lake in Prestwood Park on holidays.

The swan was taken to the *lehr*, where it would be wound slowly through the long cooling tunnel until it could withstand normal temperatures and be handled.

The taker-in brought Joe another iron and he began to blow again.

In quick succession, he made a sailing ship, a long pipe, a trumpet and a menagerie of animals, ranging from an elephant complete with trunk and tusks to a playful kitten with its legs in the air. He made a different frigger for each person in the party, and with a glance at Christina which she interpreted correctly, and answered with a nod, he made a further small selection for his own family; a flip-flap for Willy, tiny baskets for the girls. The array of gleaming birds, animals and playthings disappeared slowly down the *lehr*.

'And now,' Christina said at last, 'we would like to see you make the Chalice.'

An air of expectancy settled over the party. Joe flexed his muscles. Making the friggers had completely relaxed him. He was in command, supremely confident, knowing that he could blow the magnificent Chalice with ease. He had, after all, blown several in the past few days, and each one now stood in a cupboard waiting for the moment when the best would be chosen. He hoped that the best would, in fact, prove to be the one he blew now, but if not, it was of no matter. Everyone would go home content that they had seen the Chalice blown, and neither he, Christina, nor anyone else in the glasshouse would disabuse them.

The amount of metal brought to him this time was considerably larger than before. He felt the weight of it on the iron, the heavy, satisfying feel that came from adding lead to the mix. He could feel the difference, too, as he blew; as the searing orange of the bulb grew, ballooning under his breath, smooth and shining, its thickness kept even by the control he had mastered as a boy, its fragility unthreatened by the immense power of his lungs.

From the corner of his eye, he could see the sheen of Christina's dress, transformed to rich bronze in the luminescent glow of the furnace. It reflected in the swelling glass at the end of his iron. He saw her there, whole and tiny, gazing up at him from the Chalice that he was making for her, as if she were contained in the bowl, trapped there for him to keep. She was different today. Bright and excited, as might be expected – and yet there was more. A blossoming, like a flower opening in the sun. Coming to life, as if she'd been half-dead all these months, and yet he'd never thought her so. Perhaps he'd always known that this other Christina lurked underneath those plain dresses and dull colours; perhaps it had been to this Christina, brilliant as a peacock, that he'd been speaking with his eyes, so that she answered with bright challenge in hers.

The Chalice was complete. He sat in the chair to make the stem, rolling and shaping it carefully. As the bowl of the Chalice was to be no ordinary bowl, so the stem was to be no ordinary stem; exquisitely fashioned, with fine threads of glass spiralling inside its length and the entire stem twisted into a curving knot, it was as delicate as spun sugar, yet strong enough to support the weight of the bowl above. When cooled and polished, it would gleam as if with a light of its own; reflecting the brilliance of the sun or the lambent softness of a lamp.

He could feel the gaze of the assembled watchers and knew that Christina's must be the most intense of all, but he didn't look up. This was to be the finest of the Chalices he had made, the one that was finally chosen to represent all that was best from Henzel's, and even Joe could not afford to lose a second's concentration at this stage.

It was done. The foot was smooth and round, the stem in perfect proportion with the bowl. The punty-iron was snapped from the bottom of the foot, leaving its telltale raggedness behind, and the Chalice was borne in triumph to the *lehr*.

A sigh of released breath sounded, wafting up towards the circle of light at the top of the cone, and the onlookers stirred.

Joe straightened and wiped his brow with a clean cloth, already set by his chair for the purpose. Automatically, he looked round for ale, and when it was handed to him he took it and drank deeply, without even glancing to see who had brought it.

'Thank you, Joe,' Christina's voice said, low and smooth as she handed him the tankard. 'The Chalice is a wonderful piece of glass, the best you've ever made.' She smiled up into his eyes. 'And the friggers are delightful. We'll all treasure them, I know.'

Joe looked down at her and felt a great uprush of frustrated desire. He wanted nothing more, in the release of this moment, than to sweep her up into his arms and carry her away, out of this crowded, smoky cone, out to the clean, fresh air where grass was springing and green, not yellow and stunted, where real trees with broad grey trunks and a spreading canopy of pale green leaves grew in place of twisted hawthorns. He wanted to lay her down gently on the soft cushion of the earth and make love to her, slowly and tenderly, feeling the creamy silk of her skin under his roughened hands, the fragile strength of her body pliable and warm in his powerful arms.

As he stared down at her, he saw a change in her face, a widening of her eyes, a parting of her lips, as though she understood what he was thinking, and felt too, this surge of the senses.

'The swan's for you,' he said gruffly, knowing that he had shaped the swooping beauty of the bird with her in mind. 'The others, you can give as you want, but I made the swan for you.'

'Thank you, Joseph.' The smile was deep and luminous in her gaze and she held his look for a moment longer before stepping back. 'And now I am sure everyone wants to return to work. We have held up production long enough. Jeremy, Aunt Susan . . .' As the party began to move towards the doors, she turned back to Joe and the glowing light of the furnace fell on her, turning the alabaster of her skin to burnished copper, her shimmering dress once again to deep, gleaming bronze. Poised, she looked like a statue; only the sparkling green of her eyes betrayed in that moment the fact that she was a living woman.

'Don't forget, Joe, that you're to come to the house as soon as you've finished work. The daguerreotype is to be done then, and I especially want you to be in it. I want to be able to show it to my children and tell them – that's Joseph Compson, the finest glassmaker Henzel's ever had.'

Your children, Joe thought as he turned back to his work. Your children – and whose? Jeremy's? Or some man you haven't yet met? Jealousy stabbed him then, thrusting its sword deep into his vitals. And it was a new experience, for Joe Compson had never until then felt strongly enough about any woman to feel jealous. Nor had there ever been any need.

Maggie Haden, however, was no stranger to jealousy. And she felt it now, as she walked away from the glasscone. That Christina Henzel, with her shining dress and her curling hair! It was easy to see what she was after. Coming into the cone like that – looking at Joe with those big green eyes, making up to him. Didn't she have any self-respect at all? Didn't she know what she looked like, flirting those long lashes, flaunting her body, acting like any gay girl of the streets looking for custom? And you could see he liked it. You could see by the way he'd stood there while she gave him that ale, grinning over her like some lovelorn swain gawking at his first sweetheart. Well, so what matter? Joe knew as well as anyone that Christina Henzel would never be for him, not in any way. There could be no fear of him turning away from Maggie to go to her. Maggie could give him what Christina Henzel must keep for the man she wed – aye, and a sight better too! That class didn't know how to enjoy it anyway; they married for money or business or land, and getting children to carry on their name was all they wanted their bodies for. The women, at any rate.

No, Maggie had nothing to fear from Christina Henzel. But all the same, she couldn't forget the look on Joe's face as he'd stared down at the girl who, you might say, had inherited him along with the rest of her father's business. He might never be able to have Christina. But that needn't stop him turning away from Maggie. For hadn't she noticed a slackening in his interest lately, haste in his lovemaking that had nothing to do with passion? As if she were nothing more than a way of getting relief, yet still didn't satisfy him.

Maggie made her way through the narrow streets towards her home. She lived with her parents on the edge of Amblecote, in the basement of one of the clutters of ramshackle houses that had happened, rather than been built, around the new factories there. The Hadens were not, like the Compsons, comparatively well-off. Maggie's father Sam had never risen above footmaker, never brought home more than fourteen shillings in a week. Perhaps things would be better now that new lead crystal could be made in quantity. It ought to help all the glassmakers, not just Henzel's, though from the fuss that Christina Henzel made, you'd think they'd invented the stuff.

Picking her way through the rubbish that strewed her path, Maggie didn't notice her friend Annie until the girl was almost on her.

''Ow bin yer, Mag? You're out early. Not got the sack, I hope!'

Maggie looked up, startled from her thoughts. 'No. Bin over Henzel's to see my Joe blow that special glass her ladyship wanted. You should hev been there, Annie! All in silks and lace, they were, and that Christina the brassiest of them all. Made Fancy Nance look like the bishop's daughter. Her and her high-and-mighty ways!'

Annie raised her eyebrows and laughed. 'Sounds as though thee dosna' like her too much, Maggie.'

'Should I? When her's in and out of that glass-cone half a dozen times a day by all accounts, and never without a word for Joe? It's as plain as a pikestaff what her's after, and yet I don't think her even knows it herself.'

'If her did,' Annie remarked shrewdly, 'her probably wouldn't do it.'

'No, I don't suppose her would. Think herself too good for the likes of my Joe. But they keep their women so ignorant, that class, her never realises she's acting like a bitch on heat. An' whether her knows it or not, it's all the same to my Joe.'

'You mean he fancies her? But that'd never get him anywhere. Thee bin't afeared of losin' him, surely?'

Maggie shrugged hopelessly. 'Tell you the truth, Annie, I don't know what I'm feared of. Of course he'll never be able to hev her, he knows that as well as I do. But he'm a man, after all, an' when that young hussy flaunts herself at him the way she do –' She stopped, ignoring the stench that rose from the sewage-filled gutter at her feet. 'I tell you what, Annie, I reckon it's her he's thinkin' of when we're together. Her he's holdin' in his arms.' Her voice shook and her eyes filled with angry tears. 'I just think if he can't have her, he won't want me neither. He'll go off the whole thing, and then where will I be?'

'Here, you don't want to tek on like that.' Annie drew her friend on, through a dark, slimy alleyway where even the heat of the July sun never penetrated. 'Come on in and have a drink – I got fresh water today and our Dolly popped in yesterday with some tea, only been used once. You'll feel better after that. And I tell you what you ought to do about your Joe. You ought to get him tied up proper, and as soon as you can. I d'know why you've not done it sooner than this, if you were that scared.'

Maggie mopped her face with the end of her shawl. 'Tied up? You mean wed?'

'Well, of course I do! He's old enough to leave his mammy now, in't he? And he's getting a good wage – he could get you out of here and into a decent home, and if you ask me he ought to hev done it long since.' Annie looked round at the squalid room she had led Maggie to, and disgust twisted her face. 'What sort of place is this to live?' she demanded, with a comprehensive gesture at the mould-blackened walls, the smoke-darkened plaster ceiling, the meagre fireplace which was the only means of cooking. 'And your place is no better, Mag. But your Joe don't live like this, I'll bet Henzel's to a glass privy!'

In spite of her misery, Maggie laughed. 'No, he don't. And I shouldn't, either. You're right, Annie.' She sat down on the bed with its tumble of thin blankets, where Annie and her parents and young brother all slept together. 'Don't make tea, your mam needs it more than I do. Half a cup of water will do me.' She sipped, thinking of Annie's mother, the worn, shrunken woman who was probably out in the back shed now, labouring painfully at the nail-making that brought in a few extra shillings a week. 'It's all wrong, in't it? That Christina and all the rest of them Henzels living in luxury while we has to scrape about like this. They couldn't live that way without us, Annie. Not without men like Joe. They hev it all – and then she wants my man too. Well, she's not going to hev him!' She got up, her mouth set now with determination. 'I'll see him tonight, when he's back from this daggertype thing she wants to hev done, and I'll talk to him then. Mek him see sense.'

'And if he don't?' Annie smiled lewdly. 'There's ways of bringing a man to heel – even a man like your Joe.' She paused and then chuckled. '*Especially* a man like your Joe . . .'

Chapter Nine

Reuben Henzel lived alone in a tall Georgian house in the main street of Stourbridge. He spent a good deal of time in his study, a well-proportioned first floor room at the front of the house. From here, he could watch the comings and goings of the town. He could also see the doors and archways of the Talbot Hotel, where all the most important meetings, sales and auctions took place.

It was while he was glancing from this window one fine September afternoon that he saw his nephew Jeremy come out of the Talbot, glance to left and right and walk purposefully across the street, heading for Reuben's own front door. He waited thoughtfully until his manservant announced Jeremy's arrival.

'Show him up.' He moved away from the window and stood before the fireplace, fingers stroking his thin beard. 'Ah, Jeremy. This is an unexpected pleasure.'

Jeremy stood hesitant inside the door. 'I hope I'm not disturbing you, Uncle Reuben. I should perhaps have sent a message first –'

'Not at all, not at all. Sit down. You'll take some wine with me?' Reuben touched the bell-pull. 'A rather pleasant Madeira I'd like you to try – very suitable as an after-luncheon refreshment. You've had luncheon, of course?'

'Yes, at the Talbot. A meeting about this new Flint Glassmakers' Friendly Society. I don't know that it's worth worrying about too much, though. It seems pretty weak to me.' Jeremy dropped his hat and gloves on the table and flung himself into an armchair, stretching out his long legs.

'We'll have to keep an eye on it, all the same,' Reuben

said pensively. 'These new friendly societies, or unions as some call them, shouldn't be taken too lightly. Look at the miners, striking for more pay! Even glassmakers could become troublesome if they're allowed to develop too much power.'

'Power!' Jeremy exclaimed disgustedly. 'God knows the men in the glass trade have too much power already – they practically dictate the terms of their employment as it is, telling us how many pieces they'll make each turn, what their hours are to be, even how many apprentices we can employ.' Jeremy paused while the servant returned and poured the wine. 'Can you think of any other trade in which the men work only two days a week, Tuesday and Wednesday, as basic employment, and who only deign to work Thursday and Friday as *optional overtime*? And have three full days off? Why, the whole thing's nonsense!'

'I'm not sure what you can do about it, though,' Reuben said mildly. 'It's a tradition now, just as their "fictitious wages" are a tradition, and you know as well as I do that no one clings more tightly to his traditions than the working man.'

'Fictitious wages!' Jeremy snorted. 'The difference between the amount of glass that is agreed can be produced in an hour and the actual amount they do produce – all neatly worked out, of course, to indicate that glassmakers work far harder than they should so as to benefit their employers with a consistently high production! Who originally agreed these figures? And is a "friendly society" likely to make any changes there? None that could benefit the employers, you may be sure. In fact, I begin to wonder why they need one at all, they seem to have us very nicely by the tails as it is.'

Reuben looked thoughtfully at him. Jeremy looked unusually ruffled, his fair hair tousled as if he had been running impatient fingers through it, his brow creased in a frown of irritation. There was a tension in him, betrayed by his abrupt movements as he sat up straight and reached for the glass of Madeira.

'Are things going badly at the glasshouse? The men, this union – are they giving trouble?'

Jeremy sighed impatiently. 'No worse than usual. At least, I thought not until I attended this meeting. Now I'm not so sure.' He rose and went to the window, staring down at the street, his fingers twitching at his side. 'You're right, Uncle Reuben, these unions need watching. They could become powerful through sheer weight of numbers.' He whipped round. 'Can you imagine it? A mass of illiterate workmen, ruling us simply because there are more of them! It hardly bears thinking of. And it could happen – revolution has swept Europe in the last few decades. Even our own queen has been attacked.'

'And what do you suggest should be done?'

Jeremy returned to his chair. 'God knows, uncle. In my view, all these societies and unions should be made illegal. The men should be made to remember their place – they've acquired far too high a sense of their own importance. Look at what's being done for them now – schools, institutes, learning to read and write, it's no wonder they're becoming discontented. And what good does it do them, after all? They'd be better off knowing nothing.'

'I'm sure you're right. And is this why you came to visit me?'

'No, it's not.' Jeremy paused and stared at his wine. 'I came to see you about something quite different, Uncle Reuben.'

'Christina?' Reuben suggested when the pause had gone on a little longer.

'Yes.' Jeremy ran a hand through his thick, fair hair. 'I don't know what to do about her, uncle, and that's the truth of it.'

'I imagined you were managing very well. She turns to you for advice, does she not? Confides in you? She's

167

learning to trust you?' Reuben frowned slightly. 'If all this is true – and I took it from our earlier conversations that it was – then what have you to worry about? She's very young yet. There's time.'

'Yes, but she spends more and more time in the glasshouse, and in one cone especially. And although she still talks to me – well, her confidences seem rather less of late. It seems almost as if there's some barrier between us.'

Reuben was silent. He leaned back in his chair, lifting his glass to the light, swirling the pale liquid gently. With his other hand, he touched his beard.

'She is losing interest in you?'

Jeremy shrugged. 'That's difficult to say. There's an added awareness in her. She seems self-conscious, avoids my look, tries not to be left alone with me. She blushes easily. In another girl, I would say that this meant an increased interest. But with Christina –'

'Perhaps she is interested in someone else.' Reuben shot his nephew a sharp glance. 'Have you any idea who it might be?'

'Oh, I know who it might be,' Jeremy said bitterly. 'But it's an interest that can never amount to anything. More a useless fascination.' He got up and paced the room, stopping to stare out of the window. 'That glassblower – the one who made the Chalice – that's who she goes to see. And the whole cone laughing at her, the silly miss.'

'Doesn't she realise?'

'That they're laughing at her? She doesn't even realise what she's doing! I sometimes wonder, uncle, whether we do our women a favour by keeping them so innocent. It's all very well for girls like Adela, or Uncle Harold's daughters – they live sheltered at home. In due course, they'll all find husbands, or have husbands found for them, and they'll learn in the right and proper way. But a young woman like Christina, going out and about,

168

meeting people her sisters would never dream of having to know – it's all too easy to make herself look foolish.'

'She needs a husband of her own, of course.'

'Well, of course she does!' Jeremy wheeled back and resumed his restless pacing. 'But she doesn't even seem to realise that. Simply goes her own sweet way, thinking she can be both man and woman. And deceiving no one but herself. I'll wager that Compson fellow knows exactly what she's at and laughs harder than any of them. What he and his mates say to each other when she's out of earshot I tremble to think.'

'Compson,' Reuben said thoughtfully. 'Is that not the man you warned would be troublesome?'

'Aye, and precious little thanks I got for that. We had our first quarrel over that man, and it's been the same ever since. He can do no wrong in her eyes. Worse still –' Jeremy leaned forward '– he's taken to going to the house of an evening to show her his designs, or so she says. And she encourages him! Asks him in, if you please, and the two of them sit for hours in the library poring over scraps of paper, with no more chaperone than young Harry, working at his books! My Aunt Susan is at her wits' end and terrified that others will find out.'

'As well she may be,' Reuben observed. 'Susan values her position in local society, and this would undo all her efforts.'

'Well, there it is,' Jeremy said, sounding deflated. 'Whether she knows it or not, Christina is besotted with this man and there seems to be little I can do about it. I wondered if you might have any ideas?'

'Did you, now?' The thin fingers stroked. 'And why me, I wonder? Do you forget that I am a bachelor? I have very little experience of women on which to base any advice.'

'I'm not sure that experience is always the best basis for advice anyway,' Jeremy said a trifle sourly. 'It doesn't seem to be helping *me* much! I think I prefer to rely on your observation, Uncle Reuben.'

'Well, I have certainly had plenty of time for observation, it's true.' Reuben's pale eyes shifted to the window with its view up and down the High Street. 'I would always rather listen and watch than take part in impulsive conversation. So easy to say what one afterwards regrets, and so easy to be misunderstood . . . But I'm still not sure what advice to give you, Jeremy. Unless it is to do just that – listen and watch. Wait. If Christina is in no mood to be advised or guided by you at present, she may be later. Things change, Jeremy, nothing stays the same. This man is certain to disappoint her in some way, sooner or later. Is he not married anyway?'

'No.'

'Then perhaps it's time he was. I know the fellow you mean – a big, powerful man, the type to appeal to a good many women, I should have thought. Has he no regular fancy?'

'I know little of his life outside the glasshouse,' Jeremy said distastefully.

'Then perhaps you should find out. His marriage may be all that's needed to destroy Christina's infatuation. It might be worth approaching the girl, if you can find her. Doesn't he have some connection in Christina's staff – one of the maids?'

Jeremy stared at him. 'I believe he does! How did you know that?'

Reuben smiled faintly. 'I make it my business to know many things . . . Well, Jeremy, I think I need say little more at present. Do whatever you think best. But don't quarrel with Christina. When her dreams come to an end, she will need someone to turn to. It would be best if it were you.'

'Yes. Yes, I see that.' Jeremy rose to his feet. 'And if there's no girl – no chance of marriage?'

'Then you will have to think of something else, my boy. Something possibly better. After all, accidents do happen, in even the best-run glasshouse. And if this Compson is as good a glassmaker as Christina believes, it might benefit us all if he were no longer about . . .' Reuben smiled thinly. 'I don't mean you to take me seriously, nephew.'

Jeremy met his uncle's eyes in a long look. Then he picked up his hat and turned to go.

'Thank you, uncle. You're right, I'll find a way to be rid of this Compson, and then it will be me Christina turns to.'

Their eyes met in perfect understanding, and then Jeremy nodded and left.

Reuben sat for a moment cracking his bony knuckles, his bloodless lips twisted in a small smile. After a while, he got up and moved again to the window. A carriage was drawing up outside the Talbot. He craned his neck a little to see who was getting in.

In spite of Susan's fussing and Jeremy's condescension, Christina's dinner party turned out to be a great success.

She had invited all her father's old friends: other manufacturers of the area, many of whom had known him – and therefore her – all their lives. They represented almost every trade in the Black Country: Mr Hay, nailmaster; Henry Somers, ironmaster; Noah Gibbons who owned one of the largest collieries in the district, and three glassmakers – Mr Webb, Mr Stevens and Mr Silvers. They came with their wives, cautious, faintly supercilious but, most of all, curious.

Christina met them at the drawing room door, extending her hand to everyone and making it quite clear that, although her cousin Jeremy stood beside her, she was very much the hostess.

'I'm so pleased to see you,' she said over and over again, resting her small hand in the large paws of her father's friends and associates. 'It's so kind of you to come.' Her green eyes gazed limpidly up at the slightly red, embarrassed faces and she felt a little laugh bubble to her lips. Really, they were so *solemn*! And they didn't at all know how to behave, any of them. Simply because she was a woman, doing what they all firmly believed to be men's work . . . Well, perhaps by the time they left the house, they would have changed their minds on that.

Their wives had no doubts about how *they* should behave. They approached Christina coolly, offering disdainful cheeks to be touched, and studied her clothes with covert surprise. Clearly, they had expected her to look odd and freakish – dowdily, if not eccentrically dressed, perhaps even wearing trousers like the notorious Frenchwoman George Sand. They would all, after all, know the story of Christina visiting the glasshouse in Frederic's clothes.

Christina smiled. Her new gown, made in shimmering silk taffeta, outshone that of any woman in the room. Its neckline swooped lower, its waist was tinier, its sleeves puffier. The cut revealed the smooth ivory of her shoulders and slender neck, and the bronze and green stripes, glowing against the silvery background, brought answering lights to her gleaming eyes and the shining hair that Ruth had piled in artless curls on top of her head.

Men and women alike, they all looked at her twice; once to patronise, the second to stare.

They were still inclined to patronise when they were seated round the table and dinner began. Christina sat quietly, demurely, allowing the talk to range about her. Together with Aunt Susan, she had given a great deal of thought to the menu and she was pleased with its success.

The soup was excellent – Mrs Jenner had always been good at making soup. The fish, boiled cod, was cooked to creamy perfection, and the parsley sauce had just the right hint of tartness to complement it. And the three entrées, wild duck, saddle of mutton and oysters, served with potatoes, broccoli and new carrots, were received with enthusiasm – not mentioned, naturally, but implicit in the way only the tiniest scrap was left on each plate, for politeness' sake.

While Jeremy carved the grouse, the talk turned from international affairs – the latest news from India and the Americas – to local affairs.

'It looks as if the railway won't be too long in coming now,' Mr Silvers remarked. 'Replacing canals for transport – the Stourbridge Extension will never get the use it was intended for.'

'Only cut a matter of four or five years ago, too,' his partner Mr Stevens agreed. 'But you can't halt progress, and no doubt it will do us all good.'

'Well, I shan't be using them,' the coalmaster grunted. 'Too slow, and you'll never get trains to carry heavy freight. Barges are much more practical. In my opinion, all this steam transport is going to prove to be a dead duck. There's been fortunes lost already in failed lines.'

'And others made,' someone else said, and Christina agreed eagerly, the sound of her voice causing them all to turn and look at her in surprise.

'I shall certainly be using them,' she declared. 'I only wish they would come sooner. The line isn't expected to reach Stourbridge for several years yet – it makes things so slow when you have to obtain an Act of Parliament for each one.'

'Well, I daresay by the time it reaches us you won't be bothering your head about such things,' Henry Somers observed, and turned back to the others.

'Indeed I will,' Christina said, before they could begin their conversation again. 'Henzel's will be needing rapid transport. Tell me, Mr Somers, how is your own industry faring these days?'

Henry Somers reddened slightly, and the others smiled. They all knew of the deputation of ironmasters, led by James Foster of Shutt End, which had made its way to London to demand a discussion with the Prime Minister on ways of improving trade. Iron had been in recession then, despite the increase in industry generally. The deputation had not been a success; Peel had given no firm promises and they had returned deflated and dissatisfied.

'And yours, Mr Gibbons?' she asked sweetly, turning to the coalmine owner. 'No disturbances here, I hope, like those dreadful riots at Walsall three years ago? I should hate to see the dragoons called out against Stourbridge men.'

She smiled at the discomfited man and then let her eyes rest gently on the face of Robert Hay, the nailmaster. This time she said nothing; but all knew that she was thinking of the march the nailers had made on Dudley to demand higher prices for their nails.

The truth was that there was unrest in many industries, with half-starved workers rising up, desperate for enough money to live on. None of the manufacturers knew quite what to do about it, and many of them agreed with Jeremy that most of the danger came from the new trade unions, and there was a general feeling that they should be banned.

'Glass isn't doing so well, either,' Noah Gibbons rallied sufficiently to remark as Rose began to serve the apricot tart. 'Look at Hawkes, up in Dudley – one of the biggest flint-glass makers in the kingdom, closed down, and it'll never open again, mark my words.'

'Yes, that's a pity,' Christina agreed. 'And if they'd been able to stay in business until now, they could have been the biggest again. As it is –' she gave the other three glassmakers a dimpling smile '– it seems that it's to be left to us. Shall we make a competition of it, gentlemen?'

'A competition?' Mr Silvers looked at his companions and laughed. 'I think there is no competition! You have a nice little works, Miss Christina, and you'll be well advised to keep it like that. You'll only court trouble if you try to expand. Take my advice, let your cousins run the business with theirs, which is the only sensible course, and keep one cone as a hobby if you must. Glassmaking is not for women.'

'No?' Christina's smile lost none of its sweetness. 'Then let me show you this, gentlemen.'

Nodding at Ruth to hold back the serving of the cheese canapés, she rose and went to a small table at the side of the room. She lifted the white cloth that covered it, and stood back.

'Do come and see,' she invited and slowly, one by one, their eyes fixed on the glittering display, the men and their wives came.

The Chalice was the centre-piece. Raised slightly above the rest of the glass, standing on its own velvet pedestal, it gleamed in the soft light of the candles and lamps around the room, each one reflected in its shining surface. It was so highly polished that it struck sparks of light from its smoothly curved surface, and beneath its heavy bowl its twisted stem looked at the same time both airy and strong.

The men drew around, their eyes fastened upon it, and one of the glassmakers reached out automatically to touch it.

'Beautiful . . .' he breathed, and lifted the heavy vessel. 'And such a weight! Can I guess who made this?'

'It has to be Compson,' one of the others declared positively. 'Only he could manage that weight of glass and get such perfect results. Or do you have other secrets in your cones, Christina?'

'No, it was Joe. And this is the first piece blown with our new recipe for rock crystal.' She smiled mischievously. 'With our own secret ingredient, of course, which you won't expect me to reveal! I intend to make this piece our symbol. We are going to pack all our best pieces in boxes of dark blue, with this Chalice illustrated on it in silver. I think it will be quite effective, don't you?'

'Very effective,' her rivals agreed. 'And this other – the coloured glass?'

'Yes, I'm especially pleased with this.' Her slender fingers drifted over the other pieces that were arranged around the table. A set of wineglasses in deep ruby, with colourless stems; a water set, with tall, narrow tumblers and an elegant jug, in sea-green, and a variety of friggers – a small basket, a pipe, a walking-stick, a collection of birds and animals – in both colours. 'These are our first too, in the new colours – experiments, you understand. And I would like you to take one each as a memento of tonight.' She smiled at them again, and this time they received the full warmth of her glowing eyes, the full power of her charm. 'Please choose whatever you like . . . And now I think the cheese canapés are ready to be served. Shall we return to the table?'

And after that, it was easy. There was no more talk of running a cone as a hobby; no more patronising. The men respected Christina both as a business acquaintance, their talk proved that, and as a woman, their eyes proved this. And their wives were no more suspicious of her than they would be of any pretty young woman.

As she caught her aunt's eye and rose to lead the way out of the dining room, Christina paused momentarily by Jeremy's chair, and looked down at him, a glimmer of triumph in her eyes. His own expression was unreadable.

Distastefully, Jeremy picked his way through the streets of Amblecote, looking for the court where Maggie Haden lived.

He was aware of being watched. From broken doorways, where women leaned in sluttish languor, suspicious eyes watched his progress. Small children, too young yet to be set to work, played half-naked in the stagnant gutters from which rose a stench that sickened him. In a corner of the yard a woman was using an open privy, her brows raised in an insolent stare as he glanced her way. Only a few yards away, another woman was filling a cracked bucket with water from the pump that served the entire yard.

'It's not for the likes of a gentleman like you,' Ruth Compson had told him doubtfully, and he knew now what she meant. An old crone lolling on a stool, a grimy bottle raised to her lips, gave him a toothless and repellent grin and he looked away.

The house where Maggie Haden lived was in the corner. Jeremy stood at the top of the steps and stared down dubiously at the rubbish that strewed them; tattered rags, past even the most squalid of tasks, old bones chewed first by humans, then by the scrawny cats and dogs that slunk furtively along the walls, and finally by the rats that scattered before him as he moved. Was it really likely that a man like Joe Compson, well-nourished and tidy enough on occasions such as Joshua's funeral and the taking of that ridiculous daguerreotype, would want to marry a girl who lived in these conditions? Jeremy had only a hazy idea of the hierarchy of the working classes, but instinctively he felt that there must be some demarcation, some kind of aristocracy operating even at these low levels. Wasn't it more likely that this Maggie was no more than Joe's whore, and never likely to be anything else?

Jeremy descended the steps, half inclined to go back. There could be nothing for him here, nothing for Joe Compson. He would have to think of something else. But his hand was raised to knock at the half-open door, and even as he hesitated the dark gap widened and Maggie stood before him.

Jeremy stared at her. The first adjective that came to his mind was – ripe. She was like some luscious fruit, ready for the picking, for the eating, filled with juicy promise. He thought of green fields under a hot summer sun, with tall cool grass that could enfold and enclose. He thought of haystacks, golden under a tender autumn sky, hollowed out inside to make a warm, sweet-smelling cave where none could see. Of shady woodland hollows, where years of fallen leaves made a springing mattress and the only observers were the busy indifferent birds and mice.

Maggie's fine dark eyes watched him, already charged

with the taunting look that had tormented so many men. She raised a hand to push back her tangle of loose, waving hair, lifting her head and turning it slowly to one side as she did so. The movement dislodged her once colourful shawl, causing it to slip from her smooth bare shoulders, and when she adjusted it the only effect was to slide it further, revealing swelling white breasts almost to the nipples.

'Lookin' for someone?' she asked, her voice soft, husky and caressing.

Jeremy smiled down at her, in possession of himself once more, comfortable with a type he believed he knew. There were Maggies by the hundred, draped in every backstreet brothel, glancing up with just that challenging insolence. He had used their bodies as casually as he used a chamber-pot and this sudden swimming of the head was caused by nothing more than surprise at finding such a one here, like a macaw on a dung-heap.

'I'm looking for a certain Maggie Haden,' he said easily, letting his eyes move over her. 'Said to be a great beauty. I suppose you . . ?'

'I'm Mag Haden.' She had bridled a little at his words, and her tone was still suspicious. 'What d'you want with me?'

'Just a word, nothing more.' He glanced up to the top of the steps, where an old crone was leaning forward to peer down at them. 'Inside, perhaps?'

Maggie glanced behind her through the door. 'It in't what you're used to. Us don't live in luxury here.'

'I realise that. Please don't worry about it.' He followed her into the dark room, where a new smell hit him – the dank odour of damp and rotten wood. After a moment or two, his eyes accustomed themselves to the dimness and he could see the rumpled bed in the corner, the cracked wooden table and two or three broken-backed chairs. Apart from a few cooking utensils and a wooden chest which presumably contained what clothes the family possessed, there was nothing else in the room.

Maggie indicated one of the chairs but Jeremy shook his head. The thought of his good clothes touching anything here made his flesh shrink, and he wanted only to get out again.

'I understand you're a friend of Joe Compson's,' he said, more abruptly than he'd intended.

Maggie's face grew wary.

'What if I am? Nothing wrong with that, bin there?'

'Nothing at all. In fact, I think it's a very good thing. He's a good man, Joe. A fine workman. He should do very well.'

'I know who you are now,' Maggie said. 'You're one of them Henzels. That cousin of Miss Christina's. I seen you at the cone that day. You're Mr Jeremy. Joe's told me about you.'

'Indeed? And what has he told you?' Jeremy was momentarily diverted from the matter in his mind. Did these people really have the impertinence to discuss him?

'Only that you come into the cone sometimes, along of Miss Christina. He says you're thick as herrings in a barrel.'

Jeremy laughed. 'So that's what they say, is it? And what does Joe think of that, eh?'

'It in't his place to think nothing of it, sir,' Maggie said woodenly, and Jeremy gave her a sharp look. 'He just works for Miss Christina.'

'Yes . . .' It wouldn't do, Jeremy decided, to question her further about Joe's feelings regarding Christina. 'Now – about your Joe. Do I take it that you're as thick as "herrings in a barrel"?'

Again the suspicious look.

'You can talk to me,' he said, suddenly gentle. 'I've come specially to ask you a favour. And one that would be in Joe's interests as well as yours.'

Maggie stared at him, and he had time to realise again just how delectable she was. What could Compson be thinking of, not to snap up a woman like this, who was obviously hungry for him! Why, if things were different and he had the time, he wouldn't mind sampling what was on offer himself. But not here, not in this dingy slum.

'All right then,' she said shortly. 'What is it?'

Jeremy answered as briefly. 'I think it's time you and Compson got married. You've been walking out together for a long time, if what I hear is true. And there's nothing to stand in the way of it, is there?'

Astounded, Maggie shook her head. 'No, sir. But why should you –'

'Why should I care whether you're married or not? That's none of your business. But it's what you want, isn't it?' Mutely, she nodded. 'Then just let's say it's because I believe a pretty girl should always have what she wants! Now – are you going to get this young man of yours to name the day?'

Maggie shrugged, her lips mutinous. 'Dost think I haven't tried, sir? I've hinted and talked till I'm blue, but he won't take any notice. I don't think he *wants* to be wed, sir, that's the truth of it. He's too comfortable where he is and as long as he can get what he wants . . .' Colour swept into her face but her eyes met Jeremy's with frank boldness. 'I've even tried saying no to him, but it's no good – I think I want him more'n he wants me now. And Joe can be very persuasive.'

Jeremy drew a handful of coins from his pocket.

'The ladies I know have a trick or two you might think worth copying,' he remarked. 'A new dress, perhaps, or a pretty shawl . . . a perfume to make you smell sweet – it wouldn't hurt to try . . . And perhaps you'd let me know how things are going with you? I might be able to help you with your wedding finery as well.' His hand pressed the coins into hers, he felt the roughness of her palm, and let his fingers move very slightly to touch the fine skin of her inner wrist and linger there for a few seconds. 'I think a pretty girl should *always* have what she wants,' he repeated softly.

'Yes, sir.' Maggie stared at the coins, then looked up at him. 'You want me to marry Joe, sir, as quick as may be, is that right?'

'I think it would be a very good thing all round.' Jeremy moved towards the door, suddenly compelled to get out into the fresh air, away from the dismal room, these squalid streets. 'You shouldn't be living here, Maggie, not a girl like you. You should have your own house and husband, a family around your knees. Meet me again in – say, a fortnight from now? You'll know by then how much you need for your trousseau. But not here.' He hesitated, thinking, 'You know the Bradley Ironworks, by the canal? Meet me just past there, on the towpath, two weeks from tonight. We'll talk again then. And –' he patted her hand, closing the fingers around the coins '– I may have another little present for you. Just to help things along. Buy yourself something nice.'

He crossed the room quickly and a moment later Maggie saw his shadowy figure dim the light that filtered in through the streaked window.

Slowly, she looked down at her hand and uncurled the fingers he had touched. Golden sovereigns. Enough for food for a month. Enough for a fine dress, some paint for her face and still food for a fortnight. Enough for a pretty shawl, something good and warm for the coming winter, food and a bit to put by.

He must want her to marry Joe pretty bad. And it was time to have done with hints, with threats and tears that seemed to drive Joe further away from her rather than bring him close. Time to see to it that Joe *had* to marry her.

Jeremy Henzel's ideas were all very well for grand ladies, who didn't know what it was all about. But she knew a trick or two worth half a dozen fine gowns.

Joe's visits to Christina had become a regular event – too regular, in the opinion of the rest of the family: Aunt

Susan was unbendingly disapproving, Adela disdainful, and even Harry slightly uneasy, although since he always accompanied the pair to the library he could be certain that nothing untoward took place.

Christina steadfastly ignored them. For her, Joe's visits were becoming the brightest spot of the week. She looked forward to them, encouraged him to come again, invented excuses for him. They talked about the glasshouse incessantly, but their conversations, originally restricted to the merits of new patterns and designs, soon ranged wider and Christina found herself more and more inclined to involve Joe in other aspects of running the factory – aspects which she had once discussed with Jeremy alone, or with her overseer Charles Turner.

She already had plans for making Joe her new overseer when Charles Turner retired, as he must do soon; after years of loyal service, the old man was growing steadily weaker from the consumption that was a permanent plague in the whole district. Christina knew that her father had planned to give him a good pension as soon as a worthy successor had been found, and now she determined to make Joe that successor. In such a position, he would be her right-hand man and his own abilities, which were becoming clearer to her with every talk they had, used to the full.

Jeremy was no longer her chief confidant. Since the night when he had first told her she was unwomanly and then kissed her in that urgent, disturbing way, she had avoided being alone with him. She hadn't liked the feeling of not being in control. For a brief moment, Jeremy had gained a strange, unnerving mastery of her body. That was something she didn't intend to allow again. For if he had her body, mightn't he also have her mind – and everything else about her? Mightn't she lose, with one betraying caress, everything she had fought to keep?

There was something about Jeremy that drew her to him, yet made her want at the same time to draw back – a fascination like that of a rabbit mesmerised by a snake, knowing its danger yet unable to flee. Jeremy was dangerous. So Christina circled around him, yet perversely could not resist flaunting her womanhood at him.

With Joe, she felt safe. She knew quite well that the expression in his eyes was of admiration; she did not realise that when those dark eyes narrowed and the jaw tightened that there was frustration as well. And because of Harry's presence in the library, or that of other men in the glasshouse, their exchanges held for her nothing more than a spice of excitement, an excitement that carried her to bed and kept her lying awake for the sheer pleasure of going over them again and again in her mind. Danger there might well be – dimly, she knew that Joe's vitality was more intense than Jeremy's, that he was a much more primitive, wild being than her suave cousin. But that the danger could be held in check, she never doubted. Joe was only a workman, after all and, even with his advancement now taken for granted, she was confident that he knew his place and would never dream of stepping out of it.

So what happened on that late September evening, when the first frosts had begun to bite the air and a fire was doubly welcome in the chilly library, came as a greater shock to her than perhaps it should have done.

On the hill behind the glasshouse, looking down at the surly, smoke-reddened sunset, Maggie Haden drew her shawl closer around her and shivered.

'It's getting colder now of an evening. Don't you think so, Joe?'

'Only to be expected. It's almost October.' He sat beside her, gazing down at the roofs and chimneys of the village. They were spreading every day, it seemed; new factories rising on fields and waste ground, new chimneys stretching taller towards the skies to add their burden of smoke and sulphur to the overladen air. And the streets

183

were growing too, with hastily-erected terraces of small, back-to-back houses facing narrow yards and alleys barely wide enough for a man to walk along. Some of them had tiny gardens in which people struggled to grow a few vegetables, but the acrid air did not encourage succulent growth, and the soil was thin and sour.

'Don't you reckon it's time us stopped comin' out here, Joe?' Maggie ventured. 'Last winter – well, it were our first together and we didn't seem to mind the cold and that. But now – mebbe I'm getting older or summat, but I don't know as I wants to lie on the damp grass any more. I think it'd be nicer in a bed, don't you?'

Joe sighed. 'Mag, I've told you before, I'm not ready to settle down yet. And you can't leave your mam and dad, there's little enough going into your house as it is. Later, when things are different –'

'And what makes you think they'll ever be different?' There was a note of despair in her voice. 'Is this my life, Joe, or theirs? Mebbe it'd be better if I did leave – they could tek in a lodger then and charge a bit more. In any case, me dad drinks away all the extra, so why shouldn't I hev the money to mek my own life? And your family could manage well enough, Joe, your dad's got years of work in him yet and gaffers all mek good money.'

'And is that why you want me? Because I'm a gaffer and make good money?'

'Joe, how can you say that? You know it's not that – I love you, don't I? But you could afford to get wed, Joe. And *I* feel ready – so why don't you?'

'I don't know, wench,' he sighed. 'Mebbe you're right. Mebbe we should settle things. But, give us a little while yet, hey? Mebbe I'll feel different in a month or so.'

Maggie looked at him. His face was shadowed in the gathering dusk and she could not read the expression in his eyes. But there was a wistfulness in his voice that struck at her heart; although she'd intended to stay calm, she couldn't help the jealous anger rising.

'It's her, in't it? That Christina Henzel. You're still hankerin' after her. Oh, yes, I know, I've seen the way you look at her, all sheep's eyes like some bit of a kid. And I've heard about you, too – the pair of you. The way her's always in and out of the cone, mekkin' excuses to talk to you. And the way you're up at the house after she, hangin' round like a dog after a bitch. Mekkin' a fine fool of yourself too! She a fine lady and you nothin' but a workman!'

'That's enough!' Furious, Joe turned on her, gripping her by the shoulders. 'You can leave Miss Christina out of this! It's nothing to do with her – and she's nothing to do with you. Whether I wed you or not is between us two, and nobody else, and I've never said I will yet. And I'll tell thee this, I'm not likely to, with the shrew you've turned into these past few weeks. No, not likely to at all.'

Maggie stared at him. His face was close to hers, eyes narrow with anger, lips tight over clenched teeth. She realised that he meant what he said, and a dreadful fear gripped her. To lose Joe – it was unthinkable. And not only because she wanted him, as desperately now as she ever had. But because there was Jeremy Henzel to be considered now. Jeremy Henzel and the money he'd given her to buy this shawl, the money he'd promised her if she married Joe. That money could set them up. She could have her own home, something she'd longed for. She could get away at last from the squalor of her parents' basement. As the wife of the best gaffer in the district, she could be looked up to, respected. And she'd have Joe, night after night, in a proper bed instead of out here on the chilly hillside. If she lost Joe, she would lose everything.

Maggie struggled with herself. There was one way to persuade him, the way a good many girls had been driven to employ, but she'd always fought against it. Her knowledge of Joe told her it could arouse his resentment to such a pitch that, even though she achieved her object, it would be at the cost of any happiness she hoped to gain. And there was her pride too. Hadn't she always boasted that she never got caught? Hadn't she always looked with pitying scorn on those girls who found themselves 'in trouble' and had to get married; or, worse still, could find no man to take responsibility and lived miserable lives in the meanest holes for shelter, able only to scrape the poorest living for themselves and the unfortunate starvelings they brought into the world.

But Maggie wanted Joe more than anything and she rapidly came to a decision. She let her head drop against Joe's arm.

'I'm sorry, Joe,' she whispered huskily. 'Mebbe I shouldn't have said those things. I know you're fond of Miss Christina, and I know she's treated you well. Here, give us a kiss and tell me it's all right. You know me, I get a bit worked up and then I say things I don't mean.' She lifted her lips and let them brush against his rough cheek. 'Give us a kiss, Joe, do.'

His lips touched hers briefly and, really worried now, she gripped him more tightly. 'Not like that, Joe. A proper kiss.' Moving her body against him, she pressed her open mouth to his, caressing, wheedling, teasing. 'You can kiss better'n any man I know,' she murmured provocatively. 'Let's forget everything else, Joe, let's just think about ourselven.' She nipped at his lips, letting her tongue roam free and at last felt him begin to respond. 'Joe . . . Joe . . . forget her. You've got me in your arms, remember? Your Mag, who loves you. Kiss me again, Joe – ah, that's right, that's better, that's my lovely Joe . . .' Abandoned to her own desire, she thrust her breasts against him, almost forcing them into his hands, moving seductively as his fingers tightened on her, moaning a little as she felt his hardness grow. 'Don't stop now, Joe,' she whispered urgently, as the rhythm of his need rose to meet hers. 'Don't stop – don't be slow, I want you so much, oh, so much, Joe, my Joe, my Joe . . .'

186

Joe found himself swept along by her frenzy, all the pent-up frustrations of the past weeks finding savage relief in this willing body. His mind became a whirling maelstrom of feverish need. Images passed through his mind, the images that had tormented him through long, starving nights when all he had longed for was out of reach. Christina at her father's funeral, tiny in her dark, plain clothes, yet still alive with that unquenchable spark that he found so irresistible. Christina in her green dress, vivid as a humming-bird in the smoky cone. Christina in her library, bent over his designs, her small face absorbed, intent. Christina when he had handed her the Chalice – her face lit up as if the sun had come out especially for her, her slender hands taking it, caressing it, her jade eyes intent. The warmth in her voice as she thanked him, the soft touch of her hand in his . . .

Christina in his arms . . . in his arms . . . in his arms . . .

'Joe . . . Joe . . . *Joe*!'

He woke suddenly to the truth – that this was not Christina in his arms, but Maggie. And that the moment of climax was approaching rapidly, too rapidly. Recollecting himself, he began to pull back, knowing that in seconds now it would be too late, that what he had always managed to avoid would be a real threat. But Maggie's hands gripped his buttocks, pulling him deeper into her. His thrusting body, now completely beyond his control, drove forcefully for its mysterious target, the powerful rhythm echoed in her cries. With each pulsating retreat, he tried to withdraw, but she would not let him; her body seemed to follow his, arching beneath him while her arms clamped him against her and her throat screamed her determination. And then the moment was on them. With a final violent surge, he felt the vital energy explode from him, pumping life into the vessel that had hitherto been used only for pleasure.

With a simultaneous shudder, they both relaxed. Joe

sagged on to Maggie's soft body, his head buried in her neck. She held him close, her hand smoothing the thick, tousled hair, her voice murmuring softly in his ear. In the darkness, she smiled.

'There, Joe!' she whispered after a while, 'wasn't that better than bein' careful? It could be like that all the time, if we was wed.'

For a moment, he didn't respond. Then he rolled off her and she saw his eyes shining red in the glow from the smoke-ridden sky.

'You did that a-purpose,' he breathed. 'You meant to do it all along. You been trying to trap me, Maggie Haden.'

'And what matter if I did?' she returned, still lying spread on the grass. 'Don't tell me you didn't like it. You've always wanted it that way, and don't pretend otherwise.'

'That's different from doing it. A man has to have some care for his woman.'

'Care for hisself, you mean! As long as you didn't get me into trouble, you knew you was safe – you wouldn't hev to marry me. Well, now, the chances are you will. And a good thing too, because I told you, I'm tired of heving to sneak up this hill in the cold and the dark. It's time we settled down, Joe Compson, and if what I did tonight helps matters along, well, 'tis a good thing too.'

'And you think trapping me will do any good? I thought you had more sense! If there's any result to this night's work, I don't hev to own it's mine. That's your doing, Maggie, and nobody else's.'

She sat up quickly. 'Joe, you wouldn't leave me to fend alone? You couldn't –'

'You did it alone,' he said grimly, fastening the last of his buttons. 'That was never in our bargain, Mag, and you know it. I told you to leave it a while – if you had, happen we'd hev settled down all right in the end. But now – nobody owns Joe Compson, not you nor any brat you might hev through your own foolishness. Nor ever will.'

He was on his feet, already turning to stride away down the hill. Maggie, her dress still dishevelled, her new shawl discarded in the mud, scrambled to her knees and clutched at him, her hands scrabbling in desperation to keep him with her.

'Joe, don't! Don't go, don't leave me like this. I never meant it, Joe – I never meant to make you angry. I just wanted you, I wanted you to love me like you used to afore you knew *her*. She can never be what I am to you, can't you see that? You can never hev her. She'll never give you a son like I can.' She found his hand and dragged it against her wet cheek, down to the breasts that spilled from her bodice. 'A son, Joe – don't you want a son? Don't you want me?' Tears left smoky runnels down her face. 'Please, Joe, *please*, don't leave me. I couldn't live without you, I couldn't go on!'

Joe looked down at her. In the darkness he could see only the shine of her eyes, glittering with the tears that he could hear in her voice. He felt her hands clawing at his legs and felt a sudden disgust for the intimacy they assumed, for the frenzy they communicated. His heart was a leaden lump in his sated breast. He pulled her hands away and stepped back.

'I'm sorry, Mag,' he said. 'You shouldn't hev done it.' And he turned and began to stride down the hill.

For a few seconds there was silence. Then Maggie's voice screamed out into the night, startling a flock of small birds from the bushes, making other lovers lift their heads to listen.

'You'll be sorry, Joe Compson! You see, you'll be sorry. You're nothing but a fool, a girt silly fool – a rich woman's toy. One day she'll throw you away just like you've thrown me away, and when she does, I hope you suffer. I hope you suffer in hell for her, Joe Compson, just like I'm suffering now . . .'

Christina was in the library alone when Joe came. She had

eaten dinner with her brother, Adela having been invited to spend the night with a friend in Dudley, and Susan being confined to bed with another of the headaches that brought flashing lights to her eyes and sickness to her stomach. Afterwards, Harry had gone to his room to study.

So it happened that Ruth, passing the front door when Joe came knocking, opened it to him and let him in. She showed him straight into the study, unaware that Harry was not there, and then, having called down to Rose that there was no need for her to attend her mistress, went upstairs to sit with Nurse.

Joe stood at the library door, his bulk filling it. His head was lowered like that of a great bull, turning slowly from side to side as he surveyed the shadowy room. He saw Christina, sitting in a pool of lamplight close to the fire, and his heart stirred. Why he had come here, straight from that last furious encounter with Maggie, he did not know. Thought and reason had played no part in his storming down the hill. And now that he was here, miraculously alone with her, he feared rejection as he had never feared anything in his life.

'Joe!' Christina was on her feet, coming towards him, her face alight in the soft glow of light. For a moment, she was aware only of the fact that they were alone – that even Harry wasn't here to oversee their behaviour, to hear their conversation. Her heart thudded with sudden nervousness. There was a wildness in his bold, dark eyes tonight, a heaving of his breast, that struck and frightened her. Doubtfully, she backed away a little.

'It's all right, Miss Christina.' He had seen her withdrawal and spoke bitterly. 'I haven't come to make trouble. If I'm out of place, I'll go.' And he turned back to the doorway.

'No! No, don't go now, Joe. You've only just come.' Whatever had brought that look to his eye, it was nothing she had done, and she could have sworn he had come more for comfort than anything else, just as her brother might have done when hurt or indignant. Yet, Joe Compson, come to her for comfort? The idea was absurd. 'Come to the fire and talk for a while,' she said persuasively, closing the door. 'Let's be comfortable together.'

He thrust a trembling hand through his thick, curly hair and shook his head uncertainly. Before now, they had always sat at the long table, with Harry at the other end. The two armchairs drawn close to the warmth, with only one lamp to add to the light of the flames, brought an intimacy that touched them both with wavering doubt, caused them to look at each other with half-glances of caution as they sat down.

'Is something wrong, Joe?' Christina asked softly. 'You look – upset. Can you tell me?'

He shook his head, mouth twisting. 'I don't know why I came, Miss Christina. It's nothing I can tell a lady like you. I've just been taken for a fool, that's all. I was wrong to come bursting in here.'

'Not wrong at all.' She waited, testing the words before she spoke them. 'We're friends, I think. Is there any reason why you should not turn to your friends when you're in trouble? *Are* you in trouble, Joseph?'

Again he ran his hand through the springing hair. 'Not trouble, miss, no. Like I said, someone just took me for a fool, and mebbe it's my own fault at that, for not seeing it coming. I suppose you'd say I *am* a fool, for letting it happen.'

'Well, I wouldn't know that, would I,' Christina said reasonably, 'since I've no idea what you're talking about.'

Joe grinned at that, his strong teeth suddenly showing white in the shadows that lay across his face, and Christina said impulsively, 'That's better! Joe, you should do that more often. Smile so. It makes you look –' She

191

stopped, blushing, then went on with sudden determination. 'It makes you look very handsome.'

There was a short silence. Christina found her breath coming quickly. She wanted to lower her eyes, to hide behind her long, dark lashes, but coquetry had no place here tonight. She kept her glance steady on his, half afraid of that burning gaze, half excited by it, seeing there a sustaining strength, a power that would not change. With sudden bright perception, she knew that here was a man who could wield the same massive strength as her father, a man who could master without domination. With Joe, there would always be a challenge to meet, a battle to be fought with exhilaration, sometimes to be won and sometimes lost so that neither would ever be tyrant of the other.

'Joe,' she said, her lips barely moving, her voice little more than a thread, 'say my name.'

'Your name?' His voice, too, was husky, as if something constricted his throat. 'Why do you want me to say that?'

'I want to hear it on your lips. No –' she shook her head with impatience '– not *Miss* Christina, not that. Just – Christina.'

There was a pause. His glance narrowed and he lifted his head slightly sideways, so that he looked at her askance.

'Please, Joe,' she said again, almost resenting the intensity she had to strive to keep out of her voice, 'call me by my name – just once.'

He began to stir, to come to his feet, and Christina, without thinking about it, rose too. They stood close, barely two feet apart, each looking deep into the other's eyes.

'Christina,' she whispered, holding his eyes; and slowly, unwillingly, as if the word were being dragged from him, he returned, '*Christina* . . .'

It hung on the air, a deep-throated murmur, echoing

through the shadows beyond the pool of lamplight. The throb of it vibrated in the heavy furniture, trembled in the glasses that stood on the side table, rustled in the curtains that hung thick against the windows. It died away slowly, as if unwilling to fade, and when there was only the crackle of the fire left, Joe and Christina moved, inch by inch, as if impelled by some force both would rather resist, towards each other.

'*Christina*,' he murmured again. She swayed towards him and his hands came up to her shoulders, touching the fine silk of her dress. Their warmth burned through to the tingling flesh beneath and she felt their trembling, transmitting directly to her own quaking heart. His large fingers moved with a surprising delicacy, barely brushing her skin as he pushed the silk aside, and Christina lifted her face, a steady golden light in her lambent eyes, and searched the dark face above hers.

'Joe?' she breathed, and the deep mahogany of his eyes darkened further to smouldering black. His expression altered, so subtly that she sensed rather than saw it, and her body quivered.

Slowly, his hands still light on her shoulders as if he were holding back an emotion too powerful, too dangerous, to unleash, he bent his head. He touched her parted lips; and as the flame ignited and leapt in Christina's breast, he caught her against him with a groan that seemed to be wrenched from the depth of his soul. And Christina, her cheek pressed into a shoulder as broad as a tree, drew the strength that she had needed from the lips he gave her and from the power in his arms.

They were arrested by a small commotion in the hall. Reality, curt as a whip, broke in upon them.

Abruptly, Christina moved away. But she was still only a yard from him, still staring bemused at his intent and tortured face, when the door opened.

'Christina!'

The voice was light and sharp, its tone accusing, and it

jerked Christina out of the meshes of the dream that held her. Shaking her head like one reluctantly awaking, she stared at the newcomer, and a deep blush spread like the apricot of sunrise over her face.

'Jeremy! I did not know you were coming . . .'

'Do I have to send word in advance? Am I to join a queue?' His fury at finding his rival here alone with Christina made him turn on her. 'Is it your custom now, Christina, to receive common workmen in your home without even your brother to support you? I am surprised that my aunt allows it.'

'Aunt Susan has no jurisdiction over me,' Christina flashed. 'And I receive whom I like. Is it *your* custom, Jeremy, to burst in upon ladies uninvited? Or do you not think me worthy of such courtesy?' Her breast heaved and she turned away, wondering if Jeremy had seen her trembling.

'It depends on whether you think yourself a lady!' he retorted, and then stopped, biting his lip. 'Christina, let us not get at cross-purposes. Have this fellow leave, if his business with you is finished, and then we can be comfortable together.'

She flushed again at his rudeness and lifted her chin in the defiant way both men knew so well. 'Joe and I have not yet finished our business together, Jeremy, in fact we had not yet begun it. Perhaps you would like to wait in the drawing room – Parker will see to your needs.' She touched the bell-pull. 'Rose will show you the way.'

Jeremy's face was now a dark, angry red. He flashed a look from Christina to Joe. 'I shall not be dismissed like this! You ought to be chaperoned, Christina, and if you insist that this man stays I shall stay with you.' He turned as Rose came into the room and said curtly, 'It was a mistake, Rose, your mistress has no need of you at present. Go!' he added sharply as the parlour maid hesitated and then, turning back to the two who still stood far too close by the fireside, 'Do you not realise just how compromising your position is?'

'Don't be ridiculous, Jeremy! Joe came simply to talk over some new designs and –'

'*More* new designs? I wonder you will ever have time to make them all!'

Christina ignored the jibe. 'There is nothing compromising in our position, cousin, and I take it a gross insult that you should so imply. I think you owe both me and Joseph an apology.'

'An apology! *I* apologise to that – that *ape*!' Jeremy's laugh, bitterly scornful, rang through the room. 'Now, Christina, my sweet, you go too far. I might indeed apologise to you – were we alone and you in a more pliant mood than lately – but say anything at all to that great hulk of overblown goat's meat? There's only one thing to be said to such as he.' He turned to Joe and went up to him, thrusting his sneering face close to the man he was determined to be rid of. 'Go your way, Compson. This is no place for you and well you know it. You're making yourself a laughing stock, hanging round Miss Christina like this, a butt for every man's humour. Petticoat government they call it, don't they? And being a rich woman's plaything. Do you like being called that? Does it make you proud?' He paused, breathing heavily, watching Joe's face for reaction and finding none other than a shift of expression in the smouldering eyes. 'Stay here and be her lapdog if you must, if you have nowhere else to go for your puny pleasures,' he said cruelly. 'But know that she laughs as much and as heartily as any, once you are gone. She even calls you her own court jester and talks of having you to live in the house, so that she may call on you at any time to entertain her . . . You afford us all a good deal of amusement, Joe Compson,' he said with a cool friendliness that was not even intended to deceive, 'and I am reluctant to end it, for I like to see Christina laugh. But any joke can go too far – and

I advise you to let it end now, quietly, before it leads to unpleasantness.'

Joe moved quickly. His great hand shot out and gripped Jeremy by the shoulder, the knuckles white with the force of his grasp. Jeremy exclaimed angrily and twisted, wrenching at the hand that held him, unable to loosen the iron fingers. For a moment, he was at a loss; then, clearly afraid of Joe's strength yet determined not to give way to it, he lifted his face and sneered.

'I'd advise you to take your hands off me, Compson, before you find yourself in real trouble. Even Christina is unlikely to stand by and see me beaten by a man who is all brute force and no brain. Take your hand away, and go back to the gutter where you belong – there are women there who think you're a man. Unlike my cousin, who has enough good sense to see that you are no more than a gorilla from the zoo, with something of an aptitude for glass!'

Christina flung herself forward. 'Jeremy! How can you say such things? They're not true, Joe, none of them are true, he just wants to make you leave. Take no notice, why, you're the best man I have in the glasshouse and the one whose advice I value the highest. Joe – please, Joe –'

But her words went unheard. Joe Compson's skin was suffused with angry, humiliated colour, his eyes blazing as he thrust his way from the room. He heard nothing of Christina's frantic pleas, none of the furious tirade she directed then at her cousin. He didn't even hear his sister Ruth's anxious questions as she encountered him again in the hallway and tried without success to bar his way.

Joe Compson had taken as much as he could bear that night. And as he stormed away down the drive and back into the darkened streets, he could hear only Maggie's voice, echoing as she screamed after him down the hill.

'*You'll be sorry, Joe Compson! You'll be sorry. You're*

nothing but a rich woman's toy. One day she'll throw you away just like you've thrown me away, and when she does, I hope you suffer. I hope you suffer in hell for her, Joe Compson, just like I'm suffering now . . .'

Chapter Ten

'A Frenchman? Coming here?'

Christina smiled and went on eating, secretly amused at the consternation she could so easily produce in her family.

'Is it so strange?' she enquired peaceably. 'Our own family was French, not so very far back. Or have you forgotten our Lorrainer ancestors, who brought glassmaking to England?'

'A mere two hundred years or so,' Susan said acidly. 'A good deal of water has flowed under the bridge since then.'

'A good deal of blood, too,' Jeremy remarked, and Susan, after a brief hesitation while she debated whether this were in questionable taste, took up his point.

'Yes, indeed. Our relations with the French have not been particularly easy, even in this century.'

'All the same, some of our relations *are* French,' Christina pointed out. 'And Papa kept contact with several of them, especially those still in the glass trade. I feel sure he would have approved this move.' She gave Jeremy a cool glance; although he still came to the house, she had never forgiven him for that scene when he had sent Joe storming out into the night. He had, later, apologised for the remarks he had made – though not to Joe – saying that they had been caused only by his concern for her and, yes, if she must have it, a certain measure of jealousy for the glassblower who seemed to be awarded so much of her favour. But for Christina, restricted now by Joe's own decision to meet only in the glasshouse, and lying awake night after night longing for something she could never have, an apology was a poor thing. And even the increased responsibility Joe now had in necessitating even closer contact between them at work, did not seem to break down the personal barrier that had risen between them.

'So what are you proposing now?' Aunt Susan asked in the long-suffering tones of one who knows very well all the work will fall to her. 'To set up a French *salon* in Wordsley? I thought you had no interest in such fashions.'

'You know quite well that I have not.' Christina could not prevent a touch of irritation in her tone. 'No, aunt, all I propose is to bring one Frenchman here, that is all. A master engraver and decorator of great skill. The state of glass-cutting is pitiful. Here we are, entering one of the greatest expansion periods our industry has ever known, with more people than ever before clamouring to buy fine glass, and with engraving becoming more and more important – yet we are *still* relying on the engraver working at home, with primitive tools and nobody to oversee him.'

'And what do you mean to do instead?' Jeremy was watching her narrow-eyed, giving no hint as to whether he agreed or not. 'Employ someone to inspect these cutters at their work? They would hardly take to that idea! And where does your Frenchman come into this?'

'I don't propose anything of the sort,' Christina said impatiently. 'To me, the answer seems so simple that I wonder nobody has done it long ago. I shall build my own cutting houses, alongside the cones – I may even use the existing warehouses and build more storage space – and employ cutters and engravers on a permanent basis, men who will work for me and nobody else. Then I shall be able to build up their skills and make Henzel's glass the best decorated as well as the best quality crystal. And my Frenchman, as you call him, will come into it by teaching the best engraving methods and designing new patterns that will go well with our new shapes.'

'Your own cutting houses! But hardly any glassmaker has his own engraving house, and those that do exist are small –' As usual, Aunt Susan automatically vetoed any idea Christina might have, looking to Jeremy to support her. But Christina spoke quickly, before he had a chance.

'Exactly. Nearly all the work goes out to individual cutters, men working in their own small sheds for any manufacturer who cares to send them his work. It's true that most of the better ones remain loyal to one master – but to take the trouble we've taken to make the finest rock crystal in the country, and then send it to a backyard workshop in the middle of the slums, is to court trouble.' Christina looked at the ring of faces and spoke passionately about the subject she cared for more than any other. 'Our fine glass is far too valuable to be treated so casually. It can be lost, broken or stolen on the journey, and is in equal peril while it is there. Why –' she allowed her intensity to relax, the mischief that was never too far away breaking through '– we might find ourselves being returned a quota of Jeremy's glass instead of our own – can you imagine!'

Jeremy smiled tolerantly. 'No doubt in that case, you would keep silent, knowing you had the best of the bargain,' he said smoothly. 'But I agree with you that we ought to reorganise the decorating side of our industry and set up our own workshops. It isn't a new idea, of course. Some manufacturers have already done it and others are thinking of following their example. What I still do not understand is why you need to bring a Frenchman over to do it. Or, indeed, why he should want to come.'

'I've already told you why we need him. To show us how the finest engraving can be done. You know that we have slipped behind the work done on the Continent – the Bohemians in particular have always produced highly-decorated glass, far in advance of ours. They have had the market long enough; now it is our turn, and if we need guidance I am not ashamed to seek it.'

'Your own engravers are less likely to welcome it,' Jeremy pointed out.

Christina shrugged her slim shoulders. 'The engravers

who work for me will be pleased to have a regular job on an agreed wage. Many of them live hand to mouth on the present system, and are dependent on having premises to work in – premises which can at any time be taken from them by their landlord. They will come to work each day just as any other factory worker does. I think that for better conditions they will not object to having a Frenchman who is master of his trade to teach them new tricks.'

'And who is this paragon?' Jeremy asked after a moment.

'His name is Jean-Paul Thietry.'

There was a tiny silence. Then Susan said carefully, 'Is that the family Thietry with whom your father used to correspond?'

'I thought,' Christina said, 'that I had already made that clear.'

'You had not mentioned the family name before.' Susan Henzel's voice was tight. 'This Jean-Paul – he is one of the younger members, I imagine.'

'Yes, he's quite young, about thirty years old, I believe. I kept up the correspondence after Papa died, and I've been writing to Jean-Paul for some time now. Our ideas seem in accord and when I suggested that he might come to England on a visit he was all agreement, and even offered his services to help with engraving designs for our new pieces. He wants to see our own methods of glassmaking too – they differ in several respects from the French – and it seems likely to be beneficial to us both. Our colour and crystal in exchange for his engraving – though I doubt if he will tell us *all* his secrets, any more than we will tell him all ours,' she added with a sudden mischievous smile. 'I think it will work very well.'

'And what of your favourite glassblower?' Jeremy asked with a curl of his lip. 'I understand he is not over-fond of the engraving trade.'

'None of the blowers are – that is well-known. If you

mean Joe Compson –' Christina lifted her chin to give Jeremy a level look '– Joe believes shape to be more important, and in some ways I am inclined to agree with him. But he is not a fool.' Her straight gaze was a clear reminder to Jeremy of the night when he had called Joe just that, and worse besides. 'He understands that public demand now is for highly-decorated glass. Without the engraver, his shapes would not sell, however beautiful they might be. But without the glassblower, the engraver would have nothing to engrave.'

Jeremy inclined his head, and at that moment Adela broke in, unable to contain her curiosity a moment longer.

'Never mind all that! Tell us about this man, Chrissie – when is he coming? Where will he stay? Will he bring his wife with him?' Words bubbled out of her. 'Imagine, a Frenchman, they're so *elegant*. And the women so well-dressed. We shall have to give parties. Aunt Susan, I shall need new clothes, a whole new wardrobe!'

'Indeed you –' Aunt Susan began, but Christina spoke at the same instant.

'Monsieur Thietry is not coming here for a holiday, Adela, nor to embark on a round of social activity. Of course we shall have to give one or two parties to welcome him here, and I daresay others will wish to do the same. But he is coming to work. And he will not be bringing his wife – he isn't married.'

'Not married?' The sudden gleam in Adela's eye was echoed around the table and Christina sighed.

'Not everyone is married, Adela. And don't ask me why Monsieur Thietry isn't. Perhaps he simply doesn't wish to be. Perhaps he is squat and ugly, with squint eyes, and no one will have him. I haven't enquired.'

'If,' Susan said quietly, 'he is the son of Marc Thietry, who came here himself as a young man, I think that is unlikely.' And, as if already regretting her words, she rose from the table and moved towards the door. 'No Adela, there is nothing more to say. He was not here for long. I met the man only once myself and had no wish to do so again.' And although Adela continued to tease her as they left the room together, she clearly intended to say no more.

Christina followed them to the door, but as she passed Jeremy he caught at her arm. She paused unwillingly, looking down into his face.

'Am I not forgiven yet?' he asked in low, urgent tones. 'Don't you think you are being hard and unkind, and all over a common workman? I insulted him, I freely admit it – but I *have* apologised. And I've done penance enough, through being shut out of your confidence and denied your smiles. Christina –' Swiftly, he brought her hand to his lips and pressed them on the soft skin '– can't you see what you are doing to me?'

Christina stared down at him and wavered. His eyes, gazing up at her, were clear and blue, like a summer sky unmarred by clouds.

'Please,' he said softly, 'let's be friends again. I've missed you, Christina.'

'You've seen me almost every week – often more than once,' she said with an effort at lightness, but he shook his head.

'You know what I mean. I had hoped that we could become – more than friends. Is that really so impossible? So distasteful an idea?'

Christina's heart twisted. She remembered the night Jeremy had kissed her, the night Joe had taken her in his arms. The way she had lain awake ever since, thinking of them both, thinking of Joe, her mind confused, her body aching. Jeremy's fingers were moving gently on hers now, stroking the skin of her wrist, slipping up under her wide sleeve . . . She drew back hastily, keeping just the tips of her fingers in his.

'It's not distasteful at all,' she said, dismayed to find her voice trembling a little. 'I just – I have so many other things to think about, Jeremy. The glasshouse, the family,

I can't consider anything else just now, there simply isn't time and –'

'But I could do all that for you, don't you see? I'd take all the responsibility from you. Christina –' he rose from his chair and stood close to her, his eyes looking down on her now, both her hands somehow caught up in his and held against his breast '– Christina, why don't you admit that it's all too heavy a burden? Let me take some of it from you. I want to. I want to help you in whatever way I can, to make things easier for you, to take that tired look from your beautiful eyes, the strain from your pretty face. Let me make your worries my worries, Christina my love, and you'll see that they'll all disappear.'

Christina trembled. His eyes were hypnotic and his voice caressing. She could sense the hardness of the body so close to hers, feel his breath on her cheek. It needed only the slightest movement on her part, or his, for their lips to meet. She felt the sharp stab of loneliness – and was swept with longing.

'You would never need to enter the glasshouse again,' Jeremy said softly, and she jerked back, wrenching herself away from him, retreating from his closeness as if it were a trap.

'Never enter the glasshouse again! What are you saying? Jeremy, don't you understand yet, that would be a prison sentence to me? The glasshouse is what I live for. It's my trust, handed down to me by my father, and if it's a burden at all, it's one I carry gladly.' She turned away, clasping her hands in front of her, twisting the fingers together in her agitation. 'You talk of being friends, Jeremy, but you don't seem to understand me at all.'

Jeremy stood still, biting his lips, watching her as she paced the room. At last, he moved forward and took her hands again, holding them still in his.

'Christina, forgive me. That was a clumsy thing to say.' He smiled down at her, a smile of tenderness and under- standing. 'Of course I didn't mean that. You didn't let me finish. I was going to say – you need never enter the glasshouse again unless you wish it. It would still be yours, to go in and out of as you liked – but the *necesssity* would have been lifted from your shoulders. The worries would no longer be yours – only the pleasures.' He slid his fingertips up her arms, slowly, sensuously, as if savouring the exquisite softness of her flesh, and drew her against him. 'I always seem to be asking your forgiveness these days,' he murmured. 'Can I have absolution for all my sins, deadly though they are – so that we can begin again?'

He smiled again, beguiling, and Christina was reminded of a small boy asking forgiveness of his mother. Unable to resist him any more, she smiled back.

'That's better!' The little-boy look left his face and he was a man again, a man with needs and hungers she barely understood. 'Christina, you don't know what these past weeks have been like, feeling out of favour with you. And now –' he raised both her hands to his lips and kissed them fervently '– now we can truly start again. Your servant, my lady!' He released her hands to sweep a deep bow. 'I am yours to command.'

'Jeremy, don't be a fool!' But she was laughing nevertheless. 'And please, just let's be friends, for the time being anyway. I really don't want to think of – of anything else yet.' She felt her skin colour and looked down, hiding her eyes behind long, dark lashes tipped with the same glinting red as her hair. 'Let me have a little time.'

'All the time you need,' Jeremy said, serious again. 'So long as we understand each other.'

Christina smiled at him and then moved towards the door. It was time for her to join her sister and aunt in the drawing room, leaving Jeremy to his solitary port. As she closed the door behind her Christina wondered whether they did understand each other, and if Jeremy would accept that she didn't want to think of marriage at all yet, to anyone. Or did he believe that she had made him a promise? She was uncomfortably aware that they had said either too much, or not enough. And that this might, sometime in the future, bring more trouble. But she could not concern herself with that now. As she had told Jeremy, there was simply too much else to think about.

Jean-Paul Thietry, for example. Although she had been cool enough at dinner, Christina was really as excited as her sister Adela about the Frenchman's visit. Not, of course, because he might be an attractive and marriageable man, but because of what he might mean to the glasshouse and its future.

Nothing, Christina thought then, could ever mean so much to her as the glasshouse.

The Henzel cousins were no more pleased than Susan had been to hear of Christina's latest plan.

'A Frenchman!' Harold exclaimed with automatic disapproval. 'And what good does she think that will do?'

'She intends setting up her own cutting and engraving shops, and Thietry will teach new methods and styles. Unfortunately, I think it's a good move,' Jeremy said, sounding depressed. 'With the new shapes she's making now, and the quality of her crystal –'

'You mean you're in *favour* of it?'

'Not as far as Christina is concerned, no.' Jeremy smiled thinly. 'Or at least, not unless we had control of the glasshouse.'

'Which we seem to be as far away as ever from achieving!' Samuel gave his son an exasperated glare. 'What's wrong with you, Jeremy? I thought you had this girl in the palm of your hand. Have your charms failed you for once?'

Jeremy reddened and tightened his lips, but before he could speak Reuben intervened, his voice as thin and colourless as ever.

'I think we are all realising that Christina is more her father's daughter than we had supposed,' he said smoothly. 'Her obstinacy is not merely that of a headstrong and wilful young girl; it is more the tenacity of a strong man. And her business sense – as Jeremy says, this is a good move. We must prepare for Christina to do well, I'm afraid. And the more successful she is –' his eyes slid round to Jeremy '– the less likely she is to need an adviser and confidant.'

'So what do you suggest we do?' Samuel demanded sceptically. 'It's a pity Alfred isn't here,' he added, getting up to walk across to the window.

Reuben shrugged. 'I still think we must leave it to Jeremy. He is the only one amongst us she will trust. I suppose she *does* still trust you?'

'I think so.' Jeremy's voice was stiff.

'Then I think perhaps you should try a new direction. Stop trying to act as her adviser and confidant over the glasshouse. Treat her as she wants to be treated – as an equal, as far as glass and business matters are concerned. Treat her, in fact, as a man, while concentrating on the fact that she is indisputably a woman.'

'And just what is that supposed to mean?' Harold grumbled. 'You're far too fond of talking in riddles, Reuben.'

'I mean that Christina has taken great pains lately to prove her femininity. She dresses well, in colours and styles that suit her. Her hair is fashionably arranged. She wants to be recognised as a woman, even though all her actions seem to deny it.' Reuben looked straight at Jeremy. 'We have reason to believe that she is not immune to masculine charms. She is of an age to be married; I think it is entirely possible that she longs for the state, without even realising it. Woo her, Jeremy. Court her. Forget the glasshouse – and make her forget it too, in your arms.'

The eyes of the three men were on him. Jeremy thought of the times he had held Christina, kissed her, felt her response. Perhaps Reuben was right. She had always drawn away from him because of the glasshouse, because of his own clumsiness in offering to shoulder her burdens. She wanted more than anything else to be recognised as able to do a man's job, in the man's world of glass. It was always his own attitude towards that desire that had spoiled their relationship.

It went against the grain to submit to what he saw as her arrogant pride. But if it were the way to win her . . . Once married, he would be her master and even if she did hold a casting vote he could ensure that her days were too full for her to be able to make real use of it. Fill her with children, he thought crudely; that will take her mind off the business. And off Joe Compson too.

'I agree with you, Uncle Reuben,' he said. 'Christina must be curbed, brought to heel. And marriage is the only restraint she will recognise.'

'If she will even recognise that,' Harold said gloomily. 'I have known headstrong girls before, but never one as wilful as she. I suspect her husband, should she ever agree to take one, will have a hard time of it trying to tame her. She's like a runaway horse, never properly broken.'

'But she is still a woman,' Reuben insisted. 'She must have the female sensibilities – and susceptibilities. Jeremy has only to approach her in the right way.'

'Let us hope you are right.' Samuel turned back from the window. 'And let's hope he can do it soon. The more successful she becomes, the more difficult she will be to tame.'

Jeremy thought of taming Christina. Meeting those challenging eyes and seeing them grow soft and submissive. Taking that slender body and feeling it grow pliant; bending it to his will and using it for his pleasure. A sudden quick excitement throbbed through his body, and he felt the spread of anticipatory heat.

November. Raw, bone-chilling fog meshed uncomfortably with the belching smoke and cinders of the Black

209

Country. From the top of Dob Hill, the scene now resembled a vast man-made volcano; a swirling soup of murk, reddened by the surly glow of the fires, spitting flame from the chimneys that rose from its depths. The growl of the furnaces, the clatter of the forges and the steady pounding of the mills could be heard from Kinver to Cannock, and there were plenty of people who could recite the rhyme that was now becoming famous:

> 'When Satan stood on Brierley Hill
> And far around him gazed,
> He said, 'I never shall again
> At Hell's flames be amazed.'

November. And Joshua Henzel had been dead for a year, and still his cousins were no nearer to obtaining his glasshouse for themselves.

Maggie Haden no longer met Joe on Dob Hill. Instead, on this sullen November evening, with the fog creeping between the sooty buildings like a preying animal, she was waiting on the towpath for Jeremy Henzel.

This was their third meeting, and Maggie had nearly not come at all; what use was it, to tell him that she had failed again to win Joe back? That her lover now refused to speak to her, turned to avoid her if he saw her in the street? That there was worse than that . . . a knowledge she dared not speak to anyone . . . But she had come, all the same. If there was nothing else to do, she could still do this. And something might come of it, who knew? She didn't let herself think of the other reason that drew her back here, almost against her will; the dark, hidden secret that she saw in Jeremy's eyes; that she feared and hated, yet could not resist . . .

He was coming now; she could hear his footsteps, quick and confident, on the muddy towpath.

'Well?'

He never greeted her by name, nor ever spoke in any

way that was not brusque. But there was always that look in his eye that gave him away. Hungry, as if he had not eaten for a month; the only difference was that it wasn't food he craved, but something else to nourish his body. You'll never get it from her, Maggie thought.

'What news?' His tone was peremptory. 'Come on, girl, out with it – it's too chilly a night to stand waiting about here.'

Maggie had stood there for an hour past, for he never gave her a time for these meetings, and it would have been of little use to her if he had; the nearest clock was on Trinity Church tower, invisible at night. She drew her shawl more closely around her and lifted her brooding eyes.

'No news, sir. I'm sorry.'

'What do you mean, no news?' He came closer, his eyes glimmering in the dull glow of the lantern he carried. 'What's the trouble now? You've had long enough, surely, to bring that young man of yours to heel.'

Maggie shrugged helplessly, black misery welling up into her throat so that her voice was low and pitiful. 'It's no use, sir. I can't do nothing more. He don't want me.' She turned away from the wavering light and her voice shook. 'Joe don't want me no more.'

'Doesn't *want* you? What nonsense are you talking, woman?'

'It's true, sir. He threw me over – won't even cross the street to speak to me now. I've tried everything, sir. It in't no use.'

Jeremy stared at her. Compson had jilted this succulent piece? He couldn't believe it.

'You're joking,' he said roughly. 'Or mistaken. It's just a tiff – he'll come round. And then, when he's wanting to please you, you can –'

'No, sir, I can't. He won't hev it. I've queered my pitch with Joe, sir, and that's the truth of it.'

'He's found someone else?' Jeremy said uncertainly, and Maggie snorted.

'Only the wench that's been there all along! Your cousin, Mr Jeremy, that Miss Christina. It must be her, I'd hev heard if he'd taken up with someone else, an' he haven't.' Maggie looked up with the boldness of desperation. 'An' I can't give thee back the money, sir, it's all spenten, on food and strong boots for me father and mother.'

Jeremy gestured impatiently. The amount he had given her, though riches to the family of a footmaker, was little enough to him. The ruin of his plans was of far greater importance. Time was pressing and Christina's confidence in running Henzel's increased with each passing month. His courtship of her remained at a standstill, and although Jeremy believed that he had regained her tentative trust and never doubted that he could eventually win her heart, he knew that it would take more time than his father and uncles were willing to wait. And there was always the risk that Christina might yet escape him – a risk he believed to be increased, the longer that Joe Compson was a free man.

Nonsense! He turned abruptly away from the girl at his side and took a few paces along the bank of the silent canal. To imagine that Christina could even entertain thoughts of a common workman – it was ridiculous, not to be supposed for a moment. Yet she was a wilful girl, and often behaved with a complete disregard of convention. But to the extent of consorting with one of her own workmen . . ? He shook his head violently, but knew that the risk was there. He had himself seen the way Compson looked at her; the way she looked at him. He had interrupted them in Christina's own library – not touching, admittedly, but with a tension between them that was almost audible when he snapped it. He had seen the light die from Christina's face when Joe blundered out. The situation could not continue. And he had relied upon Maggie's power to end it.

'What does Compson expect to gain by it?' he demanded, swinging back to her. 'Throwing you over is not likely to help him as far as Miss Christina's concerned. I doubt if she even knew of your existence. All he's doing is depriving himself.' His eyes returned to the girl in front of him and another thought entered his mind too. 'Have you found another man?' he asked sharply.

'No, sir, I ent! There's not many about like my Joe, an' besides –'

'Yes? Well, girl, what is it?' God in heaven, what was the matter with the wench – she was as white as a ghost, all her haughty colour gone, her eyes as dark and empty as the canal itself.

Maggie stared up at him, her lips moving as if she were trying to speak words that would not come. He watched as she struggled; then she shook her head as if defeated, and turned away.

''Tis no good, sir. It's me own trouble – nothing you'd want to hear.' She lifted her hands suddenly to cover her face and swayed in her distress. 'It's Joe I need! Oh, if only Joe was here!'

Jeremy felt the thrust of jealousy like a knife stabbing into his stomach. Joe Compson! What did he have that these women – two as different as this luscious slut and his imperious and exasperating cousin, Christina – should desire him so?

He thought yet again of the night when he had walked into Christina's library and found Compson there with her. Compson's visits to the house had ceased after that night, according to Cousin Susan. But the situation was no less dangerous. The little scene Jeremy had witnessed had been explosive. His arrival had damped it down; but it could still be smouldering and ready to erupt. Something else would have to be done about Joe Compson.

He felt a hand touch his arm, softly, and looked down.

213

'Sir?' Maggie said tremulously. 'It – it weren't my fault, sir. I did try. I *want* to marry Joe. And now –' He saw the tears glitter on her cheeks. 'Now I don't know what I'm goin' to do. An' it's all *her* fault,' she added viciously. 'None of it would hev happened if it hadn't been for her!'

Jeremy looked down thoughtfully. The sudden flash of venom was unaccountably cheering. For a few moments, he'd thought Maggie's spirit broken, her fires quenched. But there was still a spark of the old Maggie there, and if it couldn't be turned to his advantage in one way, it surely could in another.

Jeremy had no doubt in his ability to win Christina. She must know that her infatuation for Joe was hopeless, and that marriage with Jeremy was the only solution. And he knew that he was not distasteful to her; she had responded to his kisses, her body giving way to his. Whether she knew it or not, she was hungry for marriage and all it brought. Putting the glasshouse to one side and thinking only of himself he knew that time was all he needed. And then, perhaps by Easter . . .

Meanwhile, nobody could expect him to forget his own needs or try to live the life of a monk. And here was Maggie. Deprived of Joe Compson and the pleasure he gave her. And feeling conveniently in Jeremy's debt. He grasped her chin in one hand and lifted her face towards his. Her eyes met his and widened. Her lips parted.

'You needn't worry about the money,' Jeremy said easily before he bent his head. 'You can pay in kind.'

The new warehouses were finished just before Christmas and the transformation of the old ones to cutting and engraving shops began as soon as the stored glassware could be moved. Christina had already begun to advertise for cutters and engravers, and although some of them looked on her venture with suspicion, several individual workers had already come forward.

'We'll be able to start work in the New Year,' she declared delightedly. 'Just when Jean-Paul arrives.'

Rose, who had been waiting at table when this announcement was made, carried the news below stairs to the kitchen.

'And I suppose that means we'll have Frogs here under our feet all day,' she said disgustedly, and Nellie, the little scullery maid employed to help Daisy, looked alarmed. 'I don't mean that sort of frog, you goose – I mean Frenchies. That Monsewer Tit'ry will be bound to bring a bevy of servants along with him.'

'And you know what *that* means,' Mrs Jenner said darkly, and Nellie looked even more frightened.

'Frenchies – don't they eat babbies?' she quavered. 'There was an old man used to live near us, he said in the old wars they did. An' rats.'

'Well, he won't cost too much to feed then,' Parker remarked jocularly. 'He can catch his own dinner . . . Don't look so terrified, Nellie, you silly girl. Of course they don't eat babies.'

'What do you think about these Frenchies coming, Ruth?' Rose asked. 'Miss Henzel's in a rare taking about it all, what with the extra bedrooms to prepare and the food and all.'

'I don't know why she should be,' Mrs Jenner sniffed, 'since it won't be her as has to do the work. I hope you'll be able to lend a hand too, Ruth,' she added, turning towards the end of the table. 'There'll be a lot of work and I daresay his servant won't be much help, think himself above the likes of us I don't doubt.'

'Here, what will he talk?' Rose was struck by a fresh thought. 'I mean, he won't know English, will he? How are we going to know what he's saying?'

Mrs Jenner looked at Parker enquiringly.

'We'll cross that bridge when we comes to it,' the butler pronounced. 'I don't see any problem myself. It's obstinacy as much as anything with these foreigners. You just talk a bit louder and a bit slower until they understand. Anyway, I can't see we'll need to talk to him much. He's nothing to do with us, after all – just here to look after his master.'

'He'll be eating his meals down with us, though,' Mrs Jenner said doubtfully. 'And sitting along of us of an evening.'

'That's as may be,' the butler said with disdain. 'But we don't have to *talk* to him.'

'There's a lot of excitement over this Monsieur Thietry,' Ruth observed later as she helped Christina to prepare for bed.

'Well, it's an event for us to have a visitor to stay.' Chistina turned her back so that Ruth could undo the long row of buttons on her dress. 'Aunt Susan is in a panic, of course. And Adela is convinced he's going to be the romantic prince who carries her off to live the rest of her life in a fairy-tale.'

'And Mrs Jenner just thinks of two extra mouths to feed and two extra beds to make,' Ruth continued.

'And I see him as the man who is going to make Henzel's famous!' Christina laughed. 'Poor Jean-Paul, I wonder if he realises what different roles he is expected to play.'

She stepped out of her dress and Ruth shook it out and hung it up. Christina wandered over to the mirror and unfastened her hair, letting it swirl loose. She shook her head, enjoying the feel of the auburn waves floating around her head and brushing her naked shoulders. 'Monsieur Thietry will be here after Christmas to take over the new shops and start Henzel's on their way as the most advanced glass manufacturer in Stourbridge – in *England*. And nothing Jeremy, or my father's cousins, do or say is going to make any difference!'

She danced a few steps across the room and whirled to smile at her maid, her tawny hair whisking like bronze silk in the translucent glow of the lamp.

'I think I am the most excited of us all,' she said impulsively. 'I have a feeling that Jean-Paul is going to change all our lives. Nothing will ever be quite the same again.'

1846

Chapter Eleven

The New Year came in cold and windy. Fierce gales swirled the smoke and fumes of the Black Country into a threatening pall of massed darkness that filled the cringing sky. The days were short and bitter; men, women and children left their homes in darkness, spent the few daylight hours there were in the factories and mines that were more shelter to them than the fetid rooms in which they slept, and returned in darkness to the rags that served to keep them warm through the bone-chilling nights until it was time to get up again.

And on the coldest night of the winter, driving through a vicious mixture of sleet and snow and icy rain, with the horses' hooves now slipping on the frozen stones, now stumbling into thick, half-solid mud, Jean-Paul Thietry came to Wordsley and, as Christina had foretold, changed all their lives.

He did not, as his servant knocked on the door and the family tumbled from the drawing room to see him arrive, look like one who would change lives; he looked barely capable of changing or even commanding his own as he stood swaying in the hall, clearly almost dead from fatigue and nausea brought on by the motion of the coach. His face was white and thin, his eyes dark pools of weariness in the pallor, while his hair lay in damp, curling tendrils across his forehead and his body, wrapped in a long cloak that was dark with rain and sleet, looked too slender and delicate for such rigours as a sea-voyage followed by a drive across half England in the worst weather the heavens could hurl down.

Christina, pausing halfway down the stairs, thought for a moment that he was seriously ill. She looked down on his bent head, noting the fragility of the thin neck, the sharpness of the cheekbones, and wondered if she had done the right thing in bringing this man here. He didn't look strong enough to last the night, let alone transform her glasshouse with his skills . . . She tightened her hand on the banister and, as if aware of her and of her misgivings, the Frenchman raised his head.

In that moment, Christina fell in love.

There was nobody, in that moment, but the two of them; he, below, gazing up with those haunted eyes, she, above, looking down and aware only of the message that those eyes held for her, only her, and of the hammering of her heart. She stared down, clinging to the wood of the banister as the only solid contact she had with the earth, as if by letting go she would be sucked into a vortex of emotion so powerful there would be no return.

His eyes were silver; a bright glittering silver that struck and held her captive. She gasped under their impact, as if hit suddenly by a shower of icy water, and found herself recovering with as much exhilaration. The stimulation of Jean-Paul's presence, even in his present weakened state, reached out and hit her like a tangible force, and she lifted her head and felt the strength and power streaming through her body.

'You're exhausted!'

The words broke from her as, swiftly, she descended the last few stairs and swept to his side, thrusting her way through the welter of luggage and servants.

'Aunt Susan, he's worn out. It must have been a terrible journey, and through all this appalling weather, too. Some soup, that would be the best thing – see to it, Ruth, would you? – and hot water for a wash. And wine, he needs wine.' She was beside him, her hands on his arms, almost supporting the tall, swaying body. 'It's all right,' she said as soothingly as if to a child. 'You're here now. The footman will take you to your room and bring you refreshment. Please don't think of anything but

222

resting – we'll talk tomorrow, if you feel quite recovered but you're not to stir a step until you're quite ready . . . Are you his servant?' she demanded of the man who had entered with the last of the luggage. *'Etes-vous son serviteur? Prenez les bagages en haut, s'il vous plaît.* Edward, take this man – *comment vous appelez-vous?'*

'Pierre, *mademoiselle.'*

'Take Pierre upstairs to the room prepared for Monsieur Thietry and show him where everything is. And then give him and Monsieur Thietry whatever help they may need.' She turned back to Jean-Paul and stood irresolute for a moment, as if reluctant to let him go. 'Go and rest now,' she said at last. 'We'll meet tomorrow, and then we can have a long talk.'

Jean-Paul turned his eyes on her again, and once more she felt the impact of that searing glance. A shiver passed over her body and her fingers tightened on his sleeve. Her lips moved, but there were no words for them to speak.

The Frenchman spoke at last, his voice husky with fatigue yet with a strange thrill running through it, a vibration like that of a violin when its strings have been plucked and left to fade alone.

'I am sorry to come to you like this,' he said, as if every word was an effort. 'I am ashamed. The journey should be nothing, nothing at all, but I have always been a stupid traveller. Tomorrow, I will be better, more able to appreciate your hospitality –' The weary tones faded and he swayed again, his face a sickly green under the flickering light, and Christina involuntarily stepped closer, supporting his whole weight briefly in her arms before Pierre, with a brooding look from under his lowered brows, caught his master. Jean-Paul shook his head slightly and seemed to recover. He gave Christina a wan smile of apology that struck at her heart and then, leaning heavily on his servant's shoulder, he allowed himself to be led up the stairs.

223

The family stood in the hall, still surrounded by luggage, staring up.

'Well!' Adela said at last. She turned to Christina, her eyes shining. 'Did you ever see anyone so romantic!'

Aunt Susan found her voice. 'Romantic! You call that young man romantic? A weedy fellow like that, blown in out of the storm like nothing more than a tussock of grass, swaying this way and that as if he had not a single bone in his body to support him? I'm afraid, Adela, that you're in danger of turning into a silly young miss – and you, Christina, you're just as bad, hanging on to his arms like that, why, you almost fawned upon him. No, I can see nothing romantic in that young man at all. And I think you're going to regret bringing him here, Christina. He can do Henzel's no good at all, and he may even do harm. A great deal of harm.'

Christina turned her eyes slowly away from the bend in the stairs where she had last seen Jean-Paul Thietry, and rested them on her aunt's flushed and indignant face. Her expression was soft, almost dreamy. She could see, as if he still filled it, the space in which Jean-Paul had stood; she could still feel his body in her arms, his weight resting briefly against her, his cold breath on her cheek.

'Harm?' she echoed, as if tasting the word. 'Why, what harm can he do, Aunt Susan? What possible harm?'

'Your good aunt, I think, does not like me,' Jean-Paul observed a few days later. 'Or perhaps it is all Frenchmen, all foreigners, she dislikes. I wonder which it is.'

'Not like you? What nonsense – how *could* she not like you?' Christina finished peeling an orange and handed him a segment. 'Take no notice of Aunt Susan. She knows nothing.'

'On the contrary, she may know a good deal. No one goes through life without learning something. And there is a look in her eyes sometimes – a certain expression –

224

which makes me feel uneasy. There is something, without doubt.'

'Has Aunt Susan been rude to you? Unwelcoming? I shall speak to her at once!' Christina was half out of her chair, but Jean-Paul waved a tapering hand, shaking his head and smiling.

'Nothing of the sort, I assure you. She has been correctness itself. I have wanted for nothing in your house. No, it is something else, a glance now and then, a withdrawal which I sense . . . She cannot be blamed for not liking me, Christina. Everyone cannot like everyone else.'

Christina moved her shoulders impatiently. True, she thought, in most cases – but everyone *must*, surely, like Jean-Paul! Slipping the last segment of orange into her mouth, she stole a glance at him, still hardly able to believe that he was here, and had been here for only two or three days. He seemed to have been always in her life; a part that had been missing since the day she was born, the part that she had needed to be whole. Mind and body, she yearned towards him, yet even while she yearned was content to be simply in the same room with him.

Jean-Paul sprawled elegantly on the chaise longue. He was staring into the fire now and Christina allowed herself the luxury of gazing at him, drinking in his appearance though already she knew it by heart and could picture every detail even when they were apart.

He had recovered from the sickness that the journey had caused him, though for the past two days he had been forced to rest and even now had no colour in his fine-boned cheeks. But the sharpness had receded from his face, leaving its planes smooth and cool, with only the straight lines of his dark brows above light grey eyes and the symmetry of his chiselled lips to leaven their ivory creaminess. Without the cloak that had enfolded him on his arrival, he was revealed as tall and slender as a willow, with long, sensitive hands that Christina could well imagine displaying the artistry that a master engraver must possess. He used them now to brush back the thick brown curls that covered his well-shaped head and she followed their movement, longing to run her own fingers through the tousled locks, to caress the delicate ears and stroke the slender, curving neck.

'Aunt Susan was against you even before you came,' she said thoughtfully, thinking back to the evening when she had announced his visit, to the fuss her aunt had made then and ever since. 'I don't know why – she's complained about everything, your accommodation, your servant, everything she could think of. It's not you yourself, it's any visitor, I think. But now you're here –'

'You think she will learn to like me?' Jean-Paul's white smile flashed and Christina caught her breath. 'Perhaps you are right, I hope so. But now, I have come to work, not simply to lie in your drawing room behaving like royalty. Tell me about your glasshouse.'

At once, Christina's eyes lit up. With Jean-Paul, she could talk for hours about the subject closest to her heart, talk as she could talk with no one else. Briefly, she thought of the other two men with whom she shared her interest – Joe, who had seemed to share her every thought and now seldom approached her, and Jeremy who, she could never forget, represented the rival side of the family. With both of them, there was a barrier – but with Jean-Paul there was none. She could talk freely at last, as she'd talked to no one since her father's death, and the words poured out.

And Jean-Paul listened eagerly, asking questions, reciprocating with stories of his own family's glassworks in France, telling her about the forest glasshouses that still existed, using wood to fire their furnaces as the Lorrainers had done when they first came to England. 'Many glasshouses use coal now, as you do,' he said, 'but there is still so much wood in France, so many forests, and it is easy for the old family concerns to continue in the old manner. But wood-burning has not been permitted for many years in England, *n'est-ce pas*?'

'Not since the reign of James the First, nearly two hundred and fifty years ago.' Christina looked at the Frenchman curiously. He seemed the epitome of everything elegant, everything modern, yet the glassworks he came from worked in a way that to her seemed primitive in the extreme; using methods discarded by her own ancestors over two centuries ago. 'They needed the wood for ships. That was why the Lorrainers moved from Kent and Surrey to the Midlands, and how Paul Tyzack came to found the industry here in Stourbridge.'

'But this is not Stourbridge? This is Wordsley – difficult name!'

Christina smiled at his pronunciation. 'That's right. Most of the glasshouses aren't in Stourbridge at all, but the glass is always referred to as Stourbridge glass. We've given up correcting people; so long as they buy from us, we don't really mind.'

'Paul Tyzack,' Jean-Paul said thoughtfully. 'This name was Thisac, *non*?'

'Yes, he was one of the original Lorrainer families. The others were Thietry – your own people, whose name has changed now to Tittery – Houx, who have now become Hoe, and of course Hennezel, our own ancestors. There are Henzeys and Ensells too, supposed to be descended from those original families, but it's impossible now to trace back all the lines.'

'And if they had all stayed in France, you might be there too now, the daughter of some forest glassmaker,' Jean-Paul said thoughtfully. 'We might have met there, in the sunlight amongst the trees, instead of here in cold, dark England. We might have known each other all our lives.'

Their eyes met and Christina found herself suddenly unable to draw breath. Her throat caught, contracted, ached. She seemed to be drowning in those translucent, silver pools, struggling feebly for survival in their fathomless depths, knowing that she was already lost. Her own eyes widened, brilliant with the emotion that welled into their swimming viridescence, and her lips moved, soundlessly, forming words she could not speak.

At last she found her voice and whispered, in a tone she barely recognised as her own, 'I feel I have known you . . . all my life.'

Jean-Paul regarded her thoughtfully and she gazed back, as helpless as a butterfly, her heart calling to his with a desperate urgency. Yet when he spoke, there was a reserve in his tone that was like a splash of cold water, and Christina recoiled from its impact, shocked and bewildered.

'It's kind of you to say so,' he said with a formality that was almost cruel. 'I too feel we can be friends. Now I would like to see this glasshouse of yours,' he added, swinging his legs to the floor and rising to his feet with the grace of a long, rangy cat. 'I want to see just how everything is done. Will you take me, Christina? Will you show me everything?

Oh yes, everything, she longed to cry wantonly, everything you want to see . . . and then she blushed at the direction of her thoughts. Even when Jeremy had kissed her . . . even when Joe had looked her over in that insolent way he had . . . never, even then, had she allowed such shameless thoughts into her mind. Mortified by the feeling that Jean-Paul must know quite well what they were, she dragged her mind away, back to the glasshouse. Yes, it would be a good idea to go there. Surrounded by the clatter and roar of furnace and men, able to demonstrate the skills of English glassmakers, perhaps she would be better able to control her wayward mind and body.

It was with a mixture of irritation and relief that she found Adela in the hall, just returned from a walk with Ruth. Adela greeted Jean-Paul with an enthusiasm that was embarrassingly gushing and, when she heard where they were going, demanded to come too.

'To the glasshouse?' Christina echoed, scarcely able to believe her ears. 'But you hate going there!'

'I used to hate it,' Adela corrected her, with not so much as a blush. 'But now – well, let's say I'm growing up.' She dimpled prettily at Jean-Paul. 'Taking an interest in my heritage. And after all, glass is *so* beautiful. One ought to know just how it is made.'

Christina gave her a doubtful glance. Hadn't she been saying exactly that for years, and without the slightest effect? Perhaps Adela was, in truth, growing up. But was it really glass that had captured her interest? A spike of jealousy lanced her heart as she watched her sister take Jean-Paul's arm, smiling up into his face, chattering ingenuously as he listened and nodded. Adela was fast becoming a minx, she thought bitterly, and for once found herself agreeing with Aunt Susan. It was time she was married.

Once in the glasshouse, however, Christina came back into her own. Adela, wearing a pale blue velvet cloak and kid boots that were never meant for walking on broken glass and cinders, hung back, her pretended interest in their livelihood vanishing rapidly before her concern for her clothes. Dimpling and trilling, she tried hard to persuade Jean-Paul to stay with her; but with a smile, he gently disengaged her fingers from his sleeve and advised her to go back to the house with Ruth.

'You are too sweet a blossom for this rough place,' he said in the voice that had become warm and rich since his recovery. 'Glass for you should be nothing more than a finely-cut vessel for the wine that must pass your lips, or an ornament for your dressing-table. Go back home and select one of your prettiest dresses with which to enchant me at dinner, and your sister will show me all I want to see here.'

Adela pouted a little but blushed at his compliments

and took herself off with Ruth, the two of them talking as they went of meeting Harry from school. Left alone at the entrance to the cone, Christina and Jean-Paul looked at each other with sudden gravity.

'Your sister is an amusing child.' He sounded as if he were explaining something to her, or maybe to himself. 'One day, quite soon, perhaps, she will be an enchantress – a fascinating woman.'

'And will you be fascinated by her?' Christina was unable to resist asking.

He slanted her an amused glance from those gleaming eyes. 'I? Perhaps – but I think not. It is not easy to be fascinated by more than one woman at a time, and it is too – confusing.'

Christina's eyes fell before his gaze and she looked around the cone at random, searching for something to say. 'This is the *lehr,* where the glass is annealed, and this the pot-arch where we bring the new pots to temperature before changing them. And this is the –'

'That is something I would like to see,' he interrupted her. 'The pot-setting – it is different from our way, I think. Can it be arranged?'

'Oh yes, easily.' She was relieved that the conversation was back on safe ground. 'Now, here, they're making wineglasses. They're one of our best lines – we make more of this shape than any other.' They paused to watch as Jem Husselbee blew an elegantly-shaped wineglass with the nonchalance of the true expert. 'I'll see that you are supplied with a selection of wineglasses, so that you can decide which engravings go best with each shape. Or perhaps we could use the same design on a variety of shapes, so that our customers can have the same engravings on their brandy goblets as they have on their sherry glasses.' She moved on round the furnace, pausing at each chair to speak to the gaffer working there and to introduce Jean-Paul. 'And this is my best glassmaker, and right-hand man,' she said at last, and was unable to prevent the quiver in her voice. 'Joe Compson.'

The two men looked at each other and Christina stepped back, involuntarily, as if from a sudden blast of dangerous heat. At that moment, by coincidence – it must, surely, have been coincidence – there was a brief instant of silence in the cone.

'Joe,' she said, hearing and disliking the tremble in her tone, 'this is Monsieur Thietry. You remember, I told you he was coming.'

Slowly, Joe wiped his hands on rag. His face was shining with perspiration, gleaming in the ruddy light from the furnace. Black hair sprang like curling wire from his head, spangled with damp, and smaller, tighter curls padded his chest and the muscles of his shoulders. His dark eyes smouldered like coals under the heavy brows, and beside him Jean-Paul looked as fragile as the glass Joe had only just blown; slender and brittle enough to be snapped in two by the massive hands of the glassmaker.

'Aye, I remember,' Joe said slowly. 'Come to mek mock of our shapes, is that right? Cut them about until they're bare fit to hold. I thought we had enough of your sort here already.'

'Joe!'

He gave her a sullen glance. 'I told you, Miss Christina, I'd never tek to engravers and I don't see any sense in pretending. The shape's the thing, allus has been. And I thought we agreed with me. Now you're changing everything – building new warehouses so you can use the old ones as cutting-shops, bringing over Frenchies. The men don't like it, Miss Christina, and you ought to know what they think.'

'The men will do as they're paid to do,' Christina said coldly. 'Make glass. You know as well as I do that the public taste is for decorated glass. We can't go against that. If we send our glass out unengraved, it simply won't sell, however beautiful the shape.' She paused, looking at him and felt a sudden ache of loss, of the closeness they had shared that last evening in the library before they had been interrupted by Jeremy. Quickly, she turned back to Jean-Paul.

'I'm afraid Joe is typical of many of the glassmakers,' she said with a forced smile. 'To him, shape is everything and he hates to see it cut. But I'm sure when you begin to design, and he sees what you can do, he'll change his mind.'

Jean-Paul smiled down at her. 'Perhaps. But your glassmaker is as tough as his glass, I think. It will not be easy to change his mind once he has made it up, just as it is not easy to change the shape of a piece of glass once it has begun to anneal. Both would break, rather.'

'You'll not break me,' Joe said shortly, and Jean-Paul gave an easy laugh.

'My friend, I would not wish to. I need you. I need your skills, your artistry, for I too appreciate shape. Without it, I can do nothing. I would not even wish to decorate a glass of inferior shape, of crude or ugly design. What would be the point? But this . . .' He indicated the row of glasses that stood on the *lehr*, being slowly wound down the long cooling tunnel, 'this glass, I would be proud to set my engraving tools to work on this.'

'There, Joe,' Christina said brightly, 'does that make you feel better?'

Joe shrugged. 'Do it matter what I feel? I only *mek* the stuff.' He turned away, nodding brusquely at his gatherer who went swiftly to the furnace with a fresh iron. Christina glanced at Jean-Paul and shook her head ruefully, pretending a wry amusement that she didn't feel. All these weeks, she had been feeling uneasy about Joe, knowing that he didn't come to see her any more because of the humiliation he had suffered at Jeremy's hands, knowing that he would resent the coming of the French engraver; knowing that somehow, in her hand, she held the power to put things right and inexplicably afraid to do so.

And now, added to all the other barriers between them, had come Jean-Paul. And the antagonism between Joe and him was not due solely to the traditional conflict between glassblower and engraver. There was something more, something deeper.

She looked at Jean-Paul again and knew a sudden swift rush of joy. Between herself and Joe there were, indeed, barriers, just as there were between herself and her cousin Jeremy. But here, there need be no barriers. Here was a man who could give her all she craved; even those things she barely knew she needed . . .

Joe watched Christina and Jean-Paul tour the cone and swore under his breath.

The wench was besotted; there was no doubt about it. You had only to look at the way she smiled at him, her green eyes flashing like the fire when you threw on a handful of salt, her lips parting to show those little white teeth that looked sharp enough to sink sweetly into a man's flesh . . . You had only to see the way her slender fingers lifted to touch her tawny hair, the way they lingered on his sleeve. She couldn't keep her hands off him, and that was the truth of it.

Joe was surprised and displeased by the strength of his own feelings. He had never liked sharing his women, it was true; always there had been a fierce possessiveness, a glowering warning to other men to keep off his particular patch of grass. But Christina wasn't his woman; never had been, never would be. So why did he feel this scorching fury at the sight of her with the Frenchman? Why did his body burn with an anger that no action of his could ever assuage?

Perhaps it was because of what the man was. A foreigner for one thing, alien in the clothes that Christina thought elegant and to Joe looked merely effeminate. Even his hair was cut differently from that of an Englishman, and his voice was odd too, with a mincing accent that contrasted strangely with its baritone richness. And he made too many gestures with his long, tapering hands, waving them in the air, flicking out the narrow fingers as he described a piece of glass he had engraved, a design he thought would go well with one of Joe's shapes.

And that was another thing – he was an engraver. The glasses Joe made, the swelling shapes that had been drawn from his own powerful lungs, were mere raw material to him, a base on which to practise his own invidious art. If you could call it art – the destruction of a shape that was its own beauty, flowing in harmony with the space around it to please the eye with a natural symmetry that no bristling criss-cross of engraving could match. Why, when one of those fellows had finished with a piece of glass you'd be lucky to recognise its original shape at all – lucky even to be able to tell whether it started out as a wineglass or a chandelier . . .

Joe flung down his rag and finished the jar of ale that had been standing by his elbow. The six-hour move was over and he was free to go, handing over his chair to his father's team who were already coming in through the double doors, stripping off their outdoor clothes in the sudden fierce heat of the furnace. He nodded curtly at his own men; they would meet again soon enough, in six hours' time, ready for another move, another shift of transforming the shapeless, red-hot mass to graceful, translucent crystal that glittered and shone with its own precious light. Ready, he thought with bitter cynicism, to provide more raw material for the engravers to despoil.

Joe thrust his shoulders through the double doors, barely acknowledging his father as they passed. His mind was circling inside his head, emotions battering at his brain, and there was only one way he knew to relieve the intolerable pressure of mental and physical frustration. And only one woman capable of giving him, at that moment, what he needed so badly.

Maggie Haden. The strumpet who had tried to trap him. The hussy who represented a different kind of danger – the dangers of marriage, extra mouths to feed, the drudgery of keeping a home when what was good pay for a single man became poverty for a family. Easy enough to see why Maggie wanted it, when you thought what her own home was like, but there was no appeal in basement living for Joe, not with her, not with any woman.

Since that evening when she had wound her legs tightly about him and refused to let him go, Joe had avoided Maggie and her friends. The very thought of her had brought him a disgust that was as much aimed at his own behaviour as at hers. They'd had good times together after all; she'd given him a lot of warmth during the year they'd been together and it was hard to throw her over just like that, without so much as a goodbye or a word of thanks. That was one reason why he'd avoided her; the shame that he felt when he remembered her had been too uncomfortable and he'd suspected that, faced once again with her ripe voluptuousness, he would have succumbed once more and this time without hope of escape.

But now, after seeing Christina with the Frenchman, he felt a fury and a jealousy, a surge of heat that was too compelling to ignore. He directed his steps towards Amblecote.

'Mag? Mag Haden? She don't live here no more.'

Joe stared, baffled, at the girl who leaned against the broken doorway.

'What do you mean – don't live here? They moved?'

Annie shook her head. Her eyes gleamed. She knew Joe well, although to him she was just one of the faceless wenches who surrounded Maggie, colourless beside her flamboyance. Like the others, Annie had envied Maggie her lover, seeing him as someone who stood out amongst the other men, a character larger than life in the dreary backstreets of the industrial villages. She had even tried, once or twice, to attract his attention. But he had only had eyes then for Maggie, and his obvious discomfort now pleased her, easing her resentment. She lifted her chin, taunting him.

'I'd hev thought you'd know about Maggie,' she said provocatively. 'Bein' as you were so close an' all.'

'Never mind that,' Joe growled. 'Tell me where she is.'

'Why d'you want to know?'

Joe controlled himself with some difficulty. It had cost him some effort to come looking for Maggie here; he had never done such a thing before – never had to – and his pride suffered at crawling after a woman he'd done with months ago. The last thing he needed was the knowing pertness of this brassy piece.

'Never you mind why I want to know. Just tell me where she've gone.'

Annie put her head on one side, considering. She had heard from Maggie about what had happened, and had sympathised with her friend. After all, what had Joe to complain about? What Maggie had done was nothing out of the ordinary. Plenty of girls were driven to do the same when their men were slow in coming to the point. A girl had to look after herself; marriage might be swapping one kind of poverty for another, but at least you were making some kind of provision for your old age, having children who might give a few pennies to keep you when you were past work. And a wench couldn't afford to wait too long before starting, not with the way children died young – you might have to go through the long process of pregnancy and child-bearing five or six times before raising a healthy brat.

No, Joe Compson had got away altogether too lightly, in Annie's opinion. He'd had his fun for a year or more with Maggie, and it was time he faced up to a man's responsibilities. But if he regretted his hastiness now, and wanted Maggie back – well, it shouldn't be made too easy for him.

'I dunno,' she said slowly, as if weighing all the possibilities. 'I dunno as I ought to tell thee where Maggie

236

bist. How do I know she wants you goin' round there after her? She might not thank me for it.'

'That's between me and her.'

'No, it bin't. It's me as is her mate. Seems to me you ent bin round for a while, Joe Compson. Seems to me Maggie's better off without thee.'

Joe took a step forward. 'Now look here –'

'Don't thee touch me, Joe Compson,' Annie warned him. She tilted her head back, regarding him with saucy eyes. 'Not that way, anyway,' she added softly. 'Some other way, maybe . . . Leave Maggie alone, Joe, why don't you? She's all right now. It ent fair to go upsettin' her again – and it won't do you no good. Why not forget about her? Mebbe I could help . . .' She moved closer to him, turning her shoulders suggestively, looking up and pouting her red mouth. 'Maggie's not the only girl in Amblecote,' she murmured and laid a dirty hand on Joe's arm.

Joe looked down at her with distaste. 'Tell me where she is,' he repeated in a low, angry voice, and he removed her hand and moved away.

Annie's mouth hardened. She stepped back and tossed her head.

'All right, Joe Compson.' Annie looked up at him venomously. 'I'll tell thee – and much good may it do thee! Her've gone over to Stourbridge, that's where – to Church Row, if you must know. You can look for her there if you like, but you won't be welcome, that I can tell thee for nothing.'

'Church Row?' Joe stared. 'That's good housen there. Do you mean to say her father's got a better job?'

'Who said she was living with her father, or her mother either?' She tossed her head again, relishing the moment. 'Maggie hev got her own place now, and no need to work either. Oh yes, she's a fine lady now all right, near as fine as your precious Miss Christina.' Her lip curled and she surveyed Joe with patronising disdain. 'You've left it too late, Joe Compson. Maggie's found herself another friend – one who'll keep her as she ought to be kept and give her a bed instead of a cold rough hillside. You can go and see her if you like – but you'll be wastin' your time. I don't suppose she'll even let you in over the doorstep. And good riddance to you, too!'

Joe stared at her. A sick feeling welled up in his throat as he listened to her words. He never doubted that they were true – Annie wouldn't have the imagination to tell lies like that. But Maggie, with another man – a man well enough off to set her up in a room of her own in Church Row?

'Who is it?' he asked thickly, reluctant to admit to this hussy that he still needed to know, that Maggie was still important to him. 'Who's this friend you talk of so light? Can't be anyone much, if Church Row's all he can afford!'

'Can't he, then?' The small eyes tormented him with their knowledge. 'Well, mebbe you'd better go there after all and see for yourself. Mebbe it'd be a good idea at that – you can carry the tale to your Miss Henzel then. She'd be interested too, I've no doubt.'

'Miss Henzel? Miss *Christina* Henzel?' Joe felt baffled rage rise in him, thundering in his brain, surging in his stomach. 'What in God's name does *she* hev to do with this? Stop your games, Annie, and tell me – or I swear I'll strangle it out of you, every last word.'

Annie eyed him and decided to do as he said. His temper had been well known in the streets when he was younger – he'd almost killed another boy once, simply for stealing a conker that Joe had carried through a whole season. And in the prize fights that took place most Saturdays, Joe Compson was the acknowledged champion . . . 'All right,' she said hastily, before he could come any closer. 'All right, keep your wool on . . . It's Mr Henzel that's keepin' Maggie Haden. Mr Jeremy Henzel. He goes there to see her regular. And I wouldn't be around at the same time as him, not if I were you. He can

238

be a very nasty piece of work, that Mr Jeremy – and that's a piece of advice you don't deserve for the way you've treated Maggie, and it's the last thing I'm tellin' thee too. So if you don't mind lettin' me get into my own house . . .'

Joe moved aside. His face was blank, his eyes hooded and he looked like a man in a dream. Annie eyed him again, uncertainly, wondering if it were safe to pass him. But he made no sign as she slipped by, and when she was safely behind the broken door she peered out again, still half afraid that he meant to follow her.

But Joe was already walking away down the street, his mind whirling, unable fully to take in what he had just heard. Maggie, set up in a room and kept by Jeremy Henzel. *Jeremy Henzel?* How in God's name had that come about? How had those two ever met and come together? And why was it that wherever Joe himself turned, there seemed to be a Henzel blocking his path – taunting, flaunting, aggravating. Maddening him, as men maddened a bull or boys tormented a tethered cat. Treating him as sport and laughing to see his black, infuriated misery.

Henzels! They had it all. And he hated them.

Jeremy was another who took to Jean-Paul with rather less than enthusiasm.

'But *why* don't you like him?' Christina demanded furiously one evening when Jean-Paul was out of the room. 'What is there to dislike? He is well-mannered, charming, a delightful companion, intelligent, he knows about glass, he has any amount of interesting tales to tell, he –'

'Is, in short, a perfect paragon,' Jeremy finished for her. 'Perhaps that's why. I distrust perfection, particularly in a foreigner. And I've never said I disliked him, little cousin. I simply do not view him with such unthinking approval as you, that's all. Christina, you won't be too carried away by

239

this Frenchman, will you? I grant you, he's charming, but there may be little behind it – except for his skill with glass, which nobody could deny. It was a good idea, your bringing him here to teach your own men his methods, but don't allow it to go further than that. You could be in danger.'

'Danger?' She turned to look at him, emerald eyes wide. 'What kind of danger? What danger could Jean-Paul possibly present to me? He can't take the glasshouse away.'

'And is that the only danger you can imagine? No, he couldn't do that – but he might take something else.' Jeremy rose and came over to Christina. He laid his hands gently on her shoulders and looked down into her eyes. 'He could take your heart, Christina. Have you thought of that?'

Christina stared up at him, acutely aware of his hands moving softly on her neck.

'My – heart?' she said softly, her voice husky. 'Jeremy, what nonsense is this? I –'

'I think you know very well whether it is nonsense or not. As you say, we know each other, you and I. We grew up together; we understand each other's language. I am not at all sure whether you understand the language this Frenchman speaks.'

'My French is very good, I had the best tutor in the district. And his English is –'

'I am not speaking of French and English. As you very well know.' Jeremy took his hands from her shoulders and moved away. 'I thought we had an understanding, Christina. I saw us – in time perhaps, when you have proved what a fine glass manufacturer you are – coming together more closely, sealing the bond that has been growing so steadily between us. I saw us joining our families; becoming one. Partners in life; founding a family. A dynasty. The greatest dynasty glass has ever known.' He turned back to her, his eyes kindling. 'I did

240

not think I needed to say these things to you, Christina. Perhaps I was wrong.'

Christina felt as if something had caught in her throat, making it impossible for her to speak. She stared at Jeremy, shaking her head slightly. Then she whirled and walked quickly away from him, reaching the end of the room in a few rapid steps, while her face burned and her breath came with uncomfortable speed.

'I didn't know,' she said in a trembling voice. 'I never thought –'

'And you know that isn't true,' he said quietly, his voice persuasive. 'You've always known.'

Christina was silent. Her own honesty would not allow her to deny it. The thought of marriage to Jeremy had crossed her mind more than once. At her father's funeral. At the reading of his will. And again, since then; more than once . . . But never seriously, she wanted to cry. Never as more than a passing thought. And now that Jean-Paul is here . . .

And at that moment, as if answering a call, the door opened and Jean-Paul came in.

'Christina,' he said, coming forward with both hands outstretched. 'And Jeremy too. The three of us together; now we can have what you English do so well, a family evening, *non*? For here are Adela and Harry too, and Adela has been telling me about a new song she has learned – a French song, she says, in my honour!' He gave Christina a conspiratorial smile. 'We will sing this with Adela, *non*? And then she will go to bed happily, and you and I can have a serious talk, as we did the other evening.' He bowed at Jeremy and lifted his brows in provocative challenge. 'That is unless your cousin wishes to stay with us, in which case we can easily postpone it until another time?'

Jeremy looked him up and down. 'I wouldn't dream of asking you to inconvenience yourselves on my account,' he said coldly. 'In any case, I have just been telling

Christina, I must go soon, I have matters to discuss with my father. I'll stay just long enough to hear Adela's new song – she has an exceptionally sweet voice, I've always thought – and then I'll take my leave. And thank you, Christina my dear, for a very good dinner, although one has come almost to take such things for granted in this house.' He stood for a moment between her and Jean-Paul, looking gravely down into her face. 'Remember what I've said,' he said in a low voice. 'You may well lose more than you bargain for.'

'How comfortable it is here,' Jean-Paul remarked. He stretched his long legs out towards the fire which Rose had just replenished, and smiled at Christina. 'I like your English drawing rooms. So warm; so sheltered. The carpets, the thick velvet curtains, all combine to make a fortress of the most sumptuous kind. One cannot imagine any malign influence forcing its way into this impregnable citadel.'

Christina, curled up in the big armchair that her father had always used, watched him, allowing herself the luxury of resting her eyes on his face as he gazed into the fire. The flames gave the ivory pallor of his cheeks a sheen of soft gold, lit sparks in his silver eyes, but when she tried to read his expression the shifting of light and shadow defeated her.

'Where did you learn such good English?' she asked idly. 'You've never been here before, have you?'

He turned his head and smiled at her again. 'No, never. You think it is good? I must thank my tutor when I go back to France. And my father, who has always spoken to me in English and insisted that I learn it from an early age. He had been here – yes, visiting your own family, many years ago. And I think he has always been fond of the English.'

Christina barely heard his last words. A cold hand seemed to grip her heart as she repeated, 'Go back to France?'

242

'But of course I shall go back. You did not invite me to spend the rest of my life here!'

'No – no, I didn't. But now that you are here –'

'I must carry out the task I came to do, and then return.' He was watching her gravely. 'You know this, Christina.'

'Yes, of course.' But she didn't know it – didn't want to know it. She wanted him to say something else, something quite, quite different.

'Our lives are not, alas, always left in our own hands to live as we think best,' he said carefully.

'But they ought to be!' The passion in her voice startled her, ringing through the room as if someone had struck a bell. She gasped a little, then went on more quietly, 'They ought to be, Jean-Paul. They're *our* lives. Nobody else's. We ought to be able to do as we please with them, not be hedged around with restrictions and conventions. It maddens me! Why should we be bound by idiotic rules that have nothing to do with the real things of life – with being kind to people, or making a success of ourselves? Why should women have to sit at home, playing with teacups and gossiping, when they could be doing real work, useful work? And it's only women like me, you know. The working-class women – they're expected to be strong, to haul bricks and make nails and chains, to work in factories for twelve hours a day and barely have enough to eat at the end of it. Why? Are we a different species? Is a girl like Adela really less strong than the poor scullery maid who slaves over the dishes in our own kitchens? I think Adela is probably stronger, yet no one would ever expect her to soil her hands with blacking a grate, or lifting coal.'

'You would have made a fine revolutionary,' Jean-Paul said, smiling at her. 'Down with the aristocracy!'

'Well, I can understand why they revolted. What I don't understand is why our own peasants don't do the same.'

'Because you have a different kind of revolution going on at this very moment. An industrial revolution, and everyone is too busy to think about the other kind.'

'We do have the Chartists,' Christina said thoughtfully. 'Men wanting to vote – but what's a vote, compared with a sword? It all takes so long . . . And they'll never allow women to vote, even then.'

Jean-Paul shrugged himself deeper in his chair. 'Politics! Let's forget this thorny subject, Christina, and talk of something that is closer to both our hearts – glass. That wonderful, shimmering substance that has brought us together, that shines even now wherever we look in this room . . . That piece, for example, on the mantelpiece, it is magnificent. A chalice, is it not?'

'The Compson Chalice.' Christina rose and lifted down the heavy goblet, handing it to Jean-Paul. 'We call it that because Joe Compson made it – the man you met the other day in the cone. The finest glassblower in the district. This is the first piece of rock crystal made with our new mixture, and Joe designed it himself. It's beautiful, isn't it.'

Jean-Paul turned the chalice this way and that, examining it closely. The smooth glass gleamed under the lamplight, reflecting the room in its gracefully curved sides like a witch's ball. Stars of split, coloured light flashed from its edges and sparkled in its twisted stem; the sudden leaping flames of the fire leapt in miniature within its mysterious depths.

'Beautiful indeed. He is truly a fine craftsman, your Joe Compson. But why have you not had it engraved? With some family symbol, perhaps? It is intended to be a symbol, is it not?'

'Yes. A symbol of Henzel's new beginning.' Christina hesitated. 'But – well, you know how he is about engraving. You heard him the other day. He believes shape is all that matters, and that cutting the glass spoils it.'

'I see. To me, that is a pity. I could do something very

fine with this piece . . .' He handed the great goblet back and Christina replaced it carefully on the mantelpiece. 'You love glass very much, Christina, don't you.'

'Yes, I do. Very much.' She hesitated, then sat down beside him on the sofa. 'It's the only thing that really matters to me. I love the look of it – the gleam and the shine. I love the transparency of plain glass and the beautiful colours – the deep blue that you get from adding cobalt, the amethyst from manganese, the glowing ruby from gold chloride. And it's such a paradox – so strong that only a diamond will cut it, so fragile that the pure note of a human voice will shatter it. You have only to pour boiling water into a glass, or touch it against a wall, and it will break; yet it can be kept safe for hundreds of years, and never look any older.' She paused, recollecting herself, and gave Jean-Paul a shy glance. 'I'm sorry. You must think me a foolish woman. But to me, glass is the most wonderful substance in the world.'

'And to me also,' he said softly. 'You and I think alike on this, Christina – as I suspect we do on many things.' He paused and then added, 'I wonder what fortune destines us to meet in a certain time, a certain place. Do you believe, Christina, that there is a God above us, who holds our fortunes in his hands like the reins of a horse, or like the strings of a marionette? So that we dance to his tune, even when we think we are dancing to our own?'

Christina was startled. 'I don't know – I've never thought. I go to church every Sunday – we always have done, the whole family. And I say my prayers every night. But apart from that –'

'Apart from that, you are too busy thinking about glass. And I am sure you believe you control your own destiny. After all, isn't that just what you were talking about just now? The right to control one's own destiny?'

'Yes.' Christina was bemused. Jean-Paul was making her think about things she had never considered before. But it was exciting, stimulating. 'Yes, I do think we should

245

have that right. So I suppose I can't believe in a God who pulls strings. But aren't we told that certain things are ordained? And if that's so, then surely –'

'Well?' He was watching her, his thin face curved with amusement. 'Which do you want to believe, Christina?'

There was a long pause.

'I want to believe in us,' she said at last in a low voice. 'You and me. Here. Together. Alone.' She turned to face him and her face was pale, her voice throbbing with intensity. 'I've never known anyone like you, Jean-Paul. I've never felt like this before. I need to know that you feel it as well. I want to believe that you do. I *do* believe that you do . . . don't you?'

The tiny uncertainty in her voice on the last, upward question made him smile a little, but his face was serious as he returned her look, his eyes as soft as doves' wings in the glimmering light. Leaning forward a little, he took her hands in his, the long, sensitive fingers caressing hers with a tenderness that made her ache with longing. She felt the tingling of his touch spread upwards through her own fingers, an almost unbearable ache in her palms, a lingering weakness in her wrists and arms, and so through her whole body; her breast, her stomach, her loins. Her lips softened and parted, and she swayed towards him.

'You want me to say all those things back to you, Christina,' he said quietly, his voice deep and sensuous in the quiet room. 'You want me to tell you that there has never been another woman for me, never one like you. That I too am experiencing sensations which are new to me, new and delightful and perhaps a little frightening. That I feel we have known each other all our lives – that everything that has ever happened to me has been bringing me, inevitably, a little nearer to the moment when I must meet you and my real life begin.' He smiled a little. 'The string-puller again, in the sky over our heads! Those are the things you want me to say, aren't they, Christina, the words you want to hear from my lips.'

'Yes,' she whispered.

'And if you knew how I long to say them,' he murmured. He lifted her hands towards his lips and kissed each fingertip, slowly, lingeringly, until Christina felt she could bear the cool touch of his mouth no longer. He turned her hands over and laid a kiss in each palm. 'How I long, long to say them,' he said again, and replaced her hands in her lap. 'But it cannot be, Christina. It is something that must not happen. The string-puller has tangled up his cords, Christina, or perhaps he is playing a joke on us, a joke that only he can find amusing. I can never say those things to you.'

'I don't understand . . .' Christina looked up at him in bewilderment. 'Jean-Paul, what do you mean?' she asked with a note of desperation in her voice. 'It doesn't make sense.'

'Oh, it is easy enough to understand,' he said with a touch of bitterness. 'When you consider, Christina, as you clearly have never done, my own age and the conventions of my own country – yes, I live by rules too, and it is too late for me to take control of my destiny, too late for me to make my decisions . . . I am not free to say those things to you, Christina. I have never been free since I was a small boy, barely out of the nursery. You see, my country is even more bound by custom than yours, and one of our customs is that of betrothal, at an early age; to ensure a suitable marriage. So I have never been free to choose a wife – only a mistress. And I cannot ask you, Christina, to be either.'

Christina stared at him. The room swayed around her, and when it steadied again, she opened her eyes to find him gazing at her with such sorrow in his face that the tears sprang to her eyes.

'You mean . . . you're married?'

'Not married. Betrothed. The wedding is due to take place next year.'

Christina grasped at the last shreds of her composure and dragged them around her like a tattered cloak.

'And you cannot break this betrothal?'

247

'It is not possible. Oh –' he shrugged '– it has happened, on occasion. But only on pain of being discredited, disinherited. One can never go back after such a thing. It brings shame to the whole family.'

Christina nodded; her calmness hid a creeping, gnawing agony that she knew was only a beginning. 'So you will marry her, this –'

'Marie-Pierre. Yes, it is all arranged.'

'And go back to France, and live with her, and never see me again.' She raised her face to his, ravaged with pain and tight with the effort of hiding it. 'Even though you know – we both know –' Her voice trembled and broke.

Jean-Paul took her in his arms and she pressed herself against him, clinging, her hands moving convulsively on his back as she sobbed. He moved his face against her hair, turned slightly to lay his lips against her neck, and as she felt the soft touch she twisted in his arms seeking his mouth with her own, reaching hungrily for the kisses that were forbidden. With a groan, he held her to him, his hands cupping her face, sweeping back the tumbling hair, lifting her from the soft cushions. He murmured something she couldn't catch, something in his own language that sounded liquid and warm, as if it were heated brandy running like fire into her throat. He ran his long hands down her body, his whispers soothing her feverish desire, calming the raging tumult that was consuming her. She felt his touch briefly on her breasts, soft as a butterfly's wing on the smooth, rounded flesh.

'Jean-Paul,' she whispered, her body twisting under his, frantic with a desire that was rampant in her now, a desire that had veered for so long between two men she felt barred to her, only now released by this stranger who seemed to have been a part of her since life began. 'Jean-Paul, I love you. I've always loved you. Tell me I belong to you, tell me you love me too . . . Jean-Paul, my dear, dear love!'

Slowly, Jean-Paul eased himself away from her. He planted one last, tender kiss upon her soft lips, and then raised himself and looked down at her. His eyes were opaque, like a winter's sea, and Christina looked up at him and was afraid.

'I have to apologise to you,' he said, his voice unbearably, ridiculously formal. 'This should never have happened.'

'Apologise? For the most wonderful thing that's ever happened to me in my whole life?' Christina sat up, trembling. 'How can you apologise for love? For loving me? Because you do love me, Jean-Paul, I know it.' Her voice was triumphant, victorious and she gazed proudly at him, her face suffused with desire and the fulfilment that even a kiss can bring in the early stages of love.

'I know it,' he admitted, 'but it should still never have happened. I must go back, Christina. I must return to France, to my home. And I must marry Marie.' He lifted one hand and ran it gently, tenderly, down Christina's cheek, following the course of the tear that had already escaped her unbelieving eye. 'God must be having a fine laugh tonight,' he murmured. 'And the joke will continue for the rest of our lives. I will never stop loving you, Christina.'

'Nor I you,' she exclaimed passionately. 'And I won't give you up either! I won't! You belong to me, Jean-Paul, and I belong to you.' She pressed herself against him again, pulling him close, reaching up for the lips that had brought her such piercing sweetness. 'I'll make you mine,' she muttered fiercely. 'I'll do anything, give up anything. You matter more to me than anything else in the world – yes, even more than Henzel's – and I won't let you go to another woman. I'll die before I see you marry her!'

Chapter Twelve

'I simply don't understand you these days, Christina. I don't understand you at all.'

Christina gazed helplessly at her aunt and shook her head. For once, she sympathised with her aunt's complaining. Indeed, she scarcely understood herself, never knew when her mood might abruptly change from sunny good temper to angry tears, from brooding silence to bright, chattering gaiety. She only knew that it was all tightly bound up with the sensations in her body: the exhilaration that made her want to run, to skip, to dance, to fly from a window like a bird, to swim like a fish in the stream; the sudden deep melancholy that gripped her like a vice, turning the dark winter days to black night, and life to an endless hell. And she knew that this was directly due to Jean-Paul.

I am in love, she would think when she woke to a bright, cold morning, and she would hug herself with the knowledge, convinced that everything would come right, that it must – you couldn't feel like this and not have all your dreams come true.

Slowly, languorously, she would stretch herself out in bed, revelling in the freedom of her body in the loose nightgown, laying her palm on the flatness of her stomach, touching the curve of her hip-bones, the ribs that formed a cage around the heart she had given to Jean-Paul. Her hands moved up, cupping the breasts that swelled out, full and round, from her slenderness, and she felt the hardening of her nipples as she moved her fingertips over them. Jean-Paul had touched her there, and she had felt the same instinctive tightening, the same electric tingling, whenever she remembered it.

I love him, she would think. And he loves me. We must be together. There is no possible alternative, for either of us. This girl in France – this Marie – she will have to give him up. He's mine. And once she knows that, she won't want to keep him. She can't possibly love him as I do. No one could. She probably doesn't love him at all. The marriage was arranged when they were both children. It's a nonsense. And Jean-Paul knows it as well as I do. He loves *me*.

At such times, gazing from her window at the sun-dappled trees and grass, Christina would feel her spirits lift, and she would twirl about the room, evading Ruth who was waiting to dress her, laughing with pure excitement and unshakeably certain that the world was hers, a plaything created especially for her, a jewel for her delight.

And then, without warning, would come the other times; when the sky was heavy, pressing down upon the town, ominous with doom. Christina, her hair damp and dulled by cold, sooty drizzle, her eyebrows frosted with sleet, would feel a chill that went through her warm clothes as though she were naked. The mean wind sliced through to her bones and she would stare miserably at the grim silhouettes of the factory chimneys, the long roofs that seemed to increase almost daily, and even her own towering glass-cones, and know that there was no hope.

No hope for her and Jean-Paul, no hope for a life together. He would leave her. He would go back to France, as he had said he must, and marry his short, fat Marie. And Christina would never see him again. She would go through the rest of her life alone, carrying within her a heart that had never been tested, a love that would wither and harden like an old nut until it was like a stone in her unused breast.

On those days, she would creep about the house like a shadow, all her brightness dimmed, all her assertive self-will chastened, like a lively dog beaten for a sin it doesn't even understand. Was it a sin to love Jean-Paul when he was already betrothed, a sin to want him, to long for him, to toss and turn at night, unable to sleep for the yearning that tore at her body and wrenched at her heart? A sin so great that she must bear such punishment, such torment, for the rest of her life.

'You're not listening to me, Christina!'

Her aunt's voice was sharp and querulous. Christina brought her attention back guiltily.

'I'm sorry, aunt. I was thinking . . .'

'Day-dreaming, I should have said. And I can guess about whom.'

'I don't know what you mean,' Christina muttered, feeling her cheeks redden, and her aunt sniffed.

'I think you do! What I can't believe is that you don't see what a spectacle you are making of yourself.'

'Spectacle? How?'

Susan Henzel's mouth tightened. 'I thought I had brought you up to have at least that much decorum,' she said coldly. 'But it seems that you have forgotten everything you have ever been taught. Setting your cap at a man like that – and so flagrantly. Why, everyone must be laughing at you. All Wordsley – the whole of Stourbridge – can see what's happening. I can hardly bear to go out for the shame of it, a young woman like you, unmarried, bringing a strange Frenchman to stay in your own house, pursuing him wherever he goes, clinging to him, gazing at him all the while with eyes that reveal your every thought . . . I never thought to call you shameless, Christina, but I fear that is what I must call you now. And he already betrothed! I cannot bring myself to use the words that best describe your conduct, and there's the truth of it!'

Christina was silent, gazing at her aunt.

'That's all a story,' she said at last, using their childhood term for fabrication. 'You don't like Jean-Paul, you never did. You were determined to dislike him, before he even

253

came. And now, because you can see I'm happy, you're trying to spoil it all, to make it seem shabby and mean –'

Susan broke in. 'Happy? *Are* you happy, Christina? I wonder! Oh, sometimes you are gay enough, laughing and chattering, singing about the house. But at other times, why, I don't recognise you, creeping about the walls like a ghost, unable to smile or even speak above a whisper. What is happening to you, Christina? What makes you so wretched? And how can you possibly call it *happiness*?'

Christina moved restlessly. She wanted to escape from this interview, but knew that her aunt was right. And perhaps – who knew – Susan might even be able to help in some way? She did seem genuinely concerned, and Christina knew that however much they might differ, there was a real affection behind their bickering.

'Perhaps you're right,' she said slowly. 'Perhaps it's not happiness. But it could be, Aunt Susan! If only – if only Jean-Paul were not betrothed, if only he could be free to marry me, oh, I could be so happy then, I know I could. But now, all I know is, I feel alive for the first time. As if I'd been asleep all these years and now with a kiss I've been woken, just like in the story. The Sleeping Beauty, woken from a hundred years' sleep by a handsome prince!' And she smiled.

But her aunt was not concerning herself with sentiment or fairy-tales. She was gazing at Christina with an expression of outraged horror.

'A kiss? You mean you've allowed this – this foreigner – to *kiss* you?' Momentarily, she closed her eyes. 'And what else, pray? What other liberties have you allowed him to take with your person?'

Christina snapped back from her dreamy trance and flung her aunt a look of pure dislike.

'Liberties! How can anything be a liberty, when you're in love? Yes, aunt, I *have* allowed Jean-Paul to kiss me. And I've kissed him. And more than that, I am not going to tell you.'

254

Susan drew herself up, her back as straight and stiff as a gathering-iron. Her mouth was folded into a tight, thin line and her eyes were cold and hard as stones.

'I see there is no purpose in prolonging this conversation,' she said icily. 'Indeed, I am sorry that I ever began it. Clearly, you have gone beyond redemption, Christina, and I can only beg you not to bring any more shame than you have to on this house. Try to remember your poor mother, and if that fails, think of your father. Even *he* would not have countenanced this!'

Jean-Paul was standing at the entrance to the glasshouse when Christina went down there, still smarting and indignant from the interview with her aunt. As usual, when she saw him, her heart leapt and she stopped, simply to feast her eyes on him; on his tall, slender elegance, his cool beauty, the rich shine of his nut-brown curls, the silver glint of his eyes. Christina wanted to run to him, to throw herself into his arms, tell him yet again that she loved him . . . But he was not alone. Jeremy was with him. And she went forward slowly, warily.

The two men made a striking pair. Jeremy was an inch shorter than Jean-Paul, his hair gleaming gold in the winter sunlight that had managed to filter through the smoky cloud. His figure was as slim, with a greater breadth in the shoulders, so that the general effect was of a bigger man. The extra inches lost him a little of Jean-Paul's easy grace, but Christina was aware none the less of his handsome appeal. An appeal which had once, she thought now, had the power to twist her stomach, but was now nothing more than an attractive charm; although there was still, when she looked at those blue eyes, a hint of danger which she quickly, impatiently, brushed aside.

'Ah, Christina, my sweet,' Jeremy greeted her. 'Jean-Paul has just been telling me about his new designs. We were about to go into your cutting shops so that I could see for myself . . . with your permission, of course.'

Christina gave him a doubtful glance. She was conscious of the hostility between the two men, a hostility that had been present since their first meeting. Or even earlier, she thought; Jeremy, like Aunt Susan, had been against the Frenchman's visit from the moment she had first announced it. But Jeremy had good reason for his antagonism. He wanted Christina to marry him. And he was sensitive enough to know that Jean-Paul was a distinct threat to his plans.

Whatever Jeremy's reasons for coming to see Jean-Paul's workshops didn't matter now, for the new designs would be on show soon, on sale. Even now, the first wineglasses to be decorated by Jean-Paul's team of cutters were receiving their final polish before being packed and sent to the great shops in London where they would be sold. There was no secret about them; no reason why Jeremy should not see the process being carried out. And it would serve to remind him once again how capable Christina was of running her business.

'My permission?' she said lightly. 'Since when have you asked my permission to go in and out of my glasshouse, cousin? And since the cutting-shops are more Jean-Paul's than mine, perhaps it is *his* permission you should be asking, rather.'

Jeremy bowed slightly, a tight smile of annoyance on his face, and turned to the Frenchman. Jean-Paul shrugged.

'But of course. I shall be delighted to show you around.'

Together, the three of them went into the long building that had originally been a warehouse. It had been extended and new skylights opened in the roof, so that it was now long and spacious. Under each skylight was a lathe, with its wheel for grinding and polishing, and these were driven by the new steam-engine which had been installed at the far end of the building. The noise of the wheels was piercing and monotonous, while

256

the steady thumping of the steam-engine provided a continuous undercurrent of heavy thuds. Christina never came out of the cutting-shop without a headache.

Slowly, they moved along the line of men, the half-dozen Frenchmen Jean-Paul had brought from France and the local cutters who had joined Christina. Each had his wheel set up in front of him. The glasses were set beside them on benches, each one already marked with the pattern to be cut, the mixture of red lead and turpentine used to make the marks being removed in the cutting process.

'The first man roughs in the pattern with this iron wheel, fed with wet sand from the hopper above,' Jean-Paul explained to Jeremy, who nodded impatiently as if he already knew this – as he certainly did, Christina thought with a smile, only he had never seen it operating in such a modern factory as this. 'Then the glass goes on to the next man, who smooths the cut with his stone wheel and water, and then the dullness must be polished out of them and a sparkle given by these wheels – you see, some lined with wood, others with brushes or felt and fed with these very fine abrasives.'

'Putty powder, pumice or rottenstone,' Jeremy said, as if to prove his own knowledge. 'Yes, Jean-Paul, very interesting. The way in which we've done it for some time, in fact.'

Jean-Paul inclined his head. 'So I understand. But each man working alone, in his own small shed, *non*? Not so organised as this, and with a greater risk of loss or damage.'

'Oh yes,' Jeremy said in a bored tone, 'Christina has explained to me more than once how much more efficient this will be.'

They moved along the row, watching the wheels that ground continuously round in front of the men's bent heads. The work was harder than that of glassmaking itself, Christina thought, seeing how the cutters leaned

257

forward all the time, their hands plunged into water and grasping the glass tightly to hold it against the wheel. There were boys too, whose task it was to supply the polishers with a continuous stream of putty powder, their heads bent over the trough so that they were breathing the fine powder into their lungs all the time, and it covered their hands in a film of dust. She wondered uneasily if it were true that glasscutters suffered from the conditions of their labour; there was the disease they called 'dropped hands', a contraction and paralysis of the muscles, which could only be cured by leaving the trade, and there were inflammations of the lungs too, and a history of early deaths amongst the men who did this work. But there was little that could be done about it. There was a demand for cut glass, especially now that it could be made with the glitter and sparkle that a high degree of lead imparted to it. And the men needed the work. If it were taken from them, they would starve and so die even earlier, and their families with them.

'So far,' Jeremy observed, 'we have seen nothing that could not be seen in any backyard. Do you really believe it was worth the expense, Christina?'

Christina opened her mouth to answer indignantly, but Jean-Paul forestalled her. He smiled, quite unperturbed by Jeremy's sarcasm.

'Indeed it is. Why change methods that have been proved by time? Already, Christina has saved money through the greater efficiency you yourself have mentioned. And now, please come through here. This is my pride and joy. Here is where the engravers work.'

They followed him through a door into a second part of the old warehouse, again, much altered, with more natural light and space. Here, the men were working with small copper wheels mounted on lathes which they operated by foot treadles. They were holding the glasses under the wheels, which were again smeared with abrasive – in this case, Jean-Paul explained, emery powder mixed with oil. The articles being engraved here were highly decorated, the engraver able to work in a more flowing and artistic fashion than the cutter with his designs already marked out for him. Jean-Paul paused beside a man who was engraving a goblet with an exquisite portrait which lay before him on paper for him to copy; he was adding in every tiny curl, every nuance of the lady's expression. The next man was engraving the likeness of a beautiful house, set back behind sweeping lawns; the third a glorious castle with turrets and ramparts.

Jeremy fell silent. No other glasshouse in Stourbridge, he knew, was producing work of this quality. Christina's decision to bring over a French decorator to teach his art to Henzel's men needed no further vindication.

'So,' said Jean-Paul when they were once more outside, away from the high-pitched scream of the wheels, the tooth-roughening grind of metal on glass. 'Do you not think that Christina and I should be proud of our new workshops?'

Our new shops. 'Indeed you should,' Jeremy answered politely. 'And the men's work seems to be of the highest artistic quality. You have carried out an excellent job.' He waited for a moment, then added casually, 'No doubt we'll be saying goodbye to you soon, now that your task is over.' He watched the quick reactions in both their faces; the swift betraying glance at each other, the dismay in Christina's green eyes, the regret in Jean-Paul's, immediately masked.

'Eventually I must go back, it is certain,' the Frenchman agreed in a tone as casual as Jeremy's own. 'But not yet, I think. We still have much to discuss, your beautiful cousin and I. New ideas, fresh designs. And –' he shuddered a little comically '– I have no desire to undertake that very unpleasant journey a moment sooner than I am compelled. *Mal de mer* is not my favourite sensation!'

Christina laughed, relief in her voice, and took his arm. 'You mustn't go yet, anyway,' she declared. 'Why, you've done nothing but work since you arrived! I want you to see more of England than this. Green fields, woods, springtime in the countryside, away from the smoke and noise of the towns. And summer – summer on the Cotswold hills, you must see that. And autumn, which is so beautiful in the forests, you have to see –'

'Spring, summer, autumn!' Jeremy broke in rudely. 'Why not invite him to live here, so that he need never miss a moment?' As soon as the clumsy words were out, he regretted them. He bit his lip, watching the deep colour flood into Christina's cheeks, the sudden tightening of Jean-Paul's jaw as he looked at her. Susan was right, he thought, and so were his father and Uncle Reuben. The Frenchman represented danger to their plans. He must be got rid of as soon as possible. But how did you persuade a man to return to his home when he was so obviously enjoying his visit here?

'There has to be a way,' Reuben had said thoughtfully when Jeremy discussed the matter with him and his father. 'Christina grows fond of him, you say? That is not good.'

Fond was an understatement, Jeremy thought, but he dared not tell them the extent of his own failure. So much for patience, he thought bitterly, of moving slowly, carefully, taking pains not to frighten her. While he had been doing that, this Frenchman had blown in like a leaf from the storm and captured the girl's heart; without, apparently, lifting a finger to do so. With just one look from those pale grey eyes, one gesture of those long, beckoning fingers, he had brought her to his feet. And there she seemed likely to stay.

'Oh, I don't imagine there's much to fear there,' he said with a nonchalance he did not feel. 'After all, the man's betrothed and I understand they take these things very seriously in France. There's money involved – property, dowries and so on. It would be difficult for him to break such an agreement, and probably lead to his being cast out from the family. He won't risk that. And I doubt if he would have the temerity to take advantage of Christina's foolishness – for that's all it is, I assure you. Just a rebellion against what she knows is the only sensible course for her to take – marriage with me. You know what she is – wilful to the last. She'll change quickly enough once we've tied the knot.'

'I wish I could share your confidence,' Samuel said pettishly. 'Christina has always seemed a deal too headstrong for my taste, and I don't see any improvement since Joshua died. Your mother has never liked her.'

'That's because she's never understood her. Christina has a spirit of her own – yes, she's wilful, but once she gives her heart she'll do anything to please. Look how she adored Joshua.' Jeremy paused for a moment, remembering with some discomfort the equally adoring glances Christina had directed at Jean-Paul. 'This is just a passing infatuation,' he went on, hoping vaguely that by convincing his father and uncle he might also convince himself. 'The best thing I can do is wait for it to blow over. Once it has, I'll step in and make sure of her. A quick wedding, I think, before she has time to fall in love with some other unsuitable rogue. And once we're married, I shall tame her at my leisure.' His eyes gleamed. 'I shall enjoy that . . .'

His father shot him a doubtful glance, while Reuben pursed his lips.

'I hope you're right. It still seems to me that the sooner we get this Frenchman back to France, the better. Betrothals may be taken very seriously, but they have been known to be broken, and how much would his loss be when there is a flourishing glasshouse here ready to be handed over as a wedding present? As handsome a dowry as he's likely to receive from his fiancée, I have no doubt.'

'You're probably right,' Jeremy acknowledged with some dismay. 'I hadn't thought of that . . . All the same, I don't believe there's any real danger. Cousin Susan is on my side, anyway – she's as good as told me she wants to see Christina married to me and this whole ridiculous situation resolved. She'll let me know at once if there's any sign of a serious affection developing between Thietry and Christina.'

'I suppose we'll have to leave it at that, then,' Samuel said grumpily. 'Though the entire thing seems most unsatisfactory to me. Over a year since Joshua died, and still nothing settled.'

Reuben got up from his chair, fumbling around for the cane he carried everywhere.

'Now, I fear I must leave you. It grows late and I like to be in my bed before midnight. It's been a most interesting evening – most interesting. No, I'll see myself out – I ordered a cab to be ready at your door. Good night, Samuel. Good night, Jeremy.' He held Jeremy's hand for a few moments, looking at him with his pale lizard's eyes. 'Come in and see me sometime, my boy, when you're over at the Talbot. We'll have a little talk – I enjoy our little talks.'

February was little better than January; raw cold, with thick, sooty rain which fell in a steady icy downpour, mixed with wet snow that was grey before it even reached the slime of the roads. Nobody could go out and remain dryshod and, in the garden, even the brave snowdrops seemed reluctant to emerge from the chilly soil.

Christina summoned Joe to the house. If he would not speak to her in the cone, he could not refuse in her own library, where they had spent so many companionable hours. At the thought of those times, warm with a contentment that was yet spiced with an excitement she could not define, Christina felt a pang of nostalgia. They had been more precious than she knew, she thought with a sense of loss, and she could see no reason why they should end.

Joe came, sullenly, stiff in the Sunday suit he had worn at her father's funeral. She looked at him in bewilderment;

why had he not simply washed and come in his working clothes, as he had been used to do? She felt as if the uncomfortable clothes were yet another barrier between them, and suddenly she had a violent urge to tear them away, sweep aside all the barriers and shake Joe hard by the shoulders until his face lost that wooden expression and relaxed into – into anger, into amusement, *anything*. But she could herself only speak stiffly.

'Well, Joe. So you don't pretend not to know me entirely.'

'I don't know what you mean.'

'I think you do.' She sounded as wooden as he looked! There must be some way of easing this stilted conversation, of making her voice sound friendly, unaffected, once more. What had happened to them? 'I thought you were my friend,' she said a little desperately.

'Friendship between the likes of us?' He lifted his head then and pure scorn flashed from his dark eyes. 'That's impossible, Miss Christina, and you knows it as well as I do. Friendship's for gentry, and people like you, with plenty of money. Friendship needs time, and men like me don't have much time to play around with.'

She went over to him, laid her hand on the stiff material of his sleeve. 'Joe – what is it? Why are you angry with me?'

'Angry? It in't my place to be angry with you, Miss Christina.'

'But you are, all the same,' she said softly. 'You never come to see me now. You barely look at me in the glasshouse, and if I speak to you, you say no more than absolutely necessary. And I can *feel* your anger, Joe. Please – don't deny it. What have I done?'

He was silent for a moment, as if struggling to hold the words back. Then he gave up, almost visibly, and turned on her, his face dark with frustrated fury, knowing that even now he could not tell her the depths of his despair. His eyes flashed, his fists clenched, even his hair seemed

263

to bristle with the impotent rage that had been building up in him for months, and Christina stepped back, startled and afraid of the force she had apparently unleashed.

'All right, I'll tell you, though I don't think you should need tellin' at all. You should know well enough what I'm angry about. Bringing that Frenchie into the place, settin' him and his Frogs up above our own men – aye, an' payin' 'em better wages too! What kind of a carry-on is that? How d'you expect our blokes to feel, seein' all those new workshops set up for a clutter of foreigners? Seein' them tek home more pay in a day than some of our boys has in a week? An' all to spoil our good lead crystal, too, with their fancy pictures and patterns,' he finished bitterly.

'But Joe, I explained all this before we even started converting the warehouses. The Frenchmen are here to help us. I pay them more because at present they've a greater skill than our own cutters and engravers, and because they've come a long way from home – they wouldn't have come at all otherwise. When our men are as good, they'll earn more too.'

'Those who still have jobs. What about the other Frenchies – the ones who'll be coming over next?'

Christina stared at him. 'Others? I don't understand. No more are coming.'

Joe snorted. 'Miss Christina, we ent fools. Stands to reason, don't it. These Frenchies are better than our men – worth payin' more, too. So you'll be bringing more over, putting our boys out of work – throwin' 'em on the dung-heap, and after mekkin' 'em give up their own busi-nesses too. What way's that to treat blokes who've been loyal to Henzel's all their lives?' He slapped his cap impa-tiently against his thigh. 'I tell you, I don't have much time for cutting and engraving good glass, but if it's got to be done I'd rather it were done by a lad I've growed up with than one of them fancy boys from over the Channel, and that's the beginning and the end of it!'

'You're being ridiculous, Joe!' Christina snapped. 'All

this has nothing to do with jobs at all – it's all because of your own prejudice. Just because a man wears slightly different clothes and speaks another language, you're set against him from the start. It's ignorance, Joe, pure ignorance, and I want to hear no more of it.'

Joe glowered at her. 'Want to hear no more, do you? Well, Miss Christina, that's a pity. Because I want to say a powerful lot more, and I mean to, and I mean to make you listen too. All right, I'm only a glassmaker, but I'm a good glassmaker – one of t' best in the Black Country, and you might remember that when you're being so high and mighty about what you'll hear and what you won't hear.' He stepped a little closer, towering over her. 'You axed me to come here tonight, Miss Christina, and now I'm here you'll listen to what I hev to say. Them Frenchies hev got to go.'

'Have they indeed?' Christina lifted her chin and met his angry eyes, her own flashing green sparks of fury. 'And why? Because you say so? Just who do you think you are, Joe Compson? Let me remind you, *I* own this glasshouse and what happens there is my decision – not yours, however fine a glassmaker you are. Being able to blow a beautiful shape doesn't fit you to decide who shall be employed and who shan't.'

'Mebbe you don't think so,' he growled, 'but the men do. And when it comes down to it, they're the ones who run the glasshouse. Your father knew that. And you'd better learn it too, if you don't want trouble on your hands.'

'Trouble?' She looked at him with scorn. 'What kind of trouble?'

'Strikes,' he said succinctly. 'It's happened afore. It's happening now, in other trades. Miners, ironworkers, they're all beginning to realise what the glassmakers hev known all along. Work is power. It's the man who has the trade in his hands who can dictate what's to do with it. Your father knew that if a man wor on t' gaffers' blacklist, there weren't a manufacturer in the district would tek him on. No matter how good he wor.'

'But that's entirely different! These French workers have done nothing to offend. They're here to help the expansion of the whole factory. The more glass we can sell, the more work there is for everybody. And we have to produce what the public want – decorated glass. If our glass is better than anyone else's, we'll sell more, it's as simple as that.' Impatiently, she turned away, walked a few steps, then wheeled back to him. 'Joe, you're an intelligent man, you *must* be able to understand this. Why talk of strikes? We've never had anything like that at Henzel's.'

'Well, you're likely to get it now.' His firm mouth was set in an obstinate line. 'What's the use of expansion to us, when our jobs hev been taken by foreigners?'

'But they're not *going* to be taken from you!' Christina sighed and stepped forward again until she stood close to Joe. She looked up into his face, holding his brooding glance with her own clear green gaze.

'Joe. Listen to me. And believe me, please. Why should I lie to you, anyway? There would be no point. You would soon see the truth for yourself. I am not bringing any more Frenchmen over, either cutters or engravers. Not even –' she gave a sudden quick smile '– blowers. So you've no need to worry about that. Nobody has any need to worry about it. When Monsieur Thietry returns to France –' and she hoped Joe could not see the pain that thought brought her '– the French workers will go with him. They're *his* employees, not mine. And then I shall employ a few more cutters and engravers, to replace them, and Henzel's will continue as before. Under my control, employing only good local labour.'

The doubt was still there in his face, dark as a winter cloud. He searched her eyes and she kept her own fixed on his, willing him to trust her.

'I don't know as the men will believe it,' he said slowly.

'There's been too many changes lately. Your father dyin', and you tekkin' over . . . There's plenty as thinks a woman ent fit to run a glasshouse.'

'And are you one of them?'

He reacted to the challenge in her voice, a flash of emotion she couldn't quite recognise glinting in the dark, brooding eyes.

'I'm a man, same as the rest,' he said stiffly. 'But I think your pa had a hard task when he drew up that will. If it weren't you, who would it be . . ? Mebbe he didn't expect it to be so soon, mebbe he thought you'd be wed to a man who understood the business like he did . . . But it's happened this way, that's where it is, an' we just have to shift the best we can with it.'

'You think I can't cope,' Christina said flatly. 'You're like all the rest. You think I need a man to stand with me on this.' There was a sudden fire in her eyes and she moved again, standing close enough to touch him, close enough to smell the sharp male odour of him. 'Perhaps you're right, Joe,' she said with sudden intensity. 'Perhaps I do need a man – to stand with me on issues that the men may not understand. A man who can talk to them in their own language, tell them what I'm trying to do, help them to see that these changes are being made for their good as well as mine . . . You've done so much already: designed new shapes, blown the Chalice that is a symbol of our prosperity. Can't we go on like that – working together, talking, sharing?' Her hand was on his sleeve now, shaping itself to the thick, sinewy muscle beneath. 'I need you, Joe,' she said simply, and looked up at him with green eyes wide in appeal.

Joe stared down at her. His face was dour, unreadable, his dark eyes hooded. He seemed to be turning her words over in his mind. She waited, hardly daring to breathe, knowing that this was the moment of crisis for them all. And then, slowly, unbelievably, he shook his head and she felt her heart sink.

'You're asking me to stand with you against my own mates,' he said. 'It can't be done. I'm one of 'em, through and through. I can't play the black rat against them – not against men I've worked with all these years. Not even for you.'

'But I'm not asking you to do that!' Exasperation broke through, raising her voice. 'You wouldn't be betraying your friends, Joe.' With an effort, she lowered her voice again, striving to speak calmly. 'Listen to me. For months now, you've been doing more than a gaffer's work and I've been discussing all manner of problems with you. Doesn't that show what I think of you, how much trust I have in you?' She stopped, looking at him with intense green eyes. 'Mr Turner's health is almost too poor now for him to continue to work. I want to offer you his job. You're ready for it. I know you can do it. And you can still blow our finest pieces, and train others to follow in your footsteps. We'd be working together, you and I. Making a success of Henzel's. And all I'm asking now is that you should simply *explain* to them, make them see what I have in mind –'

'And they're expecting me to explain to *you*,' he cut in. 'But you're not listening. You don't want to listen. You're just blind, blind to everything but this Frenchie an' what he can do . . .' He was standing so close, she could feel the heat of his body. 'I'm telling you, Miss Christina, it's going to bring trouble – unless you get rid of 'em now, send 'em back where they belong, aye, and him along with them.'

Christina felt the anger surge through her at his obstinacy. 'They'll stay until I say it's time for them to go!' she retorted. 'I won't be bullied by my own workers, and you can tell them *that*!'

There was a long silence. She could hear her own breathing, coming short and heavy. Joe gave her a long, measuring look, then turned and picked up the cap he had dropped on the table.

'I'd best be going now.'

'No – wait.' Without thinking, she reached out and caught at his sleeve again. Joe stopped abruptly, and she leapt back as if she had been stung. 'I – I only wanted to say, I hope we are still friends, Joe. In spite of all this.' She hardly knew why she said it, knowing only that she could not let him leave with anger between them.

At once, his face closed.

'We were once,' she said, almost pleading. 'You – you called me Christina once.'

'Aye, an' should've known better,' he growled, his face turned away as he put on his cap.

'Surely that's for me to say.' She stood looking at him, her anger quickly evaporating as she remembered how it had felt to be in his arms. 'We *were* friends,' she said again, and there was a forlorn note in her voice.

Joe's eyes were shuttered, the grimness in his face hard and inexorable. Again, he shook his head.

'Friendship ent for the likes of us, Miss Christina. I told you that. We hev our own lives. Our own mates. And I stick by mine.' He gave her a glance that withered her bones. 'I'll work for you, as blower, gaffer or even overseer, so long as it don't interfere between me and my mates. But that's where it ends.' He went to the door, paused and gave her one last glance.

'I wish you luck, Miss Christina. With the trouble you're bringing here, you'll need your friends. But don't call me one of 'em.'

The door closed behind him and Christina, staring at the impassive wood, felt suddenly cold. Alone.

Bereft.

Joe left Christina's house in a state of frustration that surpassed anything he had yet experienced.

It was not solely the increasing unrest in the glasshouse that occupied his mind. Seeing Christina again in her own home, warm and tawny like a lioness in golden-brown velvet, had refreshed the tumult of mind and body that he had tried so hard to overcome. Once again, all he could think of was what it would be like to possess her. He had held her in his arms once, for a few short moments, and it had to last him a lifetime. A lifetime of this!

Furiously, he tramped out into the wet street, slippery with its layer of icy mud. It had been a mistake to go, just as he'd known it would be. A mistake to stand there with her in the warm lamplight of the room that held so many memories of happier evenings. A mistake to look down into her green eyes, feel the warmth of her body reaching out for his, the soft whisper of her breath against his cheek. A mistake to let himself think of her again as anything but his employer.

Friends! She wanted them to be friends – as if there could ever be anything of that kind between two people so far apart in class and background. For a moment, as she pleaded with him, he'd almost given in, almost said yes, he would count himself a friend, but as soon as the thought had entered his mind, he'd known that it couldn't end there. Friendship was impossible. What he wanted from Christina Henzel was something far deeper, something raw and earthy; the physical clash of two bodies that came together because there was nothing else they could do, because they were meant to come together and always had been. The surge of fulfilment that he had never quite attained, even with Maggie; the soaring knowledge that Christina was his woman, and he her man.

And that could never be. There was Jeremy Henzel; there was the Frenchman. And there was the fact that he was no more than a glassmaker – even though he might be the finest in the country – and she owned him, in ways he didn't want to be owned. Friendship! It was impossible.

Christina. He tasted the name in his mind. Once, once only, he had spoken it to her, just like that, as if he had a right to – and he had, for hadn't she given him that right? And then, moments later, the dream had been smashed and he had been sent out into the night burning with a humiliation he swore never to repeat.

Jeremy Henzel had done that. The man Christina was expected to marry – or had been, until this Frenchie came along with his fancy coat and fancy manners. They said she favoured him now . . . But the odds were still on Jeremy. She might fancy the Frenchman, but it would be Jeremy she'd marry. And Jeremy Henzel, not content with her, not content with making Joe look a fool in front of Christina, had taken Maggie too. Set her up in a house in Church Row, visiting her whenever he liked and enjoying the pleasures of that ripe flesh.

At that moment, a carriage passed him, heading for Henzel Court. Joe looked up at it and recognised it for the one Jeremy Henzel used. He must be going to visit Christina. Probably to spend the evening there. So he wouldn't be going anywhere near Maggie tonight – not for several hours, anyway.

Joe turned and set off to walk to Stourbridge and Church Row. He stopped at a tall, thin house and looked up at the window which he thought must be Maggie's. It was lit and he knocked on the door of the house. It was answered by a thin, slatternly woman who stared at him with suspicion.

'Maggie Haden. Her live here?'

'Arr.'

'I want to see her.'

The woman shrugged and turned away, leaving Joe to follow. She pointed up the narrow stairway.

'If she don't want to see yer, mind yer comes right out straightaway, see? I don't want no trouble here, and that room's paid for regular.'

Joe didn't bother to answer. He knew all too well who was paying for the room, and he knew too that this woman was no more capable of enforcing her rule than a kitten. He guessed she was alone, too; probably her husband, if she had one, was drinking the rent away in the local inn.

Or perhaps she lived simply by renting out rooms like this, to well-breeched men who wanted somewhere to keep a whore.

Maggie's door was at the top of the stairs. It was battered and shabby. He knocked, and a moment later she was there.

'Joe!'

'That's me.' His voice was rough, his heart high in his throat as he stared down at her, seeing the figure that was even more voluptuous than he remembered, the swift colour in her cheeks, the taunting look already in her eyes. Her hair tumbled around her shoulders in the old way, and he wanted with sudden violence to gather it in his hands, bury his face in its luxuriance. 'Well, aren't you going to invite me in?'

'Joe, I don't know, I –' She looked uncertain, almost scared and he said roughly, 'It's all right, he won't be coming tonight, your fancy man. I seen him going the other way, to his other piece, up at Henzel's. We're safe, if that's what's worrying you.'

She lifted her head. 'Nothing's worrying me, Joe Compson, unless it's you. What are you doin' here anyway? Who told you you could come calling, this time of night an' all? What makes you think I want you in my room anyway?'

Joe glanced down the stairs. The landlady was standing there, peering up through the gloom, watching them in the light of her guttering candle. Maggie looked down and saw her too.

'All right,' she said ungraciously. 'You'd better come in.' She turned away and then closed the door behind him.

Joe stood just inside the room. It wasn't large, but it was clean enough. There was a chair at the window, and a small table. A fire burned in the grate, with a rag rug on the polished floorboards in front of it. In one corner stood a marble-topped washstand, in another a mahogany chest and, in the middle, taking up almost all the space, was a large bed. For many of the families in Stourbridge, a room of this size would be all they had to call home. And there would be four or five sharing a bed like that.

'Well, Mag, I hev to hand it you,' Joe said at last. 'You fell on your feet here and no mistake.'

'That's right.' She was standing close to him, her shawl wrapped around her. A new one, he thought, remembering the tattered cloth with which she had covered them on cold nights on Dob Hill. 'Right on my feet. And I means to stay on them, Joe. I ent never goin' back to the old life. I had enough of scraping for every penny, livin' hard, cold and wet. That basement my mam and dad lives in, it ent fit for a rat. I got a bit of money now, Joe. I can put a bit by. I mean to help them a bit, later on.' She tossed back the cascading hair and looked at him with defiance in her eyes. 'I don't need you no more, Joe Compson.'

Joe stared at her. The hunger that had driven him here, gnawing like an animal in his belly, had been aggravated by this sight of her, so lusciously desirable in the leaping firelight. They had never been together indoors, only out in the open, under the smoking sky. He'd never been with any woman in a bed . . .

'Don't you?' he demanded, his voice hoarse. 'Be you sure of that, Maggie?' He moved closer, took her roughly in his arms, jerking her against his body so that he could feel again the familiar softness of her breasts against his broad, hard chest. They were even fuller than he remembered . . . He slid one hand up her back to cup her head, holding it tilted to his so that she could not twist her face aside, and fastened his lips on hers, forcing the kiss, compelling her to open her mouth to his, plundering greedily and with grim satisfaction as he felt her instinctive response.

All the frustration that had been building up in him for months now, was boiling in his body like a cauldron of bubbling acid, lethal, uncontrollable, hot and fierce

enough to consume anything that dared to stand in his
way. The violent energy spread through his great body,
through the powerful limbs; with his arms, he clasped her
against his rocklike hardness, with his thighs he forced her
against the end of the bed, every inch savouring the
softness that melted against him, the shape that moulded
so readily to his own.

'Jeremy Henzel!' he muttered in bitter scorn. 'What's a
man like that got for a woman like you, Maggie? How can
you go with him, let him do this to you, and this, and this,
when you've been with me? When you *knows* what it can
be like?' His mouth was devouring her now, moving over
her face and neck, down to the swollen breasts with their
darkened nipples that stood out already, full and proud
against the white skin. 'If it's money, I'll give it to you,' he
promised recklessly. 'I'll give you whatever he gives you –
you can stay here if you like, live like a queen . . .' He
ripped at her dress, pulling it down to the waist, dragged it
from the body that twisted under his, and then stepped
back to stare at her.

Maggie lay, white and abandoned, on the blanket that
Jeremy Henzel had paid for. Her body was full, the belly
no longer flat as Joe remembered it but swelling into a
curving mound, the waist thicker, the hips wider. He
looked into her eyes and knew the truth.

'You're expectin'.'

She stared straight back at him; her eyes were like
stones. 'An' what if I am?'

Joe looked at her again. His desire had gone, leaving
him limp and flat. He looked around for her shawl, found
it on the floor and threw it over her.

'It's yourn, Joe,' she said in a hard voice. 'I knew it had
happened before I ever took up with Mr Henzel.'

'You *knew*? And you still . . ? That's my babby in
there, and you let him –'

'And what was I supposed to do?' She reared up on the
bed, clutching the shawl around her. 'Wait for you to tek

274

on your responsibilities? You'd already told me you didn't want no more of me – you wouldn't even walk down the same street as me. Was I supposed to starve in the gutter while you danced attendance on your fancy lady up at the glassworks? Not that you ever had any chance there, and you knew it – an' less so than ever now, if what I hear's half true.'

'And what do you hear?' He was shaking, confused. That Maggie might indeed be pregnant had never occurred to him. It had only been the once, the last time they were together when she'd tricked him – and her trick had worked. The fury that he'd felt then at the trap she'd laid for him surged back, so that it was with difficulty that he kept his hands off her.

'What do you hear?' he challenged her, thrusting trembling fingers through his thick black hair. 'Nothing good, I'll be bound – and nothing true, neither.'

'I hear she've got a new fancy man now.' Maggie spoke slyly, glinting her eyes at him, taunting him again. 'French, in't he? And pretty with it. I hear all the ladies are sighin' over him, an' your precious Miss Christina most of all. Reckon you might hev to learn a new language, Joe, if you wants to keep your place there!'

With a snarl, Joe flung himself on her, but she was ready for him now. Drawing her knees up, she thrust him away and then kicked him, catching him on the point of his jaw so that his head snapped back. Her other foot struck him hard on the nose, while a toe thrust painfully into his eye. He staggered back and Maggie hastily wriggled up to the head of the bed and crouched there, naked, like a wild cat ready to spring. She was breathing hard, shivering with excitement, and as he removed his hand from his face he knew that she was his for the taking now. He felt the heat in his loins, the leaping awareness of his own power. And then he saw the blood on his fingers and a sick disgust turned him away.

'All right, Maggie,' he said wearily. 'Hev it your own

way. Be a rich man's whore. I don't know what you think you're going to do when he gets tired of you – an' he will soon, mark my words, once he knows about the babby. But that in't my business. Just don't come runnin' to me, that's all.'

Maggie lifted her face. Her eyes glittered and her lips parted in defiance. 'He won't leave me, just because there's a brat around. He likes me too much for that.' She spoke the last words insinuatingly, so that Joe should be left in no doubt as to what Jeremy liked about her. 'So you go back, Joe Compson, go back to your glasshouse and your fancy piece that'll never be any good to you. And don't come down here no more – you ent welcome.'

Joe gave her a last, long look, 'I'll wish you luck, Mag,' he then said shortly, turning towards the door. 'You're goin' to need it.'

Chapter Thirteen

Spring came to the English countryside, starring hedgerows with yellow clumps of primroses, carpeting the woods with the royal purple of violets. In the fields where Christina and Frederic had run wild as children, lambs frisked in the evening shadows and birds danced their courting displays before finding sites for their nests. Blossom wafted like snow in the breeze, and a tender blue warmed a sky that had been sullen with cold.

Christina, wanting Jean-Paul to see her country at its best, took him out of the grim smoke of Stourbridge. They went to Kinver Edge and picnicked in the woods, looking out over the vale of the Severn towards the distant Shropshire hills.

'The people here,' Jean-Paul said as they meandered along the winding wooded path, 'living in these caves, who are they?'

'Just people. Mostly, they work in the iron foundries. They make rooms and homes of them. There are a lot here: Nanny's Cave, Holy Austin Rock, and the Hermitage, further down the river. They've been lived in for centuries.'

'In France also, we have the *troglodytes* – the cave dwellers,' Jean-Paul said. 'In cliffs beside the rivers, with ladders and steps crawling up the precipice . . . It is not a life I would enjoy, I think.'

Christina laughed. 'No – I don't fancy living in a cave either. But they're better than some of the houses – they're solid. They won't tumble down around their ears.'

'But not very dry, I think.'

'Perhaps not. But neither are the houses.' Christina spoke in a troubled voice. She was still unhappy about the conditions in which some of her own employees lived; still meant, sometime, to go and see for herself. But the time never seemed to come, there was always too much to think of concerning the glasshouse and the expansion which was going on there – even now, not satisfied with the success of her cutting and engraving shops, she was turning her mind again to coloured glass, experimenting with different minerals to find a colour that could be uniquely Henzel's.

She glanced up at Jean-Paul, her eyes reflecting the dappling green sunlight, her hair gleaming with burnished copper lights.

'I would live in a cave with you,' she said softly.

Jean-Paul stopped and looked down at her. His face was grave, his eyes as dark as sun-warmed slate. Christina felt her heart kick as she met his gaze. She put up her hands to touch his face and at the same moment, he bent towards her.

The kiss was as sweet and piercing as the song of a lark, and as Jean-Paul gathered her more closely into his arms, Christina felt her heart soar as if the bird had carried it into the distant blue sky. Her blood sang in her ears, tingling through her body, quivering to her fingertips, curling in her toes. A sigh whispered in her throat as he murmured softly against her lips, and she felt his lashes brush her cheek as he moved his face against hers. The sun was warm on her closed eyelids; she tilted her head back and Jean-Paul stroked his lips caressingly down her throat.

'Christina, *cherie* . . .'

'I love you, Jean-Paul,' she whispered, and her fingers moved through his hair, tousling the brown curls that twined around them. Suddenly consumed with urgency, she sought his mouth again and felt his arms tighten around her, his fingers reaching her breasts, and she turned against him, almost overwhelmed by the sensations that unfolded beneath his searching hands.

278

Jean-Paul lifted her from her feet and carried her away from the path, between the trees to a clearing where the moss formed a deep cushion beneath the dappling leaves of a silver birch.

Christina looped her arms around his neck and rested her head against his chest, feeling the strong pounding of his heart. For a few moments, she was tranquil, secure in the certainty that the weeks of agonised frustration were over. Since that night when she had first acknowledged her feelings for Jean-Paul, he had not allowed a single moment when they could be alone, had never even permitted their glances to meet in any way that could betray them to others. She had begun to fear that Jean-Paul would indeed return to France without another word of love, that he intended to go back to his fiancée as if nothing had happened – just as if he and Christina did not belong to each other, as if their destinies were to remain apart.

But now, as he laid her down on the mossy bed beneath the trees and smiled down into her eyes, she knew that her enforced patience was to be rewarded. And Jean-Paul, with his tender grey eyes and his long sensitive fingers, which had already brought such exquisite agony to her trembling body, was to become hers in every way. As she would be his. After this, she thought dreamily, he would never be able to leave her.

'My darling,' he murmured throatily. 'Christina, cherie . . . you know what you are doing, oui?'

Slowly, Christina nodded her head, and knew that it was true, and with an instinct that had been born in her, handed down from Eve, she moved and stretched and lifted herself to him. And Jean-Paul, his face grave and tender, began very slowly to make love.

He began with her face, cupping it with his hands, his lips teasing hers with little kisses, gentle nips, before travelling down the line of her jaw and to the hollow of her throat. Christina moaned softly and turned her head

279

again, seeking his mouth, and he returned his lips to hers in a series of lingering kisses that left her weak, kisses that were sweet yet pulsing with the promise of a greater excitement, a more intense delight. She moved closer and, winding her arms about his body, strained against him with desire. With one hand, he held her close; then the other began to move slowly, sensuously, his fingers as light as a whisper as they travelled down from her neck and into the bodice of her dress and began to untie the ribbons that fastened it across her swelling breasts. He touched the taut white skin and she gasped, moving suddenly against him and then he was stroking her nipple, moving it with exquisite gentleness between his finger and thumb, letting the tips of his fingers stray against the pounding heart beneath before finally burying his face in the soft, warm flesh.

Christina lay still, her hands moving involuntarily to hold his head against her. She could feel his tiny movements, his lips and teeth and tongue, and her own excitement mounting, the singing of her body as the blood thundered through her veins; yet because of Jean-Paul's tender restraint and delicate skill, she felt none of the fear or pain that her sister had warned her of in their girlish talks.

Jean-Paul raised his head and began to kiss her again. And this time his kisses were different, fiercer, more urgent, more demanding. His lips had hardened; they tore a response from her, so that she tightened her clasp on him, found her mouth opening at his implicit command, her tongue moving to meet his as it sought her sweetness. Both his hands were at her breasts now, caressing her with a trembling roughness that had her whimpering with pleasure; he drew them together and bent to kiss the deepened cleft.

Christina slid her hands down to the buttons of his shirt, unfastening them with trembling fingers, longing to feel the touch of his skin against hers. She touched the roughness of hair, spread her palm on it, opened the white linen to reveal its flat expanse. With a mutter in his own language, Jean-Paul drew against her and they both cried out as their skins touched, holding each other close and still as the sensation of warmth flowed between them and their incipient passion mounted.

Jean-Paul's eyes were dark now as he looked down at her, and Christina's were as green as the moss on which they lay. She lay beneath him, looking up without fear, smiling a little at his gravity, tasting her singing joy in the kisses he placed all over her face. With one hand, he swept the damp, dark red curls back from her forehead and with the other, he began to explore in small, ever-increasing circles, the slender flatness of her stomach and the narrowness of her waist.

Christina closed her eyes and moved restlessly. His fingers were moving almost casually, teasingly; she wanted them to explore further, deeper, to grow more intimate, and she circled her hips under his hand, trying to entice the roving fingertips into the secret places that she knew instinctively they sought. Yet at the same time, a tiny thrill of fear was spiralling deep inside her, a tremor of apprehension that made her grasp at his wrist whenever his hand moved too close. She felt him smile against her mouth before he deepened his kiss and her senses reeled. Her grasp grew weaker, fell away, returned to stroke feebly at his muscular arm, and then, as his fingers came deep against her body and began to move with rhythmic sureness, she quivered against him, aware of nothing now but the hot red darkness behind her eyelids, the warmth of Jean-Paul's body hard against hers, and the almost intolerable pleasure of his moving fingertip, touching one tiny and sensitive spot that until now she had barely known.

Jean-Paul was murmuring to her in French, words she knew were words of love. Hardly knowing what she said, aware that it scarcely mattered, she whispered back, and their soft voices mingled together, blending with the breeze and the shiver of the newly-born leaves above them, at one with the twitter and bustle of the birds, the rustle of small animals, and all the other natural sounds of the woods in which they lay.

The sound of voices broke with crude, unwelcome harshness upon their soaring joy. Jean-Paul's caressing fingers stilled; his lips left hers and he raised his head to listen.

'People!' Christina whispered in an agony of dismay. 'Who are they? *Where* are they?'

'They are coming along the path.' He glanced quickly in the direction in which they had come. 'We did not come far enough into the woods, *ma cherie*. They will see us. Quickly, sit up and rearrange yourself.' He lifted himself away from her, his fingers moving rapidly to fasten the buttons Christina had undone. While Christina, feeling shaky and a little sick, struggled with her own clothes, he swiftly unpacked the picnic basket which he had dropped beside them. As the voices came nearer, he spread the cloth and set food, plates and glasses out at random.

The second picnic party to walk on Kinver Edge that day was a family – father, mother and three young children. They took little notice of the two people they passed in a clearing under some birch trees. If they had, they would have seen that Christina's dress was improperly fastened, that her fingers trembled as she cut a slice of fruit cake for Jean-Paul. And if they had been possessed of second sight, they would have seen that within the two apparently calm and tranquil bodies there raged a fury of frustration, alongside sweet delight in each other's discovery of their love.

There was no question, after that, of Jean-Paul's returning to France.

'It will not be easy,' he told her as they made their way back along the path to where the trap waited to take them home. 'And I shall have to go back to settle things –

Marie-Pierre is entitled to a meeting at least, and there will be discusions to be held with her family, with my own father. Unpleasant discussions, I am afraid. But there is no other way. I must deal fairly with them all – for after all, I am the one who is looking forward to a lifetime of bliss.'

Christina held his hand in hers and smiled. The torment of the past weeks was over; she felt light and ethereal, and even danced a few steps, half expecting to find herself floating. The agony of the abrupt termination of their lovemaking had faded now, and she could remember only the heady delight, the sweeping, overwhelming excitement of passion. It would come again, she thought with an almost painful beat of her heart. And they would be married – as soon as Jean-Paul returned from this last journey to France, a parting which she was already dreading but knew was necessary. They would have the rest of their lives for loving . . .

'We'll tell the family at once,' she declared. 'I want everyone to know how happy I am – to be as happy as we are.'

Jean-Paul quirked a smile at her. 'And do you think they will be so happy? Your Aunt Susan, who neither likes nor trusts me; your cousin Jeremy, who sees me as a threat to his own chances – in which I am delighted to say he is entirely correct! And Adela, who I dare to believe cherishes her own romantic attachment to me, which I may say I have done *nothing* to deserve. Even your brother Harry, sensible though he is, treats me with a certain reserve.'

'Oh, Harry's always like that – he's become very protective since Papa died. And the others will come round. Aunt Susan will be delighted to have me married at last, she believes it is the only life suitable for a woman – poor Aunt Susan, she never had the chance herself and looks on it as a kind of heaven. Which I declare it is!' Christina exclaimed warmly. 'Though I never saw it so until now – it always seemed more like a trap until I met you. Tell me it's true, that I'm not dreaming; tell me it really has happened, that we really will be married. Kiss me again, Jean-Paul, where nobody can see, and tell me you really do love me.'

They stopped at the last bend, before the path came into sight of the road, and Jean-Paul took her into his arms. His eyes were like stars in the dusk of twilight. His face was sombre, as if he made a sacred vow.

'It's all true, Christina, *cherie*,' he said gravely. 'I love you. You are my heart, my body, my life. And we shall be married, as soon as it can be arranged, and live together in harmony for the rest of our lives, as it has always been ordained that we should.'

Christina raised her face to his like a child. And kissed him like a woman.

'Married! *Married*! The silly chit means to *marry* the man, and it seems we are quite powerless to stop it.' Samuel paced the room, his steps making quick, furious jabs into the thick Turkish carpet. 'And you, Jeremy – you, who assured us there was nothing to worry about, that it only needed time and patience – you have failed. Failed lamentably. Failed the entire family. God knows what Alfred is going to say – he intends to begin producing rock crystal at any time now. He needs the Stourbridge branch behind him, needs the capital, the expertise, the outlets Christina has for her lines. And now this! She'll never let it go now, not with the Frenchman to support her. They'll go on from strength to strength, and where will that leave us?'

Jeremy's eyes fell. The argument had been going on for hours, circling and blustering, always coming back to the same inevitable point – Christina's engagement to Jean-Paul and the proof of his failure. And he had his own fury and disappointment to contend with as well. He had genuinely believed that, until Jean-Paul had arrived, he

284

was gaining ground with Christina; winning first her trust, then her friendship and, finally, her heart. The force of her infatuation for Jean-Paul had dismayed him, but as long as the Frenchman was betrothed in his own country and had every intention of returning there, Jeremy had thought him to be no real threat. Indeed, the situation might even be turned to his own advantage once Jean-Paul had left, and Christina, bereft, needed a shoulder on which to weep out her loss.

And now, before anyone had fully recognised the danger, Christina and Jean-Paul had announced their engagement. Looking as radiant as if she had just been handed the world to play with, Christina had made the statement that shattered her family at a dinner at which they were all present. And Jean-Paul, though he looked somewhat self-conscious, was just as triumphant. It was sickening.

'You've let us down,' his father accused Jeremy yet again. 'Let us all down. And what do you intend to do about it, may I ask?'

'Do? What is there to do? They're engaged – he has only to return to France to sort out the tangle he has made of his life there, and he will be free to come back to England and set up house with Christina. It will be all over within a few months. What do you expect me to do? Step in and forbid the banns? Can *you* think of any "just cause or impediment"?'

'Please do not resort to sarcasm, Jeremy,' Samuel said coldly. 'We are here to find a solution to this dangerous situation. There must be *something* that can be done.'

'I agree.' Reuben, who had said little so far, removed his hand from his beard and spoke in his remote voice, as if all this had really nothing to do with him. 'We should discuss it coolly and calmly. Perhaps you could make a start, Samuel, by seating yourself.'

Samuel glared at him, but did as he was told, leaning his elbows on his knees and resting his forehead on his palms in an attitude of despair. Harold, as wooden-faced as ever, grunted.

'That's better – you've been making my head ache with that infernal prowling up and down. Logical discussion, that's what we need now. There must be some way of saving the glasshouse from this Frenchman.'

Samuel lifted his head from his hands. 'You really think he will take it over?'

'Doesn't it stand to reason? We know Christina will still hold a controlling interest, under the terms of that damned will – but what difference will that make, when she's besotted with the fellow? And in a year or two, she'll have more than the glasshouse to concern her. Children – domesticity.' He turned on Jeremy. 'Exactly the results we expected you to achieve!'

Reuben intervened before Jeremy, tired of the constant accusations, could defend himself. 'There is little point in going over all that yet again. The question is – what do we do now? It seems to me that the marriage must be prevented in some way.'

'How? She's determined – and we've all seen how obstinate Christina can be. I believe she's even worse than Joshua himself.' Samuel made to rise again, then caught his brother's eye and subsided. 'I have to agree with Jeremy here. Christina won't give in, and Thietry's betrothal is only an embarrassment to him in his own country. It can't form a legal impediment.'

'And Christina is of age,' Harold contributed. 'She needs no one's permission for marriage. I see little that we can do.'

'He might be discredited in some way,' Reuben mused. 'What does he do when he's not at the glasshouse? Does he have no unsavoury habits? He's a long way from home, after all; he might well desire a few . . . comforts.'

The three older men glanced at Jeremy. He shook his head.

'I know of nothing. As far as I know, he spends most of his time at the house, with the family.'

'With Christina,' Harold said brusquely. 'It seems to me that Susan must accept some of the blame here. There has clearly been a laxity in that house, an absence of supervision –'

Jeremy gave a sour laugh. 'Supervision! Can you imagine Christina succumbing to *supervision*? She is far too self-willed, and she's grown worse in the past year. I tell you this Thietry will have his work cut out there to bring her to the proper state of submission.'

'Nevertheless, it's a task you would have taken on,' Reuben remarked, and Jeremy coloured.

'Yes, and still would, for the sake of the family. And because there would be a certain – pleasure – in seeing that arrogant miss brought to heel. There might even be moments . . .' He shook himself. 'Well, be that as it may. I can't see that we can discredit Thietry, his behaviour since he's been in England has been, I'm sorry to say, impeccable. As for what he did in France –'

'Yes, there might be something there,' Reuben said thoughtfully. 'We could, perhaps, send some trusted emissary to do a little detection . . . Or there's this betrothal of his. I understand such affairs are difficult to resolve. Could we perhaps persuade those concerned that it would be most undesirable for a break to be made? His father, the girl's family, even the girl herself. It might, perhaps, be made so difficult for him that he comes to think the status quo might be better maintained.'

'I suppose it might,' Samuel said doubtfully. 'But you saw their faces the other night. They're both set on this engagement. And as Jeremy has already pointed out, Christina doesn't give in easily. If at all. You'd have her to reckon with too.'

'Why, what could she do about what happens in France?' Harold objected. 'Unless you think she'd take ship and go after him! I don't imagine even Christina would dare to do anything that bold.'

'I do.' Jeremy, unable to sit still any longer, got up and began to pace the room exactly as his father had done. 'No, I think Uncle Reuben's idea is the best. Thietry must be discredited here. We must find some evidence against him that even Christina would accept – something so unsavoury that even she would turn against him.'

'A woman.' Samuel spoke with decision. 'A woman of the lowest order; someone whose association with the fellow would disgust Christina to her very soul. And after all, the fellow's been in England for months; if Jeremy's right and he has never sought comfort, he should be easy enough to persuade.'

The three men turned their eyes upon Jeremy, who met them blandly for a while. Then he shrugged.

'Very well, I'll see what I can do.' He gave them a warning glance. 'Mind, it may take a little time. I shall need to make friends with him first, and he may be suspicious.'

'Just see that on this occasion you don't over-estimate the time available to you,' Samuel advised him. 'And the other question is, can you find a suitable woman?'

'Oh, there's no problem there,' Jeremy said easily. His mind went to a little room in Church Row, a room furnished with little more than a large, comfortable bed. 'I know just the one. Not a whore yet, but going down that road. And she owes me a favour.' As he and his father and uncle prepared to depart, he felt Reuben's hand on his arm.

'Stay on for another brandy, my boy. There's another little matter I wish to discuss with you.' His voice was soft and insistent and Jeremy, reluctant but curious, laid down his coat.

They sat together in Reuben's study, drinking brandy and staring into the flames of the fire. There was a silence that lengthened between them. Jeremy had a strong feeling that there was more Reuben wanted to say; suggestions he hadn't wanted to make before the others. He waited.

'I hope you will be able to carry out this new plan, Jeremy.' Reuben said at length. He too was looking into the fire, and he spoke absently, almost as if the matter were of no consequence. 'Otherwise we may have to resort to more drastic measures.'

'Drastic measures?'

'Yes. He must be got rid of, you know.' Reuben could have been speaking of nothing more than an irritating pest, a rat in the kitchen or a mole in the lawn, yet there was a chilling undertone to his words; an implication of ruthlessness. The rat or the mole would be eradicated – how hardly mattered – but there would be no thought of mercy. 'The situation cannot be allowed to continue.'

'Well, it won't be.' Jeremy spoke with more confidence than he really felt. 'I'll befriend him – a little late, perhaps, but that can be overcome – the gallant Englishman, losing with a smile on his lips, that kind of thing, and then I'll offer to show him the conveniences of the town. He'll probably even be grateful. And once he is established with this woman I know of – why, then it will be easy. The whole thing can come out and Christina will feel so betrayed, disgusted, he'll find himself on the next boat to France, with not so much as a goodbye kiss.'

Reuben's pale eyes slid round to Jeremy, 'This plan of yours may work, but it's as well to think of something else; to be prepared.'

Jeremy watched him cautiously. He had come to respect his uncle's devious mind, while being never entirely sure that he wasn't himself a victim of it.

'I mentioned more drastic measures,' Reuben remarked, still in that light, casual tone which he adopted when he wished, for some reason, to be less than explicit. 'Would you be prepared to execute those, Jeremy?'

'I don't know what you mean –' Jeremy began, but Reuben interrupted him.

'I used the word "execute" advisedly, Jeremy.'

It took a moment or two for his meaning to sink in. Then Jeremy's eyes widened; he gave his uncle a quick glance of dismay, dawning horror, even fear.

'You – you mean you think we should – *I* should – Uncle Reuben, I don't think I can have understood you aright. You're suggesting . . . '

'I'm suggesting nothing, nephew. Nothing at all. But . . . accidents happen.' The tone was still unbelievably casual. 'They happen in even the best regulated glasshouses. They can even happen at home – in the street – anywhere. It might be the best way, Jeremy. A clean break, with no repercussions, and Christina grief-stricken, needing a strong man to help her through her time of trouble. What more could you ask?'

Jeremy stared at him, shaken. 'You're talking about murder!'

'I am talking about *accidents*,' Reuben corrected him firmly.

Jeremy shook his head. 'How could we be sure it would work? If it failed – or there was any suspicion of foul play . . . How could you be sure there would be no repercussions? It's dangerous, uncle – too dangerous.'

'Repercussions can be avoided. Someone else might easily be blamed.'

Jeremy was still gazing at him horrified, then he shook his head again.

'No. It wouldn't work. It couldn't be done. And it's far too dangerous.' He spoke decisively, 'I want no part of it, uncle. I'd rather the whole glasshouse went to the wall.'

'And us with it?' Reuben leaned forward. 'Jeremy, this isn't just a matter of plain greed. We need that glasshouse! Christina is in the right market and she can't help but succeed. Her father was right, you know, she is entirely capable of running the business, and she will outstrip us all. *She'll take away all our business*, Jeremy. Already she has gone into lead crystal, fine engraving, colour. Why should she stop there? She's young, energetic, and a very clever young woman. She'll look around for fresh fields to conquer. She'll have the capital, the knowledge and the daring to do it. I warn you, if she isn't stopped now, in five years' time she will have bought us out – yes, and Alfred too, up in Newcastle. She will be the biggest glassmaker in the country.' He leaned back again, his lizard's eyes still for once, fixed on Jeremy's stunned face. 'The only way we have of saving ourselves is for you to marry her. And any threat must be removed – by whatever means possible.'

There was a long silence. Then he added, 'An accident, Jeremy. That's all it needs. And then he can be no further danger to us.'

Chapter Fourteen

'I can do nothing with her. Nothing at all.' Susan Henzel sipped her tea, the trembling of her hand causing the cup to rattle slightly against her teeth. Her customary fluttering manner had deteriorated to a constant nervous agitation. Her eyes, as she gazed at Jeremy over the rim of the thin china cup, were large and piteous.

'She is quite determined, and nothing I can say has any effect at all on her. She has always been wilful, of course; even as a child, she always set out to acquire whatever she wanted, regardless of the consequences, and I fear she is the same now.'

Jeremy sighed. He set down his cup. 'You know, Cousin Susan, I had hopes myself . . . Christina and I have always been friends. I thought that, given time, she would satisfy herself concerning the glasshouse and be ready to think of other things, more fitting things for a young lady. Marriage – yes, I had hoped for marriage.'

'And so had I. Nothing would have made me happier than to see her married to you. The glasshouse and Christina herself, both in the same safe hands.' Susan's eyes filled with tears. 'And then she must needs bring this Frenchman over – to stay in the house, too! As if it weren't bad enough that she should see him each day, he must live as one of the family! And – well, it was inevitable, I suppose. She is past marriageable age.' Susan shook her head fretfully. 'I blame myself entirely. I should have seen what was happening and taken steps to prevent – but I thought he was safely betrothed, that there could be no real danger. And now, whatever Alfred is going to say, I dread to think. I know what he wanted, what you all hoped for. And it seemed so *sensible*. And now it will never be!' She began to weep, lifting a scrap of lace to her eyes and shaking her head despairingly.

'Come now, Cousin Susan.' Jeremy leaned forward, masking his distaste for the crumpled, ugly face, taking her hands gently in his and massaging the trembling fingers. 'Don't upset yourself. All is not lost yet. They aren't married yet, after all, nor can they be, until Jean-Paul has returned to France. Where, I imagine, he will not be at all the hero Christina believes him to be!'

'No, that he certainly will not.' Susan sniffed delicately and blew her nose. 'And that only makes things worse! It means he will certainly stay here, to plague us all for the rest of his life. That is,' she added with a sudden hard edge to her voice, 'if he comes back at all.'

Jeremy gave her a quick glance. 'Why, what do you mean by that?'

'Oh, nothing. Nothing at all.' She pulled her hands away and began to busy herself once more with the tea things. 'Now, are you sure you won't have some more bread and butter? A piece of fruit cake, it's one of Mrs Jenner's best. Or perhaps another –'

'Cousin Susan,' Jeremy said firmly, 'tell me what you meant.'

'I simply meant that he – might not come back. That's all,' she said, nervously playing with her teacup.

'But why?' Jeremy asked in exasperation. 'Why shouldn't he? I don't imagine he is any more likely to be persuaded to change his mind than Christina is. Though I'm quite sure his family will try.'

'Yes, so am I. But I wasn't thinking of that either, or not entirely. Simply that – well, men do forget the ladies they profess to love. Especially when they are many hundreds of miles apart, in another country. And especially –' she lowered her eyes and colour mounted in her papery cheeks '– especially when they happen to be Thietrys.'

Jeremy stared at her. 'Cousin Susan,' he asked gently, 'I

really think you must explain exactly what you mean. What do you know about the Thietry family that might apply to our situation now?' He caught her hands again, shaking them gently, drawing her round to face him. 'Tell me, please. Don't you see, it might help?'

'Help? How could it help?'

'Cousin Susan,' he said as if speaking to a child, 'none of us wants this engagement – this marriage. I, for one, am bitterly disappointed. I was hoping very much to marry Christina – and not simply because of the glasshouse,' he added quickly. 'I love her for herself. I want to look after her, help her. I want to see her with a family – our family – clustered about her knee. And I believe that if it had not been for Jean-Paul, that is what would have happened. Now, if you know anything, anything at all, that might give me some hope, well, don't you think it is a little cruel to withhold such knowledge?' He smiled disarmingly. 'And if it can be used to help in any way, wouldn't you reproach yourself for the rest of your life, if you hadn't imparted it?'

He watched carefully and saw the indecision in her face, the wavering uncertainty. She looked at him, then quickly down at her hands, still clasped in his. He saw her bite her lip, still undecided.

'It might help you, too, Cousin Susan,' he murmured, feeling his way, 'to unburden yourself.'

At that, she raised her head quickly. 'Oh, it's not a burden! No, not at all – I've hardly thought of it, all these years. After all, we were very young – or I was. It probably would never have come to anything. No more than a childish dream, really, I came to realise that afterwards. But at the time –'

'Yes? At the time?' Jeremy prompted when the silence had gone on long enough. 'It was painful then, was it? Very painful?'

Susan met his eyes again, and her own were misty with distress.

'Yes, it was. Very painful.' She took a breath; she had obviously decided to tell him, and he waited, knowing that she could as easily retreat again. 'It was Jean-Paul's father, you see – Marc Thietry. He came over to England, just as Jean-Paul has done – there was always a good deal of communications between the two families. He stayed with Joshua and Margaret – they were living in the country then, near my parents' home at Kinver – and he and Joshua became close friends. And he and I –' her cheeks were pink but she continued to speak without faltering now '– he and I fell in love. Or thought we did. *I* thought we did.'

'I see.' Jeremy looked at Susan with new interest. 'And he betrayed you?'

'It was the same story as Christina's, just the same,' Susan said agitatedly. 'I tried to warn her when she first spoke of bringing him here. Of course, she took no notice . . . He had to go back to France, naturally, although there was no betrothal involved, I would not have allowed myself to become involved if there had been. So there were no complications at all. He was to return, and after a few months he would come back for me. We would live at his home, near Paris. I was very excited. The Revolution was safely over and things in France were settling down. The thought of beginning a new life there was like a dream. And so it proved. To be a dream – nothing more. Marc returned and I received one or two letters from him. Then nothing. Not so much as an explanation. One day, Joshua told me that he had heard Marc was married, and soon after that Margaret became ill and Joshua asked me to live with him and help care for her and the children.'

There was a long silence. A tear crept slowly down Susan's cheek, and Jeremy took the lace handkerchief from her fingers and gently wiped it away.

'Thank you for telling me,' he said at last. 'I know it couldn't have been an easy time to speak of. Have you told Christina?'

'Oh, I've tried. But she doesn't listen. She simply says that it's a sad story and she pities me – *pities* me! – but that it isn't at all the same as it is for her and Jean-Paul. Such a thing could not happen to her, she says, because she knows Jean-Paul truly loves her. And then she kisses me and goes dancing off to the glasshouse. I know exactly what she's doing,' Susan ended bitterly. 'I thought and said and did exactly the same.'

There was a bright flame of hope in Jeremy's mind, dimming every other thought. Suppose Jean-Paul were indeed to fail Christina! Suppose, like his father, he were to return to France and forget her. Could it really be so easy?

'Don't think about it any more,' he said gently. 'It's all over now. You did right to tell me, Cousin Susan. I think we may after all be able to save Christina from her own folly. And now, I must go.'

He rose to his feet, hesitated for a moment, then bent and kissed the damp cheek. Susan gave him a wavering smile, but as she watched him go her thoughts were not for her niece but for herself; for the girl she had been thirty-five years ago, tremulously in love and alive with a gaiety that had left her for ever.

Jeremy went straight to Church Row. It was unusual for him to go so early in the day; he normally visited Maggie under cover of darkness, not wishing to be seen by acquaintances who might also be in the vicinity. Every man knew quite well how his friends conducted their private lives, but the knowledge was seldom overt; a veneer of upright respectability was so strictly honoured that it was almost believable. In a few men it was even genuine.

Today, in the hour when most men would be either still at business or at home enjoying afternoon tea with their wives, there was nobody about to watch Jeremy's arrival; he did not count the urchins who rushed to hold his horse's head, or the slovenly women who sat on steps, legs spread wide as they lifted their faces to the murky sunlight. Their eyes watched, dull and indifferent, as he opened the door with his own key; if they knew who he was or why he was there, none of them had the energy to care.

'Mr Jeremy!' Maggie struggled up from a doze, the shift which was all she wore disarrayed. 'I worn't expecting you today, I hevn't got no –'

'I told you always to expect me.' Jeremy stood by the curtained window, removing his gloves, regarding her with disfavour; she was letting herself go, growing fat and blowsy. But the sight of her full breasts crowned by the rich, dark nipples made his flesh quicken.

'Is there clean bedlinen?' he demanded, and she nodded, pulling back the coverlet on which she had been lying to reveal white sheets. There were always clean sheets; Jeremy demanded them and Maggie never slept between them when he was not with her, lying instead on top of the bed under a thin blanket. Now, she slid between them, enjoying as always the feel of the cool linen against her naked skin.

Jeremy removed his clothes. There was no passionate haste, no urgency, more a cold determination to have satisfaction, much as a man might strike a bargain for a horse he wished to buy. Nor was there any emotion in his dealing with Maggie. To compensate for its absence, he was compelled to experiment with a number of different practices which Maggie ascribed to a better education. Certainly none of the men she had known previously had conducted their lovemaking with such startling imagination; nor with such a cool pleasure in inflicting small, but exquisite, pains.

She often wondered what it would be like to be free of Jeremy, free to go out when she chose, speak to whom she pleased, love with innocent warmth and tenderness again. Joe had been rough at times, but nothing like this . . .

And she was beginning, too, to fear for the baby growing inside her. Freedom, however, was a luxury Maggie could not afford. The thought of giving up his protection, returning to the grinding poverty she had known before, was unendurable. And she had given up her job, might not be able to get another; even with new factories being built every day, it seemed, there were still men and women who could not find work. Without work, there was no money, no food or shelter; only the workhouse at Wordsley, where you worked in the fields or made bread or nails to earn your keep. She was lucky, Maggie thought as she lay beneath Jeremy Henzel and tried to close her mind to his latest excesses, to have this room and good food, and money for a new shift. And it was little enough to endure, after all . . . just a few times a week.

It was in the last few moments, as Jeremy Henzel reared above her, bellowing news of his climax to the world, that the baby moved; and with that tiny, fluttering kick of life, everything changed.

It had been moving for some time, of course, its kicking and stretching increasingly active. But this was the first time it had happened while Jeremy was with her. She felt the kick as he uttered his last, long groan; then again as he sank down on top of her, and knew that he must have felt it too.

Immediately, his body tensed. He rolled off her, his eyes on her rounded belly, and this time the movement was visible; a tiny protuberance, there and gone as a minute foot thrust, pressed against the wall of her womb and was withdrawn.

'What in hell . .?' he breathed; but, like Joe, he knew.

For a moment, she debated telling him it was his. But the thought was discarded as soon as it appeared. Jeremy Henzel was no fool.

She watched fearfully, waiting for his reaction.

'I take it it's Compson's,' he said at last, harshly.

Maggie nodded.

'Does he know?'

'No, sir. It was the – last time –'

He looked at her with sudden understanding. 'Is this why you parted?'

She snivelled and hid her face. 'I tried, I wanted him to wed me. He wouldn't, an' I thought if a bairn was on the way –'

Jeremy's face twisted with disgust. 'The age-old trick! And Compson wouldn't wear it, eh? Well, I don't blame him. And then I suppose you thought to try the same game with me.'

'Oh no, sir! No, I never dreamed –'

'Save your tears,' Jeremy advised her, standing up and reaching for his clothes. 'You're going to need them.' His face was closed, with no expression to reveal the distaste he felt. Pregnant by Joe Compson – the slut! And he'd been lying with her, reaching into those mysterious dark spaces where another man's child was already forming. He felt an urgent need to get home, to call for hot water and sink into a steaming bath, knowing that he would never visit Maggie again. But there was something he had to do first. And for that, he needed her. Once dressed, he sat on the small chair and looked thoughtfully at her, still lying spread upon the damp, sweat-stained sheets.

'I want you to do something for me,' he said abruptly.

'Of course, sir.' She was snivelling still, pathetically grateful that he had not already stormed from the room.

'It's for a friend of mine, really, but it will be a favour to me, too, you understand.' His mouth twisted a little. 'Or, not a favour exactly – a service, shall we say? A service for which you'll be well paid.'

'A – service, sir?'

'Yes. You've heard of the Frenchman staying at Henzel's? I'm sure there's been talk. Miss Christina is rather attached to him.'

'Yes, sir.' Maggie watched him warily. At least he did

300

not seem angry about the child – although you could never tell with Mr Jeremy.

'I want to do him a favour,' Jeremy said easily. 'After all, he's a visitor here – a long way from home. Miss Christina doesn't understand a man's needs – how could she be expected to, after all? Well, I thought it was time we showed him that England isn't quite the dark, dull country foreigners may think. I thought we ought to show him that we, too, understand how to enjoy life.'

Maggie made no response. She always had to take time to work out just what Mr Jeremy meant; he had an odd, twisted way of saying things.

'You and I have had some very pleasant times together,' Jeremy went on, giving her a smile that chilled her blood. 'I'd like Monsieur Thietry to enjoy the same delights. It's a way of extending our hospitality towards him, don't you think?'

Maggie stared at him. 'You mean you want me to be a whore.'

Jeremy laughed a little irritably. 'A whore! That's rather an extreme way of describing what's really no more than an act of friendship . . . After all, I'm not asking you to entertain the entire French fleet! Now I'm sure you're going to be sensible over this, Maggie, you do owe me a good deal. I want Monsieur Thietry to come here, and I want you to behave exactly as you do with me.' His voice was harsh as he continued. 'I'll pay you extra – just for his visits. But only when you've given satisfaction, understand. I want to know the goods have been delivered – to everyone's satisfaction.'

'Goods? I ent goods!' To her own surprise, Maggie felt the old fire coursing through her veins, the fire she had almost forgotten. Pride and indignation, the combination that had brought a sparkle of defiance and challenge to her eye and had attracted first Joe Compson and then Jeremy Henzel, flashed again in her angry glance. Forgetting the dependence on Jeremy that had coloured so

301

much of her life during the past few months, she went on with bitter wrath, 'I ent a parcel to be given around to your friends as a – a present. I may be poor, but I was brought up respectable, and I got me pride. I kep' meself for you once I come here – an' I don't fancy goin' with no foreigner, neither. There's plenty of other women, real whores, who'll do that for you, go an' ask one of them.'

Jeremy's eyes were cold. 'I think you *will* do it. If you're wise.'

She shook her head. 'I won't. I told you, I've kep' meself for you – I don't want to go with no one else. I'm happy with things as they are.' She looked at him pleadingly. 'Find someone else, Mr Jeremy, please. It won't make no difference to you. I could tell you a few names, they'd be just as good as me. Honestly, Mr Jeremy –' she dragged together all her courage '– would you still want me, after I'd bin with a Frenchman?'

She had believed it to be her trump card. But Jeremy merely looked at her with eyes of ice and said 'Want you? Of course I won't want you again – Frenchman or no Frenchman. With your belly filled with another man's brat . . . ? In any case, I've been growing rather tired of you lately. I was going to give you a last, quite generous present today, and the visits from Thietry would have been, I imagine, a quite welcome bonus. But since you've taken this unreasonable attitude –' he stood up and his eyes raked her cruelly '– I'm afraid we'll have to forgo the present. You've done very well out of me as it is.'

Maggie's eyes widened with disbelief. As he moved towards the door, she scrambled across the bed, reaching out, grabbing at him in her anxiety to keep him there. She was trembling, her body ungainly as the sheets fell away to reveal the thickened waistline and bulging stomach. Her face was ashen, her eyes like hollow pits against her pallor.

'You don't mean it, sir! You can't – you can't leave me. Not like that, not after all these months. What'll I do? Where will I go? Me mam and dad will never tek me back now, they say I've brought shame on them . . . Mr Jeremy, sir, say you never meant it, say it was a joke, say you won't leave me like that, or I'll kill meself!'

Jeremy looked down impassively. He removed her clinging hands as he might have removed a trailing branch.

'I doubt if you'll kill yourself, Maggie,' he remarked. 'And as for what you'll do and where you'll go, how on earth should I know, or care? Now, please don't be so hysterical. You knew this would come to an end. You cannot have imagined I would continue to use you as you grew bigger and uglier, nor once you had a brat squalling around you. Now, take your hands off me, I have to go. And please don't follow me down to the street.'

He left without a backward glance, leaving Maggie slumped half on the bed and half on the floor, her eyes and mouth open wide as the tears of silent despair began to fall. She remained there for a considerable time, frozen and numb. I'll do it, she cried inside her head, I'll do it, I'll do anything . . . But she knew that, in the end, it would make no difference. Jeremy had gone for good. And however handsome his 'present', it would have disappeared all too soon, leaving her facing just the same black pit of poverty as she faced today.

If Jeremy, his pony and trap clattering through the streets, felt any regret at all, it was only a brief one. A momentary vision of the green, flower-filled meadows and the warm, scented haystack, that had never been; that had degenerated into a squalid little room in a dirty backstreet, where a woman's body had never been given the chance to fulfil its early ripe promise.

More important to him now was finding someone else to take part in his plan.

Christina was conscious of a change in the atmosphere of the glasshouse.

It had been happening slowly, too slowly for her to

recognise at first. A sideways glance here, a reticence there from men she had known and felt easy with ever since that first day when she'd delighted them all by coming here in Frederic's clothes. Now the comradeship had gone, seeping away like molten metal through a cracked pot. Blithely happy in her love for Jean-Paul, she had been blind at first to the change. But her confrontation with Joe had opened her eyes; she realised that it was a long time now since any of the men had paused in their work as she passed by, to exchange the cheerful remarks, the casual yet respectful banter that she had been accustomed to.

Uneasily, she thought of Joe's accusations, that she intended bringing over more French workers. She had assured him there was no danger of that, but he hadn't believed her. She had hoped that he would do so when he'd had time to think, when his anger had quietened and reason returned. But perhaps it hadn't. What if he were even fanning the men's unrest, urging them to take the action he'd threatened – strike?

There had never been a strike at Henzel's. Joshua had always maintained a good relationship with his workers. If there were to be one now, it could only mean that Christina was failing in the task he had set her.

If only Joe were still on her side! His position in the glasshouse was such now that the other men, even the older ones, looked to him for leadership. If he were to reassure them, as Christina had tried to reassure him, they would settle down again, their grievances forgotten. But she came back again and again to the unpalatable fact that Joe didn't believe her.

'I have the feeling he doesn't *want* to believe me,' she told Ruth. 'It's as if he wants to be angry with me. There's something else – some other reason. He's your brother, Ruth. Do you know what it is?'

Ruth shook her head. 'No, Miss Christina. He don't talk to me much these days. He seems different, somehow

304

– angry all the time. As if he don't want to be happy – like you said.' She frowned. 'Mind, he've allus had a temper on him. But I haven't ever known him like this before.'

Christina sighed. 'It's so difficult. None of the men will talk to me. I can't explain to them what the situation is – they won't give me a chance. And I'm afraid they wouldn't believe me anyway, if I told them the Frenchmen were going home soon and there were no more coming. It's natural, in a way – they're all afraid of losing their jobs. But there really isn't any risk of that.' She looked at her maid. 'Could *you* tell him, Ruth? Tell him all that I've told you – tell him that I was speaking the truth when I said there was no danger. Otherwise, I'm so afraid something dreadful will happen.'

'I'll try, miss,' Ruth said dubiously. 'But I don't suppose he'll listen to me any more than to you.'

'And you really don't know what the trouble is – why he's so angry?' Christina asked wistfully. 'I feel sure there's something more than the French workers . . . We used to be friends, Ruth, and now we're not any more. It makes me very sad.'

Ruth looked at her. It seemed impossible that her mistress should not be aware of the truth. But there, they said love was blind, and it seemed it was true. Joe wasn't the only one who had changed lately. And she strongly suspected that the cause in each case was all too similar.

'Them Frenchies!' she muttered as she went down to the kitchen to collect Thomas's supper tray from Mrs Jenner. 'More trouble than they're worth – the whole blessed lot of them!'

Christina had been saddened by Aunt Susan's tale of her own unhappy love affair so many years before. But she didn't think it was fair to burden Jean-Paul with the sins of his father.

'I did know something of this,' Jean-Paul had confessed when she told him. 'My father has spoken of your aunt and when he knew I was coming here he told me the whole story. It is a pity she will not listen to me now – the truth might ease her heart.'

'What is the truth? Did he find he didn't love her after all? Was there someone else?'

Jean-Paul shook his head. 'Not at once, no. My father was young – marriage plans had not been made for him when he came here; the years of his youth had been too unsettled for such things. But it was expected, nevertheless, that he would marry a girl from a good family, a wealthy family. The business depended on it, you understand. The times of the Revolution had been hard; many of the old forest glassmakers had lost their homes, their businesses, everything. Nobody had been buying glass during the troubles, and little could be exported. It took a long time to recover, and the Thietry glasshouse was not the only one to suffer.'

'So Aunt Susan was simply not rich enough for him?' Christina's tone was a little hard and Jean-Paul smiled and touched her cheek.

'Do not sound so disapproving, little one. You are very like your aunt yourself when you speak like that . . . No, it was not simply a matter of wealth. My father knew all that, and he was determined that he would make the business succeed without a large dowry. With your aunt at his side, he felt that anything could be achieved – yes, do not look so astonished. He saw your aunt as a very different person, as indeed, I have no doubt she was, thirty-five years ago, and when she was in love and happy. And my father was in love with her, also.'

'So what happened? Why did he never come back? Why did he stop writing?'

'Within two days of his return,' Jean-Paul said quietly, 'his own father died. And everything was in disarray. There were debts – obligations which must be met immediately. The glasshouses needed attention: there was rebuilding to be done, essential if production were to continue; there were men, workers and their families, who depended upon the business for their living, who would have starved if they had been turned away without jobs; there were materials to be bought – oh, the problems went on and on. And nobody would wait. If my grandfather had lived, they would not have pressed him so, but he had died and nobody was sure of the very young man who was my father, and who had just been to England and come back with stars in his eyes. They were afraid – and the only solution was the wealthy marriage that had been planned. He was not betrothed, you understand – there was nothing so firm as that. But my mother's family, for reasons of their own, wished her to be married quickly, and they were willing to give all the help needed.'

'He didn't have much choice then,' Christina said.

'He had no choice.'

Christina was silent for a moment. Then she said, passionately, 'But why didn't he *tell* her? Why just stop writing? She must have been so hurt . . .' For the first time, she began to understand her aunt, to comprehend the reasons for the bitterness that sometimes broke out, the tight disapproval of anything unconventional – anything that might later bring pain. 'Surely it would have been better if he'd told her the truth.'

Jean-Paul shrugged. 'He thought not. He knew the unhappiness it would bring. He felt it better that she should be angry – anger is an emotion that brings energy with it, whereas sadness takes life away.'

'I think he was wrong,' Christina said positively. 'Aunt Susan might have accepted the truth – but never to know it, always to wonder . . .' She turned quickly in his arms. 'I would rather have known,' she said with an intensity that brought the darkness of deep forest shadows to her eyes. 'If anything like that happened to us, Jean-Paul – anything – you'd tell me, wouldn't you? You wouldn't just leave me to rot through the years, always wondering why . . .'

'No, I would not do that. But nothing is going to happen to us.' He smiled and tipped her face towards him. 'Our love is safe,' he whispered against her lips. 'Nothing will stand in the way of our happiness. I swear it.'

Christina quivered in his arms. She longed for his touch, to feel his hands on her body, his mouth on her breasts, his fingers bringing that strange, exquisite sensation that was something she'd known only a hint of in her dreams. And she wanted more than that; the revelation of the mystery, the consummation of a love that tormented her even while it delighted her.

But there had never been another chance since their walk in the forest at Kinver. Never a moment when Aunt Susan, or Adela, or Harry might not come into the room. Never a moment when other eyes were not upon them, other ears not ready to hear.

'Jean-Paul,' she murmured restlessly. 'It seems so long to wait until we are married.'

He smiled at her, his teeth white and even in the sculptured face. 'I know, my dear one. I too find it difficult. But it is usual – *n'est-ce pas*? – for a bride to go to the altar a virgin?'

Christina blushed. 'Yes, but does it *matter*, Jean-Paul? Who would know but ourselves? And – and I want your love so much. I want to give you mine. And it might be weeks – months – and you're going away, so soon.'

'The waiting will make it all the better when it comes,' he promised her. 'And it will be all the better for being right – in our own room, with a privacy we know will not be interrupted. I do not want to hurry this, Christina, it is so important, the first time, for a woman. Trust me in this, my darling, and be patient.'

His kiss was gentle, not designed to arouse, and Christina sighed and relaxed, and her thoughts now turned on Jeremy and his apparent acceptance of the situation.

That was the one bright spot that lit up the cloud of her worries over the glasshouse. It brought her a good deal of comfort – more than she had expected, since to be in opposition had always exhilarated rather than disturbed her. But that was when the opposition was directed at herself and became a challenge. When it was directed at Jean-Paul, it was quite another matter. And now Jeremy was beginning to change and Christina felt that it was a good sign. The rest of her family, Aunt Susan, Alice, Adela, respected Jeremy and his opinions – Aunt Susan especially. If he gave Jean-Paul both approval and friendship, they would do likewise.

And he certainly seemed to be doing just that, unbending from his previous chilly aloofness to engage Jean-Paul in conversation, showing an interest in French glassmaking, a desire to involve the Frenchman more closely in their own methods. He had taken Jean-Paul to his father's own factory, explaining the making of crown glass which was their speciality; Samuel had invited him to dine, with Christina, and his two brothers had been there as well; taking trouble, putting themselves out to welcome the stranger.

At first, Christina had been suspicious, afraid that they were trying to steal his expertise away from her. But that was nonsense; they had made no effort until after the engagement was announced, and even now there was never any suggestion of his switching allegiance. Samuel and Harold were, she was sure, too ingenuous to be playing a devious game, and although she could never be certain enough to say the same of Reuben, his lizard eyes met hers with a bland innocence that she had to be satisfied with. And in Jeremy's smile there was nothing but genuine friendship.

'We'll have to have a night out together before you go back to France, Jean-Paul,' he said, stretching himself lazily before the fire which they still needed on those cool spring evenings. 'You've had no fun at all since you came here, nothing but hard work. And a little courting, of course,' he added with a teasing smile at Christina.

'That would be pleasant,' Jean-Paul answered, accepting coffee from Lavinia. 'But I fear there will not be time. I am leaving sooner than I had expected, in only a few days. I have done all I can here for the time being, and Christina thinks it best that I take my workers away from the glasshouse before there is serious trouble.'

'Trouble?' Samuel looked up sharply. 'These rumours are true, then? There is unrest amongst your men, Christina?

Christina bit her lip, wishing Jean-Paul had not spoken. She had hoped to keep her problems quiet . . . 'Yes, I'm sorry to say there is, uncle,' she answered quietly. 'All totally unnecessary and very foolish – but they persist in thinking the French workers will take their jobs and there is even talk of a strike. I can't risk that; it would undo all the good Papa did and I have tried to do.'

Harold frowned. 'I heard there'd been violence too.'

'Yes. One of the Frenchmen, set upon and beaten on his way home one evening. There is no proof that it was a glassmaker and I don't believe it was. But these things can inflame others. There have been enough riots, with the Chartists and the Irish problems . . . I can't be responsible for any more.'

'So I return to France at the end of the week, taking my men with me.' Jean-Paul smiled at Jeremy. 'There will be few evenings left before my departure, and those I would like to spend with Christina. And therefore I cannot accept your offer of a "night out" – attractive though it sounds. Perhaps when I return.'

Jeremy was silent, his mouth sullen. He felt eyes on him, and turned his head to find Reuben watching him. The message was clear, and he steeled himself.

'Then I must find some other way in which to entertain you,' he said heartily. 'No – I insist. We have done little enough to welcome you into the family . . . Perhaps there is something else you would like to see, some other process in the glasshouse I could show you. Or something else, nothing at all to do with glass. Some of our famous sights perhaps at Dudley, or Warwick or Coventry.' He was floundering and he knew it. There could be nothing that Jean-Paul wanted to see again. But there had to be some way of arranging that the man should be alone with him – some way in which to carry out the plan that Reuben had proposed, dreadful though it was. He felt his forehead grow suddenly cold and damp with perspiration as he thought of it, but he could not draw back now.

Jean-Paul smiled a little, as if taking pity on this Englishman who was so pathetically anxious to make amends for his former rudeness.

'But yes, of course there is something,' he said, his eyes moving lazily from Jeremy to Christina. 'I was going to request it myself anyway. The changing of the glass-pots – so dramatic – that I should certainly enjoy seeing again. And in Christina's own glasshouse, I think, so that I can carry back with me the memory of her there, in the place she loves best.'

'The pot-setting?' Christina said. 'But you must have seen it time and time again.'

'It is something of which I never tire,' Jean-Paul said simply, and Jeremy cut in quickly, as if afraid he might change his mind.

'Of course you must see it,' he agreed warmly. 'And you're right – it's the most interesting thing of all. It will be a pleasure.'

Three nights later, Christina rose from her bed. She went to the window and drew back the heavy curtains, looking out at the night. For once, the smoke of the factory chimneys was less thick, no more than a copper mist over the garden. A full moon rode high, lighting the trees and bushes, throwing dense shadows on the dewy grass. It was red; as red as blood.

Christina drew her nightgown close around her. Restlessly, she roamed about the room, her feet bare and

311

soundless on the thick rug, only the moonlight casting its unearthly reddened glow across the floor. She looked at her bed, wide and empty, the sheets thrown back, and longing rose in her like a consuming fire, devouring her, tormenting her, refusing to be doused. For a moment or two she stood quite still and, finally, with a movement so quick that her nightgown swirled about her, she turned towards the door.

Jean-Paul was asleep. He lay half on one side, his arm flung out. His shoulders were bare, unhampered by any nightshirt, and his skin gleamed in the glimmering moonlight. He had evidently drawn back his own curtains before going to bed; perhaps he too had stood at the window, only yards from Christina, gazing up at the same moment, suffering the same yearnings . . . She closed the door softly behind her and stood watching him.

She had never seen a man sleeping before. His face looked as if it were carved from marble, the beauty of a Greek god warmed by the russet glow of the copper moon. It looked calm, restful, yet vulnerable to danger as anyone is when asleep. Her desire was pierced by a sudden fear for him, a fear that there was danger lurking . . . She pushed it away. There was no place for danger here, not for him, not for them. Their love was inviolate; as clear and lovely as crystal, and as tough as adamantine.

'Jean-Paul,' she whispered, and bent to touch him. 'Jean-Paul.' He stirred a little but did not wake. A brief smile touched his face; had he heard her voice in a dream? Christina knelt by the bed, her face only inches from his. 'Jean-Paul.'

This time, his eyelids fluttered and the silver of his eyes glinted for a moment, then vanished. There was a moment of stillness and then they opened again, more slowly now, and she saw them stare and widen.

'*Christina!*' he whispered unbelievingly.

Christina laughed, a giggle of excitement and fear of the unknown.

'I had to come,' she whispered. 'I couldn't sleep . . . I wanted you so much. You're going away again in a few days. I couldn't bear to let you go without – without once knowing . . .'

Jean-Paul watched her with that beautiful gravity which always brought a surge of love into her heart. His eyes were dark with concern – and their own burning desire, to which he would not give way.

'Christina, my love, what is wrong? Do you fear that I shall be like my father, and never return?' A smile curved his lips. 'I think our story would be very different. *You* would not sit at home waiting and wondering!'

'No – I'd be on the next boat, coming to see what you were doing!' Christina laughed a little, a nervous gaiety dancing in the eyes that were like deep green pools, then the laughter faded and she was as grave as he. 'Jean-Paul, my darling, I just want us to be together. To know each other properly – fully.' And she stood up, raising her arms to lift the nightgown from her body. It came over her head like a web of gossamer, so that her body was outlined mistily against the brightness of the window. With a graceful movement, she lifted it away from her and dropped it in a pool of white on the floor. Her loosened hair fell in a tawny cascade around her shoulders, the copper tendrils curling down over her breasts and reaching like strands of shimmering silk to her nipples. There was the faintest sheen of light in her darkened eyes.

Jean-Paul slowly pushed back the covers and rose from the bed. He stood naked before her, his slender body white and straight. He reached out and took Christina's hands and they stood linked, studying each other in shy, yet frank, appraisal.

Christina felt her breath quicken. Her heart had begun to pound, slowly and forcefully, driving the singing blood around her body. She felt it pulse through her veins,

313

tingling in the fingertips that Jean-Paul held in his, curling her toes. She looked at Jean-Paul's body, so gloriously, positively male, at the desire that revealed itself so unmistakably. She felt his eyes on her; moving slowly down from her face to her shoulders, to the fullness of her breasts with the nipples already standing out, proud as pegs; down to the dark copper triangle of hair between her creamy, rounded thighs. She lifted her chin, in that characteristic gesture of hers, and offered him her lips.

He did not take them at once. Instead, he laid both hands on either side of her face and gazed down as if memorising every tiny detail.

'This will be our wedding night,' he said softly, his voice deep in his throat. 'The night that is ours alone. Other wedding nights – everyone knows about them. But this one is entirely private.'

He bent his head then and kissed her.

Christina felt herself lifted on her toes, lifted from the floor as he held her against him. Joy pulsed between them with sudden, rocking violence, as if every muscle, every vein, every fibre of skin and bone and sinew were part of the same body. There was no restraint in their kisses now as their mouths opened to each other and their tongues entwined. There was no restraint in their bodies, straining towards each other with an eagerness that nothing could deny.

Jean-Paul turned to lay Christina gently on the bed. She was trembling, her body burnished by the glow of the moon that rode high and red above the window. He looked down at her for a moment, then ran his hands lightly down the length of her body and laid himself beside her.

At first, it was sweetly familiar; the movements and sensations that she had first experienced on the ridge above Kinver, with dappled sunlight shining down through the trees. She began to move, driven on by urges she barely understood, instincts which told her that her

314

body knew better than she. She moved against him, delighting in the subtle friction of his silky hairs against her own smooth skin. He thrust against her body and she pressed harder, feeling the strange hard smoothness, the throbbing rigidity. Jean-Paul disengaged himself and knelt beside her. He began to kiss her, slowly and thoroughly, from her lips, down her arched throat, to her breasts. He bit gently at each nipple, circled each breast with tiny pecks, cupped their fullness in his hands and laid his face in the burgeoning softness, and then he moved on, trailing more burning kisses down her stomach, to the fine, silken skin on her inner thighs, and to the secret spring between, which brought a shuddering gasp to her breath, a whimper to her throat.

Christina lay supine, unable to move. She felt as if he had paralysed her, as if his kisses had contained some strange, exotic ingredient that drained the strength from every muscle, slid the very bones from her body, leaving only the thundering heart, the singing blood and the whirling, scorching desire. The need for a climax to this intolerable tension, this burning, throbbing, overwhelming compulsion.

Jean-Paul paused once more. He rose above her, looking down, and his eyes were now as dark as her own. Christina felt her heart skid to a stop. And then she lifted herself to him.

It was as if it were a signal. There was an end to the gentleness and passion took its place, an unthinking, mindless meeting of bodies that were now totally in the control of their ageless instincts. Limbs met and meshed, twined and parted; lips devoured the flesh that was so freely offered, searching every crevice, discovering every pulse. And Christina, who had wondered if she would, when this moment finally came, understand what was required of her, realised that there had never been any cause for concern. Her body settled under his as if it had been born there; her thighs parted to accommodate him,

315

clasping him firmly as he came to her; there was one sharp pain, a feeling of something tearing, a momentary recoil, and then a soaring ecstasy.

For a few seconds, Jean-Paul lay still and quiet, enclosed by her arms, her legs, her warm, pulsing body. At last he began to move, gently at first then with increasing vigour. And Christina moved with him, catching a rhythm that was as old as time, the very heartbeat of the earth. Her arms tightened around his body, drawing him further and further in. He slipped one hand under her buttocks and his body struck at hers, was met joyfully and relinquished. The crescendo of sensation mounted, and peaked with an exquisite explosion that seemed to fill the room with stars.

Jean-Paul fell against her. She held him close, feeling his damp hair tangle with hers. Slowly, the pounding of her heart began to calm. A warm peace rose like a tide through her body and into her mind.

'Christina,' he murmured, and laid a soft lingering kiss on her throat. *'Je t'aime.'*

'I love you, Jean-Paul,' Christina said quietly. 'I love you very, very much.'

They lay entwined for the rest of the night. And it was only early in the morning, when the birds woke them and little Daisy, in the kitchen, had already begun her day's work, that Christina left his bed and went back to her own; where Ruth found her later, fast asleep with her hair tousled and a smile of pleasure curving her bruised lips.

Chapter Fifteen

It was on his last day in Wordsley that Jean-Paul went with Jeremy to watch the pot-setting.

They had spent a good deal of time together in the past week. Christina, relieved and grateful for Jeremy's apparent change of heart, had overcome her desire to be with Jean-Paul at every possible moment, and had left them alone, to sit for hours discussing glass or, Jeremy's other abiding interest, politics. Jean-Paul had a considerable knowledge of the French Revolution, which had taken place within the memory of many of the older men in his father's glasshouse, and Jeremy showed great interest and never tired of asking questions about this turbulent period.

'There are fears that it could happen here, even now,' he remarked one day. 'The Crown fell into disrepute in the last century, and is still by no means as stable as it ought to be, even with the young queen and her consort. There are plenty of people who think he is trying to govern the country through her, and the British don't take kindly to the idea of being ruled by a German. And with this Chartist movement so strong still . . .' He shook his head.

'Ah, democracy is the only way,' Jean-Paul declared. 'The principles of *liberté, égalité, fraternité* – these are what will make France great again. You English are still bound by the feudal system – the master and his servant. It will not do any more. This is the nineteenth century.'

'Yes, but this idea of working men being given the vote!' Jeremy moved impatiently. 'How could they possibly know what is good for the country? Uneducated, uninformed, living in conditions I wouldn't wish on a dog . . . they'll vote for anyone who promises them more ale.'

'Then educate them, inform them, pay them higher wages, so that they can live in better conditions. It is all so easy.' Jean-Paul quirked his brows humorously, 'It is better than going to the guillotine, *mon ami*!'

Jeremy gave him a sharp glance, then smiled in return. 'I think it is as well you are returning to France, you speak as though you approve of these Chartists and their demands. You should watch your tongue, someone might take you seriously, whereas I know you're only joking.' He lifted his glass and drank. 'No, it's simply not possible. The working class is in the place where it belongs now. It will never be lifted out of it. They're just not capable of education, you see. Not capable of understanding the complexities of parliamentary business or financial affairs. Why should they be? They have their trades, at which they are accomplished, and to tell them of other ways of living would only make them discontented, to no good purpose.'

'And their housing? Their insanitary conditions? I know that Christina is not the only one to be disturbed about this.'

Jeremy snorted. 'A lot of nonsense! They *like* living like that – they know nothing else. And there is no possible way in which it could be relieved, without causing a great deal of trouble. You see –' he leaned forward '– if we gave them better housing, as we have in the case of the better workers, like the gaffers, there would be even more competition between them for work. That would have the effect of *reducing* wages – bringing them back down to subsistence level once more. And if it didn't, they would simply have even more children than they do already, with more surviving, too, so once again living conditions would deteriorate, right back to where they are now. No it's a natural law and any improvement is simply a foolish dream. I've tried

318

again and again to explain this to Christina, but she can't see it.'

They talked like this for hours, arguing good-naturedly, although occasionally Jeremy's lips would tighten with irritation and he would have difficulty in controlling his retort. But Christina was happy to see their friendship apparently deepen and increase, and as long as she could have Jean-Paul to herself for these last few nights, she didn't mind so much seeing less of him during the day.

And now it was Jean-Paul's last day. It was just six o'clock when they entered the glass cone together, Christina between the two men and Ruth following quietly behind. The usual echoing clatter of the irons, the men's voices and the hundred and one other noises of the glassworks, were dying as the men finished their work and did what tidying-up was necessary for the weekend. Joe Compson and his chair, together with some of the teasers from the furnace mouth down below, were clearing the space in front of one of the gaping red mouths, ready to take out the old pot and replace it with the new one, already waiting in the pot-arch nearby.

Jeremy, Jean-Paul and Christina arranged themselves in a small semicircle a little distance away, and waited.

There was an odd hush. The men who had been leaving, paused at the door and turned back. Joe, who had been in the act of lifting a jug of ale to his mouth, lowered it again. The young taker-in who had been shovelling red-hot metal from the pot which was to be changed, stopped and stared, sideways, as if afraid to be seen looking directly.

'What's wrong with them?' Jeremy muttered.

'They are angry because I am here with Jean-Paul.' Christina spoke calmly, but her heart was thumping sickly in her throat. She knew that they had reached a crisis point. This afternoon's visit was being seen as a significant moment. A statement by her as to what the future was to be.

And she too saw it as significant – a moment in which,

once and for all, her authority over these men which had been challenged both overtly and subtly, was to be either confirmed or rejected. If they were to declare battle now, it was a battle she had to win, or she might as well hand the whole business over, lock, stock and barrel, to her father's cousins, the rival Henzels who wanted it so much.

And I won't do that, she told herself fiercely, and felt the old exhilaration surge through her, bringing her a strength she desperately needed. Opposition! As always, it brought out the best in her, defined the qualities which had caused Joshua to leave the glasshouse to her. So they wanted a battle – well, so be it! Christina could fight as long and hard as any man there, and that included Joseph Compson.

She lifted her chin and looked directly at him.

'We're waiting, Joe. Is there any reason why you shouldn't begin?'

Joe returned her look steadily. He glanced round at the men, now forming a silent semicircle behind him. Deliberately, he drew the back of his hand across his lips and then wiped it down his dusty trousers.

The silence in the cone was almost tangible. The other men watched, unmoving. Their faces were grim; some of them held glassmaking tools – punty-irons, pucellas, battledores, shears. And held them as if they were weapons.

Beside her, Christina felt Jeremy stir. Without taking her eyes off Joe, she put out a hand, motioning him to be still. This was something she had to deal with herself, and deal with alone. This was the moment on which her future in the glasshouse depended. Her behaviour now was crucial.

'Joe.' Her voice was steady, remote, as cold as an icicle. 'We are waiting for you to begin. Please don't keep me waiting.'

There was a slight stir amongst the men, as if her voice had broken some spell. But she did not glance at them.

320

Her eyes, clear as a green mountain pool, were holding Joe's, absorbing that smouldering brown stare, bouncing her own defiance back at him in a battle of wills as savage as a sword-fight. Her chin was up, her small, slender figure straight as an iron; danger was in the firm set of her lips. For all the difference in their sizes, she had never looked more like Joshua.

Joe wiped his lips again, the gesture a studied insolence. He let his eyes shift from Christina to Jean-Paul, and he jerked his head.

'We ent working with him in the cone.'

There was a rustle amongst the men, a low murmur of agreement. With difficulty, Christina kept her temper – how dared he speak in that way, assuming an authority he certainly did not possess.

'Let me remind you, Joseph, that this is *my* cone, and I shall bring here whomever I wish. And you are my employee – for the present.' She paused to make sure he understood the implication. 'Now, will you please begin.'

Joe's eyes flashed. He glanced around him again. 'When the Frog's out of it,' he said, and Christina felt a surge of fury.

'You will *not* speak to my guests in that fashion. Apologise at once!'

'Christina,' Jean-Paul murmured beside her, 'there is no need. Don't make matters worse. He has to make a stand – but he would probably like it to be resolved without trouble as much as you would.'

Christina wavered. She looked at Joe again and saw only implacability in the powerful face.

'My guests and I stay here,' she said firmly. 'And I shall not ask you again to begin.'

'That'll save us all a deal o' trouble, then,' Joe said and turned away. He faced the silent crowd of men. 'You hear that, lads? It means we're out – on strike. No more work until the Frogs hev gone – every last man jack of them,' he added, turning back to shoot a look of venom at Jean-Paul. 'And gone away to stay away.'

321

'*No!*' Christina stepped forward. Her face was pale, even in the ruddy glow of the furnace, and her eyes flashed, fiery emeralds set in the ivory of her cheeks. 'There will be no strike!' She stood, small and proud, on the flagged floor, gazing round the throng of faces. 'How can you even think of such a thing?' she demanded passionately. 'You, who have worked for Henzel's all your lives, some of you the latest in a long line of glassmakers, workers who have given my family generations of loyalty? How can you sink to withdrawing your labour, the only thing you have which gives you self-respect?' She swung round on each man in turn. 'You, Jem Husselbee. You and your father and your grandfather have been part of Henzel's ever since it began. You, George Scrivens, Sam Sheldon, Tom Cartwright – you've known me ever since I was a child. Why do you no longer trust me? Why do you think I mean to take your jobs from you? Am I such a fool that I don't realise I have the best glassmakers in the Black Country? Am I so likely to throw away the skill and craftsmanship it took your fathers and mine to build up?' She turned a look of venom on Joe that was equal in ferocity to his own, and added with withering scorn, 'Why do you believe *him*? He may be the finest gaffer in glassmaking, but he is still only a glassmaker. And that's all he ever will be. My great-grandfather was the same, but he became his own man and founded Henzel's. And I mean to carry it on, with or without Joe Compson or any other man who dares to tell me what to do.' Her eyes were as hard as agate as she raked them over Joe again, and then turned away as if he were of no account. 'Joe Compson will never be his own man. And if he doesn't want to be mine, he needn't. But he will have to be someone's, if he doesn't want to starve.'

When she finished speaking, there was a silence, broken only by the steady burning of the furnace, diminished to ease the difficulties of the pot-setting. The men were shifting uneasily, glancing at each other, looking at the floor, the dome in the middle of the cone – anywhere but at Christina.

'Trust me,' she said softly, and lifted her hands in appeal.

Jem Husselbee walked across to his chair and laid down the iron he was holding.

'Reckon I'm going.' He walked towards the door, watched by every person present. Christina felt her heart jerk painfully in her throat: was he still backing Joe, making himself the first man to walk out of Henzel's in protest? The tension stretched between them, thin almost to breaking-point as he paused and looked back.

'Don't you be late now, next Tuesday,' he admonished the young taker-in who had recently become apprenticed on his chair. 'There's plenty others want jobs here if you don't. And there'll be foot-ale to pay, too, if you're caught talkin' to the wenches again over Sunday.'

He went out. The doors slammed behind him. And immediately, the cone was in uproar.

Every man turned and started talking to his neighbour. Every man raised his voice, determined to be heard. Christina stood quite still, conscious of the two men beside her. Had she won, beaten Joe Compson, and proved to them all, finally, that she was the mistress of Henzel's?

It all depended on what happened next. Jem Husselbee had made his own declaration by laying down his iron and leaving the cone. For any man in doubt, that final admonishment to the young taker-in had made it clear: Jem would be reporting for work on Tuesday. He had accepted Christina's plea. He was not on strike.

The men were silent, watching her, glancing at each other. She met their eyes steadily, proudly, knowing that this was the moment of decision. The tradition of generations, matched with the emerging restlessness of a new age.

George Scrivens was the first to break the tension that had mounted within the cone. With the deliberation of a man who has come to a decision, he marched across to his chair, laid down the pucellas he was carrying, lined them up with the other tools, turned to the men and said, loudly, 'I ent never striked afore, and I don't reckon to start now,' and walked towards the doors.

'Aye,' said his brother Tom, who always followed where George led, 'and that goes for me, too.'

And then the noise broke out again. Voices, the clatter of tools being replaced, dropped, left lying on the chairs or stood beside them on the floor. The tramp of boots on stone, sounding like a military charge as the men flocked towards the door. There was a struggle to leave, to get away, out into the air – and probably the tavern – where the whole thing could be discussed far from Christina's ears. The cone emptied as quickly as if it had suddenly caught fire. And Christina knew that she had won; the men were leaving in peace, meaning to report for work on Tuesday.

Now only Joe and the members of his team stood between Christina and the furnace. She turned slowly and rested her eyes once more on Joe. In that moment, she was as imperious as a queen.

'I think we have waited long enough,' she said coolly. 'You may begin now.'

Joe flung her one glance of such smouldering resentment that strong men would have quailed before it. Christina met it without flinching. The anger that boiled inside her was a match then for any fury of Joe's and as their eyes met she knew that he recognised it. He also recognised that he had – this time, at least – failed. Like a great bear baulked of its quarry, he turned to the rest of his chair, who still stood waiting nervously for his orders, whether they were for work or strike. He jerked his head.

'All right, then! What are you all gawkin' at? Let's get this pot changed and get home to our suppers. Sooner we get this done, sooner we can be gettin' a bit of clear air into our lungs – and better company besides.'

With a relief that made her feel weak, Christina watched the team begin to take up their positions for the pot-changing. Beside her, she felt the two men relax. She turned to Jean-Paul and smiled.

'Why didn't you tell him we were leaving?' he murmured. 'It would have been easier, surely.'

Christina shook her head 'It would have resolved nothing. It wasn't just about you, Jean-Paul, it was about the whole situation here, my running Henzel's – everything. I had to prove to the men that *I* was in charge – not Joe. If I'd taken the easy course then, there would have been another problem soon, and it would have been all the harder to resolve because I'd evaded it this time.'

Jean-Paul nodded slowly. He looked across her head at Jeremy and said with a smile, 'I think we have a very clever lady here, *non*? She would make a good diplomat.'

Christina laughed. 'Then you're the only person who thinks so! I've always been told I speak before I think, and often don't think at all. I'm sure Aunt Susan still believes I'll bring disaster to us all some day.'

'No, you are not made for disaster. For a little adversity maybe, for you are a fighter, my Christina. But disaster, *c'est impossible*.'

'You see, he is an accomplished fortune teller as well,' Christina began, turning to Jeremy. 'Perhaps he will read your palm, like a gypsy and tell you what the future holds for you.' Her voice trailed away as she caught sight of his expression in the shifting red gloom. 'Jeremy? Is there anything wrong?'

Her cousin was staring at her almost as if in the grip of some strange horror. His eyes were wide and dark, black holes torn in a paper-white face flushed only by the furnace glow. He seemed rigid, paralysed.

'Jeremy!' Christina shook his arm, her voice frightened. 'What is it? What's the matter?'

With a visible start, Jeremy came to himself. He blinked, shook his head and stared at her for a moment as if he were not quite sure who she was. He glanced across at Jean-Paul, his brows drawing together a little as if in faint puzzlement. Then he smiled and shrugged in his familiar, casual way.

'What's wrong?' Christina repeated, her eyes wide with anxiety.

'Wrong? Why, nothing. I was just thinking of something else for a moment . . . You're quite right, Jean-Paul, Christina is a very clever girl. Her father certainly knew what he was doing in leaving the glasshouse in her hands. Look! They're just about to pull out the old pot. You can see right into the eye of the furnace itself. Let's go closer – feel the tremendous heat.'

'No, please, it's not good to go too close,' Christina began, but Jeremy laughed.

'Nonsense! It's perfectly safe. The men do it all the time. And you can't see properly from here. Jean-Paul, I want to show you – take that piece of smoked glass Christina is holding, it'll make her happier. Now, come over here and see this . . .'

The two men approached the mouth of the furnace, with the fire clearly visible around the pot which stood isolated now in its own inferno. As they did so, Joe and the team approached with the pot-wagon, its long curving spike ready to be inserted under the pot and used as a lever to draw it out. The heat then would be intense, blazing almost visibly from the gaping red hole left in its jaw like that of a tooth recently pulled.

With the spike almost in position, Joe paused, gesturing to his team. His face was grim, angry. He left the wagon and, with his gatherer, went towards Jeremy and Jean-Paul, close now to the searing heart of the open pot. The four men shifted in the blinding heat, their images blurred and whitened in the darkness of the smoked glass: images that hesitated, wavered, merged . . .

What happened then, Christina could never clearly remember. Perhaps the horror of it was too great; perhaps she had really not seen. All she could ever picture was a sudden movement, a commotion: a shout from Joe, a cry from Jeremy and then they were all around the mouth of the furnace. And there was a long, thin scream which seemed to belong to nobody, but which Christina, paralysed where she stood, recognised at once as the sound of a soul being torn from its body.

It seemed an age, an eternity of panic and confusion and shouting around the searing heat of the furnace, before they came to tell her what she already knew; that Jean-Paul was dead. And then she and Ruth were being led from the cone, led by a Jeremy who looked as white and shaken as they, who trembled and shook his head and, once outside, had to stop and be sick. And although she begged, they wouldn't let her see Jean-Paul, not even for one last goodbye, not even to bring home to her the truth that she knew but could not face. It was better not, Joe said, his voice rough. It wasn't a sight for ladies, not even for the gentleman's affianced wife.

Later, they told her that he had fainted and fallen headlong into the merciless heat. Apart from the moment when he had screamed, he could have known nothing.

His face had been burned quite away.

Chapter Sixteen

The days that followed Jean-Paul's death took on a dimension of their own, following no rules, either of time or place. An hour would pass without Christina even being aware of it; an hour, two hours when she would not move, would simply stand at the window staring blindly out into the garden, or sit at the empty fireplace, gazing into flames that did not exist. And the very next hour would drag, so that she could scarcely convince herself that it was still the same day, and would snap impatiently because things she wanted done appeared to have been neglected.

She would be walking under the trees with Ruth, dry-eyed and stony, and then, without knowing how the change had come about, would find herself in her room, lying on the bed in a paroxysm of grief while Ruth sat with her arms round her shoulders, giving what comfort she could and knowing it could never be enough.

'Why?' Christina would cry, beating the pillows with her fists. 'Why did it have to happen to him? Why should it happen at all – they hardly ever have accidents, serious ones, in the glasshouse. Why Jean-Paul? I loved him! We were going to be married.'

She spoke in a tone of bewilderment, as if the fact of their loving each other should have been enough to keep him safe, a talisman against disaster. And she thought of Jean-Paul's words about disaster.

'*You are not made for disaster*,' he had said. '*For a little adversity maybe, but not for disaster.*'

They had been almost the last words he had said to her. Why did his last words have to be so dreadfully, horrifyingly wrong?

'What *happened*?' she demanded of Jeremy, who came

to see her with a face as ashen as her own. 'What caused it? Aunt Susan tells me not to think about it, but I have to. I can't help it. I have to know what happened, and you were there. You must know.'

Jeremy sighed and shook his head. His corn-gold hair was the colour of dried grass now and even the blue of his eyes seemed to have faded. When he raised his hand to smooth back the dusty strands, his fingers shook.

'God knows, Christina. There were several of us at the furnace as they started to lift out the pot. Jean-Paul, Joe Compson, the gatherer. There was a splash of metal, I think, perhaps it hadn't been sufficiently emptied, I don't know. We jumped back, all of us, and Jean-Paul seemed to slip. I reached out, grabbed at his arm, but it was too late.' His eyes avoided hers. 'It was so quick, Christina. There was nothing anyone could do.'

'And that's all that happened?' She tried to visualise the scene again, the glimmering darkness, the sudden huddle of bodies, the cries, the confusion. 'Joe shouted something. Was that when Jean-Paul slipped?'

'It may have been.'

There was something in Jeremy's tone she didn't understand. She looked at him searchingly and saw his eyes slide away. She took his hand.

'Jeremy, you must tell me everything. I have a right to know. And it was in my glasshouse. I – I'm *responsible*.'

'No! Nobody could blame you, Christina. You weren't even near –'

'It was in my glasshouse,' she said steadily. 'It could have been one of my men. I would have been held to be responsible. Please, Jeremy – tell me exactly what happened.'

'I have,' he murmured, but she shook her head.

'No. Not everything. Look at me, Jeremy, and tell me. *Please*.' The intensity of that last word made her voice tremble. With an effort that was as great as any she had ever made, she kept the tears from her eyes, but their

330

message was clear. Jeremy, forced to meet them, sighed again.

'Very well, Christina. And then, perhaps, we may talk of something else. This is painful to me too . . . I don't know exactly what happened. There was some confusion, and the heat was intense – perhaps he fainted. But . . . I am not sure that Joe didn't move then too. Somebody did, quite violently. I know I cried out, thinking how dangerous it was, just before Jean-Paul fell. I – Christina, I've tried not to think this, not even to let the thought enter my mind, but it keeps nagging at me. I'm not sure I can even say it, but . . .'

'You think Joe pushed him.' Her voice was small and flat, the voice of total despair, the voice from the bottom of a dark, deep pit from which there is no escape. Jeremy waited for a moment; then, reluctantly, he moved his head.

'It could have happened, Christina. I'm not saying it did – I can hardly believe it myself. I don't *want* to believe it. But – well, we all knew how Compson felt about Jean-Paul. He'd made it clear only a few minutes before. And when you defeated him so admirably –'

'So it's my fault!' Frantically, Christina began to weep again, her face buried in her hands, the tears streaming through her fingers. 'I brought Jean-Paul's death on him, as surely as if I had pushed him myself. I thought I was so clever, too, winning that stupid battle with Joe. Refusing to tell him the French were leaving, because he hadn't believed me before. Thinking I had to show him who was mistress of Henzel's. And none of it mattered! I could have told them the truth and averted a strike, and Joe would not have hated me or Jean-Paul, he would never have done such a dreadful deed . . .' She raised her face, her green eyes magnified by the tears that burst from them like water from a breached dam. 'But he did it, didn't he? You didn't want to say, but you know he did it. And he'll suffer for it, Jeremy. I shall see that he suffers for it – for the rest of his life. As I shall suffer.'

'It would be difficult to prove –' Jeremy began uneasily, but she cut in sharply.

331

'Oh, I don't need proof. I know you're right. I think I must have known all the time . . . That look he gave me when I told him to start work; the way he looked at Jean-Paul . . . I don't need a magistrate to help me punish him, Jeremy. I can do that myself.'

Jeremy looked at her. Her face was set in hard, bitter lines, its gaiety and mischief obliterated by grief and angry determination.

'What do you mean to do?'

'I'll see that he never works again in Wordsley,' she said slowly. 'Or anywhere in the Black Country. I mean to reduce him to nothing, Jeremy. I mean to be able to go out from here and see him scavenging cullet from the streets; picking up broken glass to sell to whatever crib is desperate enough to buy it. Once I've seen that, I'll be satisfied. After that, he can starve.'

Jeremy passed his hand over his hair. He shook his head thoughtfully.

'Christina, if that makes you any happier, then do it. But I'm not sure that it will. Wouldn't it be better if Joe Compson were simply removed from here? If you simply never saw him again, never knew what had happened to him, wouldn't that be better? No bitter reminders; no sad memories. Isn't that the answer?'

Christina lifted her eyes to his. They were heavy with grief, her face thin and drawn with a pain she could not cope with, a pain even worse than the one she had suffered after her father's death.

'Joe Compson's presence will make it even worse for you,' Jeremy said gently. 'You don't need any more suffering. Let him go . . .'

'Go where?' she said dully. 'Joe only knows Wordsley and the Black Country. Where could he go?'

'Leave it to me,' Jeremy said.

The funeral was held a week later, and to Christina it seemed like a macabre re-enactment of her father's funeral, less than two years earlier. This time, the weather was warm and sunny as if in reminder of Jean-Paul's youth; only thirty years old, and dead through a tragic and avoidable accident. Her tears flowed freely at this service, attended by so few mourners – herself and her family, the Frenchmen who bore the coffin and a few sombre, black-suited gaffers from the glasshouse. Joe was not among them, and Christina was thankful not to see him, yet bitterly resented his absence.

Flouting all convention, past caring now what Stourbridge society thought of her, she followed the coffin to the grave and stood with her heavy veil blowing gently in the summery breeze, listening to the final words. *Dust to dust, ashes to ashes* . . . The bitter irony of their meaning struck at her heart, and when she stepped forward to throw a handful of soil on the coffin before it was finally covered from her sight, she threw tears as well.

She stayed after the others had walked slowly away, refusing Jeremy's arm, silently determined to have these last moments alone with the man who had taken her heart into the next world. The heavy veil moved in front of her face, casting shadows over her vision. When at last she looked up and moved away, the shadow before her was large and heavy; too solid to be anything but real.

'Miss Christina, I wanted to talk to you . . .'

The voice was deep and roughened with the local accent, sickeningly familiar. How many times had she listened to this voice in the glasshouse, in her own house, listened for hours in the warmth of the library? Anger flooded in, a hot rush of fury that scorched through her body and brought a painful clarity to her mind.

'Joe Compson. What do you think you are doing here?'

He shrugged, looking as nearly helpless as she had ever seen him. She lifted her veil, let the icy coldness of her eyes strike at him, saw him flinch and rejoiced.

'I wanted to see you, Miss Christina. And I thought I ought to be here – to pay my last respects, like.'

'Respects? You? What do you know of respect?' Her voice lashed him, thin and cutting as a whip. 'And how can you dare to come here – to have the insolence to stand by the grave of a man who was a finer man than you will ever be? How can you dare to approach me, on this of all days?'

'I had to.' There was desperation in his voice, a desperation she heard and was glad to ignore. 'I had to tell you . . . I never intended him harm. What happened at the furnace – it wor an accident. I'd never hev set out deliberate to – to . . . His voice broke and he shook his great head. 'Please believe me.' He was humble then, humble as he had never been before, but to Christina it meant nothing now.

'Believe you? Why should I believe you? Did you believe me, when I told you the Frenchmen were going back to France? Did you stand by me when I needed you?' She slashed him with a contemptuous glance. 'You don't even believe yourself,' she said clearly. 'You know what happened at the furnace, and so do I. Don't try to pretend otherwise. And now – go away. As far as you can. I don't want to see you again, anywhere near this grave – anywhere near *me*.' To her dismay, she felt the tears burning yet again in her eyes. 'Just get out of my sight,' she said, her voice breaking. 'I never want to set eyes on you again, Joseph Compson. Never.'

Marc Thietry arrived too late for the funeral; by the time a message had been sent to him and he had arranged his journey, it was all over. They had hoped – Aunt Susan, especially, had hoped – that he might not come at all. But it was inevitable, Christina knew, that he would.

'And we must invite him to stay here,' she said to her aunt as they sat drearily discussing what must be done next. 'We cannot do otherwise.' She hesitated and glanced at Susan, feeling a deeper sympathy for her than she had ever known before. 'I'm sorry,' she said finally. Since the

334

funeral, her own emotions seemed to have died; she felt nothing now but a vast emptiness, stretching ahead of her like an endless desert. The rest of her life was to be nothing but a hopeless plod across it, with no chance of ever reaching an oasis.

Susan threw her a glance of bewilderment from eyes that seemed these days to be continually reddened. 'Sorry? You're sorry? I don't understand, why should *you* be sorry?' Without giving Christina a chance to answer, she got up and began to walk restlessly about the room, her hands clasped in front of her. 'It's I who should be sorry. I behaved so badly. I was inhospitable, discourteous, yes, even unkind. I did all I could to make him feel unwelcome. I took my revenge on him for what his father did, before Jean-Paul was even born. And I shall suffer for it for the rest of my life!'

Christina watched her helplessly. Her aunt's face was lined with remorse so bitter that it was painful to see. 'But you never really hurt him,' she said. 'He understood why you behaved like that. He was sorry for you, he hoped all the time that one day you would be friends.'

Susan turned and looked down at her, and her face crumpled. Christina rose quickly and caught the older woman in her arms. For the first time in their lives, aunt and niece clung together and wept; for a common grief.

It was unthinkable that Christina should allow her aunt to be alone when Marc Thietry arrived; which he did just as they were having afternoon tea, a few days after Jean-Paul's funeral. When Rose announced him, Christina flung a brief, questioning glance at her aunt's whitened face before asking the girl to admit him. In the tiny pause that followed, she was conscious of Susan's tension, her rapid breathing, the tightness of her clasped hands. She covered them with her own, and gave a reassuring squeeze. She was thankful now that her own feelings seemed to have been deadened, her grief numbed. If they had not, she would scarcely have had the strength for this meeting herself, and could certainly not have sustained her aunt as she knew she must.

But she was unprepared for the man who came through the door then and stood looking at them both, his eyes going from one to the other, his hands held out.

Jean-Paul! It was Jean-Paul as he would have been – in twenty-five, thirty years' time. The slender body a little thicker, broader, the hair receding, grey as iron now but still curling over the well-shaped head; the face delicate still but with an added gravity, a hint of wisdom. And the movements, the gestures, Jean-Paul all over again. No wonder Aunt Susan had found Jean-Paul's presence here so painful.

'Susan.'

The voice was deep, with an added richness to the timbre of Jean-Paul's caressing tones. Christina heard her aunt's gasp and moved slightly, to be closer to her. But there was no need. Susan was already on her feet, moving forward, her own hands held out. And he had taken them; was gazing down into her eyes, as oblivious as she was of their surroundings and the eyes that watched.

'Marc.' It was all Susan said, but there was a world of meaning in the tone; a world of forgiveness, of acceptance, the bitterness of the years discharged in one short word. And there was more. All the sorrow and sympathy she felt for his son's death. The remorse that more than equalled the bitterness that had come before it. The knowledge that Jean-Paul's fate overshadowed their own affairs and stripped them of the importance they had been given over the years. All that in one short word and the tone in which it was spoken.

'And this is Christina.'

Marc Thietry nodded and turned his attention to her, meeting her jade-green eyes with a glance that hit her like a blow. For a dizzy moment, she was back with Jean-Paul, looking into eyes that spoke of love . . . And then the impression vanished. Marc Thietry was not looking at her

336

with love: he was looking at her with a mixture that was composed of wariness, speculation, assessment and, perhaps, just a little pity.

Did he know? Christina wondered, feeling the warmth of his hand close around hers. Perhaps Jean-Paul had written and told him. He had said not – but there was more than ordinary interest in Marc Thietry's eyes.

'We are all so sorry that your visit has to be such a sad one,' she said formally. 'It was a great shock to us all, we were so fond of Jean-Paul.' Her voice trembled and broke, the emotions threatening to come to life again, and ruthlessly she thrust them away. She could *not* give way before this man. 'It was a terrible thing to happen,' she finished simply.

Marc Thietry nodded. 'Terrible indeed. The kind of accident one fears . . . And which so seldom happens, simply because of that fear. Do you know how –' He did not need to finish.

Christina shook her head. 'Nobody knows what happened.' She thrust away, too, the thought of Joe, his malevolent glance before they started work, the shout he had given just before Jean-Paul screamed . . . Nobody could say for certain, Jeremy had said, nobody could prove it. 'There were several of them there, and Jean-Paul wanted to see more closely. I had given him some smoked glass to protect his eyes – perhaps he just didn't see properly, or perhaps as they thought, he fainted with the heat . . . It was all over very quickly.' She thought of that scream which had seemed to go on and on, tearing at her mind, her heart, until her own screams had taken its place, and turned aside to hide her tears.

'I understand,' the Frenchman said quietly. 'I lay no blame.' He pressed Christina gently into a chair then and sat down himself, accepting a cup of tea from Aunt Susan. 'Now, I would like to see where the accident happened, and I would like to see my son's grave. Then I will go, and leave you to try to forget this terrible business. It is all any of us can do.'

'It is more than I can do,' Christina said in a low voice; and then, more firmly, as he turned towards her, 'Monsieur Thietry, I think you should know that your son and I wished to marry.'

She heard her aunt's gasp but did not turn her head. Her eyes were on his, drawing on the silvery light that had been Jean-Paul's. She did not know whether they were expressing understanding or shock, and she barely cared. She knew only that there had to be honesty between them.

'Yes,' he said quietly. 'I know.'

'You *knew*? Then he did tell you! But I thought –'

Marc Thietry cut her short, lifting one hand. 'No, he did not tell me. But I know – knew – my son well, Christina. I knew that something had happened. After a little, when he wrote to say he was coming home, and had something important to discuss, I knew what it must be. After all –' he flashed a glance, half-humorous, at Susan '– I knew just how delightful the Henzel ladies can be. And I was as certain as I could be that the lady in question this time must be you. When I saw you, there was no possible doubt.'

Christina held her eyes on his and saw his expression soften a little. Her glance fell then, and she said in a low tone, 'I didn't want to hurt Marie-Pierre. But she didn't love him, and I – I loved him so much.' Her voice was a cry of anguish now. 'We belonged together. We had no choice.'

Marc Thietry smiled slightly. 'Ah, you English, with your notions of love and romance! And Jean-Paul – I had thought him a better Frenchman than that. It is as well, I think, that I have had my own experience; otherwise I might have found it more difficult to understand.' His smile at Susan this time was apologetic. 'I am sorry, Susan, if that gives you pain. But we must understand these young people, must we not?'

Susan bowed her head. 'I'm afraid I didn't, Marc. I did

338

not welcome Jean-Paul here at first, and I did not want him to marry Christina . . .' She lifted her head and her eyes glittered with more tears. 'I was not kind to him, Marc, and I am deeply sorry for it now. Because I did like him, really. I could have become very fond of him. I believe I had already begun.'

'Then that is all that should be said.' He tasted the tea. 'I had not intended to speak of these matters until we had all had time to become accustomed to one another. But perhaps it is better that we have come to them so soon. We can be easy with each other now. We understand. And we can share our grief.'

He left a week later, taking with him Jean-Paul's belongings and the French engravers who had accompanied his son to Wordsley. On the last evening before he left, he came to Christina alone with a package.

'Jean-Paul wanted you to have this,' he said. 'I understand it was to have been a surprise for you. Jacques gave it to me this afternoon. It has been in the engraving shop all this time, forgotten.'

Christina took the package and opened it. Inside was a box, and inside the box lay the Compson Chalice. It had been engraved. Its curving shape now was etched delicately with a flowing representation of Wordsley, seen from the slopes of Dob Hill. The houses, the close-packed streets, the chimneys and the cones, they were all there, as Christina had seen them so many times before. And her own cones were in the foreground; larger, more imposing, more important than any of the others. The picture stretched three parts of the way round the glass. And on the fourth face, entwined like lovers, were the initials C and J.

Christina and Jean-Paul. Entwined, as they had been during those nights of rapture that she had believed set the seal on their future. Engraved for ever on the Chalice, as they were on her aching heart.

She held it in her hands and the tears fell on to its

gleaming surface, blurring the exquisite tracery, glimmering and magnifying.

The Chalice. Joe had made it for her, and Jean-Paul had engraved it. She had promised Joe that she would never allow it to be engraved. And Jean-Paul, not knowing that, had removed it from its shelf and taken it away to do this. And she had never even missed it.

'That's good of you, Ruth, to bring fresh tea and a cake,' Sal Compson said, sucking the thread before she inserted it carefully into the eye of the needle. 'I hope it's all above board, you won't get into trouble for it, will you?'

'Of course I won't!' Ruth set her gifts down on the scrubbed table and pulled off her shawl. 'Mrs Jenner knows all about it, she gave me the cake herself, and Miss Christina said I was to have it.' She didn't add that Christina had thought the Compson household might be in need of a little extra help now that Joe had lost his job. It was an aspect of her action that had occurred to Christina only after her furious dismissal of him; and although she had no intention of taking him back, she did not want his family – and Ruth's – to suffer.

'I don't want charity, mind!' Sal said sharply, as if reading her daughter's mind. 'Your father's wage is enough for us to manage on, aye, an' keep Joe as well, if need be.'

'What's that about keeping Joe?'

The two women jumped as the passage door opened and Joe came through with his father William. As usual on a Saturday night, they had been to the tavern together. Sal's eyes, missing nothing, took one glance and then narrowed. She gave Ruth a quick look and then jerked her head at the younger children.

'Up to bed, you three, and no arguin'. Your father's home, you can see that, an' he don't want you under his feet. Go on now, look sharp, I don't want to have to tell you twice.'

Willy and his sisters scrambled up from the floor, where they had been playing with some spills, and offered their faces for a goodnight kiss. William gave his absently, Joe with a casual indifference. But Ruth looked at the small faces and touched them with her fingers, gently, before kissing them with a rush of tender pity. All too soon they would be forced out of the secure warmth of this little room and sent to earn their own livings in the world.

'Goodnight, bairns,' she said softly. 'Sleep well. I'll bring you some more of they pictures next time I come, an' you can cut them out and make puzzles. Go on, now.'

She watched them go up the steep, narrow stairs that led directly from the room – Willy, looking more like Joe every day, and his sisters May and Ada, big enough to make rugs and wash dishes. It couldn't be long now before they had to do those things for other people, and she could only hope that they would find kindness; although even if they did, they were still doomed to work long, exhausting hours for little more than their keep.

'Come out of that dream, our Ruth,' her mother said sharply. 'Can't you see your father's got summat to tell us?'

William grunted. He was sitting in the best armchair, the one he had made for himself when he was married. It had a slatted seat with a cushion on it, and a back that could be adjusted so that he could lean back comfortably and go to sleep. When he was at work, Joe used the chair, but when they were both at home, at weekends, Joe sat on one of the kitchen chairs that were kept tucked under the table. Sal had her own, smaller armchair by the range. She sat there now and motioned Ruth impatiently to take a seat by her brother.

'Well? What's to do?'

William filled his pipe. He glanced up momentarily, his eyes as dark as Joe's under white brows, and jerked his head at his son.

'Ten't me got news for you. Ax our Joe here.'

341

Sal turned her head. Her eyes were as bright as a bird's and as suspicious as a cat's. 'What have you done now? Isn't getting the bag enough for you, without bringin' more trouble down on our headen?'

Joe's face flushed angrily. 'Who says I'm bringing trouble? An' what trouble hev I brought thee, anyway? It's my job that's lost and I'll be out from under your feet as soon as mebbe, an' then you needn't think about me no more!'

'All right, Joe, no need to snape. I jes' don't like hevin' the neighbours look at me as if my son's a murderer, that's all.'

'If you think that –' Joe began to rise and Ruth put out a hand and touched his arm.

'Don't, Joe. Can't you see she's upset? It's hard to understand – why Miss Christina should act as she has, if there was no blame on you. Hard for me mam, anyway, not knowin' the mistress, like.'

'Hard? I'm fair bamfoozled by it all,' Sal declared. 'But our Ruth tells me Miss Christina's so put about she scarce knows what she's doing, and with her being young an' all, we hev to try to mek allowances.' She looked at Joe and her thin, tired face softened, 'Of course I don't believe what they say, Joe. I know thee better than that. But you've come in early tonight, you and your father, and I can see there's summat up, so you'd better out with it an' tell us – what's happened now? We might as well know the worst straightaway.'

Joe subsided. His face was still dark, the brown eyes wary like those of an animal too badly hurt to trust again. The line of his mouth was bitter; his tone, when he spoke, defensive and rebellious.

'You might not think it worst at all – I don't. Best thing that ever happened to me.' He glanced at his father, still pushing the tobacco into his pipe. 'Truth is, I've been offered another job.'

Sal laid down her mending. 'A job? Already? Well, I

342

can't say I'm surprised, stands to reason someone'd snap you up, a fine glassblower like you. I'm right glad, Joe, that I am, an' you must be too. Who is it? Richardson's? Stevens and Williams? Whoever 'tis, they'll be lucky to hev you.'

Joe shook his head. He looked at his father again, but received no help from the lowered head. Ruth watched him, waiting for what she was sure was going to be unwelcome news – though she could not imagine what it might be.

'You won't guess who it is,' he said at last, and shot his mother a quick, half-guilty glance that nevertheless was tinged with triumph. 'It's Henzel's.'

'Henzel's? You mean she's taken you back? Is it me that's moithering, our Ruth, or him? Can *you* mek head or tail of what he's sayin'?'

'Not Henzel's in Stourbridge,' Joe said as if they ought to have understood him to start with. 'The other Henzel's. Henzel Brothers. They've offered me a job. And a better one than I had before, too,' he added, his voice rising a little. 'I'm to be in charge of a new cone, mekkin' lead crystal and coloured glass. I'll get more money than Miss Christina was paying me an' I'll hev more independence. I'll be overseer of the whole lot – what do you think of that?'

Sal and Ruth stared at each other, then turned their eyes back to Joe, who looked uncomfortable in spite of his declared satisfaction. Sal picked up her mending again and stared at it as if wondering what it was. She stabbed half-heartedly at it with the needle, then laid it down again.

'I still don't understand. What new cone? I never heard of one being built. An' why should they mek you overseer? It must be because they're trying to hurt Miss Christina in some way. I wish you wouldn't do it, Joe, and that's the truth. I know you hevn't allus seen eye to eye, but her father was good to thee, an' she's only a wench when all's said and done. And your own father's still workin' for her, too. I don't think you should go over to the others.'

Joe's face darkened again. 'So what should I do? Pick up cullet? Start my own crib in the privy? I hev to eat, don't I? Anyway, it's not the glasshouse here. I won't be working for Harold or Samuel Henzel. It's Mr Alfred that's offered me the job. Alfred up in Newcastle. And I mean to take it, whether or no. It'll be good to shake the dust of Wordsley off my boots, and that's straight.' He felt in his pocket for his own pipe and began ramming the tobacco into the bowl as if the entire Henzel family were under his thrusting thumb. 'Mek a new start,' he added without looking up again. 'That's the best way all round.'

The room was completely silent. Sal sat, her thread halfway to her half-open mouth, needle poised in her other hand, eyes wide. Ruth felt suddenly cold. She looked at her mother, at her father, but Sal's attention was fixed on Joe and William was staring at the range.

'Newcastle?' Sal said at last, and her voice was dry and rasping. 'You'm going to Newcastle?'

'That's right. It's all arranged. I'm to go as soon as the journey can be fixed – I'll be going by train part of the way! And I'm to be gaffer still, as well as overseer, with my own chair. I can hev a free hand, that's what Mr Jeremy said, a free hand to mek my own designs, an' a bit of respect to go with it. And I'll –'

'Mr *Jeremy*? What's he got to do with this?'

'Why, he offered me the job. Said his uncle wanted me. Sent a message that I should go as soon as mebbe.'

'I thought,' Sal said, threading her needle at last, 'that you hadn't got much love for Mr Jeremy Henzel.'

'Well, no more I hev,' Joe muttered, avoiding her eyes, 'but that don't mean I can't be civil to the man. An' this was a business talk, man to man. Nowt to do with anything else.'

344

'I just wonder why he should put hisself out for you,' Sal observed.

Joe moved impatiently. 'He *ent* putting himself out for me! He's getting me for his own uncle's glasshouse, before one of t'others snaps me up, like you said to begin with! You know they've all been wanting to get into flint glass – that little bit they've been mekkin' in't enough to get 'em a name. And there's none to speak of at all up in Newcastle, it's nearly all flat and bottle glass. That's why they want me up there. They're going to start a new line, and they need someone who can design shapes and blow them.'

'You,' Sal said.

'Mr Jeremy said it. Not me.'

Sal looked at her husband. 'And what do you think of this, William? You're very quiet over there.'

'I wanted to let you hev your say.' William Compson's voice was as deep as Joe's but the rich timbre was rusted. 'Don't seem to me there's much sense in thinkin' anything. Joe's a grown man, it's time he made his own way. And this is the best time to do it. Stourbridge ent no good to him no more, not as things are.'

Ruth watched her mother and saw her mouth suddenly work and tremble. Her eyes were fixed on her work again, but Ruth could see by the way she held the needle, the way the garment she was sewing – one of Joe's shirts, having its collar turned – shook, that she could not see what she was doing. The tears hung and shivered on her lashes; impatiently, she brushed them away.

'Well, that's that, then. You're off. All we can do is wish you luck and hope things goes well for you.' Her mouth was compressed into a tight line and her voice sounded almost angry, defying the tears to fall. 'You'll keep in touch, I hope. You can write a letter now and then.'

'I won't forget thee, Mother.' Joe too recognised the meaning behind Sal's brusque tones, and his own voice was softer now, the angry resentment gone. 'An' I'll be back, someday. I'll not let Stourbridge forget me, you can be sure of that. Nor Christina Henzel either,' he added, and his voice hardened until it rang with the force of iron. 'One day, she'll know the mistake she made, and she'll wish she'd never sent me away.' His dark eyes flashed with the old fire, and he lifted his chin in a gesture that was uncannily like that of Christina herself. 'She may regret me,' he said proudly. 'But she'll never forget me.'

And Ruth, staring at him, knew that he spoke the truth.

Joseph Compson left Stourbridge on a cool day towards the end of May. In spite of his bravado, he felt an odd panic as the day drew closer. He had never before been further afield than Dudley, to see the castle on top of its hill. The journey to Newcastle-upon-Tyne, so far north and on the other side of the country, was daunting; the thought of leaving all his mates, the men who had worked with him, the family and neighbours he had grown up with, and going amongst strangers, was even worse.

He could not, of course, admit these feelings to anyone. He spent his last few days at home swaggering the streets, behaving like a gentleman of leisure: an hour or two in the public house, a walk by the canal, a climb up Dob Hill to look down on the town – but that reminded him too strongly of Maggie and he didn't go more than once.

He thought of Maggie several times and wondered if he should go to see her. The baby must be due about now – when had it been that she'd pulled that trick, last September? He felt a twinge of conscience – maybe he should have married her, it was his bairn after all. But she hadn't wanted him then, had she? All set up for a fine lady with that Mr Jeremy – the man he'd sworn hatred against because he seemed to have everything Joe wanted, and yet was now proving to be his saviour. Without Jeremy Henzel and his offer of a job, Joe wasn't sure what he'd have done. Well, if Mr Jeremy wanted Maggie, bairn and all, why shouldn't he have her? If truth were told, Joe felt nothing for her now – hadn't for a long time.

Christina Henzel, now – she was different. He still couldn't rid himself of a mixture of feelings when he thought of her; feelings so strong, so powerful that he could feel them churning inside him, surging like sickness in his stomach, bringing a slow, painful pounding to his breast, an aching soreness to his throat. Anger: a bitter, resentful rage at the way she'd treated him. Taunting him with Mr Jeremy; letting him visit her at home and then standing by when the other man humiliated him. Spending time with him, consulting him over the new crystal, and then kicking him aside when that French engraver came over, almost laughing in his face over the question of shape or decoration, scorning the ideas he'd confided in her.

There were other things, too. The way she'd stand there in the smoky shadows of the cone, the red fire gleaming on her hair and turning it to copper, the colour of her eyes shifting from green to gold in the flickering dimness. Tiger's eyes. And a tiger inside that slender, upright body, too. He knew it, knew instinctively that Christina Henzel would be like a flame in a man's arms. scorching her way into his heart. She'd known it too, even if she'd never realised it. She'd known that if things had been different – if there hadn't been the barriers of class and trade and all the other obstacles that could never be overcome – she would have been Joe's woman, and he her man. But instead she hated him.

He'd despised himself for being so weak over a mere woman, and one that was out of his reach. He'd told himself it would pass, it was just a madness that would eventually leave him. But it didn't. And by now it had become a part of his life, a constant nagging pain that he had learned to live with because it was all he had.

It would be a good thing when he was out of here. Up in Newcastle, things would look different. There, he might at last be able to forget the bronze hair, the flashing eyes and become his own man again.

There was little preparation needed for his departure. Apart from his one good suit and his whippet, which he was leaving with William, there were simply his working clothes and a few bits and pieces – his pipe, the daguerreotype Christina had given him the day he had made the Chalice, the pewter tankard he drank his ale from, and little else. He looked at the daguerreotype for a long time, half inclined to throw it away. But he couldn't quite bring himself to do so. He had never before had a picture of himself. And although Christina was in it too, and his senses told him that it would be better left behind, he packed it just the same, in the old carpet bag he had bought from one of the cellar shops that were forever appearing on the pavements – pitiful attempts to make a bit more money, by women who could not go out to work or men crippled by disease and doomed either to starvation or the workhouse.

'I'll mek you a bit of bread pudding to tek with you,' Sal said a day or two before he was due to leave. 'And Ruthie said she'd get you summat from the kitchen there – Mrs Jenner offered a pie, I know that, an' mebbe there'll be a bit of fruit cake left over from their teas.'

'And what will Miss Christina hev to say to that?' Joe asked cynically. 'Or won't Ruth tell her? Like to see me starve, I heard – I can't see *her* sending me pie and cake. She dunna even know I'm going.' He had discovered that from Ruth, and made her promise not to tell her mistress where he was bound. 'Don't even tell her I've left Wordsley,' he added, his mouth grim. 'Let her wonder – if she ever thinks of me at all. She said she never wanted to see me again, well, that suits me too, an' she needn't know where I am either.'

Ruth, her eyes saddened by his bitterness, had agreed not to mention him again to Christina. 'And I don't think she'll ask,' she said regretfully. 'She still believes you – well, that you may have been clumsy at the furnace that day.'

'You mean she thinks I pushed the Frog,' Joe said flatly. 'Well, I told her I hadn't, an' if that's not good enough for her . . .' He paused, remembering that he had not believed Christina's word either, and shrugged angrily. 'It's better she forgets me,' he said with a rough indifference, 'an' better I forget her too. And that's what I mean to do, once I gets to Newcastle. It'll be a new life for me up there, and I mean to mek it a good 'un.'

But forgetting wasn't as easy as he pretended. And the memory of that last day at the furnace was the hardest of all to erase. Over and over again, his sleep was disturbed by a re-enactment of those last horrific moments. And always distorted. Sometimes it was indeed he who pushed Jean-Paul, taking the slender shoulder in one great hand and forcing the resisting body forward until the head, still frantically straining backwards away from the heat, was thrust into the merciless radiance. Sometimes it was Jeremy Henzel whose hand gave the fatal impetus, flashing a look of evil triumph at Joe from those bright blue eyes as he did so. And sometimes, in the worst of the dreams, it was Christina herself, suddenly amongst the little knot of men, her small hands held before her, palms outwards, fingers curled like claws, reaching, reaching . . . for whom?

Once again, those needing tranquillity in the Henzel household were drawn to the nursery, Thomas's nursery at the top of the house where the boy lived quietly and undemanding, playing eternally with his wooden bricks, his Noah's Ark and the farm.

For Christina, the nursery was a haven. Partly, she knew, because her aunt so rarely went there, and although

349

she and Susan were closer now, it was a closeness that became at times almost claustrophobic. Susan hugged her grief to her, wearing it like an outer garment, always on show. She went about the house like a spectre, her eyes huge and reproachful at any sign of normality – a laugh, a smile, a joke, all seemed to be a minor blasphemy to her – and because she knew that Christina's own sorrow must be even deeper than her own, she sought constantly to share it, to take it out and examine it, endlessly to discuss and wallow in it.

Christina bore this with as much patience as she could muster. She had learned from Jean-Paul during their brief courtship; she had learned compassion for her aunt, come to understand more about people, and her own loss had deepened that compassion, but she still yearned to escape occasionally, to breathe a freer atmosphere. Thomas's nursery, where her brother played in happy ignorance of the disaster that had occurred, gave her the rest she needed.

The best times, she found, were those when she could be alone with Thomas, the nursemaid dismissed to the kitchen for an hour or two. Her brother was thirteen now, able at last to tell a camel from a zebra and to hold long, rambling conversations about the small events that made up his day. His flattened features could split in a smile of endearing sweetness and he demanded no more than a hug, a kiss, and a few kind words spoken in a soft tone; his dislike of harsh voices was as strong as ever.

There were other times when Ruth sat with her in the bright rooms at the top of the house, and Harry too. The three of them developed an easy companionship: Ruth always with something to do, some mending or sewing which kept her hands busy and her eyes down, Harry – taller than ever now that he was almost eighteen – sprawled in the armchair with his legs half across the room, Christina curled into another chair with her eyes fixed on the child who sat on the floor, innocent as she would never be again.

Harry was coming to the end of his schooling now, and leaving King Edward's at the end of July. His future had been discussed before Jean-Paul had come to England, and it was arranged that he should go on to Oxford to study mathematics. This would be a better grounding than an immediate apprenticeship in engineering and although Harry fretted at the delay, averring constantly that by the time he obtained his degree it would all be too late, the railways built and the great engineering achievements over, he finally agreed and was now looking forward to becoming an undergraduate.

Their sojourns in the nursery were oddly silent. Christina would turn her eyes from one to the other, wondering what was going on in those still heads, while her own thoughts pursued each other endlessly through her weary brain. Still prominent, a perpetual shadow over her mind, was the death of Jean-Paul, that last horrific moment when there had been a sudden stir amongst the men at the furnace, a shout and then the long, thin scream that had sliced through her heart and still woke her in the night, leaving her cold and trembling.

There was Joe, the man she tried so hard to force from her mind, but too inextricably entwined in her memories to be expelled. Over and over again, she tried to untangle the confusion of her feelings about Joe. There was the way he had looked at her, insolent and audacious, when she had first inherited the glassworks. The way his slightly defensive challenge had thawed, warmed into the promise of friendship; a companionship that had grown slowly, tentatively like a delicate flower during those evenings in the library. But the promise had withered and appeared to die after Jean-Paul had arrived. Joe had hated Jean-Paul. He had thought him a threat in the glasshouse, a threat to the jobs of many of the men if not to his own. Had he thought him a threat in any other way? She shook her head; how else but through their work could Jean-Paul have threatened Joe?

351

And now she had lost them both. Jean-Paul had left her only an engraving on the Chalice Joe had made and a grave in the churchyard at Holy Trinity, close to her father's last resting-place. And Joe – no one had seen him since the week after the accident; nobody knew where he was or what had happened to him. Maybe it was best that way. She had told him she never wanted to see his face again, and she had meant it. This ache inside, this empty hollowness that seemed to fill and encompass and surround her, was more to do with Jean-Paul than Joe; it had to be, she wouldn't allow otherwise. And one day perhaps it would begin to fade, to hurt her less, so that she could go on with the long, hopeless trudge across the desert that life had become.

Meanwhile, there was the glassworks. And Harry, and Ruth and Thomas. They weren't enough. But they were all she had.

In this, however, Christina was wrong. Slowly, in the weeks that followed the accident, she began to return to her normal way of life, going to the glasshouse each day, talking to the men, consulting with the overseer and general manager. There was plenty to do. The new cutting and engraving shops were a success, the incessant high, whining scream that came from them testifying to the amount of work being carried on inside – and keeping Christina effectively out, for not only did the long workshops remind her too forcibly of Jean-Paul, the thin scream was too much like the last memory she had of his voice . . . She went into them only when compelled, forcing herself because she knew the men needed the approbation she gave so willingly to the glassblowers. And the work they did was excellent, bringing even more honour to the house of Henzel, well deserving of her praise.

Painstakingly, she moved along the benches on which the polished glass stood before being packed. Wineglasses, vases, epergnes, goblets, ewers and decanters – the range glittered in the light that fell from the skylights, the sun catching an edge with the sparkling iridescence of diamonds, the darkness of a passing cloud seen with menacing blackness in the curving belly of a bowl.

Joe's shapes, all of them. Cut and engraved with Jean-Paul's designs.

Christina lifted a fruit bowl, turning it this way and that, her hands spread delicately to cup its shape, her eyes following the exquisite tracery of the flowing design. A common fern, its fronds open like a hand in supplication, each tiny notch perfectly etched. She thought of it in palest green, the colour completing what had been started by shape and continued by incision . . . Yes, it would certainly look even more beautiful in colour.

And a lustre, its central column faceted to match the long, pendent drops that swung from its splayed top, it too would be improved by colour – a deep ruby, perhaps, overlaid with enamel painting and gilt. The vogue for coloured and painted glass was growing stronger and Henzel's, one of the first glasshouses to experiment with new processes, must continue to lead the field.

She turned away and left the cutting shop, hesitating before the cone where Joe had worked and where Jean-Paul had died. She had not yet been able to bring herself to go in there, though she knew one day she must. Nobody could be a successful glass manufacturer and be afraid to enter one of the most important parts of the glasshouse. For a moment she longed for Jeremy, who had been unfailingly kind and understanding since the horror of that April day. And then she took herself almost physically in hand. This was something she had to do alone; and it might as well be now.

With no more time for thought, Christina pushed open the outer doors, and then the inner ones. The noise, the smoke and the heat hit her like a blow. She let the door close behind her and stood there, in the shadows, her heart hammering.

It was just as she had remembered it – although what changes she expected to find, after only a few weeks, she couldn't have said. But its very sameness astonished her. Surely there ought to be some difference, some dramatic and radical alteration in this place where one powerful personality had worked and another died?

There was nothing; no hush, no diminishing in the noise and clatter she had always taken for granted; no respectfully lowered tones in the voices of the men, still calling to each other, shouting for ale, for a rag, for more metal; no lingering, shadowy memories lurking like ghosts in the corners; no imprint of bitterness, of jealousy and hate, of fear and sudden, violent death. It was as if nothing had ever happened here other than the making of glass.

Nobody haunted the cone; neither Jean-Paul, who was dead, nor Joe who was – where? And Christina, forcing herself away from the smoky wall which tapered up to that disc of sky, seen only intermittently between gusts of soot-laden smoke, began to walk round the chairs. The men were right – the work had to go on. Ghosts had no place in a glasshouse. So why did she faint, when she had almost completed her tour and was approaching the chair that had been Joe's? Why then, when she had overcome so much?

Ruth knew why. She was in Christina's bedroom when they brought her home, lifting her slight figure carefully from the carriage and carrying her into the hall under the shocked eyes of Parker and Rose. She looked down and saw them arrive, saw their anxious faces and the tenderness with which they handled their burden, and ran down the stairs so quickly that she afterwards declared she must have flown.

'What is it? What's happened?'

'Miss Christina,' one of the men said tersely and she recognised him as one of the glassmakers – Jem Husselbee, who had worked the next chair to Joe's. 'Fainted in the cone. Caught the heat, I reckon, but she dunna look well. Right thin and poorly if you ax me.'

They laid Christina on the couch that stood in the hall and Ruth bent over her, feeling the limp wrist, gazing in consternation at the fluttering eyelids, the pallor of the small face. She was conscious of the others crowding behind her, and quickly, she gestured to them to move back.

'Don't crowd her! She needs air. Rose – fetch some water. Mr Parker – get Edward to help you carry Miss Christina upstairs. Where is Miss Henzel?'

'Upstairs, lying down. I'll fetch her –' Rose was off but Ruth stopped her sharply.

'No! We'll deal with this ourselves. I've no doubt it's only a faint. She just needs to be in bed, quiet-like, and a glass of water to sip when she comes to herself.' Ruth stepped back reluctantly as Edward appeared. 'Take care with her,' she admonished as the two men lifted the fragile figure. 'She ent a rag doll.'

Parker gave Ruth a shocked and disapproving look and Rose sniffed and muttered something about 'cheeky hussy'. Ruth ignored them both. A year or so ago she would have shrunk from their disfavour – but then she would never have dared to give them orders. She was surprised herself at the changes that had taken place.

She followed them up the stairs, slipping ahead as they reached the landing to go into Christina's room and turn down the sheets. She watched as they laid her down, and then nodded sharply.

'That'll do now. If you'd just fetch that water. Rose, you can send Daisy up with it. I won't be needing nothing else.'

'Well, really!' Rose exclaimed, but she looked again at the still figure on the bed and hastily went out.

Ruth unbuttoned Christina's dress and slipped it off, pulling her mistress up against her to do so. Her shift came off more easily; then the ribbons of her stays could be untied and the tight whalebone construction removed. Ruth could almost feel Christina's relief, and to her joy the blue-tinged eyelids fluttered again. A moment later, they were open.

'Ruth?' Christina whispered. 'Ruth, what happened? I – I'm at home. I thought – I thought I was in the cone . . .' The thread of sound faded and died; a small frown of bewilderment creased the fine brows.

'You were in the cone,' Ruth said gently. 'You fainted, miss, but you're all right now. I expect it was the heat.'

There was a knock at the door and she got up quickly to take the water Daisy had brought, shielding the room from the inquisitive eyes. 'Thank you, Daisy. You needn't wait. I'll ring if the mistress wants anything more.' Ruth took the jug to the washstand and poured water into the glass already there.

'Thank you, Ruth. That feels better.' Christina sipped and lay back. Her eyes were fully open now, fixed on Ruth's face. 'Did you say I fainted? Why should I do that, I'm not ill?'

'I don't think so, miss. But you've had a sad time of it lately – you're tired and unhappy. Maybe it was that and the heat, like I said just now. I don't suppose it's anything to worry about.'

'But you look worried, all the same,' Christina said shrewdly. 'What do you think is the matter with me, Ruth?' Fear leapt suddenly into her eyes and she reared up on the bed, remembering her brother, the epidemics that had killed so many, so quickly. 'You don't think it's the cholera come back, do you? Oh, Ruth!'

'No – no, I don't think that. I haven't heard of any cholera this year, though it's been hot. Nor smallpox either – not where you're likely to go, anyway.' Both diseases were in fact making their periodic appearance in

356

the more squalid areas of the town, but Ruth was not going to mention that. 'I don't think it's anything catching, miss – not in that way.' She sighed and added, 'Mebbe you'll wish it was, before this lot's finished.'

Christina stared at her. 'Ruth, what do you mean?' The fear was there again. 'What are you afraid of? What can I have that's worse than cholera, or smallpox?'

Ruth gave her a long look. Then she went to the big chest that stood in the corner and opened a drawer. It was filled with white linen; strips of cotton, used each month, washed out by the scullery maid, aired and then ironed before being returned to the drawer for the next month's use. Ruth stepped back and Christina stared, a dawning realisation in her eyes.

'I haven't used them for two months – more. Since before Jean-Paul . . .' There was fear of a different kind in the look she gave Ruth now. 'Ruth . . . I thought it was just the way I am sometimes, a little late, because of all the distress, all the upsets. It happened when Papa died as well . . . It could be that, couldn't it?'

'I thought so too,' Ruth said. 'But you were sick yesterday morning, weren't you? And again today. I heard you.'

'It wasn't much,' Christina said, almost pleadingly. 'Hardly anything, in fact. I felt quite well again after a few minutes.'

'It don't hev to be much,' Ruth said grimly. 'Well, we'll wait and see. You might be lucky yet.'

They waited a few days; a week. And then Christina was compelled to admit the truth. Jean-Paul had left her more than an engraved chalice and a patch of earth in the churchyard on the hill. He had left her the seed of his child.

Chapter Seventeen

While Christina was discovering her own pregnancy, Maggie Haden was coming to the end of hers.

The months since Jeremy had abandoned her had been long and hard. At first, she had been unable to believe that he wasn't coming back. She had barely ventured out of doors, sending the woman who owned the house for the few items of food she dared to buy. She had kept the room clean and warm, fresh sheets on the bed as he liked and had sat by the window, staring out through every daylight hour in the hope of seeing him. But, slowly, the hope had faded and died; soon, she had been forced to acknowledge that he was not coming again, and that her position was desperate.

She counted her money: enough for less than a month in this house, and then she would have nothing. And her pregnancy a month nearer its end, her body that much thicker and more cumbersome, her usefulness more limited. Doing her best to stave off the evil moment when she would have to find somewhere else to live, Maggie began systematically to starve herself. She ate nothing but bread and the few scraps of meat and vegetable she could beg from the local shop; she drank nothing but water from the pump. Her body, swelling all the time with the vigorous life that grew within it, was nevertheless thin and bony, so that she looked distorted. Her face was white, her eyes hollow, and she was gripped frequently by cramping pains in her stomach that made her fear an early confinement; something that would be fatal for the child and dangerous for her.

As the weeks dragged on, her desperation increased. With less than a month to go before the birth, she was almost at the end of her carefully-saved money. She had not paid her rent for a fortnight and knew that Florrie Hayward, the slummock who kept the house, would not wait much longer; she had taken to locking herself in her room and moving quietly, as if the woman might forget she were there. The only food she had was a hunk of dry bread and a half-bucket of water. Her back ached, her stomach gnawed and she felt sick in the stale heat of her airless room. In a few weeks the child would be born, and what she would do then she had no idea.

A sudden loud hammering on her door brought her out of her chair. With thudding heart, she stared at the door, then wildly out of the window. There was no horse below, no vehicle that might have brought Mr Jeremy. Her agitated speculations were cut short by a voice, and her shoulders sagged once more.

'Mag Haden! You in there? Open up, I wants a word with you.'

The slattern from downstairs. Drearily, Maggie crossed the room and slid back the bolt.

Florrie Hayward stepped into the room, her hair as straggled, her dress as torn and greasy, as it always was. She was a thin woman, with narrow, crafty eyes and a hard mouth. She had never made any secret of her dislike for Maggie; but since she appeared to dislike everyone she met, Maggie had taken no notice. Besides, she had considered herself several cuts above a woman like Florrie Hayward, with her admirer, the gentleman friend who paid for her to be here and would look after her when her baby was born.

Florrie was chewing something. Maggie, conscious of the gnawing in her belly, watched hungrily. It wasn't until the other woman had finished chewing and swallowed that she spoke.

'Hevn't seen your gentleman friend round here lately, Mag.'

'He's away,' Maggie said quickly. 'He'll be back.'

'That ent what I heard.'

They looked at each other cautiously. Florrie was trying her out, Maggie decided. She knew nothing really. She wouldn't risk losing a good tenant, not without proof that no more rent would be paid.

'I heard he's got another fancy-piece, up Brettell Lane way,' Florrie said finally, and Maggie reacted at once.

'Where d'you hear that? I don't believe it.' She regretted the words at once and added lamely, 'He'd hev told me,' knowing all too well that he wouldn't.

Florrie laughed scornfully. 'Would he? He's a bit unusual then, in't he? Clever, too, seein' as he ent bin round here for over a month.' Her eyes hardened. 'You're overdue for your rent. I'll hev it now, if you please, or you're out.'

'Now? But I can't – can't you wait a bit, I'll hev it for you next time he comes. He's bound to come soon, he's bin away, he –'

'It's overdue. I wants it right away.' She planted her feet a little more firmly on the floor and fixed Maggie with an eye like that of a fish. 'Before I leaves this room,' she said implacably, and Maggie knew she meant it.

She pleaded, of course. Begged, cajoled, promised. She would work for her board, do anything, scrub, clean, cook . . . But Florrie Hayward wasn't interested in cleanliness and she bought most of her food from the pie-shop on the corner. She laughed in Maggie's face, demanded her rent once more and, when it wasn't forthcoming, told Maggie to get out. At once.

'It ent winter now,' she said callously. 'Nights are warm enough and you won't be the only one sleeping rough. I done it meself in me time. And there's allus ways a piece like you can make a bit of money.'

Whoring, Maggie thought bitterly as she gathered together the few things she possessed and went out into the street. That's what I'm down to now. Whoring. And

361

no hope even of that, not with this great lump of Joe Compson's inside me and kicking me to death.

All the same, she left Church Row with her head high and her back straight; she wasn't going to give that old bitch the satisfaction of seeing her beaten now! It was only after she had turned the corner that she allowed her despair to overwhelm her. She had nowhere to go. Her parents had washed their hands of her, clinging to their shreds of respectability in the squalid basement. Poor they might be, her father had said, but they'd always been decent. Maggie had brought shame on them; not only by being in the family way by a man who wasn't going to marry her, but living as a rich man's judy as well. She was no daughter of his any longer, he'd said, his moustaches quivering with an indignation he rarely had the opportunity to feel, and her mother, sitting in the corner on the pile of rags that served as a bed, had nodded blearily and scarcely seemed to know when Maggie turned to leave. They wouldn't take her in now, even if she went back. And they couldn't afford to keep her.

Annie would help if she could, but she and her family were as poor as the Hadens, their cellar as crowded and as damp. Another bulky body would take up room needed for the men of the family who brought what money there was, and for the children Maggie had never been able to count. And Annie's mother was going the same way as Maggie's, barely able to work at her nail-making now for the fuddled state she was always in, soaking away her troubles with gin in the hope that they might be nearly tolerable.

Maggie wandered that night, her possesions tied up in her shawl, until she was too exhausted to wander further. She had no idea where she roamed, only knowing that there was nothing else for her to do. When dawn broke, she was in a part she had never seen before, a part that was worse than any slum she had yet known. A dirty river ran close by and cottages built of mud instead of bricks, scattered in no especial formation so that the streets and alleys wound between them more by accident than design; unpaved and rough, with holes that were filled with black, malodorous slime that seemed yet to provide a play-ground for the children who were already running about or sitting in the dust, many of them almost naked. She stood there, unnoticed for a few moments, staring at this little community, so different and isolated, with its dark-skinned inhabitants that might have come from a different world, and wondered just where she had come, and what would happen to her next.

And then she knew. Mud City. The jeering name that the rest of the Stourbridge area had for the place known as the Lye. The Lye Waste. A name that was all too appropriate. There was nothing here but waste – waste land, fit for nothing, and waste humanity, equally dismis-sed, self-contained and hostile.

And as the first pain gripped, her heart thudded in sudden fright.

'That's it, duck. Bear down, hard – here, grab ahold of my hand. Shout if you like – yell as loud as you can, it all helps squeeze the little brat out. Down . . . down . . . down . . . and let go. That's it. That's it. You're coming along fine, you'll soon have a bairn to suckle.'

Maggie lay back, panting, feeling the sweat cold on her brow. The woman with her spoke her encouraging words in a rough, grating voice that sounded as if it were more accustomed to swearing and cursing. She was as slatternly as Florrie Hayward, but her small eyes were kind and her mouth grinned as Maggie clung to her hands.

'That's it,' she said again as a fresh wave of pain spread from the small of Maggie's back, tightening its iron grip around her swollen stomach. 'Hang on – bear down again, real hard, hard as you can. It won't be long now – I can see its head, all black hair it is – harder, harder – no, it's slipped back again. Next time we'll have 'un.'

363

Her grin revealed that she had several teeth missing, but her ugliness meant nothing to Maggie; to her, the woman was nothing less than an angel.

The whole of the Lye Waste was, as far as Maggie was concerned, inhabited by angels. Only angels would have treated her with such kindness, rough though it was; only angels, seeing her at their doorsteps that morning, would have immediately recognised her condition and, without question, taken her in and ministered to her. It was true that she had always thought of angels, when she thought of them at all, as living in golden palaces, with every luxury around them, and these people lived in a poverty even greater than she had known. But they had seen her and taken her in, and now this woman – Em – was seeing her through her labour.

She rested again, moaning. The pain was worse, far worse than she had ever imagined. It began as a gentle warmth, quickly igniting to a burning heat that scorched a path around her body, turning then to a mail-clad fist that held her in an inexorable grasp; tightening, tightening, tightening until she twisted and writhed in a vain effort to escape it, crying and screaming, swearing her bitter protest at the torture her body was suffering. You couldn't live through this; nobody could. She was going to die, die, with the baby she had never wanted, the baby who had lost her Joe, stuck half in and half out of her torn and battered body. She gripped the woman's hand and stared up into the haggard face that hung above her, advancing and receding through waves of red, grinding pain, and begged for help.

'You're all right, love. You're doing well. It'll be over soon, trust old Em . . . Bear down . . . *down*, hard, it helps. Work with it. Every pain's pushin' the little toad out. *That's* right, girl, that's right. Push. Push. *Push*. He's comin' . . . he's comin' . . . One more, an' that'll be it.'

Maggie felt the hard head between her legs, the thrust which was beyond her control. She felt the opening spread wide, wider than she could believe possible. It was splitting her apart, ripping her from groin to navel, tearing her flesh open in its furious desire to be free. Vaguely, as if from a great distance, she heard Em's voice, urging her yet again to push. Push? And help that selfish brute inside her to open her body even further, to slash her stomach as if with a knife she felt sure it must have . .? The pain tore into her again, clenching, wrenching, demanding submission, release, life. She shook her head violently, rolling it from side to side in hopeless rejection, and then kicked herself backwards, jerking her distorted body in a futile effort to escape.

'I can't!' she bellowed. 'I can't, I can't, I can't! Tell it to stop – I can't do it any more, I *won't*!'

'One more, now.' Em's voice was calm, coming from a long way off; she was busy further down the pile of rugs that Maggie lay on, holding Maggie's feet braced against her shoulders. 'Only one more and it's all over. Real hard now . . . here it comes . . . an' *push*. And that's it! You've done it, girl. You've birthed it.' With a sigh that dragged itself from the roots of her being, Maggie fell back on the rags; and heard her child's first cry.

'What is it?'

There was a fractional pause, but it was long enough for Maggie to struggle up again, suddenly afraid. 'Is it all right? What is it? Hev I got a boy, or a girl?'

Em lifted the baby in her arms. It was crying furiously now, a purple, slippery creature smothered in grey slime. The cord that still attached it to Maggie was like the black liquorice she had once been given at Christmas – twisted and rubbery, protruding grotesquely from its belly. Its head was covered in thick black hair.

'It's a little wench,' Em said, and laid it on Maggie's breast. 'A lovely little wench, God help her. Why they're in such haste to get into the world, I don't know – better off where they are, I allus say. Still, I reckon *you're* glad 'tis all done. Now, there'll be just one more pain or two in a little while, to get the afterbirth away, an' then it's all over. I'll just get this cord cut away. You have a look at your babby.'

Maggie found that she had automatically closed her arms around her child. She felt the small body, warm against her own sweating skin, felt the beat of the tiny heart against her own. The eyes were closed, the lids blue against the red and crumpled face, but even so she could see Joe in the child that lay on her breast. Joe's hair, Joe's expression, Joe's dogged determination; all were reproduced there in miniature, in the first few moments of life.

'There, that's done,' Em remarked. 'We'll hev the afterbirth in a few minutes now, I reckon, an' then it's all over. What are you going to call her?'

Maggie hadn't given it a thought. Until now, the baby had been nothing more than an idea, a means to an end in the first place, then a burden that grew increasingly and finally threatened to kill her. She had felt nothing for it but dismay, dislike and despair. As a person, it had never existed.

And now it was here. *She* was here – her daughter, square-faced and dark-haired, already nuzzling at her breast as if determined to stay alive come what may. Determined, like her father . . . but wholly, solely Maggie's. A slow warmth spread through her body. For the first time in her life, she had someone who belonged only to her. Someone who depended on her, someone who must, would, love her. Her daughter. *Her* daughter. Nobody else's.

She discarded at once any idea that she might be named after Joe. Or anyone; after all, what had her family, her friends, done to help her when she needed it? Only these people, the inhabitants of the Lye Waste, with their reputation for roughness and brutality, their isolation and their hostility, had given her help. They had taken her in without question, given her food they must

366

need for themselves, shelter and, in her final extremity, courage and comfort.

She looked up into the skinny face that had given her that comfort, had taken her in and worked with her to produce this new life, this bright new hope. Em. She knew no more of her than that. It was enough.

'I'll call her Emily,' she said. 'After you.'

A baby. The idea, the reality, filled Christina's waking thoughts and haunted her dreams. She had no doubt at all that Ruth was right. Those stolen nights, the blissful hours spent in Jean-Paul's arms, they had to be paid for. If she and Jean-Paul had been married, there would have been no question as to the rightness of it. Because they had not, in the eyes of the world it was a sin.

Christina spent the whole of that first night sitting by her window, staring out at the garden, at the red glow that burned in the sky from sunset to dawn. Her hands moved slowly, compulsively, over her stomach; could there really be life growing there?

She thought of her aunt's reaction. This would over-shadow even the horror of Jean-Paul's death. The shame, the stigma – it was one of the few sins that couldn't be concealed. Men, as she knew from gossip amongst her sisters and their friends, could have their doxies and dollies, but women were expected to go as virgins to the altar. The fact that she had expected to go to the altar with Jean-Paul was irrelevant; she would be seen as a sinner, and treated as such.

Desperately, she yearned for Jean-Paul's presence, for his strong arms around her, his calm reassurance that all would be well. But it wouldn't; it would never be well again. Jean-Paul was dead and she was carrying his child.

'What am I going to do?' she asked Ruth, but the maid's face was as pale and frightened as her own.

'I don't know, miss. I've never known anyone – there was a wench in our street, only sixteen she wor. Her

367

father threw her out; she went to the workhouse but she died when the babby was born, and the bairn with her. I heard she could have gone to someone – an old woman, lives up Beauty Bank way – but she left it too late. And another girl who went there, she died. I don't know what you're going to do, miss, and that's a fact.'

'Well, I'm not going to the workhouse,' Christina said with grim humour. 'Nor to any old woman in Beauty Bank, and nobody can throw me out of my own house, either. So if I don't have to do any of those things, I suppose I shall just stay at home, and *have* my child. You see, it's quite easy when you think clearly.'

Aunt Susan, however, did not see it so clearly. Her reaction was just as Christina had predicted.

'A baby? A *baby*?' Her face whitened, the blood draining away and then returning in a flood so that her cheeks were stained with ugly colour. 'Christina, it can't be true. It's some cruel joke – you're hysterical, losing your reason. Please, don't talk such nonsense.'

'It isn't nonsense, Aunt Susan. It's true. I am expecting Jean-Paul's baby. Ruth and I think it must be due about January of next year.' Christina spoke calmly enough, but her heart was beating fast. She put out a hand, as if seeking comfort, but her aunt drew back sharply.

'You mean you've already discussed this with Ruth? A servant?' The shocked eyes moved from one to the other. 'Oh, Christina, the disgrace, how could you, how could you do it? None of us will be able to hold our heads up in respectable society again. You are so selfish, so thoughtless of other people – but then you always have been, haven't you? Wilful, determined always to have your own way regardless of the cost to others. I warned your father – over and over again, I warned him what it would be, but he would take no notice. Leave her to me, he said, leave her to me – and now see what his foolishness has brought about!'

368

'How dare you talk about Papa in this fashion!' Christina said sharply. 'Do not mention him in this respect again. As for Harry and Alice and Adela, none of them is at fault in any way and I don't see why their lives should be "ruined" or even affected by this. *I* am the one who is likely to suffer.'

'You know that isn't true,' Susan said more quietly. 'The whole family will bear the stigma. It always does.' She rose and walked about the room, twisting her hands together as she always did when agitated. 'There is only one solution. You will have to go away.'

'Away?'

'Yes. As far as possible. Abroad, perhaps. France – no, not France. Italy. Many people go to Italy. Rome or Florence; a tour of the most cultured places. I shall come with you, of course.' This was said with an air of martyred courage. 'We will stay away until the child is born, and when we return nobody will be one whit the wiser. It is often done, I believe,' she added ingenuously.

Christina's lips twitched, but she was too concerned with what, to her, was the crux of the matter to take her aunt up on that last remark.

'And what would happen to the baby?'

'Oh, that would be easy enough to arrange.' Susan's confidence was growing, her agitation lessened now that she had thought of a solution. 'There are people who look after such children – homes, institutions. Or you could engage a young woman of good character and set her to look after the child, somewhere in another town, of course, or in the country.' Her eyes strayed to Ruth. 'You needn't bother yourself with it, of course; simply provide the money for its upkeep.'

'You mean desert it,' Christina said flatly. 'Give it away. Bury it in an institution, as the family wanted Papa to do with Thomas. Forget it ever existed.'

'It's the only way,' her aunt said pleadingly.

Christina shook her head. 'No. It's not the only way.

There must be others.' Christina rose and went to the door. 'This is my baby, Aunt Susan. Mine and Jean-Paul's. I cannot – I *will* not abandon it.'

Brave words. But, as the days went by, frightening ones too.

The house, already saddened by Jean-Paul's death, became oppressed by the emotions that hung unspoken in the air. Susan spent long hours alone in her room, appearing with reddened eyes and a reproachful look; her migraines came more frequently and more severely than ever. Adela, aware that something was seriously amiss, was resentful that she had not been told; she was eighteen now, she declared, surely old enough to know what was making Aunt Susan so unhappy, and why Christina no longer came to breakfast. Harry, equally aware but uncomfortably sure that the secret was something he would rather *not* be told, kept away from the family as much as possible, spending all his time with his books. He had examinations to pass, he said, preparations to make for Oxford, and took to disappearing the moment meals were over.

The kitchen was full of speculation.

'There's something more to it than just hankering after that Monsure Tittry,' Rose declared. 'I mean, we all saw how Miss Christina was over that – and no wonder, for she saw it happen. But this is something new – something that's only happened in the last week or two.' She gave Mrs Jenner a meaning glance and lowered her voice. 'Or maybe something that happened in the last *month* or two.'

Mrs Jenner looked quickly at the two young maids, Daisy and Nellie. 'You two get along out to the scullery and see to them dishes. I wants them properly scrubbed, mind, and no listening at the door.' She turned back to Rose and mouthed the words. 'You mean you think she might be – *you* know? Surely not!'

Rose shrugged. 'Tell me why else she don't take

breakfast no more. Or why Ruth suddenly says she'll do all Miss Christina's washing – ah. *That* one knows a bit about it, if you ask me. But she's closer than ever – won't say a word.' She stopped speaking abruptly as the door opened and Ruth came into the kitchen, flushing as the two women turned their eyes on her. 'Come down for summat for Miss Christina, then?' Rose asked innocently. 'A bit of dry biscuit, perhaps? Or a cup of tea? Feeling *faint* again, is she?'

'That's enough, Rose!' Mrs Jenner said sharply. 'Whatever ails Miss Christina, she's still our mistress and deserves our respect. You get whatever you want, Ruth, and don't take no notice.'

'Yes, thank you, Mrs Jenner.' Ruth finished loading her tray and slipped quietly out, passing Rose without a glance. The parlour maid sniffed, but Ruth, her colour high, took no notice.

All the same, she thought as she made her way up to Christina's bedroom, where her mistess lay waiting for the tea and bread and butter that was all she could face today, it was high time something was decided. There was gossip in the kitchen; it would not be long before it reached the glasshouse. And then it would be all over Wordsley. Whatever course of action Miss Christina was going to take, she ought to take it soon.

The gossip did, as Ruth had dreaded, reach the glasshouse. Christina could feel it about her, an atmosphere of discomfort, palpable embarrassment. She saw it in the sidelong glances the men gave her, the measuring look in the eyes of some of the bolder ones.

Something had to be done, and done soon. But she was still undecided when Jeremy came to visit her one afternoon, a grave look in his eyes.

Since Jean-Paul's death, they had drawn slowly closer. Each had been present on that dreadful day, each deeply, horribly shocked. Jeremy had brought Christina home afterwards, had supported her at the funeral. He had told her what had happened, keeping nothing back, even those details which he had felt might hurt her and which she had demanded to know. And he had – somehow – rid her of the continual reminder that Joe Compson's presence would have been. Where he had sent Joe, she never asked. She looked at him now, doubt in her eyes. Desperately, she needed someone to confide in, someone who might help her. But, she feared the moment when she told him the truth. She feared the look of disgust, of rejection that she felt she must see in his eyes. She feared the loss of his friendship, for then she would be more alone than ever.

Jeremy, however, forestalled her. He sat beside her on the sofa and took her hands in his.

'There's talk in the glasshouse, Christina. Unpleasant talk.' He paused. 'I don't like to repeat it to you – it can only be hurtful and upsetting. But I mean to stop it and first I have to hear from your own mouth that it's not true.'

'And what is this talk?' Christina asked after a moment.

'Forgive me. The whole matter is so indelicate, I hardly like . . .'

Christina looked at him and knew she must tell him the truth. He would know in time anyway.

'I can guess what this gossip is about, Jeremy,' she said briefly. 'Let's put it plainly, shall we? I am in what is called an "interesting condition". In other words, I am expecting a baby. Jean-Paul's baby.'

The words seemed to hang in the air, falling slowly into the silence. Outside the open window, a bird sang. Inside, nothing moved.

Jeremy said nothing. He seemed to be considering his response and Christina felt a stirring of impatience. She opened her mouth to speak again, but he laid a finger on her lips.

'You poor, poor child.'

His words took her breath away. She stared at him, nonplussed. His eyes met hers, and he smiled and took her hands.

'Do you think I should be shocked? Do you think I should condemn you – turn away from you? Ah, Christina, little cousin, do you not know me better than that? Don't you know that I would do anything to help you – whatever your trouble?'

She shook her head mutely. The tears were in her throat, making it swell and ache; they fell from her eyes and splashed on Jeremy's fingers. He drew her closer and with a small sigh she let her head fall to his shoulder.

'Tell me what you want me to do,' he said softly.

Christina could not speak. The relief of not being rejected was too great; the tears flowed as they had not done since the days after Jean-Paul's funeral, and now they were tears of healing rather than sorrow. She clung to Jeremy, pressed herself against his heart and wept. His arms were strong around her and she thought briefly how once they would have stirred her. But that was before Jean-Paul; before she had grown up.

'There is nothing anybody can do,' she said at last, shakily. 'Aunt Susan wants me to go away – have the child in Italy and then send it to an institution or pay a woman to bring it up . . . I can't do that, Jeremy! This is my baby – mine and Jean-Paul's. I can't abandon it, I have a duty to bring it up as I would if we had been able to marry. I owe it to Jean-Paul as well. And besides – I love it already.' Her hands were on her stomach, not caring that the gesture might seem indelicate. 'It's all I have left of him,' she said softly. 'I can never give it up.'

'So you mean to have it even though that may mean being ostracised? Even though life will certainly be impossibly difficult, for you and your family?' Jeremy shook his head but his eyes were tender. 'So like my brave Christina! And so unnecessary.'

'Unnecessary?'

373

'Of course. Are you sure you have thought of every-thing, sweet cousin? Every alternative – every possibility?'

'We have thought until our heads whirl with thinking,' Christina said wearily. 'Aunt Susan, Ruth and I – we have asked ourselves every question, and found no answers. I will not go away to have my baby – I am needed here, at the glassworks. And I will not hide until the child is born and then abandon it as if it was never mine. I will *not*.'

'And so you shan't.' His voice was easy and confident, and Christina glanced at him with a new, dawning hope.

'Then what? Jeremy, don't tease me, please. What else can I do? What else is there?'

'There is the most obvious answer of all,' he said com-fortably. 'An answer that will, I hope, please everyone. Yes, even Cousin Susan.' His blue eyes smiled into hers. 'You may stop looking so frightened, little one. I am proposing nothing that should alarm you; at least, I hope not. Only marriage.'

'*Marriage*?'

'Had it never occurred to you?' he asked in an amused tone.

'No, of course not! Who would marry me? Jeremy, I asked you not to tease, and this is a particularly cruel joke –' She recalled her aunt using those very words and stopped. Jeremy was laughing openly now, and she turned her head away to hide her mortification.

'Cousin, I am not joking! I would like to marry you. As soon as possible – I think that would be best, don't you? And when the child is born, it will have a father as well as a mother, to care for it as it should be cared for. Well – what do you say?'

'I don't know,' Christina stammered. 'I had truly never thought – but Jeremy, I can never love you as I loved Jean-Paul. I am fond of you, of course, I've known you all my life and you've helped me and been so kind – but marriage, I don't know, I have to think –'

'Think then, little cousin,' he said quietly. 'Think, but

374

not for too long, for time is growing short. As for love, how many marriages begin with love? It grows later, and grows all the stronger for it. I have no worries on that score.' He bent and kissed her gently, 'Think, little cousin, and imagine how it will be when I can call you "wife".'

He left her then, sitting alone in the dusk that gathered in the shadowy library. The birds outside had fallen silent; stars were beginning to appear through the haze of the twilit sky. There was no sound from the rest of the house.

Christina looked up and saw the Chalice shining softly in the light from the single candle. She stood up and lifted it down, and ran her finger over the engraved initials. C and J. Christina and Jean-Paul.

Or Christina and . . . Jeremy?

Time, Jeremy had said, was growing short, and Christina knew that her decision must be made soon. The few weeks' respite given her before her condition was apparent to everyone were passing all too quickly; and even if she married Jeremy now, the birth of the child in February would have people counting the months.

'Why are you waiting?' her aunt begged her over and over again. 'Jeremy has always wanted to marry you. You are fortunate that he is still prepared to take you, more fortunate than you deserve. Many men would refuse a young woman in – in your situation.'

'I'm well aware of that, aunt.' Christina was weary, weary of discussing the subject, weary of thinking about it. Weary as she had never been before. It was natural, Ruth said the early weeks were often the most tiring of them all. But I haven't *time* to be tired, she thought rebelliously, and knew that even the energy needed for thinking was more than she could gather together.

'You should be careful you don't prevaricate too much,' Susan Henzel said shrewdly. 'He could change his mind yet. And then what would you do?'

'If he's waited for me all this time –' Christina began, and broke off. *Had* Jeremy 'always' wanted to marry her? Or had he discovered her attractions only since her father had died, leaving her the glasshouse? She passed a hand over her hot forehead. 'I don't know,' she said dully, and her aunt sniffed.

'The truth is, your wild ways have brought you into real trouble this time, and you don't know how to get out of it. And you do hate to accept help, don't you – to feel obliged to others!' Christina looked up, startled by this perceptiveness, but Susan swept on. 'Christina, can't you see that this time you *must* accept help! You cannot deal with this alone. And the help that Jeremy is prepared to give you – marriage, his name, the respectability you seem to think is so worthless and unimportant – it's help that you cannot refuse. If you will not think of yourself, think of the rest of us.' Her mouth worked and her eyes filled. 'And if you'll think of none of us, Christina, think of your child – born without a name.' And she sank into a chair and covered her face with her hands.

Christina watched her, reflecting on the irony that whether she married Jeremy or not, the child's name would be the same – Henzel. But what a world of difference there was in whether the name had been bestowed by the father or the mother.

So, the name Henzel, given by Jeremy, could affect them all: Adela's marriage prospects, Harry's opportunities, at Oxford and later in his career, her own 'respectability', which Susan said was so important. Each must be weighed against the tiny doubt, the niggling unease, that she still felt about her cousin.

Christina rose and walked to the window. She looked down at the closely-packed buildings beyond the garden, at the cones that dominated the landscape. She thought briefly of her father, knew one last stab of longing for his bluff, vital presence. What *would* he have said and done about her present predicament? But Joshua had gone. She had to make her own way now.

376

'Very well,' she said, turning back to where her aunt sat gazing hopelessly into space. 'I'll do it, Aunt Susan, I'll marry Jeremy.'

Susan Henzel's face was transformed, alive with sudden joy. But Christina felt nothing. Nothing but an increased weariness, tinged with dull relief at having made a decision at last. And a small, icy coldness around her heart.

'Marrying Jeremy?' Adela's eyes widened so much that Christina feared they would drop out of her head. 'But it's so soon – I mean –'

'So soon after Jean-Paul's accident,' Christina finished quietly. 'Yes, I know. And it doesn't mean I loved Jean-Paul any the less. But Jeremy has asked me to marry him, and Aunt Susan thinks I should, so it seemed unnecessary to wait.'

'And do *you* think you should?' Harry asked shrewdly.

'I think I must. Yes, I think I should. There are – many reasons.' Why not tell them, she thought wretchedly, hating the dishonesty, the subterfuge. Why not tell them she was carrying Jean-Paul's child and needed Jeremy for a name and respectability.

They would know soon enough, just as anyone would who remembered her wedding date. But she could not bring herself to tell them the truth now.

'Be happy for me,' she said, almost pleadingly, but Adela was already into a flurry of excitement, her head full of bridal gowns and attendants. 'I *shall* be the bridesmaid, shan't I, Chrissie? Or must it be Alice, because she is married?' And Harry looked at her with grave concern.

'I hope you'll be happy, sis. I'm sure if *you* think it's the right thing to do, it is.' He paused as if about to say something else, then ducked his head and left the two sisters alone in the cluttered drawing room.

'Isn't Harry funny?' Adela said, laughing. 'You'd think he didn't *want* you to get married! Well, *I'm* pleased for you, Chrissie – though I was beginning to think Jeremy might get tired of waiting and look to me instead!' She gave a coquettish laugh. 'Now I'll have to find another man to appreciate me, won't I? But not until we've got you safely wed. Now, have you thought about your gown? There really isn't much time. We shall have to have Mrs Biddle here at once. I shall embroider mine myself, of course. Oh, there's so much to do – must it really be so quick, Christina? Do you *have* to be married within the month?'

Christina smiled faintly. 'Jeremy's tired of waiting, just as you thought,' she said. 'He insists. I think he's afraid I'll change my mind.'

She wouldn't, of course. She had to go through with it now. But the thought did, just for a second, bring a touch of warmth to that icy place around her heart.

It would go eventually. After all, she was still grieving for Jean-Paul, still lying awake at night aching for him, sleeping only to suffer hideous nightmares about those last few minutes in the cone, before he began to scream . . . And Jeremy was very understanding. He knew, told her that he was suffering in exactly the same way, dreaming and waking in horror, convinced that it was all happening again. Seeing his whitened face, his haunted eyes, Christina had believed him. And she had never felt closer to him than when he caught her hand in his and said, 'We'll be each other's comfort, my dear. From now on, when either of us dream, the other will be there to share the pain. And when you cease to grieve for him, I'll be there, waiting. Love will grow, Christina; believe me, love will grow.' She had to believe him.

There was rejoicing in the other Henzel homes when the news of Christina's engagement to Jeremy became known.

'It's to be just a quiet wedding, Mamma,' Jeremy said when he made the announcement. 'In view of what's happened, we thought it best. And soon, too – the middle of August.'

'August? But that's barely a month! How can we possibly prepare for a wedding in that time? And what will people say at such speed? It's positively indecent!' Lavinia fussed agitatedly with the flowers she was arranging. 'It can't possibly be so soon as that, Jeremy.'

'It can, and it will. Papa agrees with me, Christina is still in a highly volatile state. She is quite capable of taking back her word. If I'm to wed her, it must be done quickly before she has a chance to break away.'

'I really can't see why you want to marry her at all,' Lavinia grumbled. 'She's hardly likely to make a good wife. So unpredictable . . . I do hope you've thought this over carefully, Jeremy. Marrying the wrong woman can bring such a lot of trouble, and it's for the rest of your life, you know.'

'I understand that, Mamma. You needn't worry. I know Christina very well by now. I anticipate no problems, once we are married.'

'I suppose she imagines that she will continue just as she is now – visiting the glasshouse, talking with the men, running the business.' Lavinia sighed irritably. 'Surely she sees that as a married woman, she will have other responsibilities. I fear you are in for a trying time, Jeremy.'

He smiled. 'I told you, Mamma, don't worry. Christina will come to terms with married life. Meanwhile, just let her have her head. It's not for much longer, after all.'

His father and uncles had said much the same thing. After congratulating Jeremy on his long-awaited success – though making it clear that it had been rather too long a wait – they had settled down to discuss their plans for the future. A future which now included Christina Henzel's glasshouse, with its three cones and new cutting and engraving shops.

'It will further our own production of flint, that goes without saying,' Harold declared. 'Going from flat glass and bottles into fine tableware has proved more difficult than I had anticipated; Christina has so much of the market. Now we can take over her cones, we'll be able to make more and more of the cheaper glasses that people are beginning to buy now – the sort of people who never bought glass before. That's where the profit is, in producing for the lower middle-classes, who want to ape their betters and at last have the money to do it.'

'We still ought to make some quality ware, though,' Samuel objected. 'And colour – there's scope there for both kinds. Christina has been working with colour for some time, after all.'

'Indeed she has – one of her cones is producing entirely ruby glass now, and another is working on blue and green. I think we should keep them so, too. Of course, there is nothing we can do before the wedding – I dare not let her suspect that we intend to make any changes with what she considers "her" glasshouse.' Jeremy smiled slowly. 'But afterwards, I see nothing to stop us from going ahead with any plans we may care to make.'

'My dear boy,' Harold slapped his shoulder, 'you've done well. Henzel's is as good as ours. Alfred will be equally pleased, I know. With the new glass that that fellow Compson is beginning to make up there, and the prospects opening for us in Stourbridge, I can see no reason why Henzel Brothers shouldn't soon be the biggest and best-known glassmakers in the land. Yes, you've done well – very well indeed.'

'And what,' asked Reuben, who had so far not spoken, 'of Christina's majority share?'

There was an immediate silence. The other men turned and looked at him. Reuben returned their looks, his thin fingers stroking his beard.

'Yes,' Harold said slowly. 'I'd forgotten that.'

'I hadn't,' Samuel snapped. 'Presumably Jeremy hasn't either – or have you?'

'Perhaps they've discussed it already,' Reuben said

slyly, and Jeremy glanced at him with caution. He rarely saw his Uncle Reuben these days; since the death of Jean-Paul, he had not visited the house opposite 'The Talbot', and he had evaded any occasions on which they might be alone together. There was a question in Reuben's eyes sometimes when he looked at Jeremy: a question Jeremy did not feel disposed to answer.

'We haven't discussed it,' he said shortly. 'There's no need for discussion. Christina will hand over all her rights in the business to me as soon as we are married. I have seen Henry Ambrose and had the papers drawn up; he doesn't like it much, but he'll have to be satisfied when Christina signs them of her own free will. As she most certainly will.'

'You seem very sure of this,' Reuben said thoughtfully. 'Considering that you have not discussed it.'

Jeremy met his eyes squarely. They were bright and inquisitive; the lizard coming out into the sun. Jeremy saw the question in them and ignored it.

'Oh yes,' he said easily. 'I'm sure.'

'You have good reasons, of course.'

The best there are, Jeremy thought. A pregnancy by another man; a family she needs to look after – brother, sister, aunt, not to mention that idiot in the nursery. Reasons that Reuben, at least, would appreciate. But Jeremy had no intention of outlining them now, or ever.

'Oh, I think I know Christina well enough now to be sure,' he answered casually. 'She's come to her senses over our marriage, after all. I have no doubt that she'll be ready enough, once we are married, to hand over all responsibilities to me. It will be a relief to her.' He smiled complacently and studied his fingertips. 'Yes, I think we'll find my sweet cousin more – shall we say malleable? – from now on. *Much* more malleable.'

Chapter Eighteen

Maggie Haden was desperate. It had taken her some time to recover from the birth of her child. Starvation, which did not seem to have affected the infant in her womb, had taken its toll of her body, leaving her thin and under-nourished. She had little milk in her drooping breasts, and the baby, so lusty at birth, began to weaken. Its wails penetrated the walls of the mud cottage in which she lay, and Maggie wondered if this were the end for them both.

'It'd be best if it was,' she said to Em. 'What sort of a life's the bairn going to have anyway? Look what I've had – what you've got. Nothing. Nothing but grind, hard work and poor living. What sort of a world is that to bring a babby into?'

'It's the same world as we all has to share,' the old woman said cheerfully. 'An' it in't so bad at times. You've 'ad a bit of pleasure yourself – or you wouldn't have the babby. Or did you get caught down some dark alley sometime and never even saw 'is face?'

'No, it weren't like that. An' I did have a lot of good times with my Joe. But, when it all comes to an end, you wonders if it's worth it. An' now look at us. Another mouth to feed, an' what with? We can't keep cadgin' off you. I dunno what we're going to do.'

The baby, who had been sleeping fitfully on Em's lap, woke and began to cry. It sounded like a kitten mewling; the bawls with which it had first split the air grew feebler each day. Em got up, carrying the child in one arm, and fetched a cup of milk. She twisted a piece of rag into a point, soaked it in the milk and inserted it into the open mouth. The baby began to suck, and after a moment Em removed the rag and dipped it again. She crooned gently as she did so, and Maggie watched, feeling weak tears come to her eyes.

'You bin good to me, Em. I don't know what I'd hev done without you.'

'Anyone down the Lye would've done the same,' the old woman said. 'Look, it's different down here – didn't they ever tell you that? Oh, I know what they thinks of us, up in Stourbridge and Amblecote and the like. Lowest of the low, that's what we are. Well, so we are, too. We ent got *nothing*. Never did hev. So we had to turn to and shift for ourselves. The folks that first come here – gypsies, they say, don't they – they got together and started to build these mud houses.' She dipped the rag again. 'Well, they're all right, keep us dry and out of the wind. You can even light a fire, if you got the wood.' The baby choked a little and Em lifted her against her shoulder, rubbing the small back before continuing with the feeding.

'They had to live their own way down here then – nobody wanted to know 'em. There was no church, so they didn't bother with marrying. Course, it's all different now. Us've had Chapel now since I were a girl. And a church, that was built when Lye Waste were two villages, an' we've got the Reverend here now, Mr Bromley, and a rare man he is too – meets the men from work and teks their wages off them before they can spend 'em down the beer-shop, and anyone he catches gambling in the street he'll give a good whipping to.' Her toothless mouth opened in a silent chuckle. 'Not that everyone took to him at the start – old Bill, up at Careless Green, he was a surly bloke and rare fond of his drink, an' Mr Bromley told him one day, "William," he said, "if you don't turn, you'll burn." It's become a kind of saying now – don't turn, you'll burn.' She grinned at Maggie. 'Anyway, what I'm sayin' is, rough we may be, but we sticks together, an' if you want to stick with us too, well, there's allus nails to be made an' cullet to be picked up. You can stop here, you an' your babby, as long as you've a mind to.'

384

Maggie lay still, letting the words flow over her. Much of it she had already heard, for although Em liked to talk her conversation was limited. But there was no mistaking the matter-of-fact kindness in the tone, or in those last casual words.

'You bin good to me, Em,' she said again, and the old woman shrugged.

'When you got nothing, it's easy to share. It's folk up at the big houses, who got plenty, that can't give it away. You want to keep clear of them, Maggie girl. They ent no good to the likes of us – none of 'em.' She wiped the rag round the now empty cup and gave the baby the last few dregs to suck. 'Her'll do all right. And there's Milly Crip just had her sixth, she'll hev plenty of milk – we'll get her to give young Emily a suck along of hers. An' as soon as you feel up to it, you can come along of me out to the nail-shop – you ever made nails?'

Maggie shook her head. 'I tried once or twice, as a little 'un – me mam did it, but I was too slow. I worked as a packer in one of the glasshouses.'

'Well, it's nail-makin' here, children an' all, a thousand a day, that's the rate.' Em looked her over critically. 'An' I don't want to hurry you, Mag, not when you're feeling poorly still, but I could do with a bit of help, so if you could start learnin' soon . . .'

Maggie had taken the hint. The next morning, still weak, she had gone with Em to the slitting mill to collect the bundles of iron rods needed to make the nails. Slowly and clumsily at first, she sat with Em and two or three other women in the dark, dirty hovel where a fire made the August heat almost unbearable, and helped to heat the rods, hammer out the shape of the nail and cut off the required length; over and over again. Take a rod; thrust it into the fire; hammer, hammer, hammer; cut. And so on, for hour upon hour upon hour.

It was bitterly hard work. For her share, she received only a few shillings – just enough to feed herself and pay

Milly Crip for suckling Emily, with a few pence to Em for her lodging in the small mud hut. There was nothing left for new boots; to save the ones she had, she went barefoot. The shawl she had bought with the money from Jeremy Henzel had gone long since, replaced by the ragged remnant in which she wrapped the baby. And although it was hot enough now, winter loomed ahead like an ominous cloud on the horizon. There was disease in the community: smallpox, fever, nameless diseases that felled the strong and the weak alike. Every week, every day, someone died. One day, it must be her.

When Emily was a few weeks old, Maggie wrapped her carefully in the old shawl, pushed her own feet into the broken boots that she had kept for the winter, and made her way to Wordsley.

She had never been to Henzel Court before. She knew where it was; had peered through the big gate at the house that stood back from the road, looking down over the town. She had known about Joe's visits there, suffered the dark pangs of jealousy at the thought of him, in there with Miss Christina. But the idea of entering that gate, approaching the big front door at the top of the steps, had never entered her head.

Nor did she dare to do it now. She went through the small gate at the side and along the path to the kitchen door.

Mrs Jenner looked at her with disfavour. 'No gypsies or beggars here, if you please'

'I ent a gypsy, nor a beggar neither. I wants to see someone.'

The housekeeper's face hardened with suspicion. 'And who would a hussy like you know here?' she demanded. 'Get away, before I gets the dogs set on you.'

Maggie stood her ground. 'I wants to see Ruth Compson. She works here, I know that. She knows me.'

'Ruth? She won't know you. She's a respectable girl.'

'She knows me,' Maggie repeated stubbornly. 'Tell her

it's Maggie Haden, an' I wants to talk to her about her brother Joe.'

'Joe?' Mrs Jenner looked at her doubtfully, her glance taking in the baby in her arms. Maggie saw her mind work, and comprehension dawn.

'Please,' she said desperately. 'I got to talk to Ruth.'

'Well, all right. Just for a minute, mind. Ruth don't have time to gossip on the doorstep.' Reluctantly, Mrs Jenner turned away and called to Rose. 'Run up to the nursery, Rose, and tell Ruth there's a party wanting to see her. Maggie Haden, her name is – got something to say about Joe.'

Maggie waited, jiggling Emily in her arms, and a few minutes later Ruth appeared at the door.

'Maggie! What is it? I'll have to be quick, Miss Christina was in the nursery with me and she's just as likely to come down to find out who's here. What's that?'

'What do it look like? It's my babby, that's what – your niece, Ruth Compson.' Maggie looked at her with some of the old hauteur. 'Don't you see the likeness to her daddy?'

Ruth parted the shawl and stared at the small, square face. 'Joe's?'

'Of course it's Joe's! And all the more trouble because of it – Ruth, where is he?' The hauteur disappeared and desperate pleading took its place. 'Where's my Joe? I can't manage by meself. I know I did wrong, but it's his babby, and he ought to give me somethin' to help out. You don't know what it's bin like, Ruth – I bin down the Lye for weeks now, mekkin' nails, an' with her growin' all the time an' winter comin' on, I don't know what to do. Tell me where he is, Ruth, for God's sake.'

Ruth looked at her with pity. Maggie Haden, once so proud, reduced to this poor wreck of a woman, her thick, tousled hair now a greasy mat, her valiant colour drained to leave cheeks that were grey and pinched.

'I don't know as I should tell you,' she said unhappily.

'He made me promise . . . He didn't want anyone to know, only the family.'

'And ent his babby family?' Maggie asked. 'Tell us, Ruth. Please.'

'You'll not be able to go there, it's a long way off.' Ruth hesitated, struggling between pity and loyalty. 'It won't do no good, Maggie, look, I've got a few shillings put by, I'll give you them, and –'

'I want to know where he is. I got a *right* to know.'

Ruth wavered. Behind her, she was conscious of the sounds of the kitchen; the scullery maids' whispering voices, the footsteps of people moving about.

'All right,' she said, speaking quickly. 'I'll tell you. But it won't do no good, he's too far off. He's in Newcastle, Maggie. He went up there to work for Mr Alfred Henzel. Mr Jeremy fixed it for him, just after the accident. An' he's doing well – I don't think he'll ever come back to Wordsley.'

There was a moment's silence. A hasty step in the kitchen. And then Ruth felt herself jerked roughly aside.

'What are you doing here? What impudence made you think you could come to this house, demanding to see the maids?' Jeremy Henzel stood on the step, his pale face livid. 'Get off this land, and see you don't come back, or I'll have you before the magistrate.'

Maggie's eyes flashed. Her desperation was such now that she would have faced Satan himself – and in her mind, Jeremy Henzel and Satan were coming very close. She took a step closer and blazed at him, the old fire in her eyes, a spot of coarse red colour in each ash-grey cheek.

'Get off this land?' she repeated bitingly. 'Is it yourn already then, Mr Jeremy? I heard you and Miss Christina were wedding, but I didn't know it had happened yet. An' if I'd thought she would listen to such as me, I'd hev been pleased to come and warn her agen it – knowin' what I knows about you and your ways. Do she know about me, I wonder? Do she know you kep' me in Church Row for

388

months, when you were courting her an' all? Do she know you wanted me to be a common whore for that Frenchman, so she'd not want to wed him? Or hevn't you got around to tellin' her that yet? Savin' it for the wedding night, mebbe!'

Jeremy, white as bone now, took a quick glance behind him into the kitchen. The cook and maids were standing, mouths agape, listening. And, thrusting her way through them, eyes dark with shock but lips compressed with determination, came Christina.

Jeremy grabbed Maggie roughly by the arm, his fingers biting cruelly into her flesh. He jerked her away from the step and down the path, out of earshot of the rest. His tone low and hard, he spoke quickly into her ear.

'Get out of here, Maggie Haden. There's nothing for you at this house. And if I ever hear you've been repeating your foul slanders again, to anyone at all, I swear I'll have you deported. It's a long way to Australia, Maggie, and many don't survive the journey, so just remember that.'

'And why should I?' She had nothing to lose now; turned away from here, she could only return to the Lye, to the cruel slavery of nail-making and the constant threat of disease. Ruth was right; she could never follow Joe to Newcastle, and there was nobody else to help her. 'Why should I care what happens to me now?' she demanded bitterly. 'Hev me hanged if you like, it'd be better than this misery, an' better for my babby too.'

'Hanging's too good for you,' he retorted, and thrust her away so that she stumbled and almost fell, the baby held even then so that no harm should come to it. 'If I had the chance, I'd serve you the same as I served the Frenchman, so get out of here and don't come back, unless you want to burn. And keep your mouth shut!'

Maggie stared at him, fear and comprehension dawning in her eyes. Instinctively, she held her baby closer, and her mouth shaped the words which sounded only on a breath.

'You did it – you killed him – my God, you're not a man, you're a devil, the Devil himself, an' I bin bedded by you!'

He moved towards her again; but a sudden touch on his arm had him wheeling, face aflame.

'*Jeremy*!' Christina was at his side, Ruth close behind her, her face anxious. 'What in heaven's name is going on? Do you realise half the servants have heard this commotion? Who is this woman, and why is she here?'

'She did not come to see me,' Jeremy said grimly. 'She came for your maid here. And if I were you, I should think again about the type of girl you employ, Christina, for this one at least seems to keep very poor company.'

Christina stared at Maggie, her brow creased. 'But I've seen her before somewhere! Surely – surely you're the woman Joe Compson –'

'That's right, miss, I'm Maggie Haden.' Even now, there was a spark of arrogance left in Maggie as she answered. 'Joe's woman. And this is his babby.'

'His *baby*? Then – are you married?' Christina thought briefly of her expressed wish to see Joe starve. Had she condemned this woman and her child to the same fate?

Maggie's lip curled. 'No, miss, I ent wed. Joe would have none of it, and afterwards when he would, I sent him away . . . I come to see if Ruth would tell me where he was, miss. I didn't know what else to do, but if he's in Newcastle, there's no hope. I can't get there. And –'

'Newcastle?' Christina rounded on Ruth. 'He's in Newcastle, and you never told me? Why did he go there? Why didn't you say?'

'He made me promise not to, miss.' Ruth's voice was wretched as she explained for the second time that day. 'And, I thought it better if you forgot him, like.'

'But why Newcastle? How –'

'Mr Jeremy sent him,' Maggie said, and as he made a sudden movement towards her, 'Ruth knows! She'd tell now – an' Miss Christina means to find it all out anyway.' She thrust past him and went close to Christina, her chin high. 'All right, so I bin a fool. But he's worse – Mr Jeremy. He teks people an' twists them. He twisted me,

390

made me a whore when before I'd only ever bin with a man I loved. An' he twisted Joe, let him think he –'

'That's enough!' Jeremy cut her short. 'Christina, you cannot want to stand here in your own garden and be harangued by this common slut. You've heard from her own lips what she is, let me haul her off now to the magistrate. A few nights in a cell will cool her down and teach her manners, and she'll bother you no more.'

'She's not bothering me now.' Christina brushed him aside and stepped forward. 'You say that this is Joe's child? Does he know of it?'

'He ent never seen her, miss. But he knew I was in the family way, aye, an' I think he would hev took me then, only Mr Jeremy was lookin' after me, like, an' I told Joe to go away. I come to see if he were anywhere near – I thought he might help me now, seein' how I am. But if he's in Newcastle –'

'Mr Jeremy was looking after you? In what way? And why?' Christina was conscious of Jeremy's quick movement beside her, his objections in her ear, but again, without even looking at him, she gestured him away. 'Jeremy, I *will* hear this – now, Maggie.'

'He give me a room,' Maggie muttered with a sideways glance at the man who stood glowering at her, his fury kept only just under control. 'He give me money . . . I'd rather not say no more, miss. I'll go now. Mebbe I shouldn't ever hev come.'

'No, I think it was as well you did.' Christina hesitated and looked again at the weary, haggard face, at the baby wrapped in its ragged shawl. She felt in her pocket and took out a bead purse heavy with coins. 'Take this, it will help you for a little while, I hope. Buy the baby something warm for winter – and yourself, too. And come to me again if you need more help.'

Maggie put out her hand slowly and took the purse. Her face moved, her eyes narrow as she calculated its value, while her lips worked as if she were about to weep. She

391

looked at Christina as if faced with something beyond her understanding.

'Why should you give me this?' she whispered, her voice dry and husky. 'I ent nothing to you. It's *him* as should be helping me –' with a jerk of her head towards Jeremy. 'Not you.'

'I disagree. I think that, somewhere in all this, I am very closely involved with what has happened to you, especially in the part my cousin played in it. But we'll talk no more now. You're exhausted. Buy yourself some food before you walk home. And remember, I expect you to come again, when you need more help.' She smiled suddenly, filled with a tender compassion for the girl for whom she had once felt only sharp jealousy. Maggie stared again, then looked down once more at the purse she held in her hand. With a brief bob of thanks, she turned away, and Christina felt her eyes grow hot as she watched the other girl move slowly towards the gate.

'I feel I ought to have done more,' she murmured as the worn, shabby figure disappeared. 'Ruth, follow her, ask her where she lives. There may be something –' She turned at Jeremy's touch.

'Christina, don't be a fool. The slut's a whore by her own admission, and a beggar too. You've no need to ask where she lives, after the little present you've just given her, she'll be making her home on our very doorstep. Follow her by all means, Ruth, but only to get that purse away from her again. Tell her it was a mistake, give her a shilling or two for her pains, on condition she never comes here again – and if she makes a fuss, threaten her again with the magistrate. Or shall I do it for you?'

'You'll do nothing, Jeremy!' Christina's voice was sharp, cutting across his words as clear and piercing as a newly-sharpened sword. 'Let me remind you that I am still mistress of this house, and I still give the orders. And while we're on the subject, this is still *my* doorstep. And now, let's go inside. I have some questions to ask you.

And I am quite sure you will not want me asking them out here, in the garden, for everyone to hear.'

'Questions?' Jeremy asked, a sneer in his voice. 'Why, what questions can you have for me? If they arise from anything that slummock told you, I can assure you they're not worth the asking.'

'I think they are.' She paused and faced him. 'And if you'd rather answer them here, then listen. Why did you set that girl up in a room in Stourbridge? What did you want her to do for Jean-Paul, and why? And why is she now in such a dreadful condition?'

She waited a moment, while Ruth went down the path after Maggie and the silence grew. Jeremy turned away. His face was very pale and a pulse beat quickly in his throat.

'And why did you send Joe Compson to Newcastle?' she asked quietly.

It was in the library, Christina reflected, that all the important events of her life took place. In here, she had spent many hours with her father, discussing glass, learning the secrets of the business which her family had carried on ever since they had come from France two hundred years or more ago. In here, she had sat with Joe, examining the new patterns he had cut so painstakingly from old books and newspapers. In here, he had held and kissed her and called her by her name, and in here, she had planned her future with Jean-Paul. And now, in the room that had already seen so much, she was about to take what might be the most momentous decision yet. She turned to face her cousin; the man she had promised to marry.

'Now will you answer my questions?' she asked quietly.

Jeremy looked faintly exasperated. 'Christina, you are meddling in affairs you don't understand. Things a lady should not concern herself with. What men do – well, it isn't always easily understood by young women who have

393

been delicately reared.' He came towards her, his hands held out. 'Your tender heart does you credit, my dear. But why not leave it at that? The woman's a slut. She'll go the way she's set, whatever you try to do to help her. And her child will die, like as not, and the best thing for it, poor brat.'

'I want to know,' Christina said, ignoring his outstretched hands, 'what you had to do with her. *And why is Joe in Newcastle?*'

Jeremy stared at her for a moment, then dropped his hands and shrugged. His voice was cold.

'Very well. Since you insist upon knowing, although these are matters I would much prefer *not* to have to discuss with my future wife. Maggie Haden described herself very precisely in a word which I do not propose to repeat. She sold her favours, in other words. I met her after Compson had tossed her aside, pregnant and homeless. I felt sorry for her. I arranged for a room for her to live in, rather better than the hovel she shared with her parents, and I gave her a certain amount of money. I hoped that by doing so I might encourage her to live a decent life and to make something of herself, if only for the child's sake. Obviously, I failed and she now lives a beggar's existence in some slum, and deserves no further help from anyone. I'm sorry if this all sounds rather sordid, but you insisted on knowing.'

Christina met his eyes steadily and he turned away. She considered, and after a moment asked again, 'And Joe?'

'You told me that you wanted Compson out of the area. I arranged for him to go to Newcastle. Is that not far enough away, then?'

'And he works in Newcastle? As a glassblower?'

'As chief glassblower, general overseer and probable future partner. More responsibility than you ever gave him, Christina, in spite of all your fine promises.'

She flushed, but refused to rise to his taunt, asking merely, although she already felt sure of the answer, 'At whose glasshouse?'

'Oh, now, enough of this questioning!' Jeremy exclaimed.

'What odds is it? He's far enough from your ken – let that be sufficient.'

'Does he,' Christina asked slowly, 'work in Cousin Alfred's glasshouse?' She waited a moment, watching the colour sweep into Jeremy's face. 'I see that he does. And just why did you think to send him there?'

'The man's a fine glassblower, you've said so yourself. An artist, you've called him. It was ridiculous to waste his skills when Uncle Alfred was just setting up the new flint house – when we're all set for expansion.'

'Expansion? We? What do you mean?'

Jeremy sighed and ran his fingers through his gleaming hair. 'Look, Christina,' he said, sitting down. 'Let's have things clear between us. Ever since your father died, you've been pulling devil and baker over this glass business, boasting how you could manage it yourself, how you needed help from no one – yet ready enough, when it suited you, to come to me for advice or consultation, without ever thinking that I might have my own family interests to put first. Isn't that true?'

'You offered me your help and advice – said you wanted to give it. You told me you believed in me.'

'I was hardly likely to tell you otherwise,' he said drily, and as she began to understand, Christina felt the colour drain from her face.

'You've wanted everything your own way, that's the truth of the matter,' he told her brutally. 'So proud and arrogant – nobody must have the best glassblower, nobody set up the best engraving shop, nobody but Christina Henzel who was going to make her glasshouse the best in the country – could you really believe that I was equally eager for your success? No, I was waiting, waiting for your downfall. It must come, I thought, in one way or another it must come.'

'But it wouldn't have come, if Jean-Paul hadn't died,' she reminded him, her voice trembling as the pain of her loss struck her yet again. 'You would have lost everything, Jeremy, if he had lived.'

There was a strange, brief silence. Jeremy's eyes changed

colour, from cool, summer blue to the darkness of the midnight sky. His face, already pale, whitened further. A thought slid into Christina's mind and out again before she could grasp it. She opened her mouth and Jeremy spoke quickly, stabbing out the words.

'Nevertheless, it *has* come, hasn't it, little cousin, soon to be wife? The trouble you're in now is at last too great for you to resolve alone. You've come to me for help again, help that this time you can't refuse. You need marriage, Christina. And I need your glasshouse.'

Christina stepped back, feeling as if she had been struck in the face. She sank into a chair, her eyes like holes in the paper-white of her face.

'You can't touch my glasshouse! I have the holding share.'

'I can do whatever I like,' Jeremy said easily. 'I'm sorry about this, Christina. I hadn't intended that we should discuss it until after our wedding. But perhaps it's as well to have everything out into the open now.' He leaned forward, his eyes alight again, smiling with the smooth arrogance she remembered from their childhood days, when he had taken over, and invariably spoilt, many of the games she and Frederic had played so happily together.

'My father and uncles and I intend to merge the Henzel glasshouses together, to make one business,' he said. 'Uncle Alfred, in Newcastle – aided of course by the admirable Compson – has already begun to produce fine rock crystal. Here in Stourbridge, we intend to turn over completely to window-glass. Blown cylinders of good quality, slit and then opened out –'

'I know how it's made,' Christina said tensely. 'But you can't possibly –'

'There's going to be a huge demand for window-glass,' Jeremy told her. 'Look at the building work that's going on now. Houses, public buildings, factories, schools. New churches being built, old ones restored. And there's the fashion for conservatories. *Houses* made of glass! All of them wanting window-glass. Acres and acres of it.' He leaned back complacently. 'That's where the future lies, Christina. That's where the biggest profits are. Fine table-glass – yes, there'll always be a market for it. But beside window glass, it's a mere frippery.'

'How can you say that?' she demanded passionately. 'How can you call it a frippery? We produce beauty – quality. Glass that people love to hold, to look at, to use. What are windows? Nothing but holes in the wall, glazed to let in the light and keep out the cold.'

'But necessary, my dear Christina. *That's* the beauty of window glass.'

'And what of the men? They're skilled glassmakers – are they to forget their skills and spend their days blowing cylinders and ironing them out like any laundress?'

'If they want to keep their jobs, yes,' Jeremy said indifferently. 'If not, there are plenty of others anxious to eat.'

'I won't allow it,' Christina said, and he smiled again.

'You will be unable to prevent it, my dear. You will be my wife, and therefore obedient to my wishes. You will do exactly as I say.'

Christina raised her head and looked at him proudly in the eye. 'And if I refuse?'

'Oh, I don't think you'll do that,' he said pleasantly. 'After all, there's your child to consider, the child you conceived with Jean-Paul. I am happy to give it a name, especially since it is the name it would bear anyway. I am even prepared to give it a home and respectability. But if you want it to be treated as one of my children, sweet Christina, I think you will soon learn to behave as a wife should.'

'I don't understand . . .' she breathed.

'Do you not? Then think for a moment of the idiot child upstairs – Thomas. Most families would have sent him to an asylum as soon as his disabilities were discovered,

397

as indeed he shall be very soon. Who will be surprised if another such child is born to the Henzel family, especially when it is born so early, as I fear yours will be, my dear. Two such – how we shall be pitied!' He stopped and watched Christina's frozen expression with interest. 'Don't look so horrified. It needn't happen – not if you are sensible about this.'

'You'd do that . . .' she whispered. 'You'd pretend my child was not normal, you'd send it to an asylum, and Tommy too . . . You're inhuman.'

'A flattering opinion indeed. Fortunately, I care little for your opinion.' He moved suddenly, grasping her by the wrist so tightly that when she tried to pull away, the flesh burned under his fingers. 'Let's be completely honest with each other now, sweet cousin. You have never had any love for me, always I had to come second, and it seems that any man is good enough to come first, your brother, your father, a common workman and finally a French engraver. Who would be next, I wonder – Parker, the footman, the gardener's boy? No, you're mine now, or soon will be, and then we'll see who's master. You'll do as I say, Christina, and if you want your precious by-blow to be treated as one of mine, you'll keep to the boudoir and the nursery, and forget glass. Leave it to those who ought to have been managing it all along, and we'll rub along very well together.'

Christina shook her head, furious with the tears that threatened to fall. She pulled ineffectually at the iron fingers, scratching at his hand, jerking her arm in her vain efforts to escape him. Her hair began to escape from its confining ribbon, copper curls tumbling forward over her face. She raised her head, her eyes sparking anger into his face, and spat her words at him.

'Let me go! Let me go at once! How dare you hold me like this?'

Jeremy looked at her and laughed. Enraged by the mockery in his eyes, she bent her head and sank her teeth sharply into the fleshiest part of his hand. She felt the shock run through him, and then he released her sharply, jerked his hand away and used it instead to deal her a sharp slap on the face.

'Why, you little wildcat!' He was nursing the hand now, staring at her while Christina put up her own fingers to touch her burning cheek. 'Bite me, would you!' His eyes narrowed and gleamed, and he reached for her again. 'It's time you were taught a few lessons, my little minx.'

'Don't touch me!' She was behind a chair, clutching its back, eyes like green fire. 'Don't you dare touch me! If you do, it'll be you who will be before the magistrate, for common assault, and I'll call Maggie Haden as a witness to your character.'

Jeremy stared at her and laughed, his laugh ringing out in the big, high-ceilinged room. The sound of it turned Christina cold. There was no humour in that ringing laugh; only cruelty and sneering contempt for her, the woman he had professed to love and meant only to cheat. She felt a sickness deep inside her, and her hand moved automatically to her stomach to protect the life within.

'Common assault! And with Maggie Haden as a character witness! You've taken leave of your senses, Christina, gone mad as your father did before you. Calm down, child, and remember I am your affianced husband. Nobody would blame me for attempting to restrain your excesses – indeed, any man who knows you already would commend me! In less than three weeks from now, you'll be my wife and compelled by law to obey me, so why not start now?'

'Your wife?' Christina's eyes moved over him slowly, as if in wonder that she could ever have agreed to any such arrangement. Jeremy's wife . . . until now, she had had no idea as to what that meant. Now she saw her life laid out before her, the life she had dreaded since her early girlhood. A life of boudoirs, needlework and gossip; a life of being subservient to a husband who cared nothing for her other than that she should bear him children. A life no longer hers.

'I am not your wife yet,' she said steadily. 'Nor shall I ever be. I was mistaken in you, Jeremy, but I see you clearly now. I shall never marry you.'

He laughed again. 'And what will you do about the child you are carrying? Not many men will take on a woman almost three months' gone. You'll be hard put to it to find another willing to be your husband, glasshouse or no.'

'I don't wish to find another man. I don't want a husband. I've managed very well alone so far, and I'll continue to do so.' She thought briefly of Aunt Susan, the scandal, the gossip that must ensue and knew that none of it could be as bad as the future planned for her by Jeremy.

His laugh was uneasy this time. 'Don't be so ridiculous! You know quite well that's impossible. Unless you plan to do as your aunt first suggested, and go abroad to have the child. Perhaps Alice will go with you and pretend it's hers. Or Ruth.' His voice was heavy with sneers as he taunted her. 'But don't forget, your secret's no secret any more. *I* know the truth about your child. Humiliate me by breaking our engagement now, and I'll see that everyone else knows too!'

Christina faced him squarely. Her head was tilted back, her green eyes calm after the storm that had shaken her during the past hour. She had faced the alternatives and knew her choice, and knew that it was right.

'You may tell everyone,' she said coolly. 'I intend to do so myself, anyway. I will not go away to have my child, Jeremy. I will have it here in Wordsley, and I will bring it up as my own. I am not ashamed of what I've done – it is no more, I suspect, than many a woman has done before me.' Her hands moved over her stomach, proud and unassailable. 'I'm thankful that Jean-Paul has

400

left me his child. Whatever it is, boy or girl, it was conceived in love, which is more than any children you would have fathered would be. And it will be the heir to Henzel's.'

She smiled at his baffled, angry face. 'You see, there is nothing you can do now. You'll never have the glasshouse, you and your father and uncles. And you'll never have me either. I'll go on as I started. Alone. And make my own future, mine and my child's.'

She swept past him, her face serene in the knowledge that at last she was travelling the proper road. And Jeremy, his face dark with fury, was left alone in the library that now would never be his.

As summer ran into autumn, Joe Compson began to settle down in Newcastle-Upon-Tyne. It was, after all, not so very different from Stourbridge. Larger, but that mattered little to a man who had rarely left the confines of his native village. Scarcely more crowded, the narrow streets teemed with people in just the same way, were littered with the same rotting debris, stank of the same stagnating effluence. The air pounded with the same clatter of forges, mills and foundries, and the public houses smelt in the same way of good rich ale and strong tobacco. The big difference was in the river. The Tyne wound very close to the glasshouse where Joe worked his six-hour moves, and whenever he had daylight hours to spare he made his way to the bustling quays and docks, fascinated by the ships that plied up and down on the tide, watching the cargoes that were loaded and unloaded and listening to the voices that seemed to speak in a strange, foreign language.

It was the language that proved his greatest difficulty. Joe had never heard anything but the dialect of his own Black Country and the lilting voices of the Irish navvies who came to dig the canal cuts and, more recently, the railways. There were Irishmen here too, and he could understand them well enough; but the local Tynesiders – Geordies to those who wanted to abuse them – with their tongue-twisting accents and words that defied translation, baffled him.

It would have gone hard with him indeed, if he had not had two qualities which forced the local men to an admiration that was at first grudging, then wholehearted – his skill with glass, and his prowess with his fists. Prize-fighting was as popular here as in Stourbridge, and there were few Saturday nights when Joe did not come home triumphant after a bout behind some tavern – 'The Old Dolphin', 'The Brown Jug' or 'The Hawthorn'.

In the glasshouse, he very quickly reigned supreme, and even the older gaffers gave him credit for the work he produced. Suspicious at first, some of them never conpletely accepted him; but their views were overridden by the men who saw that Joe Compson's word was law where their employer was concerned and were content to let him lead them, as he had once led his mates in Wordsley.

'It was a good day's work when my nephew sent you up here,' Alfred Henzel told him one day as they stood together in the packing-house, assessing a new batch of wineglasses made to Joe's design. 'Their loss is my gain, I think. Now, what are your lodgings like?'

Joe shrugged. Neither worse nor better than the home he'd left, the terraced house where he rented a room hardly mattered to him at first. It was somewhere to lay his head between moves, that was all. He didn't expect the comfortable familiarity of home; like Ruth, happiness or enjoyment of life was not something he looked for. But he was beginning now to feel a strange restlessness. A discontent with the life of six-hour moves, a few drinks in an inn, a woman and what sleep he could snatch. He wanted something more.

And, by God, he could *do* more! Those evenings spent talking to Christina in her shadowed library had opened his eyes to a different way of life, a new world. And the added interest of the new responsibilities she had given him at the glasshouse had widened his view of glass itself. It was no longer raw metal, to be blown into shape and then forgotten. It was a part of himself that went out into a world wider than he could ever know. His glasses were handled and used in great houses and palaces, not only in England but in countries like France, Germany, Italy – places that until a few years ago he hadn't even known existed. People in America, Australia – people on the other side of the world, thousands of miles away, who would never meet him or hear of him, they all held in their hands glass that had been blown from his breath. The thrill caught at his vitals, and he knew that simply to blow a piece of glass and then forget it would never again be enough. He wanted to follow that glass through; to know what mixture went into producing the metal, who ordered it, how it was sold. He wanted to be implicated in every stage of its production and sale. He wanted to become the equal of people like Alfred Henzel. And that would show Christina Henzel just what she had lost when she told him to go!

'The room's not bad,' he said now to Alfred Henzel. 'But I think I ought to hev something better, being over-seer as well as master glassblower.'

'Something more in keeping with your status,' Alfred suggested, and Joe looked at him doubtfully, wondering if he was being mocked. He decided to assume the suggestion was serious – after all, if he did not take himself seriously, who would?

'That's right,' he said. 'I want to get on now, Mr Henzel. I think there's a place for me in glass, summat more than just blowin', and I think now's the time to start doin' summat about it.'

Alfred looked thoughtfully at the dark, rugged face of the glassblower. Here in Newcastle, away from his brothers, Alfred had developed his own personality which was remarkably like that of his dead cousin Joshua. Tied to them by the bonds of business, he had yet retained his own independence; the glass he produced was different from theirs, with different markets, and he had been left mainly to his own devices. He was keen now to strike out in the new direction that lead crystal opened up before him, and he was well aware of the value of the man who had so fortunately, as it were, dropped into his lap.

'You should have something better than a room in a terraced house,' he observed. 'And some education might not come amiss. You can read and write, I know, but I doubt if you can do much more. Did you ever go to school?'

'Dame school for a while. And then Mechanics' Institute. I learned to draw and reckon – I can look after accounts too, and work out the measures for a glass mix.' He stopped for a moment before adding, 'I worked a bit at that sort of thing with Miss Christina. Reckon I knows as much about the glasshouse now as she do.'

'Indeed.' Alfred thought of the sons he had never had, of his search for a man with skill and ideas to help him put the Newcastle branch of Henzel's firmly on the map. But Joe Compson was a rough diamond, coarse and un-cultured. Could he really be the man to become a future partner? Diamonds, however, could be polished. It might be worth trying.

'We're a long way from Stourbridge here,' he observed. 'So far, the glasshouses there have had the cream of the markets. Now, with lead freely available, there's nothing to stop anyone from forging ahead. My niece knows that. My brothers do too. They may imagine that here in the north-east we are content to be a minor power in the industry – well, I'm not, for one. I would be happy to make the name of Henzel as important here as it is in the Midlands. *More* important. By some happy chance, I have the finest glassblower in the Black Country, and the freedom to develop my own quality lines.' His sudden smile was very like Joshua's. 'You and I could do well

404

together, Compson. Educate yourself, and there's no knowing where we could go.'

'You and me?' Joe studied the older man, his eyes dubious. 'A Henzel and a common glassmaker?'

Alfred Henzel snapped his fingers impatiently. 'Think, man! The best glassmakers have always been those who know glass from its very beginning, the glassblowers themselves, gaffers like you. Look at old Joshua Henzell of Newcastle – died nearly eighty years ago, a rich man yet not ashamed to blow glass with the rest of them. He worked as a gaffer until he was in his seventies.' He laid a heavy hand on Joe's shoulder, meeting his darkened glance eye to eye. 'You could follow him. Make the name of Compson as famous as that of Henzel. We could help each other. But you need to be able to meet other manufacturers, our suppliers, our customers too, on equal terms. Talk with them without their looking down on you. And that means education.' He turned away and moved to the door, staring out at the crowded buildings. 'There are other glasshouses out there. The Northumberland Works, the Newcastle, the Closegate. I don't want them outstripping Henzel's, Joe. So, if you're interested, you'll have to go back to the Mechanics' Institute and if that's not enough I'll arrange some extra tuition for you. And I'll find you somewhere better to live.'

His words echoed in Joe's head as he paced the quays, looking across the river. Over there, on the top of the steep cliff, stood St Mary's church where the old glassmaker, Timothy Tyzacke, was buried. Joe had been to see his tomb in the chancel, where it had stood for a hundred and sixty years. He had laid his hand on the smooth stone, run his fingers round the ornate carving. *Timothy Tyzacke, Merchant Adventurer*, who had become a burgess, an overseer of the poor, a leading personage in the town and warranted his own coat of arms with foreign words on it – words that Jean-Paul Thietry would surely have understood – and a picture with lambs and acorns and God knew what else cavorting about all over it. There'd been Henzels in the family too, though it would be difficult now to trace back and find the relationship to the present-day Henzels. They'd spelt their name with two l's then, like old Joshua. And they'd married in All Saints' on the Newcastle side, facing across the river to St Mary's. And so Timothy Tyzacke had their crest on his tomb too: a thunderbolt and a fireball.

Well, there were fireballs and thunderbolts in the Henzel family still, he thought, remembering the way Joshua's voice would set the cone trembling with his roar, and the way Christina's eyes would flash brighter than the furnace when she was crossed.

They'd all come up together in glass, the Tyzackes and the Henzels, and the Compsons. Yet the Tyzackes and the Henzels were the ones who had the coat of arms and the grand tombs, while he was still living in a terraced house and working six-hour shifts.

He looked up at the church again, and thought of Alfred Henzel's words. It sounded as if he wanted to break away from the Stourbridge lot and make his own way. It sounded as if he wanted Joe Compson to help him.

All right, Joe thought, I will. I'll get the education he thinks I should have. I'll learn to speak like they do. I'll help him break away from them down in Wordsley – after all, I owe them nothing, nothing at all. But I'll do it on my terms.

If Alfred Henzel wanted to make his glass famous, he would have to change the name of his business to Henzel and Compson. But he needn't know that; not just yet.

And then there was Sophia.

Sophia was the daughter of Ralph Armstrong. He owned a forge not far from Alfred Henzel's glasshouse and, like Christina Henzel back in Stourbridge, Sophia was the apple of her father's eye and always in and out of the foundry. She was also a frequent visitor to the glasshouse; particularly after she and her parents had been to supper with Alfred and Jane Henzel and met Joe there, slowly acquiring the polish that Alfred wanted him to have. She said little to him on that first meeting, simply watching him with her wide blue eyes. But the next day she appeared in the cone.

'I hear you're the finest glassblower in the country,' she said to him, her head lifted to one side so that the pale blonde ringlets brushed her cheek. Her blue eyes gleamed provocatively. 'Make me something – a frigger. I'd like to see you do it.'

Joe looked at her. He had a quota to fulfil, but Sophia was the daughter of his employer's friend and clearly popular with the men who were all watching her admiringly. He nodded to his gatherer, who thrust his iron deep into the glowing pot.

'What would you like, miss? I can make birds, animals, a walking stick, to keep off disease, whatever you choose.'

'A ship,' she said without hesitation. 'A cutter in full rig. Don't you think they are the most romantic sight, sailing up river, loaded with silks and spices from other lands . .? I'd love to sail in one – if I were a man, that's what I'd do. Make me a ship, Joe.'

Joe thought briefly of Christina, who also wanted to do a man's work and could do it too. How many young wenches were there like this, wanting to break free of the bonds that held them? He took the iron from the gatherer and began to manipulate it, swinging the metal to lengthen it, blowing, teasing it into long, fine strands with his pucellas, cutting it with the shears; working swiftly and surely to produce a ship like those he had watched coming up the Tyne.

The ship, when finished, was a masterpiece of spun glass, the rigging and masts a delicate filigree above the swooping decks. Sophia clapped her hands with delight and watched anxiously as it was placed in the *lehr*. Her eyes danced and her small red mouth curved in a smile of pleasure.

'That's delightful, Joe! They were right, you *are* a wonderful glassmaker. Now, what else can you make for me?'

'Nothing today, Miss Sophia,' he said firmly. 'Mr Henzel wants these wineglasses finished by the end of the week and then I'm moving over to the caster-hole chair to make some big pieces. There won't be time for friggers.'

'Oh.' Her mouth pouted with disappointment, and then she smiled again – an enchanting, fairy-princess smile that had Joe transfixed. 'Never mind. I shall have my sailing-ship to look at and enjoy. And I shall see *you* again, Joe, I know.' She began to move away and then paused. 'Mr Henzel tells me you're taking lessons in the evenings.'

'That's right.'

'Well. I wonder.' She was tilting her head again, slanting a look from those cornflower eyes. 'I know you go to supper with Mr Henzel, we met there last night. Perhaps you'd like to come to supper with me one evening?'

'With you, Miss Armstrong?' He was startled, and Sophia laughed enchantingly, her head thrown back a little, small white teeth gleaming. He watched her, liking her amusement even though it might be directed at himself.

'With my parents as well, naturally.' She smiled again. 'Don't worry, I already have their permission. My father was most impressed with you last night.'

Joe glanced uneasily round at the men who stood, a short distance away, waiting for him to begin work again. He wondered what they were making of all this. Sophia seemed to understand his concern; her smile deepened.

'All right, Joe. I won't tease you any more. Mr Henzel knows about it too, and he and Mrs Henzel are both coming tomorrow evening. We shall expect to see you then. And don't say you have a lesson, for I know you don't!' Her eyes flashed a twinkling message of mischief at him. 'And don't dare to be late!'

She fluttered away, leaving Joe bemused. Supper with the Armstrongs! And Mr Henzel knew and approved. Well, it must mean he wasn't doing so bad, hadn't made a sight of himself at dinner, managed to use all the right knives and so on. The Henzels had taken quite a bit of trouble with him, after all.

He thought of Sophia Armstrong for the rest of that morning. Her face was in every wineglass he blew, her laughter in every tinkle of glass he heard. Her smile flashed with the sunlight that filtered down through the smoky cone, and the gaiety of her voice sounded constantly in his ears. Sophia Armstrong, he thought, was like a butterfly, dancing in and out of his mind. She would never own any man, never want to. Filled with a happiness that must have been born in her and that bubbled over and infected everyone with whom she came into contact, she would never have to try. Men would flock to her side at the lift of one pretty finger, and do her bidding almost before she had spoken it.

And she had asked him, Joe Compson, to supper . . .

'And you must sit there, Joe, next to me.' Sophia was flitting about the room, organising everyone. It was her party, she explained, her mother had allowed her to do everything, from deciding on the menu to arranging the flowers and planning the seating. 'And it's all been such fun! Aunt Jane, you're to be at Papa's right hand so that he can talk to you all evening. I'm afraid that leaves Mamma with Uncle Alfred, but I know she'll be very good about that, she has the patience of a saint, or so she's always telling me!' The cornflower eyes sparkled with mischief as she teased her guests, and Joe realised that the two families must be very close.

'Patience of a saint, indeed! I must have acquired it through being the mother of a minx,' Harriet Armstrong declared. 'You've no idea how this child tries me, Mr Compson. Don't allow her to tease you; she has no mercy. Come and sit by me instead and tell me about yourself. Mr Henzel tells me you are a superb glassblower.'

During the course of the meal, she kept him firmly in conversation with her, apparently oblivious of her daughter's pouting efforts to attract his attention. Joe, who had begun the meal in a state of nervous apprehension, ended it feeling comfortably at ease and immensely grateful to the kindly woman.

'And now we'll leave you men to your port,' Mrs Armstrong said at last, rising, 'and when you join us in the drawing room, Mr Compson, you shall talk to my daughter, that's if you still wish to after hearing nothing but her chattering voice all evening.'

'Mamma, that's nothing but slander!' Sophia cried. 'I've hardly spoken to Joe – you've monopolised him disgracefully. I shall *insist* on his company for the rest of the evening.' And this being a plan to which Joe was not at all averse, that's just what she did, drawing him out with merciless determination.

'Tell me which books you've read. I'm reading *Wuthering Heights* – such a powerful book. You must try it, I know you'll be interested. And Dickens, I adore Mr Dickens. I read every word. *Oliver Twist*, have you read that? Joe, you must! What *do* you read?'

'I hevn't read much at all, Miss Sophia,' he admitted. 'I've never had that much time.'

'Then you must start now. I'll tell you what we'll do, we'll read together. You can come to supper every Tuesday night and we'll read something. Yes, Joe, it's essential,' she said firmly before he had a chance to protest. 'I know Uncle Alfred wants you to get on, and how can you if you don't read? And, if you won't be offended, Joe, I'd like to help you with your speech, too.'

'My speech? I don't hev to make a speech, do I?'

Sophia laughed. 'Of course not! I mean the way you

talk. It's, well, it is just a little *broad*, you know. I think if you could just learn to say things like – well, *have*, instead of *hev* – that sort of thing, it would make things easier for you in society.' She smiled and laid her small hand momentarily on his. 'And I do want you to get on, Joe. So, will you come? On Tuesday nights?

'All right, Miss Sophia,' he said, mesmerised by the bright eyes and the laughing mouth, 'I'll come.'

Chapter Nineteen

Breaking the news to her family was only the first of many difficult moments for Christina. But that, she thought, was what she must expect of life from now on. Difficulties; disapproval and censure, for everything she did.

'Not marrying Jeremy!' Aunt Susan exclaimed. 'Christina, you can't mean it. Everything's arranged, the service, the wedding breakfast. What will everyone say? Samuel, Lavinia –' A fresh thought struck her. 'And what of the – the –' She floundered, glancing with agitation at Harry and Adela, her neck flushing its unbecoming red. 'Christina, tell us it's just a silly joke,' she said pleadingly.

'I'm not joking, Aunt Susan.' Christina found her voice came with difficulty from her aching throat, and sounded dry and thin. She had barely had time herself to come to terms with her new situation; had lain awake all night, going over the quarrel again and again; remembered the way Maggie Haden had looked at Jeremy and hissed her venom at him, the roughness with which he had handled her. Clearly there was even more in their relationship than she could guess at – she didn't believe Jeremy's version of what had happened between them, and she felt certain that Maggie knew more about Jeremy than she had said. Something terrible, that brought fear and loathing to her dulled eyes . . .

When the family were gathered at breakfast the next morning, Christina, knowing that it could not be put off, had made her announcement and must deal with the consequences.

'But why doesn't Jeremy want to marry you any more?' Adela's eyes gleamed suddenly. 'Is it – is it because he loves someone else?'

Christina sighed. Already, Adela was beginning to build up her own hopes again. 'I don't believe Jeremy loves anyone. Certainly not me.'

'Stuff and nonesense!' Susan flung down her napkin. 'Christina, this is nothing more than a lovers' tiff. You're taking it far too seriously. By teatime, you'll have made it up and everything will be rosy again. Now, if we could just go over the guest-list once more –'

'Aunt Susan!' Christina heard her voice crack with a tension that was close to breaking-point. 'Please listen to me! I am *not* going to marry Jeremy. This is no "tiff" – it's something far more serious. I told him last night and I don't imagine we shall see him here again.'

'Not see him here again? But –' Adela's face fell and she stared accusingly at her sister. 'Chrissie, what have you done?'

'Did he hurt you, sis?' Harry's newly deep voice sounded for the first time as he stretched a hand across the table. Christina took it and gave him a grateful look. 'If you want me to do anything . . .'

'There's nothing anyone can do. No, Aunt Susan, I am *not* going to tell you what happened between us. All you need to know is that the wedding is cancelled. Everyone will have to be told, and that will be the end of it.'

'But it won't be!' Again, Susan's neck was scarlet. 'What of – of –'

'The baby?' Christina said crisply, and heard Adela's gasp. She turned to her brother and sister. 'You may as well know the truth. In plain words, I am expecting a baby. That is why I accepted Jeremy's offer of marriage.'

There was a stunned silence. Then Susan rallied herself to protest at Christina's brazenness, and to protest at this new turn of events.

'Oh, Christina, how could you? With everything so nicely arranged – Jeremy so *generous*. Nobody would have known – well, they might have suspected, but with the wedding safely behind you they would have been indulgent enough. But now, you don't seem to understand what this means. What it will do to you – to all of us.'

'I understand very well. Please believe me, it was the only course I could take.'

'The *only course* – when it means being ostracised, having a stigma on the whole family! Christina, I truly believe you have taken leave of your senses –'

Adela broke in, unable to contain herself any longer. 'But what does it mean? How can Christina be expecting a baby when she isn't even married?' She caught their glances and suddenly blushed deeply; probably Alice had been talking to her too, Christina thought wryly. 'Surely you'll *have* to marry Jeremy now,' she finished in a mumble.

'That would certainly be expected,' Christina said, 'if Jeremy were the father.'

Into another silence, Harry said diffidently, 'I take it that Jean-Paul –?'

'Exactly. Jean-Paul.'

'But Jean-Paul's *dead*!' burst from Adela.

Christina looked at her. At eighteen years old, when many girls were already married, she still had only the haziest idea of what brought children into being, and none at all of the consuming passions which began the process. It was wrong, she thought, that so many girls should go ignorant to the marriage bed, unaware of what was expected of them.

'Adela,' she said quietly, 'sometime soon, you and I shall have a talk. But for now, believe me that Jean-Paul was the father of my coming child, and Jeremy would merely have given it his name. And now –'

'*Merely*!' Susan expostulated. 'Christina, even now it seems that you do not fully understand. You propose to bear a child who will be nameless – illegitimate. A child without a father. The scandal will be all over Stourbridge. None of our friends will want to know us. The young men who would have courted Adela: James Richardson,

415

George Benton, Stanley Bardsley, none of them will wish to call now. Not only that –'

'Aunt Susan, is that true? Will nobody want to marry me now?' Adela turned frightened and accusing eyes on her sister. 'You can't let that happen! My whole life ruined by your selfishness. And just because of a stupid quarrel with Jeremy. Aunt Susan, Harry, tell her she can't do it, make her see reason.'

'Christina see reason?' Susan gave a high-pitched laugh. 'As well ask the world to stop turning! Oh, I knew it would come to something like this. No, Adela, there is no persuading your sister once she has made up her mind – we should all know that by now. We must make up our minds to a life of seclusion, that is all, for we shall have no friends once this business is known. But so long as Christina has her way, we must all be content.'

'But *why*?' Adela asked piteously. 'Why have you quarrelled with Jeremy? Surely you can make it up. Now that you know what it means to us. Whatever reason you have for wishing to break off your engagement, it can't be so serious as that.'

'It can. It is.' Christina's hands were tight on the edge of the table, her fingers white with the pressure. She looked around at the little ring of faces; two accusing, one bewildered. 'It *is* serious,' she insisted. 'Very well –' she paused, choosing amongst her reasons, hoping without much hope that one would satisfy them. 'If you must know. Jeremy has threatened to send Tommy to an asylum. Our dear Tommy! And not only that – unless I do exactly as he wishes, he will do the same with my baby. He means to tell everyone it was born abnormal because of a premature birth, and to place it in an institution. *Now* do you see why I cannot marry him?'

The faces were shocked now; shocked and unbelieving. Susan spoke first.

'*Jeremy* said that? But why? He spoke so generously before. Christina, are you sure you understood him? I cannot believe that Jeremy –'

'What did he mean,' Harry asked, 'by saying *unless you do exactly as he wishes*?'

'Yes,' Christina said. 'That's the point, isn't it. You see, Aunt Susan, there are terms to Jeremy's offer. I have to hand over the glasshouse to him, lock, stock and barrel, to run as he wishes – he and his father. They'll take everything that is good from Henzel's and transfer it to their own business. They'll take our best men – and they already have the best of all, Joe Compson, who I learn now is in Newcastle with Cousin Alfred. They'll take all our secrets, all the processes and recipes we've developed. They'll take our designs, our new engraving shops, and they'll turn it all over to Henzel Brothers. The business my father and grandfather worked so hard to build up will be gone – they'll even take our history. My cones will produce nothing but sheet glass and in a few years we'll be forgotten.'

'Then there's nothing to worry about!' Susan said triumphantly. 'As usual, Christina, you're making a great deal out of nothing and putting the glasshouse before your family. What does it matter who runs the glasshouse or what it's called, so long as it still produces an income. Now let's have no more fuss, you must go straight to Jeremy and tell him that you'll agree with his plans, which seem perfectly sensible to me, and all will be well.'

'*Perfectly sensible*? Aunt Susan, it's exactly what Papa tried to avoid – exactly why he left the glasshouse to me. I have a trust to do as *he* wanted. I can't betray that trust – I won't!' She swept a defiant glance around the table. 'No, not even to please the rest of you. Yes, I shall have my baby and it will bear *my* name – and what better name could it bear, I ask you? And if people choose not to know me, so be it. I cannot – *cannot* – see why they should extend their disapproval to the rest of my family, but if they do I wonder if they are worth calling friends.' She paused and then added very quietly, 'I had hoped that you might stand by me.'

'And I shall,' Harry declared loyally. He reached across to take her hand again. 'Count on me, sis. I think you're doing the right thing. I never liked Jeremy much anyway,' he added. 'Send Tommy to an asylum indeed! He'd have to break the door down to reach him first.'

Susan sighed. 'Very well, Christina, since you seem set on this lunatic course, I suppose I have very little choice but to stand by you. And heaven knows, it isn't the child's fault that its entry into the world will be so unfortunate.'

'Well, *I* won't,' Adela said loudly. 'I think you're being exceedingly selfish and I won't spend a moment longer in this house than I have to. I'll go to Alice and perhaps in Warwickshire I shall be far enough from any scandal to have a chance of finding a husband. Which is more than *you* will ever do now!' She jumped up from the table and ran from the room, her voice breaking into tears as she flung that last accusation at her sister.

Christina sat quite still, biting her lip. Then she rose to her feet. Outside, the sun was already warm, shining down through the haze on to the dusty garden. The clatter of the town drifted up through the air, a background noise she scarcely noticed now.

'It's not just a trust I hold from Papa,' she said, as if speaking to herself. 'I hold it for my child, too. His grandchild, the first of the new generation of Henzels. I shall see that he – or she – inherits what I have helped to build up. And I shall make it a worthy inheritance. Henzel is a name to be proud of now. I mean to see that it always is.'

'Even though you've besmirched it yourself?' Susan said with a bitterness that seemed to shock even herself.

Christina turned and surveyed her; an ageing woman, disappointed and embittered by her own experiences, with nothing to show for her life but a scatter of nephews

418

and nieces, none of them with any real regard for her. She crossed the room and knelt beside her aunt, laying one hand on her sleeve and looking up into the unhappy face.

'Go with Adela, if you'd rather,' she said softly. 'Go to Alice – you'd be welcome there, I know. You could make new friends, live as you would like, without all this talk of glasshouses and business which you hate. You don't have to stay with me, if you don't want to. I can manage.'

'Alone? I wonder how you would get along!' But her face softened a little and she touched Christina's hand. 'Do you want me to go? Would you rather I left you to do as you please, without my constant disapproval?'

'No,' Christina said simply. 'I'd like you to stay. The house would seem wrong without you. But only if you want it too.'

Susan sighed. 'I must be as mad as you are,' she said wryly. 'But now that you've given me a choice, I find that I don't want to leave after all. Very well, I'll stay with you. Whatever there is to be faced, we'll face it together.'

They smiled tremulously into each other's eyes. And then Susan, with a return to her accustomed querulousness, added, 'Mind, I still think you could make it up with Jeremy. He couldn't *really* have meant those things about Tommy and the new baby . . .'

The rift between Christina and her father's cousins had never been wider.

It was like a vast chasm. On one side, alone as if on a bleak, featureless moor, stood Christina; on the other, massed like a hostile army preparing to invade, were the cousins, and their children, headed by Jeremy, their eyes covetous as they watched and waited for her downfall.

And now Joe was amongst them, Joe whom she'd depended on, trusted; Joe, who had caused such a turmoil of confused emotions within her, and had then caused Jean-Paul's death. She had sworn she never wanted to see him again, and she repeated it with a bitter passion that warred with the longing which even now still haunted her dreams; dreams from which she woke in a rage, furious at the involuntary betrayal of her grief for Jean-Paul. Not only Joe, she thought during the long weeks and months that preceded the birth of her child. Adela had gone to the other side too. She was now living with Alice and John in Warwickshire – and they too had made no secret of their shock and horror at what had happened – and, according to her letters to Aunt Susan, living at last the life that suited her: parties, balls, rides and drives in the leafy countryside. There were times when Christina envied her the simple, uncomplicated round of pleasure that now seemed to be hers. But never for long – always the glasshouse would draw her back. That and the trust she felt so strongly, handed down through her to the son – it must be a son – that she now carried.

Even her aunt, who had loyally declared her intention of standing by Christina, would rather be over there with the rest of them, at peace within the conventions of the community instead of here, beyond the pale. Only Harry, who never raised his head long enough from his books and drawings to notice other people's reactions, was wholeheartedly on her side. And by October, Harry was in Oxford.

There was Ruth, of course – Ruth, the staunchest of allies. But even Ruth seemed, these days, to be a little distrait.

'Your father thinks you oughter come home,' Sal declared every time Ruth visited her in the little house with its stiff, uncomfortable parlour and warm, cosy kitchen. 'These stories about Miss Christina – be they true?'

'If you mean is she having a baby,' Ruth said bluntly, 'yes, she is. And you needn't look so shocked, Ma. Let's talk straight about it if we hev to talk at all. It's not me dad wants me home anyway – it's you. *He's* still working for Henzel's.'

'That's different. He's in the glasshouse. In't it natural

for a mother to want her girl out of a house where there's goings-on? I allus brought you up to be respectable, Ruth, an' –'

'And so I am respectable. And so's Miss Christina. She got caught unlucky, that's all, and don't tell me she's the first. She'd hev wed Mr Titt'ry and nobody would hev worried if they'd had a seven-months bairn. Don't you think she've had enough upset, with him gettin' killed that way?' Ruth demanded passionately. 'She needs me, Ma. An' I'm not leaving her now.'

Sal sighed and gave in; she'd never expected Ruth to come home anyway, and secretly she was as sorry for Christina's trouble as her daughter. 'What a tangle it all is,' she said. 'How's it all goin' to end? An' what'll she do next?'

'With Miss Christina,' Ruth observed, 'nobody knows what she will do next.'

The cousins were wondering the same thing.

'Stupid, obdurate miss!' Samuel fumed. 'And slipped out of our hands again, just when we might have felt secure. The more I consider the matter, the more certain I am that there's a streak of madness in that side of the family. Probably through poor Margaret. How can any well-brought-up young woman even *contemplate* the course Christina has taken? The girl must be completely off her head.' His eyes gleamed. 'Perhaps even now we could bring a charge of insanity against her – get a doctor to certify that she isn't fit to control her own affairs.'

'It wouldn't work,' Jeremy said. 'Christina would never let a doctor into the house. And Cousin Susan would stand by her too, not to mention Harry.'

'Susan! Harry!' Samuel exclaimed dismissively. 'Pawns in the wench's hand. And you, Jeremy – by what reason do you think we should listen to anything *you* say! A few weeks, that was all you needed and we would have had control of everything, yet you could not hold her even that

421

long. Why? What happened? Are you *so* distasteful to her? Is it only the women of the streets who'll accept your attentions?'

Jeremy flushed with angry humiliation but before he could reply, Harold intervened.

'It's no use continually railing at Jeremy. Quite clearly, the girl is totally uncontrollable and unpredictable. She was spoiled, as we all know, by her father who filled her head with wild ideas before dying untimely and leaving her in control of the business. Added to which, she has involved herself immorally with a foreigner, witnessed his death and is soon to bear his child. Rational behaviour can hardly be expected in these circumstances –'

'Or in any circumstances, where Christina is concerned,' Samuel interjected sourly.

'It is a great pity that this coming child made haste imperative,' Harold went on in his wooden way. 'Given time, I believe that Jeremy would have succeeded.'

'Well, he didn't. The question is, what do we do now?'

Harold shrugged. 'What is there to do? We can only wait. Christina will be her own executioner. Nobody can pursue the wild courses she does without eventually coming to grief.'

Reuben's thin voice sounded from the corner where he had settled himself.

'I think a great deal will depend on the sex of Christina's child. If it's a girl, we may not have too much to worry about. She will still need a son to carry on the name. If it's a son –'

'What difference will that make? Christina will be only too pleased to bring a daughter up in the way she has gone herself – wilful, thinking herself as good as a man, learning to manage the glasshouse and taking a sight at her elders and betters. She'll take a positive delight in it!'

422

'But a girl will marry,' Reuben pointed out. 'The Henzel name will die. Whereas a son, born to Christina and taking her name for his own, even though it comes from the wrong side of the blanket . . .'

'Yes, I see.' Harold frowned. 'With a daughter, we still have a chance – with a son, there is none.'

'I would not go so far as to say that,' Reuben said gently. His eyes slid round to Jeremy's, holding them in a glance that sent the colour from his nephew's face and left it grey as ashes. 'Life is a strange business – all manner of unexpected things may happen. No, I would not lose hope yet, not for a long time.'

'Well, there seems to be little we can do at present anyway, so I suppose we will just have to wait,' Samuel grumbled. 'But for how long? Just how much time do we have?' He shot Jeremy a baleful glance that clearly indicated that he had not yet forgiven his son. 'Christina's child is due in a few weeks now. Perhaps we'll know then what the future is likely to be.'

'Oh, we can never know that,' Reuben interposed softly. 'As I said, unexpected things may happen.' His eyes moved to Jeremy again. 'But I agree, it will be interesting to see whether Christina gives birth to a son or a daughter. Very interesting indeed.'

It was a matter which interested a considerable number of people in Wordsley, Amblecote and Stourbridge. And it was resolved on the sixth day of February, 1847, a Saturday, when Christina, after a labour that took her eighteen long, hard hours, gave birth. Her child was, for a newborn infant, long and slender, with a fuzz of nutbrown hair and eyes that bore only a tinge of milky blue in the soft grey that showed in their first baffled stare at the world. Its cry was loud, long and peculiarly penetrating.

It was a boy. She called him Paul.

Motherhood came as a revelation to Christina.

At first, her pregnancy had come as a shock – innocent though she had been, she was aware of the disgrace of illegitimacy and she was not so independent as to be able to dismiss entirely the society of her friends. It had taken more strength than her aunt had supposed to declare her situation openly and accept the consequences, and the defection of her sister Adela and others who had turned their backs, had hurt her considerably.

She had also found the pregnancy itself irksome and uncomfortable. The sickness she had suffered in the early days had not worn off after a few months, but had dogged her all through. And her increasing and cumbersome size had irritated and wearied her until there were times when she had wondered whether she would ever again know what it was like to move freely, to run and skip and dance.

'As if our clothes were not restriction enough,' she grumbled to Ruth as they went through the busines of dressing yet again. 'But I suppose babies *are* born, eventually.'

'I've never known one that wasn't,' Ruth agreed. 'And you'll feel different when it's here, Miss Christina. You'll love it then.'

'I love it now. It's all I have left of Jean-Paul.' Christina rested her hands on her swollen stomach. 'It's just the process of getting it that I don't love.'

Even less did she love the labour that came at the end, the waves of pain that washed over and took control of her agonised body, the screaming muscles that were brought into action for the first time, the last wrenching thrust that pushed her son into the world. But when she held him in her arms, and looked down at the crumpled face with its down of soft brown hair, she felt a surge of love that she knew would stay with her until the end of her life.

As Paul grew bigger, Christina's love grew with him. She took a constant delight in him: in the tiny fingers and toes, the soft brown hair that rubbed off and then grew again into strong curls; the first tentative smile at six weeks, the chuckling laughter at four months. She fed him herself, disdaining her aunt's suggestions of a wet-nurse, and when he grew big enough to take solid food she spent every meal-time with him, patiently teaching him the use of a spoon and a cup.

Inevitably, the glasshouse slipped into the background of her mind. She was aware of this and excused herself: the cones were producing fine glass now, some of it coloured, the cutting and engraving shops were settled and busy, the market assured. She still visited it at least once a week; the embarrassment caused by her condition as she had grown larger was no longer there, and the men had accepted the situation, but there seemed little cause for concern.

However, in the year of Paul Henzel's birth, there were great changes taking place in the glass trade, and in the Black Country generally. Christina, playing with her son in the new nursery next door to Tommy's, was aware of them; but she did not at first realise their significance.

The Smethwick firm of Chance Brothers had developed a new method of making sheet glass; so had Hartley's of Sunderland, and the two firms were in fierce competition. As more and more buildings were erected – many of them large houses for wealthy manufacturers or public buildings, needing vast areas of glass for windows – the demand for flat glass increased. The Henzel cousins began to expand; they still cast greedy eyes at Christina's three cones and told each other that one day she would fail, and soon enough, too, if she continued to neglect her business – and then they would buy her out.

In Stourbridge, the two daughters of Joseph Silvers, of Silvers, Mills and Stevens, married and their husbands, Will Stevens and Samuel Cox Williams, became principals in the firm and changed its name to Stevens and Williams. Typical, Christina thought with scorn, of the way most women were treated by their menfolk, for the daughters, whose inheritance the glasshouse truly was, were no more than stepping-stones for their husbands' ambition. But in Dudley, to Christina's delight and Aunt Susan's disapproval, a woman founded a brewery. Julia Hanson and Son, it seemed, was the only brewery in the country with a lady's name. She sent Julia Hanson her congratulations and good wishes. In her own glasshouse, circumstances were less favourable.

She was in the nursery one afternoon, just after luncheon, when Rose came to say that there was a 'person' waiting to see her downstairs.

Christina looked up at her. For a moment, sharply, she was reminded of that first evening when Joseph Compson had come to show her his designs for the new glass, and Rose had almost forbidden him the house. Her heart leapt, startling her with the reaction which left her momentarily weak and trembling. But almost at once, she fought down the response and when she spoke, her voice was calm and steady.

'A "person", Rose? Someone with no name?'

The parlour maid coloured. 'He's from the glasshouse, Miss Christina. Husselbee, he said. Shall I tell him you're not at home?'

'Husselbee?' Christina's brows lifted. 'Why should he come here? No, Rose, of course you won't tell him I'm not at home. Show him into the library, I'll see him there.' Where I used to see Joe, she thought involuntarily, and closed her mind against the flicker of pain.

She laid the baby back in his cot and left him with the nursemaid. There was no question of a chaperone accompanying her now; Christina had gone beyond such conventions. She saw Jem Husselbee alone, facing him across the table where he sat twisting his cap in his hands.

'Well, Jem, and what brings you here? There's no trouble, I hope? No accident?' Her voice sharpened.

426

'No, miss, nothing like that.' The gaffer was ill at ease, out of his element in the comfortably furnished room, so different from his own home. Yet Joe had been out of his accustomed surroundings too, and he had never looked out of place; only right, and assured, as if he belonged there . . . Christina jerked her mind away and waited while Husselbee sorted out his thoughts.

'There's naught really *wrong*, Miss Christina. It's just that, well, things ent right, either. The men don't seem to hev the heart they used to. And the new designs, they're not as good as the ones Joe Compson did, there's no getting away from it. And I hear orders ent coming in so fast these days, either.'

'No, they're not.' Christina frowned. Honeyborne and Turner had both spoken to her of these things, but she had brushed them aside as being the normal worries of an overseer and manager. But the order books could not be brushed aside, and their evidence had been plain enough. 'It's nothing serious, though, Jem. Only a slight drop. It's all this Bohemian glass, so much cheaper than our own. But we have the quality – theirs cannot touch ours for craftsmanship and brilliance. And I refuse to compromise quality for profit.'

'That's all very well,' Jem said bluntly, 'but we has to make a living out of glass and if we can't sell it, we starve.'

'Nobody's going to starve!'

'Firms hev gone bankrupt before,' Jem said. 'Even glassmakers. Even Henzel's.'

Christina was silent. It was true enough that a Henzel had once gone bankrupt, many years ago. But that was before Roger Henzel; before old Joshua himself. It could not happen again.

'You're making far too much of this, Jem,' she said, striving to keep her voice clear of the doubt he had sown in her mind. 'Henzel's is doing as well as ever, and will continue to do so. We've had thin times before, and no doubt we will again, but I don't believe this is one of them. A few lost orders mean nothing.'

'Begging your pardon, miss, but they mean a lot.' Jem had overcome his nervousness and was speaking up boldly now. 'A few lost orders are like straws in the wind – they show which way it's blowing. If these Bohemians are taking our customers, we got to do something to stop them. Put our prices down. Mek a different sort of glass. Something to get folk to buy.'

'Put our prices down! Do you realise how much wages have increased in the past three years? And as for making a different sort of glass, what are you suggesting we do? Start press-moulding? Never! My father trusted me to continue to make fine quality glass, and that is what I shall do. I told you, Jem, we'll weather this storm, if storm there is at all.'

'There may not be yet, but believe me, there will be.' He spoke doggedly, standing his ground. 'It ent just the orders, miss. It's the whole feeling in the glasshouse. It ent the same. There don't seem to be no one to egg the men on, if you know what I mean. You don't come in so much as you used to –'

'No, I know. I've been – occupied. I'll put that right, Jem. I'll visit each cone regularly, just as I used to. I'll talk to the men, set their fears at rest if I can. Will that help?'

'It will, a bit.' He paused and his colour deepened. 'But it ent just you they're missing, if you'll pardon me saying so. It's Joe Compson too. He were only young, but the men looked up to him. They knew him for what he was – the best glassmaker hereabouts, and a man that had summat more about him too. He could lead the men, Miss Christina, and there's nobody else just the same.'

'But Joe Compson is in Newcastle,' Christina said, and her voice came with difficulty.

'I know, miss. We wondered if – well, he might come back. It could make a deal of difference if he did.'

Christina turned away. She was disturbed and confused, unable to sort out her own emotions. Joe Compson, back in Stourbridge! What would it mean to her, seeing him again daily, with all the memories that would bring? Could she tolerate such a thing, even for the sake of the glasshouse?

'He might not come,' she said. 'He may be settled in Newcastle.'

'Couldn't you ask him, Miss Christina?' Jem Husselbee leaned across the table, clutching his cap between fingers that showed suddenly white. Clearly, this was the crux of what he had come to say. 'Couldn't you tell him we need him here? This is where he owes his loyalty, after all. I tell you this, miss, if we don't get Joe Compson back, with his hold on the men and his new designs, we'll be facing trouble in less than five years. And it might be a trouble you can't get out of – this time.'

Christina gave him a sharp look. But she could not censure Jem for his impertinence. He was one of the older glassblowers, a gaffer who had worked for her father, had begun his apprenticeship under her grandfather. He had a right to a certain freedom of speech. And besides, he was obviously in earnest over this: he would never have come uninvited to the house without a very powerful reason.

All the same, to ask Joe to come back . . .

'Isn't there anyone else?' she asked with some desperation. 'There are always glassmakers looking for work – isn't there anyone who can make designs as well as Joe? What about the younger men, the servitors, are none of them ready for promotion? I can't believe the future of our entire business rests upon just one man!'

'Ordinarily, perhaps it wouldn't,' Jem said. 'But times ent ordinary. And Joe Compson's no ordinary man.' He stood up and looked at her with sombre eyes.

'There's trouble brewing in all sorts of ways,' he said. 'Not just in the glass trade – in everything. Men are beginning to understand what their rights ought to be. The new unions – they're going to get stronger. And with machines takin' over more and more, we're going to get the old skills giving way to new methods, an' in my opinion it's for the worse. I'm not sayin' that bringing Joe Compson back will put a stop to all the trouble, Miss Christina. But he knows the men and the men know him, and it's here he ought to be, not up in Newcastle.'

'And are you asking me for the men's sake or for mine?' Christina asked with sudden bitterness. 'As I recall, he wasn't much use to me during the last dispute. And it was because of what happened then that he is in Newcastle now.'

'And there's plenty,' Jem returned, 'who'd say that wasn't justice. But it's for you to decide, in the end.'

He nodded to her and went out, settling his cap on his head as he walked through the door. Christina stayed where she was; sitting at the table, staring unseeingly after him.

Ask Joe Compson to come back? *Ask* him? Go begging, pleading with him to come back, just as if he had never quarrelled with her over the French workmen, just as if he had never given the push that sent Jean-Paul to his death? Never. *Never*.

She walked to the window, her steps short and quick, and gazed out. What had Jem meant by that last remark? Not justice? Not justice to send Joe away, when he had killed the man she loved and meant to marry, even though he'd denied all guilt?

She remembered the day of Jean-Paul's funeral, when Joe had come to her in the churchyard and implored her to believe him. And she had sent him away, angry that he should even dare to approach her, hating the sight of his dark, unhappy face, and had shown him no mercy. What if he had, indeed, been innocent?

430

Restlessly, Christina paced the room, her skirts rustling over the thick carpet. For months now, she had tried to close her mind to the memory of that dreadful day. It would do no good to keep going over it, Ruth said, and besides it might harm the baby. And Christina had agreed, and tried hard to forget. But now all the old pain returned, the horror of those last few minutes, the endless scream . . . And with the pain came the fury, the rage she had felt towards Joe when Jeremy had told her, the consuming desire to see him suffer as Jean-Paul had suffered and –

She stopped in her tracks. *Jeremy*. It was he who had told her that Joe had – could have – given that fatal push. And Jeremy who had sent Joe to Newcastle. It was Jeremy who had offered her marriage, in order to acquire control of the glasshouse. It had suited Jeremy's purpose to have Joe out of Stourbridge. And it certainly suited his father and uncles to have Joe working for them, even though it must be in Newcastle. Nobody else had suggested that Joe might have killed Jean-Paul. Only Jeremy. And she had never doubted him then, nor given it a thought since. Perhaps there had been an injustice. But even so . . . Joe's return would stir up memories best forgotten – emotions best left sleeping. Even *if* he agreed to come.

Ruth was very doubtful, when Christina broached the subject with her later.

'He's settled up there now, you see,' she explained. 'I don't like to say this, Miss Christina, but since you ask me, he seems happier. He writes to me, and me mam and dad, and he's talking all the time about his work and the new place he lives in and his mates and the lessons, and I really don't think –'

'Lessons? What lessons?'

'Why, he goes to the Institute of an evening, miss – like the Mechanics' Institute in Stourbridge, I suppose it is, the one they're talking of turning into a School of

Art, and he learns all kinds of things. And then there's Miss Sophia and the books they read and –'

'Miss Sophia?' Christina said sharply. 'Who is this Miss Sophia? Some retired governess or teacher, eking out a living by reading stories to mechanics?'

'Oh no, miss. She don't work at the Institute. She's the daughter of one of Mr Alfred's business friends. He says she's helped him no end.'

Christina frowned. 'A spinster, I suppose, like Aunt Susan, with some education but unmarried and having time on her hands. Very commendable, to help people like Joe, but I don't really see what she expects to achieve.'

Ruth eyed her and smiled. 'I don't suppose she reckons to achieve anything much,' she remarked casually. 'But our Joe seems to get along all right with her. And I don't think she's as old as Miss Henzel – from what he says, I'd be surprised if she was twenty yet. I reckon she likes him all right, too,' she added as an afterthought.

Christina turned away and busied herself with the things on her dressing-table. She looked at her ringless fingers, moving amongst the pretty, cut-glass bottles and silver-backed brushes. She picked up a mirror and gazed into it, seeing the sadness of experience that shadowed the green eyes, the slight droop in the once laughing lips.

Jem had said that there was trouble ahead, for everyone. He had said that Joe Compson might be able to keep the glasshouse from going under, should hard times come. There was a new barrier between her and Joe now, higher than ever before. She wondered if they could forget what had happened, put it in the past, and whether he, if she were patient, might once again become her friend and ally, a man she could talk to and trust.

'I'll go to Newcastle,' she said without turning her head. 'I'll talk to Joe, and I'll bring him back.'

Jem was right. Joe Compson belonged here in

432

Stourbridge. Not up there in Newcastle, blowing good glass for her cousins, making a reputation for them in the world her own side of the family had ruled for so long. There was this Miss Sophia, too. Somehow, Christina didn't like the sound of her.

Chapter Twenty

Autumn came early to the north-east, touching the trees with flame. By the middle of September, when Christina made her journey north, the brilliant leaves had been quickly torn from the branches by the gales that swept in from the North Sea, and the bite of winter was creeping in with the cold morning mists that rose from the river. Harry and Ruth accompanied her, both excited by the journey and, away from home, all three relaxed; the conventions of Stourbridge did not apply now and they could behave as friends, equals.

The reaction of the Newcastle Henzels was, predictably, unfavourable. Especially as Christina had refused point-blank to stay with them, and had put up instead at a hotel in the centre of the town.

'They don't want me there,' she told her aunt when the usual expostulations at this plan had been made. 'I don't suppose Cousin Jane would even receive a fallen woman like me under her roof. I could only be an embarrassment to her. And Cousin Alfred is too closely involved with the other cousins. He still wants to take over my glasshouses, like the rest of them.' She paused, and then added with a little smile, 'Besides, I intend to steal his best man from him. I can hardly accept his hospitality at the same time.'

'I am surprised that you concede that Compson *is* his man,' Susan said with acerbity, and Christina laughed outright.

'I don't! Joe's mine, I'm merely going to reclaim my rightful property. But Cousin Alfred won't see it like that.'

Her own words gave her an odd sensation, however. Joe hers, her 'rightful property'? She could imagine just

435

how Joe himself would react to that statement, and yet, there was a feeling of truth about it, a feeling that somehow she had laid her finger on everything that was at present wrong with her life.

'Well,' Susan said, giving in, 'I insist that you at least call on Alfred and Jane. It would be most discourteous not to do so.'

'Very well, Aunt Susan, I'll call. But,' Christina continued, with a flicker of her old impishness, 'I doubt if they'll be pleased to see me.'

And she was quite right. She and Harry called on their first afternoon in Newcastle, arriving at the conventional time and giving the parlour maid their names. There was a long pause – while they discussed the pros and cons of even allowing her over their doorstep, Christina thought with grim amusement – and eventually the parlour maid returned, a curious expression on her face.

'The mistress is at home,' she said, her eyes resting avidly on Christina. 'May I take your coats?' and then she showed them into the drawing room, where Jane and Alfred were having tea. The two faces were stiff and unwelcoming.

'This is a surprise, Christina,' Jane said, offering her cheek. 'What brings you to Newcastle? It's a long journey for you to make.'

'Oh, I felt in need of a little holiday,' Christina said lightly. 'And Harry kindly agreed to accompany me before going back to Oxford . . . And how is the glasshouse doing, cousin Alfred?'

Alfred Henzel looked startled and muttered something into his beard. Christina looked at him sadly. He was so much like her father. If only they could have been friends – even partners. But it was plainly out of the question.

Jane Henzel changed the subject.

'And how are you enjoying Oxford, Harry? This is your second year there, I believe? Oh, and you must tell me about dear Susan, is she well? And Alice, and her husband and baby? And Adela, such a sweet child, I've always thought.' She did not ask after Thomas, whose existence she preferred to ignore; nor after Christina's son Paul. Indeed, as the hour wore on, it became clear that she would have preferred to ignore the existence of Christina herself; most of her conversation was addressed to Harry and if she did speak to Christina, she hurried on before there was a chance to answer.

Christina sat quietly, aware that Jane could quite easily have refused to receive her at all and had probably agreed to admit her only out of curiosity. She glanced once or twice at Alfred; he was as silent as she, staring into his cup and rousing himself only once or twice to talk to Harry about his engineering ambitions. Nobody, she thought, was sorry when she said that it was time to go.

'You must come again,' Jane said insincerely. 'There will be several messages I shall want to send to Susan. Come on a Tuesday, none of my friends call then, and we can be cosy together.'

And you won't need to introduce your scandalous cousin to them, Christina thought with a twitch of her lips. She touched Jane's cheek with hers and offered Alfred her hand.

'Thank you so much for the tea,' she said. 'It's been delightful. And when may I come to see your glasshouse, Cousin Alfred?'

The grey whiskers bristled. He stared at her.

'Well, you must know how interested I am,' she said gently. 'It *is* true that you're making lead crystal now, isn't it? I should so much like to see how your methods vary from ours.'

He recovered himself. 'Not possible! No. Couldn't be allowed.' He paused, as if casting about for a reason. 'The men wouldn't have it,' he said at last. 'Women in the glasshouse – no. I'd have a strike on my hands.'

'Oh, but surely –'

'I said no!' He was on firmer ground now, it was his

glasshouse after all, who better to say who went in and out of it? 'I'm sorry, Christina, it's out of the question. There'll be no visits to my glasshouse. And that's final!'

His glare reminded her irresistibly of her father's. And when had she not been able to persuade him . . . ? But this was Cousin Alfred, she reminded herself, and he had Joe Compson in his glasshouse and must know why she had come. She smiled sweetly and inclined her head.

'Then of course I accept it, Cousin Alfred. Though I own I'm disappointed. However, Harry will be able to tell me all about it.'

The dark eyes bulged. Alfred looked at Harry, then back at Christina.

'Well,' she said reasonably, 'the men can't object to Harry, can they? And I know he'll be interested. Tomorrow morning, shall we say? He might want to go several times, mightn't you, Harry?'

'I should think it very likely,' Harry said, his face quite straight as he looked back at her. 'Very likely indeed.'

And there was really nothing that Alfred could say. He said a good deal more later on, though, as he and his wife prepared for bed.

'She's got something in her mind,' he declared, sitting down to remove his boots. 'Mark my words, my dear, she hasn't come all this way just to kiss our cheeks and wish us well. She means to take Compson back, that's what it is, I'll stake my life on it.'

'Compson? Joseph Compson, that Sophia Armstrong thinks so well of? Well, and mightn't it be a good thing?' Jane sat up in bed, her cap pulled tightly down over her papered curls. 'I know Harriet is not altogether pleased at her fancy. She was anxious for Sophia to marry nobility.'

'Aye, that's so, but the child's unlikely to make a catch like that, pretty though she may be. And Ralph thinks highly of Compson too. He'll not gainsay her if Compson's the man she wants. The lad's changed a lot since he came here, you know, smoothed out the rough edges and

438

turned into quite a prepossessing fellow. Young Sophia could do a lot worse.'

'I suppose that's true, especially if you decide to make him a partner, though I'm still not sure about that, Alfred. After all, he *is* only a common glassmaker.'

'Now that's just what he's not. There's nothing common about Joe Compson – no, he's a very uncommon man indeed. Young Jeremy did well to snap him up and send him here, and I'll do my best to keep him. We need men like that, Jane, men who understand the work of glassblowing and can lead the men as well as design new patterns. And we need them on our side – the manufacturers'. If these unions become as powerful as it seems they might, we don't want men like Compson at their heads. That's why I'd like to see him wed Sophia. He'd be one of us then and bound to stand by us, and he'd be a good man to take into partnership, along with Ralph's concerns. He'd stand to inherit them too, you see. We both need heirs. We've got to look for new blood.'

Jane Henzel was silent, turning over her husband's words. 'So you think that Christina is here to take him back?'

'If she's got any sense, she is. She'll realise the truth of what I've just said, worked it out for herself, no doubt. There are no flies on that lass. More's the pity,' he added as he got heavily into bed.

'And will he go?'

'That,' Alfred said, humping himself into a comfortable position for the night, 'depends on young Sophia Armstrong.'

Sophia and Joe, meanwhile, had become increasingly friendly. The Tuesday evening suppers were an established routine. Ralph and Harriet Armstrong were always present, of course, and often there were others too. Friends and acquaintances, carefully chosen at first so as not to embarrass Joe's newly acquired social skills, and then asked at random when Sophia realised that Joe wasn't the man to let a small thing like using the wrong fork upset him. He was willing enough to go along with such niceties, he implied, but they didn't really *matter*. They weren't important. Not like being able to blow fine glass or run a successful business. It was a point of view that hadn't occurred to her before, but having thought it over, she appreciated it.

'Very well, Joe. It doesn't matter in the least which knife or fork you use. It doesn't make you any less of a glassblower or Freddie Birkett any less of a fool for laughing at you. And nobody has to look twice at either of you to see which is the better man . . .' Head on one side, she surveyed him. 'But I really do think one of those new jackets would suit you far better than they do him. You've got the figure for it . . .'

Another time, discussing a book they'd read together, 'Yes, of course Heathcliff was treated badly. But you see, he never took any *trouble*. It's so easy to make people behave as you want them to do, if you just take a little trouble over it. Look, let's try with Stanley. He doesn't like you and you don't like him. But why not try to *make* him like you?'

'I don't especially want him to,' Joe said.

'No, I know you don't. But if you're going to get on in the world you have to be able to make people like you. He's just practice. Try it tonight, Joe. Ask him about himself. People love talking about themselves and they like anyone who listens. You see.'

Joe tried it, and to his surprise it worked. Stanley Hacker, who had treated him from their first meeting with lofty disdain, was delighted to find someone who would listen to his long monologues about Himalayan plants. And to his own immense surprise, Joe found that by the end of the evening his own feelings towards the older man were a good deal warmer.

'He's not a bad chap after all,' he told Sophia, and she laughed.

'You see! An added benefit.'

Often, there was nobody else to supper, and then Joe would spend the evening virtually alone with Sophia, sitting with her at one end of the drawing room while her mother sewed peaceably at the other. Then their talk would range far and wide, and he found himself becoming increasingly attracted to the pretty butterfly with the cornflower eyes. He began to wonder if Sophia had any suitors or if her father had anyone in mind for her. It was never mentioned. And he speculated upon whether there was any possibility that if he himself worked hard, rose to the top position in the glasshouse and perhaps even became an equal with Alfred Henzel himself, he might be considered acceptable. He began to picture a home – one of those in Jesmond Dene, perhaps – with Sophia in it as his wife.

And if these pictures were marred by the intrusion of a small, slender sprite of a girl with tawny chestnut hair and flashing tiger's eyes, he thrust her firmly out of them again. Christina Henzel was in the past. He'd be better off forgetting all about her and starting again.

Now that she was here, in the same city as Joe and perhaps only streets away from him, Christina found herself strangely reluctant to meet him. Too much had happened between them. She couldn't visualise his reaction to seeing her again, and tried to decide if he would be pleased, resentful or – after all this time – merely indifferent. She hoped desperately that he would consider returning to Stourbridge and that her journey wasn't simply a waste of time.

'You're just nervous, now it's come to the pinch,' Ruth told her. 'And you don't even have to go up to him cold, like. Mr Harry will see him first and find out how the land lies. All you have to do is wait for him to come back from the glasshouse. And I reckon that ought to be any minute now.'

441

Christina paced the hotel room.

'He may not have seen Joe. We don't know which move he works.'

'Then if he hasn't seen him, he'll go back this afternoon. He's got to be on one or the other. Listen, that's him now. I know his step anywhere.'

Christina turned to the door. Her heart was beating fast. Her brother came in and she looked at him, unable to speak.

'Well,' Harry said, throwing his hat on to a chair, 'he's there. I saw him and I spoke to him. But I couldn't say much, Cousin Alfred was by me all the time and watching like a hawk. I found out this, though, he's intent on improving himself, just as Ruth said. And Cousin Alfred's all for it. I think he means to make Joe up to overseer – maybe even more.' He paused and glanced at his sister. 'I think he could even be intending to make Joe some kind of partner.'

'*Partner? Joe?*'

'He could do worse,' Harry pointed out. 'Joe's a brilliant workman and designer. And it wouldn't be the first time a glassblower has risen up to run his own business – look at the Stuarts.'

'Yes, indeed.' Christina paced the room again.

'The thing is, does Joe realise what Cousin Alfred has in mind? If he does –' Harry shrugged, lifting his hands and letting them fall again.

'He isn't going to come back to Wordsley as a common gaffer,' Christina said thoughtfully. 'No, you're right, Harry. I should have to offer something very worthwhile. But a partnership . .? Well, we shall just have to see.' She straightened her shoulders. 'The whole question is, whether Joe knows of Alfred's plans, and whether he wants to come back anyway. And to find that out, I must see him. Did you discover whether that might be done, Harry? A meeting arranged?'

'I found out where he lives from the address Ruth gave

me. She could go to see him, arrange a meeting,' Harry said. 'But I think I have done better than that. This Miss Sophia Armstrong –'

'Yes, yes, I know. What about her?'

'Miss Armstrong was at the glasshouse this morning. Apparently she often goes there. So much for Cousin Alfred's talk of strikes if the men see a woman in the cone! Anyway I talked to her and told her how you run the glasshouse down in Wordsley.' Harry paused, a look of triumph on his face. 'She's invited us both to supper tomorrow evening. And Joe will be there too. How do you like that!'

By the time she was ready to go to supper at the Armstrongs' house the next evening, Christina had tried on all her dresses at least three times and discarded each one.

'Nothing's right!' she said at last in despair. 'I shall have to say I can't go.'

'Nonsense!' Ruth exclaimed strongly. 'You look lovely in every one of them. Try the blue brocade again.'

'No, it's too grand – suitable for a mayor's ball rather than a supper party. I can't think why I brought it,' Christina declared. 'And don't suggest the rose-pink again, it looks dreadful with my hair. That leaves only the crimson, which is no better, and the bronze silk.'

'And that's the best of all.' Ruth held it up, admiring the shimmering folds. 'Its just the colour of your hair, and these stripes bring out the green in your eyes. Why don't you wear it, Miss Christina? You know you look beautiful in it. You'll make that Miss Sophia look nothing but a washed-out doll.'

'A fine way to repay one's hostess,' Christina murmured. She looked at the bronze gown and sighed. Ruth was quite right, it did something for her that no other dress had ever done. Brought out a brilliance in her eyes, a wildcat, gypsy bearing to her body. It made her

443

feel different too – reckless, primitive, as if she would dare all for what she wanted most . . . So why didn't she want to wear it?

Because she was afraid of meeting Joe Compson, that was why. Afraid of the sparks that might fly between them; the consequences of the clash that must result when his vibrant personality struck at hers. And this dress would tell him too much about her; remind him of things that were better forgotten.

'I wish I hadn't come,' she said aloud, and Ruth shook the dress impatiently.

'Don't talk ridiculous, Miss Christina! You don't wish that at all – you're glad you came and you're glad you're going to supper at Miss Sophia's tonight, and you're going to wear this dress and show them just what a Black Country girl is made of. And if you're scared of meeting our Joe,' she added shrewdly, 'then you needn't be. I reckon he's a whole lot more scared of meeting you, that's if he knows you'll be there at all. And serve him right!'

Christina stared at her maid, then laughed. Her tension dissolved and she held out her arms.

'Very well, Ruth. I'm behaving childishly, I know. Let's put this gown on again and see just what effect it has on your brother. Imagine him taking supper at one of the best houses in Newcastle! It seems most unfair that you can't be there too.'

'Oh, I'll see him soon enough,' Ruth said, and slipped the silk over Christina's head. 'But I wouldn't mind seeing his face when he claps eyes on you.'

Christina remembered the remark when, less than two hours later, she entered the drawing room at Sophia Armstrong's house to find Joe Compson already there. And she could not prevent her own hesitation on the threshold; nor hold back her own gasp of shock at seeing him again after so long.

For a few heart-stopping minutes, time ran backwards. She was in her father's cone again, watching the men at

444

work, her eyes drawn irresistibly to the one who stood head and shoulders above the rest; waiting for him to turn and notice her, waiting for the slow stare which would quicken her heart and bring colour to warm her cheeks. The past years were, for that brief space of time, wiped clean; none of it had happened and she was waiting to start again.

And then Joe turned and saw her. Time ran forwards again and clicked into place. Nothing had changed, yet everything had changed. Her heart beat fast as she moved forwards, and she answered the familiar challenge in his eyes with the same proud tilt of her head.

'Good evening, Joe. You look well.'

He watched her cautiously. His eyes glimmered and she caught her breath, seeing danger there. But he answered her coolly enough.

'Good evening, Miss Christina. I didn't expect to see you in these parts.'

His voice had changed. The roughness of the Black Country accent had been smoothed out, leaving a timbre that was cultivated enough to take him into any society, yet still rich and deep and unashamedly coloured with his origins. And the smart fashionable evening clothes he was wearing were a far cry from the dark ill-fitting suit he'd worn at her father's funeral. She gazed in some surprise at the black tail-coat that fitted his body so admirably, displaying to the full his breadth of shoulder and tapering elegantly to the narrow trousers. And she almost gasped at the vivid splendour of his richly embroidered waistcoat. Embroidered by whom? she wondered, with a bitter flash of jealousy that was quashed as quickly as it appeared.

'I needed a short holiday,' she said casually. 'It seemed a good idea to come to Newcastle to visit my relatives. You've been here, let me see, would it be a year, just over?'

'About that,' he agreed sardonically and Christina felt her colour rise. He was mocking her! she thought indignantly. Of course she knew well enough when he had left, but she didn't want him to think his departure important enough for her to remember. And he knew that and was mocking her. As insolent as ever! Perhaps he hadn't changed so much after all.

There was little opportunity for private conversation during the supper, but Christina had plenty of opportunity to observe Joe and her amazement grew. He was no longer the common workman, being patronised by his betters. He was one of them – able to talk articulately, argue with cogency and conviction, proving with every word he uttered that he had a mind of his own and could use it. He was no man's mouthpiece, she thought with increasing admiration; he came to his own conclusions and wasn't afraid to say what he thought. And the way that pale, insipid Sophia flirted with him, gazing up at his dark face with those adoring eyes, sickened her.

Supper over, Sophia swept them all out into the garden to walk in the evening air. Ralph and Harriet Armstrong soon found a seat and sat down to enjoy the sunset; Sophia and Harry disappeared for a game of croquet and Christina found herself sitting alone in a shady corner with Joe.

'Well,' Christina said at last. The barriers were there again, all the old constraints of class and position, together with the bitter memory of Jean-Paul. 'You seem to have done very well for yourself, Joe.'

'I'm not sorry I came,' he acknowledged.

'Not sorry! I should think not – you have your feet well under the table here, it seems. What would they think back in Wordsley, I wonder?'

'Since I'm never likely to find out, it don't worry me too much,' Joe returned.

'No, I can imagine you'd not want to return to us – what country bumpkins we must seem to you now. Scraping by in our poor way – I wonder you stood it as long as you did. We certainly wouldn't be good enough for you now!'

'I never said that!'

'You don't have to say it, it's plain for anyone to see.' Christina looked him up and down, her eyes kindling with scorn. 'Such fine clothes, Joseph! And such tidy hair. Why, I hardly recognised you.' She waited for a moment and when no response came, went on, driven by the bitterness that burned in her breast. 'Do you know what you are, Joe? What you've become? A rich lady's plaything, a toy, a dressed-up monkey on a stick. How do you like dancing to her tune, Joe? Tell me that. How do you like playing Heathcliff to her Cathy? Or had you never realised what was happening – had you never understood that she's using you just as a game, acting out these books you read like a play in a theatre? Only much more entertaining, of course – for *her*.'

'That's enough!'

Joe moved so swiftly that Christina was barely aware of it until he was upon her, his hands gripping her upper arms, jerking her hard against him. His face was suffused with dark, frightening fury, his eyes smouldering as he glowered down at her. She caught the familiar odour, the faint scent that was Joe and only Joe, and felt a dizziness sweep her body.

Roughly, he dragged her into the shelter of some nearby bushes. He was holding her too tightly for her to fall, and he did not even seem to realise her condition as he began to speak, all his pent-up anger and frustration pouring out like poison from a suppurating wound. Christina heard his words like blows punching from his body, battering her mind; but the sense of being in his arms again, even though he held her in anger, was too much for her and she could do nothing but droop against him, weak and helpless, as he raged around her.

'Monkey on a stick! Lady's plaything! That's rich, that is, coming from you. Don't you know that's what they used to say about me in Wordsley? Isn't that what your fine cousin Jeremy said about me, that I was your plaything, that you

447

laughed at me behind my back? And now you dare to say it about me and Miss Sophia! You come up here after me – oh yes, I know, I can see it in your eyes, you came after me – and you dare to sneer at what you find. What's it been to you, this past year, what was happening to me? What have you cared? I could have starved for aught you worried – it was what you wanted, wasn't it, to see me starve? But I didn't, did I? I came here and found myself thought worthy. Worthy of a good position in the glasshouse – and worthy to court Miss Sophia too.' He paused and thrust her suddenly away, still keeping his grip but holding her so that he could stare down into her widening eyes and blanched face. 'You don't like that, do you. You don't like to think that I might make good without you and your lady bountiful help. But I will. I *have*. And I mean to do better yet.'

'I always thought you worthy –' she began faintly, but he shook his head.

'No, you didn't. Never. You never thought of me at all – not really. You didn't know what life was about then – you looked at me with those great tiger's eyes and promised what you didn't even know was yours to give. And when you found out, you gave it to another man.' He snorted his contempt. 'A weedy Frenchman! When I could have – well, never mind. It's over now.'

He released her suddenly and turned away. But Christina, rubbing her arms where the marks of his fingers must surely show purple already, followed him across the grass. She caught at his sleeve and pulled him round to face her, and now her eyes were shining, as green as summer streams, light sparking from them as it sparked from water caught by the sun.

'You could have what, Joe? Tell me.' She lifted her face, consciously provocative now, her heart thundering as she remembered the evening when he had kissed her. Do it again, she begged silently, and let her gaze move down from his eyes to his mouth. Her own lips parted in anticipation and she tilted her chin.

With a swift, almost involuntary movement, Joe swept her into his arms, so fiercely that the breath was pushed from her lungs. He scooped her up against him so that her slender curves moulded perfectly with his broad, muscular shape, and for the second time in their lives, he bent his head and laid his mouth on hers.

Christina felt herself drawn swiftly, deeply, into another world; a world that was composed of nothing but herself and Joe, a swirling vortex of darkness and heat and aching need. The touch of his lips, exploring, plundering, shaping hers, the feel of his body moving in arrogant demand, called forth a response that shook and frightened her. In her experiences with Jean-Paul there had been nothing like this; none of this sense of hidden violence, this dark undercurrent that brought her panting against him, returning kiss for kiss, caress for fierce caress, tangling her fingers in the dark, curly hair and straining her body futilely for a closeness that only nakedness could achieve.

With a muttered oath, Joe wrenched his lips from hers and thrust her away. They stood apart, breathing rapidly, watching each other like antagonists waiting for the signal to take up the battle again. Christina raised a trembling hand and found her hair loosened, tumbling around her shoulders. She touched her lips and found them already swelling. Joe was staring at her. She saw the darkness in his face, the smouldering in his eyes, and interpreted it as bitterness and hatred. The violence in his hands, his arms, his lips – it had been a punishment for all that she had caused him, the injustice that had been done. She turned away. It was all too late. Too much had happened, too much had been said. For Joe's sake as well as her own, it had to be stopped. Now.

'I'm going indoors, Joe,' she said faintly. 'In fact, I think I'd better leave. You can tell Sophia and her parents that I felt unwell. No doubt she won't be too upset . . .'

Shakily, she found her way to the edge of the shrubbery and turned. 'I think you're right, Joe. Newcastle is the place for you. I'm sorry I came.'

'*No!*'

The violence in his tone was like a physical blow. 'No, you can't go like that. Not just because of a kiss. You started it, you know. You asked for it, plain as a baby crying for its mother's milk. And you're not going to end it there, not even if you did get more than you bargained for.' He moved slowly closer. 'We're going to get to the truth of all this now, what's between us two, and sort it out for good and all.' He towered over her, and Christina shrank back against a tree. He raised a hand and she trembled; but he only touched her lips, very gently, with one big and infinitely tender finger.

'Meet me tomorrow at this time,' he said. 'Out on the road to Town Moor. We've things to say to each other that can't be left any longer. Will you do that?'

Christina looked up into his eyes and saw with incredulity that the darkness was the darkness of a more tender passion than hate. She felt her own body grow soft and weak, and she longed, as she had never longed for anything in her life, to fall forward into his arms, rest against his broad rock of a chest and feel his heart under her cheek.

'Tomorrow,' he whispered, and she nodded her head.

'I'll be there,' she said, and slipped out from the shadows of the trees, making her way back to the house.

The Town Moor lay just beyond the boundaries of Newcastle: a bleak, windswept upland where children could run wild and free, and courting couples find seclusion.

Christina went there by hired trap, accompanied by Ruth and Harry, who had both refused point-blank to allow her to go there alone. And she was glad of their company, for her wildly swinging emotions had kept her

450

awake for most of the night and continued to plague her through what seemed to be an exceptionally long and irksome day; now, as the moment approached, she was almost ready to turn around and go straight back to Newcastle. Her pride, however, kept her from voicing these ridiculous fears to her companions and, as they drove sedately along, she gave no hint of what she was really feeling.

The light was already beginning to fail as they approached the Moor. The sun had disappeared ten minutes since, leaving the pale sky flushed with thin wisps of apricot cloud, high up, like a gossamer scarf across the heavens. Already, the first bright star had appeared, low down near the horizon, and the air, warmed during the day by a sultry September sun, was chilling with the wind that blew sharp and cold from the North Sea. She left Harry and Ruth in the trap and went on to meet Joe alone.

He was waiting for her, a shadow amongst the shadows of a clump of trees. He stepped out and stood before her. They looked at one another, wary again.

'I didn't think you'd come,' Joe said at last, and Christina laughed, the high-pitched laughter of nervousness.

'I didn't think *you'd* come! Oh, Joe,' she said, suddenly serious, unable to conceal her feelings any longer, knowing that now there could be no hiding from the truth between them, 'it *is* so good to see you again.' She lifted her face. 'Say my name. As you did before – you remember. Say it to me now.' She challenged him with her eyes and saw, with a great leap of joy, the challenge met and answered in his.

'Oh, God – *Christina*!' he ground out. He took her by the hand and drew her quickly along the twisting paths, into a secluded dell. It was surrounded by bushes, too dense for anyone either to see through or force a way. He stopped and immediately Christina was in his arms.

'If you only knew how I've wanted this,' he muttered

against her mouth, his hungry lips making an attack on cheeks, eyes, ears and throat. 'If you had any idea how you've kept me awake at nights, thinking it could never happen, telling myself what a fool I was . . . Christina, Christina, Christina . . . there, is that enough for you? Three times I said it, will that do?'

'No, no, it will never be enough, never.' Her head hung back, her throat arching itself to his kisses, and she moved restlessly in his arms, knowing at last what it was she craved. 'I want to hear you say it for the rest of my life. I want to hear your voice every day, see you every day, do this every day.' With sudden energy she lifted herself against him, moving sensuously so that he gripped her more tightly still. 'We belong to each other – it's true, isn't it? You know it too.'

'I've known it ever since you first started coming to the glasshouse.' He looked down at her, his eyes gleaming. 'I knew you were my woman, that's why no other was ever enough for me. But I never thought – do you know what you're saying, Christina? Do you really know what that means?'

'It means I want to marry you, Joe.' She shifted so that she could look up into his face, shadowed from the glow of the sunset. 'I can't afford to wait until you ask me – so I have to be like the queen and ask you! You will, Joe, won't you? Marry me and come back to Wordsley? We need you, Joe.' She laughed a little. 'I came to fetch you back, if you would come, because Jem Husselbee told me that. The glasshouse couldn't survive without you, he said. It was only when I saw you again that I realised – neither can I.' She was trembling with the discovery she had only just made, and the desperate need to convince him it was true.

'Nor I without you.' His kiss this time was deep and lingering, rousing a passion that had her panting and whimpering, before he released her. 'It's been good for me, this year away. And I owe Miss Sophia a lot, I think

452

she may be disappointed to lose me. But she's young and nothing goes too deep with her. She'll soon find another chap to read to and teach to speak well, and dress up like a – a monkey on a stick.' He took Christina's face between his palms. 'I'll take payment for that remark,' he threatened. 'But not until we're wed – I don't want you worrying about a second by-blow on the way.'

Christina felt her cheeks flood with scarlet.

'I was going to tell you about that, Joe. I didn't realise you knew.'

'I knew,' he said grimly. 'Ruth kept me in touch . . . And I wished it could have been me you turned to, instead of that cousin of yours. But at least you had sense enough to put a stop to it, and even though I had no hope, I was glad of that. He's never the man for you, Christina.'

'Nobody is,' she said soberly. 'Only you.'

'And the Frenchman?' He was watching her intently.

'I loved Jean-Paul very much,' she said honestly. 'I can't tell you otherwise, Joe. But it wasn't the same as what I feel for you. Jean-Paul was – oh, sweet and romantic and delightful. He taught me gentleness and kindness when I was in danger of becoming hard. He taught me about tenderness. He made me very happy.' She felt Joe stir and knew the pain of jealousy that was lancing him. 'But I think in time, I would have needed more. He could never have given me what I know you will. And I could never have given him what only you can call from me.' Passion shuddered through her and she caught her arms around his neck, pulling him down against her. 'Joe, I want you so much,' she whispered against the roughness of his cheek. 'Let's be married soon – here in Newcastle if you like, or back in Stourbridge. Anywhere, so long as it can be soon and we can be together at last.'

They were married three weeks later, in the Church of

All Saints where so many glassmakers had made their vows. Alfred and Jane, disappointed and annoyed, had finally consented to attend. The Armstrongs did not.

Christina and Joe left Newcastle then to return to Wordsley and to tackle the difficulties they were sure to find there. Some of them were, as she had expected, overcome without very much trouble. Others, more insidious, would rock the foundations of her marriage almost before it had begun.

Chapter Twenty-One

Married! To Joe Compson! The news went round Stourbridge like wildfire. It came first to Henzel Court, arriving by one of the new telegraphic communications – enough in itself to send Susan into hysterics, as much at the expense as at the fright it gave her. And when the contents of the message sank into her consciousness, she had, predictably, a fresh – and worse – attack.

'Married! To that *workman*!' she kept repeating. 'Oh, how *could* she? The shame of it!'

She had only just begun to hold her head up after the birth of Paul, who played in his nursery upstairs, oblivious of the fresh scandal his mother had brought upon the house. Now, she felt certain, the entire family would be completely ostracised. It never occured to her that Christina was rapidly becoming one of the 'characters' of Stourbridge, and that her doings were gleefully watched and commented on by most of the bored matrons of local society. Nor that Susan herself, as emissary from the eccentric and fascinating world of Henzel Court, was becoming more welcome in more mundane households than ever before.

The latest news, however, startled more than the upper ranks of Black Country society.

'*Married*?' Sal Compson said to her husband when he brought the news home from the glasshouse. 'Our Joe, married to Miss Christina? You've got it wrong, Will. It can't be true.'

'True it is. Mr Honeyborne told us all today. They were wed a week ago and they're comin' back soon. Hevin' a sort of holiday first – a honeymoon, he called it.' William sat down heavily and shook his head. 'I don't understand it. I thought as he wor settled up there in Newcastle. Doin' well. And then, all of a sudden she ups an' goes up there after him and then this!'

'You did say Jem went an' towd her the men wanted our Joe back,' Sal reminded him, her fingers going back automatically to her podging.

'Ah, that's right, but her din't hev to *marry* him to get him back. Or mebbe her did – I dunno. I daresay he'll be round soon's they're back, and we can ask him ourselves then.'

'That's if he still wants to know us,' Sal said darkly. 'Mebbe he'll want to forget where he came from, now he's married well. An' our Ruth – what'll this mek her?' Her head shook in imitation of her husband's. 'I dunno, I'm sure. I dunno what'll come of it.'

The same sentiment was being expressed in the kitchen at Henzel Court.

'I thought as we were going to have Mr Jeremy as our new master,' Rose said tearfully. 'I always liked Mr Jeremy. A real gentleman . . . And now we've got to bow and scrape and touch our hats to that Joe Compson, who's no better than any of us. What got into her, that's what I'd like to know? What made her do it?'

'On the rebound,' Parker declared. 'That's what it was, mark my words. Had some silly tiff with Mr Jeremy and never got over it. And a woman's never the same after a babby . . . 'specially not a high-strung young woman like Miss Christina – Mrs Compson, as I suppose we'll have to call her now.'

'If you ask me,' Mrs Jenner said darkly, 'there's a weakness there, in the whole family. Look at Master Thomas. And that will that Mr Henzel made. It was the shock of the Frenchman getting killed that brought it out in Miss Christina. This won't be the end of it, mark my words.'

By the New Year, Joe's return to the glasshouse had already begun to have its effect there. Startled at first by the manner of his return and his new status, the men had treated him with some caution. Was he now an employer's man, the old ways forgotten, set amongst them to spy and report back to Miss Christina? Their first reaction to him was covertly hostile, and it was only when Joe threw off his coat and let his old, rich Black Country accents bellow through the cone as he shouted for ale that they began to feel he was still the man who had grown up and worked beside them.

'I have to get their confidence back,' he told Christina, 'and that means working with them just as I used to. I may be master over them all now, but unless I can still blow a good piece of glass and show them I'm still the same old Joe, I'll lose their trust. And if that happens I'd be better to have stayed in Newcastle.'

'I hope you don't mean that,' Christina said, reaching for his hand. 'After all, you were virtually my overseer before you went to Newcastle – we were only waiting for poor Mr Turner to retire – and Cousin Alfred was on the point of making you his partner.' She held his hand against her cheek, turning it to nuzzle into the cupped palm. 'You're the equal of any manufacturer now; you deserve to be master by virtue of your own skills, and the men know it.'

He glanced sideways at her, his eyes darkening in the way that made her heart leap, and his fingers stroked her wrist. Immediately, she was invaded with weakness and her eyes closed. It was almost too much, this effect Joe had on her, and it was growing stronger. There were times when he only had to look at her, and her body moved for him.

And yet . . . There was still something that eluded her; something that, after every lovemaking, she felt was missing. A tiny piece of the puzzle not fitted into place, like a segment from one of Thomas's dissected pictures lost beneath a chair. Perhaps it was due to the problems of fitting Joe himself into the Henzel household. It wasn't easy for Susan, for instance, to find herself living in the same house, on equal terms with a man who until recently had been no more than an employee, who she certainly wouldn't have recognised in the street.

Christina was well aware of her aunt's feelings, but took the view that there was little to be done about them. Joe's manners and speech were perfectly acceptable – for which, grudgingly, she had to thank Sophia Armstrong – and he was polite without being fawning, friendly without being obsequious. He knew that there would have to be adjustments on both sides, and he was willing enough to make his. Aunt Susan would simply have to make the best of it.

Joe's decision to continue working at the factory did not, she had to admit, make things any easier. Although he no longer worked the strict six-hour moves, he was liable to decide to go into the cones at any time of day or night if something were happening he felt he should see, and she found it disconcerting to have him arriving in her bed some time after midnight, only to leave it again at five. And then he was often around the house in the afternoon, which upset Aunt Susan further. Afternoons were times for calls to be paid and now that her friends were beginning to include Henzel Court again on their calling list – partly to indicate forgiveness for Christina's disgrace, and partly out of curiosity over this new marriage – she did not want Joe about the place, dwarfing everything in her cluttered drawing room and making the house shake with his laughter and his bellowing voice.

'It's almost like having Joshua back,' she said to one particularly close friend, 'and while I loved my brother well enough, this man is *not* my brother. That makes all the difference.'

'I should think so indeed,' said the friend, and went off to spread the news that all was not well in the Henzel household, as people still thought of it. News that quickly reached the ears of the Henzel cousins.

'All is not lost, even now,' Reuben remarked to Jeremy. 'As we've agreed before, events can often take a surprising turn.' But Jeremy, soured by the whole situation and burning with hopeless hatred towards Joe Compson, turned away. Of all the family, he was least welcome at Henzel Court. He never went there now, nor to the glasshouse. The sight of Christina, radiant and blooming, filled his mouth with a bitter taste and tore his body with a frustration that could not be assuaged.

Everyone was affected in some way by Joe's arrival. The servants had found it difficult to accept as master of the house a man they had previously looked down on. For Ruth, the situation was even more difficult, but Christina took this matter into her own hands.

'We're sisters-in-law now, Ruth,' she said as soon as they all returned to Wordsley. 'You can't possibly be my maid. But would you be my companion? Stay with me as a friend? You're the only real friend I have, after all.'

'I don't know, miss, it's all so queer. I don't see how –'

'I'm not *paying* you to be my friend,' Christina said with a smile. 'You'd be one of the family, with your own allowance. Joe will arrange that with you. Please say you'll stay. I don't think we could manage without you – I certainly couldn't, and Tommy would break his heart. And there's Paul, too.'

So Ruth stayed, and Susan had to accustom herself to a former maidservant also joining them at meals. At this rate, she told her friend, they might as well all move down to the kitchen and eat there, since half the staff seemed to be in the dining room. And the friend, agog for more information about this increasingly curious household, invited Susan to her own forthcoming *At Home* and thus set the seal on her return to Stourbridge society.

The only ones who were wholeheartedly pleased by Joe's arrival were Thomas, who took immediately to this big, bluff man, in spite of the loud voice and laugh which, however he tried to temper it when he was in the nursery, still set old Dobbin rocking, and baby Paul. And for this, Christina felt, she would forgive him anything.

It had been her biggest worry, the relationship between Joe and Paul, for there could be few men who would willingly accept their wives' illegitimate children as theirs. Joe, however, seemed to be one who could; perhaps because he remembered only too well that he had fathered a child of his own. He had not asked about Maggie Haden, perhaps supposing that she was married herself by now, and Christina did not volunteer any information. Some day, she might tell him that she was still sending money down to Maggie at the Lye; but not yet.

She wondered sometimes whether it was Maggie who was coming between them, whether Joe still hankered for her and remembered her in the most intimate moments he shared with Christina. Or could it be the memory of Jean-Paul? She had seen Joe's face darken when he had first caught sight of the Chalice in its position in the library. He had lifted it down, turned it this way and that, his dark brows lowered ominously before he finally gave her a glowering look.

'You had it engraved, then.'

'He did it without my knowledge,' Christina said defensively. 'He wanted to please me. And he didn't know of my promise to you.'

'You said you'd never have it engraved,' he said as if he hadn't heard. 'And now it's got his initial on it – his and yours.'

Christina came to his side. She wanted to point out that it was Joe's initial too, but she knew it would only anger him further. He wasn't ready yet to accept any compromise; his own position was still too fragile.

'It doesn't really matter,' she said softly, leaning against him. 'It's only a piece of glass. And you made it for Henzel's, not just for me. I still have the swan.'

He had put the Chalice back then and turned to kiss her, and she knew that what came between them was not

460

his jealousy of Jean-Paul, any more than it was her jealousy of Maggie Haden. It was something deeper than that; something more sinister.

It wasn't Sophia; her fluttering prettiness had, Christina thought now, already begun to pall. But there was definitely something that still raised a barrier between them, something indefinable. Like the glass that had first brought them together; transparent, invisible, yet diamond-hard. If she could only discover what it was maybe it could be as easily shattered.

These thoughts did not occupy her mind all the time. There was too much to do. The business of the glasshouse, which had receded from her during her pregnancy and the first few months after Paul's birth, was now as absorbing as it had ever been. The joy of her marriage had given her back all her old zest; she found herself brimming with energy, delighting in a life which was full of interest and variety. There was never a moment when she wasn't busy: attending to the business of quotas, marketing, design and finance in the mornings, spending the afternoons with Joe and baby Paul, working again at her papers in the evenings. There were visits to be made to the cones, poignantly mischievous when she approached Joe's chair, and meetings with other manufacturers. She began to give dinners again, on the evenings when Joe would be at home. And, slowly, invitations began to come again to Henzel Court, addressed to Mr and Mrs Joseph Compson.

And there were the nights, those few short hours between midnight and dawn, when Joe would hold her in his arms and capture again the magic of their love. A magic that was as fierce as it was potent, as their minds were abandoned, and bodies and senses took control. Christina found herself swept, time and time again, to new peaks of desire, new heights of rapture. Stretching her body to Joe's, she was vibrantly aware of the burning touch of his skin, the rough friction of hairs against her own silky smoothness, the intoxication as his fingertips traced every

461

hidden contour and roused her to wilder and wilder frenzy.

But although her frenzies were invariably rewarded, by a climax that was as varied as Joe's lovemaking itself, she was always visited, when it was all over, by that same tiny doubt, scratching away at the back of her mind and bringing an indefinable sadness to her heart.

In February, Harry came home for Paul's first birthday party.

They were a small gathering. Adela was still with Alice, refusing to have any contact with Christina, especially since her marriage to Joe. None of the other Henzels came: they were still having difficulty in acknowledging Christina's son, and Lavinia, for one, could not countenance the idea of drinking tea with 'that man' as she referred to Joe. So it was only Christina, Joe, Susan, Harry and Ruth who celebrated Paul's first year of life. And since they were so few, Christina said, they might as well take their tea in the nursery with the baby and Thomas, and make it a real birthday party.

It turned out to be the most successful family event since her marriage. Joe made an excellent bear, crawling around the floor with a hearthrug draped across his back, and Susan forgot her dignity and played spillikins with Thomas by the fire, laughing as heartily as anyone when Harry and Ruth joined forces in order to beat her. Christina held Paul on her knee, feeding him cake, and felt a warmth creep into her heart as she remembered the words Harry had spoken long ago, about the secure happiness he always felt in the nursery. They were on the right road at last, she thought dreamily, hugging her son to her breast, the whole family was coming together. Now if only Adela could forget her grievances, all would be well.

Later on, Joe went off to the glasshouse; he had promised to give some lessons to some of the more promising apprentices. Christina and Harry stayed in the nursery, and they were still by the fire, talking quietly, when Rose came to say that there was a visitor downstairs.

'A visitor? To see me? Mr Compson's at the glasshouse now.'

'Yes, miss – madam. He asked to see you, particular.' There was a suppressed excitement about the maid's face. 'It's Mr Jeremy, madam.'

'Jeremy!' Christina gave a quick glance at Harry. 'He hasn't been here since – well, for over a year.' And had played so small a part in her life since then that she had almost forgotten him.

'He asked 'specially if you'd see him, madam, but he said he'd understand perfectly if you were otherwise engaged.' Rose spoke with an air of having learned her words, and Christina smiled a little. She was half inclined to say that she was indeed otherwise engaged. But curiosity won the day.

'All right, Rose. Show him into the drawing room. I'll be down in a few minutes.' She waited until the parlour maid had gone. 'Do you want to see him, Harry?'

'Not unless you want me there.'

'Then I'll leave you here. I don't think I need any help in dealing with Cousin Jeremy – not after all this time. I wonder what he can possibly want?'

Jeremy was waiting in the drawing room. He was looking at Susan's collection of shells when Christina came in, his back towards the door. As she entered, he laid down the huge cowrie which was Aunt Susan's pride and joy, and turned to face her.

It was a surprise that he looked so much the same. In the eighteen months since they had last met, Christina felt that she had been through a lifetime of experience, which must surely show on her face. Yet Jeremy seemed untouched; still the same corn-gold hair, still the same blue eyes, the faintly smiling mouth. They looked at each other in silence for a moment.

'Well, cousin.' The voice was the same as ever too,

smooth and cultivated. 'As beautiful as ever, I see. You should always wear those shades of gold and brown – except when you wear kingfisher blue, of course, to bring out the auburn in your hair, or jade to match those dangerous eyes. But I daresay your husband tells you these things often enough.'

'Often enough,' Christina agreed steadily. 'You look well too, Jeremy.'

'Oh, I manage, I manage. I brought a small gift for the birthday boy.' He laid a small parcel on the table.

In spite of her distrust, Christina couldn't help feeling a spurt of pleasure. 'Oh, how kind! Not many –' She broke off.

'Not many people have remembered him. I thought as much. The sins of the fathers, and the mothers. Rather unfair, don't you think? So I thought perhaps I might be allowed – well, to take an interest. To show no hard feelings, you know.' He paused. 'There *are* no hard feelings, I trust?'

Christina shrugged. 'I haven't really thought about it.'

'Ah, now, that can't be true. It can't have mattered as little as that. No, I would imagine you've thought about it a good deal – not, perhaps, so much since the admirable Joe came back into your life, but still . . .' He eyed her brightly, head on one side. 'Christina, let's deal honestly with each other. It was a difficult time for both of us. Things were said – well, let's say in the heat of the moment, a good deal was said that ought not have been. Things that weren't really meant, weren't even true. I was hasty and unwise, I freely admit it. But I've been punished, haven't I? I lost you, after all.' He moved closer to her. 'Let's be friends again, shall we?' he murmured persuasively. 'Forget the past: start again. What do you say?'

Christina looked up at him, wavering. It was true that she had not thought much about Jeremy since her marriage. But now, seeing him again, all the old feelings were coming back; all the confusion of doubt and trust, friendship and anger. She tried to think clearly.

'Wordsley's too small for feuds,' Jeremy continued. 'And glassmaking is too closely tied with tradition. We have long lives to live, you and I, and I don't want to be a bitter old man with a family he doesn't see. Look ahead, and tell me what you see for us in forty, fifty years' time. Shouldn't we make it up now?'

She smiled at the picture, seeing herself and Jeremy in two invalid chairs, refusing to acknowledge each other as they were pushed along the street.

'That's better,' he said quietly.

'Oh, very well. We'll be friends again.' She gave him her hand. 'Come to supper next week – Saturday. Joe will be home.'

'And if I'm to be friends with you, I must be with him too. Well, so be it. I hope he agrees!' Jeremy took out his pocket watch. 'And now I must be going. You'll give little Paul my present, won't you? And next time I hope you'll allow me to see him. I hear he walks now.'

'He learned a week ago – he can manage a few steps and then he falls.' Christina watched as he went to the door. 'Thank you for coming, Jeremy.'

He sketched a bow. 'Thank you for receiving me. I'm glad this threshold is not forbidden to me any more. It's been a long, sad time for me, Christina – little cousin.'

The door closed behind him and Christina stood quite still. It had been a strange, disturbing day, filled with memories and echoes from the past. She had woken to thoughts of Jean-Paul – on his son's first birthday, it would have been strange if she had not. And there had been Joe, leaning over her with passion already in his face, reminding her of the love they shared. And now, Jeremy, coming to offer friendship.

She was still not sure about his plea. But there was nothing he could do to harm her now. The glasshouse was safe in her hands and Joe's, with the men settled again and production increasing every day. There was really no reason to refuse Jeremy's outstretched hand.

As she went back up the stairs to the nursery, Christina felt a great contentment fill her heart. Life from now on was going to be good. She had Joe; she had Paul, and in time there would be other children. And although she was no longer a Henzel, there was her son to carry on the name. The house of Henzel would continue and go from strength to strength.

Nothing could prevent that.

Chapter Twenty-Two

Cholera.

Ever since the great outbreak of 1832, it had scourged the crowded towns and cities, laying its dead hand over the helpless population. In that first dreadful epidemic, striking Stourbridge in July and spreading rapidly, it had taken at least two thousand Black Country people by the time autumn came to touch the trees. Churchyards filled quickly; in Dudley, by September 1st, both St Thomas's and St Edmund's were full and victims had to be taken to Netherton for burial. Since then, its spectre had stalked the land. Sporadic outbreaks occurred, and nobody knew why. It was the miasma from the raw sewage that flowed in the gutters, said some, and people went about with handkerchiefs pressed to their noses. Or it was rats; and impossible to rid the streets and alleys of their scurrying presence. One of these outbreaks had killed Frederic Henzel. And now the menace walked again.

There was cholera in Stourbridge; in Coseley, and in the Lye, where Maggie Haden still lived with her daughter.

Emily was just two years old and toddling with the other children. Her playground was the gutter, her toys an old, broken peg and a piece of rag she called her dolly. She clutched them to her wherever she went. Most of her days she spent in and around the nail-shop where Maggie worked long, hard hours, heating, hammering and cutting a thousand or more nails a day.

They still lived with old Em, in the mud house. Life was a little easier for them than for most, because Maggie was given a few coppers each week by Mrs Jenner at the Henzel back door. Since the day when she had gone there in desperation to seek Joe and found compassion in Christina, she had returned regularly and the money was always there. And often there would be a fresh-baked loaf to go with it, or a dish of scraps left over from the kitchen table. Maggie would accept it all without question; her haughty pride had gone long since.

She had been to Henzel Court on the day when Em died.

'She wor all right when I left this morning,' Maggie told her neighbours frantically as they came crowding in. 'Just had a bit of a backache, like, but that weren't nothing. She wor talkin' about the old days – cheerful as a cricket. An' now this! What is it, for God's sake?'

Milly Cripp, who had suckled Emily along with her own Ben until Ben had died, edged nearer to take a look at the contorted body.

'She didn't die easy, look. Holdin' her stomach, see. And look at her face – that's pain, that is.' She moved away quickly, her face frightened. 'That's cholera.'

'Cholera!'

They all moved back, staring fearfully down at the old woman on her bed of rags.

'Her'll hev to be buried,' Maggie said, clutching Emily to her. 'What shall I do?'

'What shall we all do?' Milly muttered. 'The hot weather's startin' and cholera allus comes with the heat. Get the minister, Maggie – burying's his work. An' he might do a bit of prayin' as well, God knows, we're goin' to need it.'

She turned and followed the rest of the neighbours out of the house. And Maggie, left alone with her baby and the corpse, felt loss settle over her like a dreary, grey cloud.

'She wor my friend,' Maggie said aloud, looking down at the crumpled body that lay shrunken in death. 'I never had no other friends.'

Maggie hadn't cried for a long time. But now the slow, difficult tears fell from her eyes and dropped on to the silent body. And before she went to fetch the minister, she said her goodbyes to the only real friend she had ever known.

That was the beginning of the cholera outbreak. Within three weeks, a quarter of the inhabitants of the Lye had caught the disease; within a month it was a third. The death cart, hauled slowly through the narrow streets to collect the bodies of the victims, became a regular visitor. Pits were dug for mass graves, and the services held over them were brief.

Maggie went once to Henzel Court and was told sharply by Mrs Jenner not to go near the house again. 'You can have some extra money and a pie,' the cook declared, feeling sorry for the ragged girl in spite of her own fear, 'an' don't come back till it's all over down there.' That's if you're still alive to come back, she added silently, looking at the thin, haggard face. And if you haven't brought it to us as thanks for the mistress's kindness.

Maggie had not brought it to Henzel Court. But already she was marked down by the killer. And it was only a few days later that she felt the first cramping pains, the first break of sweat on her brow, and knew that she was doomed.

Christina, having tea, was surprised when Rose came into the room with a scared face and told her there was a 'person' at the kitchen door.

'The *kitchen* door?' Christina said. 'Whoever is it?'

'I don't know, madam. I've never seen him before. He says he's come with a message and it's got to be given to you, personal.'

'Well, I'll come, then. I daresay it's someone from the glasshouse – a muddle over a new mixture we're trying, or which pots are to be changed today, or something of that kind.'

The messenger was a boy, barely twelve years old by the look of him. He was barefoot and grimy, clad in filthy rags, his arms and legs like sticks. He was delving into a bowl of bread and soup given him by Mrs Jenner, scooping the food hastily into his mouth with his dirty hands as if he expected that at any moment the bowl would be torn from his skinny grasp.

'Well, who are you?' Christina asked, looking down at the urchin. 'What message do you have for me?'

He scraped out the last few scraps and licked his fingers. His eyes were frightened, darting swiftly this way and that, but he answered readily enough.

'It's for Mrs Compson.'

'I am Mrs Compson.'

'Well, then, it's Mag Haden, her that lived with old Em down Lye Waste. She've got a babby, says you give her money.'

'Maggie Haden? Did she send you here with a message for me? What is it?' Christina eyed him with suspicion. It seemed more likely that he had heard Maggie talking about her and come to see what pickings there might be for himself. And wasn't there cholera in the Lye?

His words confirmed her thought. 'She's sick, miss. Can't get out of her bed, and like to die. Liggin' there like a dead 'un already, but she told me to come up and fetch you to her. There's summat she wants to tell you, summat you got to hear.'

Christina stared at him. Maggie, dying, and asking for her. Wanting to tell her something – what could Maggie have to tell her? Her mind went back to the day when Maggie too had stood at this back door, screaming abuse at Jeremy as the tears streamed down her face and she clutched Joe's baby to her bosom. Where was that baby now? Dying with its mother?

'Wait,' she said, 'I'll come.'

Mrs Jenner had been standing behind her at the door, convinced that the urchin meant to steal whatever he could lay hands on.

470

'Go to the Lye, madam?' she exclaimed, scandalized. 'You can't do that!'

'And why not?'

'A hundred reasons!' Mrs Jenner's outrage sounded in her voice. 'They've cholera there, for a start – why, the boy says Mag Haden's dying of it. And even if they hadn't – 'tis no place for a lady to venture into. Why, there's the worst housen in all Stourbridge down there, an' the worse folk too – always has been, ever since them gypsies first come. Give 'un a penny or two, madam, and send him back – God knows what he's brought here already.'

'Tell Jake to bring the trap round immediately, and prepare some food and milk, Mrs Jenner,' Christina said as if she had not heard the cook's words. And she hurried away to gather together a few clean towels and cloths.

In her haste there was no time to think of why she had been summoned by Maggie. Within minutes, the trap, with the small boy huddled wide-eyed in one corner of it and Christina in the other, rattled away down the drive. Only as they passed the glasshouse did it occur to her that she ought to have sent word to Joe.

It was not long before the trap, driven by a reluctant Jake, turned away from the streets Christina knew and began to penetrate areas she had only heard about. And nothing she had heard prepared her for the squalor that she saw now on every side. She sat, stunned into silence, only her eyes moving in disbelieving horror. This was what she'd always meant to investigate, and had never found time for; in streets like this, people lived and brought up their families. And she had never really known. The Lye was, as everyone said, the worst of all. And the stench of sickness hit her as the pony's head turned towards the foul streets. Jake reined in and turned to her.

'Don't you think I'd better go back, madam? This is no place for you, and it's dangerous to venture further. The master –'

'Where does Maggie live?' Christina asked the boy, cutting across Jake's words.

He nodded his matted head. 'Over there, miss. That house.'

'Then I'll get down here. You needn't wait, Jake, if you'd rather not. I can find my own way home.'

Jake's snort indicated what he thought of this, and in grudging silence he flicked the reins and the pony ambled on, coming to a halt outside Maggie's house. Christina stepped down.

'Hand me the bundles. You can bring the food,' she said to the boy, and went inside.

It took her a moment or two to accustom her eyes to the dimness and rather longer to overcome the nausea induced by the smell. But as soon as she could see, she went forward and bent over the woman lying on the makeshift bed in the corner. The child was beside her in a cot, made from an old box and padded with sacking.

'Maggie? How are you feeling?'

The once proud head, with its mat of greasy hair, turned and dull eyes stared at her. She doesn't know me, Christina thought, and then saw recognition creep in, and tears ooze slowly on to the sunken cheeks.

'Miss Christina?'

'That's right. I've come to see how you are.'

'Poorly, miss. I ent got long now.' The voice was dry and cracked, a bare thread of sound. 'I'm glad you come.'

'I've brought some soup. Won't you sit up a little and try to take some?'

The head moved slowly from side to side. 'I couldn't swallow it miss. It's too late for that now. I'd like some water, though.'

'Water.' It was the one thing Christina had not thought of. She looked around but there was none, only a cracked cup and an empty bucket.

'Go and fetch water,' she said to the boy, but he shook his head.

472

'Tap's not turned on, miss.'

'The tap –?' She stared at him uncomprehendingly and then turned impatiently back to Maggie. 'Milk, I've brought milk, have some of that. Look, I'll pour it out –'

'Give it to Emily, miss. She ent sick yet. She might live, if someone takes her on. Give it to her and let me see her drink it – there, ent that good, my lovely?'

Christina fed the child, her heart torn with pity. She looked at the small, square face with its dark brown eyes and frame of dirty black hair, and saw Joe. Joe's daughter, living in squalor, surrounded by disease, while her own son lay in a comfortable cradle and spurned food that children like this one would think a feast.

'Is there nothing I can do for you, Maggie?' she asked. 'I've brought fresh bedding and towels.'

'There ent no ease for me now, miss. I just wanted to see you, to tell you . . .' Her eyes wandered from Christina's face. 'They tell me you wed my Joe.'

'Yes, that's right.'

'He allus wanted you. I were never first with him. And that Mr Jeremy . . .' She raised herself slightly in the bed, her eyes lightened by a tiny spark of urgency. 'You want to watch him, miss. He ent no good, that one. He's bad – bad all through.' Her words were coming rapidly now, on short, panting breaths, as if she were afraid she had not the time to say all she needed to say. 'Wanted me to be a whore, he did, for the Frenchman. I wish I had now! He'd still be alive today if I'd done as Mr Jeremy said – aye, and you wed to him as 'twas meant, and Joe and me in our own house as we ought to hev been all along. But I didn't know – how was I to know what'd happen?'

She fell back, breathing hard, moans of pain issuing between her clenched teeth. Frantically, Christina dipped her finger into the milk and spread it on the cracked lips. Maggie's tongue came out, black and swollen, licking with painful desperation, and Christina gave her more.

'Tell me what you mean,' she said when Maggie's

breathing had eased a little. 'What was it you didn't know? What did Jeremy want you to do? *Why would Jean-Paul still be alive?*'

'I told you, he wanted me to be a whore, so that you'd not want to wed the Frenchman after all. He wanted you for himself – you and the glasshouse. I wouldn't do it, though I'd hev done it if I'd known what it meant – for him and me. I'll be glad to die now, and that's the truth, for this is no life here, and I don't suppose my babby'll be long in following.'

'But why would Jean-Paul – the Frenchman – why would he still be alive? What did you have to do with his death?'

The weary eyes turned to her face. 'I didn't hev nothing to do with it, miss. But Mr Jeremy did. He told me, that day in your garden. He threatened to do the same to me. He never said as much, but he pushed your Frenchman into the pot that day and killed him. That's what he meant, anyway. That's my belief.' She lifted herself again, using the last of her strength as she did so. 'That's what I wanted to tell you, miss. They blamed my Joe, I know they did. *You* did. Well, he never did it. It wor Mr Jeremy and he ought to hang for it too. Hang by the neck, up on Gibbet Hill.' She told her story with long pauses between the words, pauses in which she sank back and Christina feared she had died. But it was as if she could not die until she had finished, as if she were driven to tell the story she had kept to herself for so long.

When it was all over, she lay back. Christina gave her some more milk and the tongue came out and licked, more slowly now, as if it really didn't matter any more. And then a film came over the dull eyes and the lids dropped slowly to conceal them. The slight, faint breathing stopped and Maggie lay still for ever.

Christina left the food for the boy who had brought Maggie's message to her. She left money to pay for the burial and to buy himself more food when that had gone, and she told him to come to the glasshouse when the epidemic was over and ask for a job. His name, he said, was Ben Taylor, and she promised to tell the overseer she had sent him.

She wrapped Emily up in the clean cloths and towels she had taken for Maggie, and took her out to the trap. They went back to Wordsley, travelling as fast as Jake could make the pony go over the rough roads. And as they passed the cone, Christina saw Joe coming out with the old pot, white-hot, to send it rolling on the ground, and with one flash of memory knew the nature of the spectre which had haunted her marriage. The doubt, tiny but destructive, which had come between them, was clear to her at last.

She called to Jake to halt the trap and went across to where Joe was standing with the other men, taking a moment to catch their breath before starting to set the new pot. He looked down at her in surprise, his brows raised as he saw the bundle in her arms.

'Look, Joe,' she said, 'this is your daughter. Emily. I've brought her home.'

Christina's arrival with Emily caused almost as much consternation as there had been when she came home married to Joe Compson.

'From the Lye!' Susan exclaimed, throwing up her hands. 'But there's disease there – cholera! Christina, what have you done?'

'Simply brought Joe's daughter home to him, where she belongs.' Christina looked down at the small face, bewildered yet stoical, already set with the lines that indicated the same stubborn determination as Joe's. 'Now that her mother is dead, who better to take care of her?'

'But she's a – a –' Susan thought better of her words and stopped. 'You say her mother is dead? What did she die of?'

'Cholera, I believe. She lived for only a few minutes after I arrived there. I brought Emily away immediately.' Christina raised her eyes and fixed her aunt with a gaze that was full of appeal. 'What else could I have done, Aunt Susan? Who else would have taken her? And how could I leave her in such conditions – it's appalling there, quite unbelievable.'

'Naturally something should have been done for the child, the workhouse would have taken her, no doubt. But to bring her here, when she almost certainly has the disease already upon her – I simply cannot understand what possessed you to do such a thing. And why did you go there in the first place? You must have known the dangers. If you'd no care for yourself, you might think of others. Your own child . . . The disease spreads, it's carried on the air. You breathe it in; you touch it on the skin. We shall all have it now, and die horribly, and all because of a woman who was no better than she should be and a by-blow of your husband's.' Susan covered her face. 'What will you do next, Christina? Are you determined to kill us all, if you cannot bring us to ruin?'

Christina was silent. She held Emily on her hip, looking into the dirty face. It could not be said that Joe's child was pretty, but food and a good wash ought to bring an improvement. And she did not look ill, in spite of having shared a house with the dreaded King Cholera.

'We'll put her into that little room near the kitchen,' she said. 'There's a door into the garden; she can play outside. I'll engage a nursemaid for her and they can stay there alone for a while. If Emily has caught the disease, it will soon show and if she hasn't she can share the nursery with Paul.'

'You mean you intend to keep her here?'

'Aunt Susan,' Christina said steadily, 'this is Joe's daughter. Why shouldn't I accept her? He has accepted my son.'

476

In fact, Joe seemed to find it more difficult to accept Emily than Paul. After that first shocked stare, outside the cone, his face had darkened and he had turned abruptly away. And when he returned home and came into their bedroom, and Christina told him what had been arranged, he merely shrugged.

'Do what you think best. If that's what you want.'

'What *I* want? Isn't it what *you* want? Your own daughter, here, being brought up as one of our own children?'

'Look, I never knew her as a daughter,' he retorted. 'She was Mag Haden's through and through; I was tricked into giving her that child, so that she could force me to wed. And afterwards, when I would have helped her, she told me to get out. All right, I'm sorry she's dead and for the way she died, but there's plenty of others gone the same way – my own sister Sarah for one. And I never asked you to go and get the bairn. So do whatever you want. But don't imagine it's what *I* want.'

'All right,' Christina flashed, 'I will. I *do* want Emily here, and I want to bring her up as our child. So you'll please act like a father to her, just as you do to Paul, do you understand?'

'I understand you're coming the fine lady over me again,' he said with a glint in his eye. 'Don't forget I'm your husband now. You promised to love, honour and obey.'

'I do love you! And I honour you. But as for obeying – you've just told me to do as I please over Emily.'

'And *you've* just told *me* how to behave in my own home.'

'Your own home, perhaps – but not your own house. This is *my* house, Joe, and don't you forget it. And I say who comes into it.'

'Like your cousin, Jeremy, I suppose, to sneer and air his fancy ways. Of course, I know I'm only a common workman and you miss his fine company, but you married *me*, don't forget – asked me on your bended knees, if I remember right and –'

'I did no such thing!' Christina stopped suddenly. 'Joe, what are we quarrelling about? Are you really so angry that I brought Emily here? If you could have seen her, the conditions she and Maggie were living in, you'd know I couldn't possibly have left her there, with no one of her own to take care of her.' She stepped close to him and slid her hands up his chest, feeling the muscles beneath the thick working shirt. 'Let me keep her, Joe. She reminds me so much of you. You needn't see her if you don't want to.'

'And how do I do that, go blind?' he muttered, and slipped his hands round her waist. 'All right, Christina, you have your way. Emily stays here. I just didn't want you hurt – seeing another woman's child every day. You're sure it won't upset you? Certain?'

'I could hardly say that, when I have my own son by another man in the same nursery,' she smiled. 'Let's say we begin equal, shall we, Joe? One each – and the next will belong to both of us.'

He drew her close. She could smell the odour of the glasshouse on him, a combination of sweat and soot and tangy metal. There was an urgency in his hands that transmitted itself through her body, and she felt the now familiar heat course through her veins, weakening her knees and tingling low in her stomach.

Joe's fingers were already working on the buttons that fastened the back of her dress.

'Let's make a start on that now, shall we?' he whispered. 'Let's seal it with a bit more than a loving kiss.' He slid the dress from her shoulders and laid a kiss in the hollow of each collarbone, while he pulled at the fastenings of her stays. 'Come to bed, Christina.'

She went; but even at the height of their passion she could not rid herself of the memory of Maggie's voice, telling her in dry, cracked tones what had really happened that day in the glass cone.

Jeremy or Joe? What was the truth?

She asked Jeremy to come to see her on an evening when Joe would be at the cone and Susan out at dinner with Samuel and Lavinia. Ruth was dispatched to her parents' house, and when Jeremy arrived she told Rose that she would not be needing her again that night.

He stood just inside the door, regarding her with wary eyes and a faint smile on his face.

'This is an unexpected pleasure, sweet cousin, an invitation to visit! Does your husband know?'

'Never mind about Joe,' Christina said crisply. 'I have something I want to ask you.'

His eyebrows rose. 'A royal command, no less! So I am here to answer questions.'

'I went down to the Lye last Friday. I saw Maggie Haden.'

Now he did look surprised. 'Maggie! That trollop! Now, why on earth should you do that? And at the Lye, too, nasty, unhealthy place, I hope you didn't bring back more than you bargained for.'

'As a matter of fact, I did.' She thought briefly of Emily, already filling out and developing the colour of wild roses in her cheeks. 'But that needn't concern you.' She paused, watching him. 'Maggie told me something very interesting.'

'Indeed?' he said with a yawn. 'Christina, if you've brought me all this way to discuss Maggie Haden, I suggest you'd find out a good deal more from your husband. He knew her *much* better than I.'

'He didn't know this. Maggie Haden came here, if you remember, quite a long time ago. She accused you of wanting her to help you trick Jean-Paul, to prevent my marrying him. And when she refused, she says you took other measures – more desperate ones.'

She was watching him closely now and saw the change of colour in his face. And evidently he felt it, for he turned away, laughing in an artificial, forced way that he immediately turned into a cough.

'Desperate measures indeed! Was she perhaps delirious? I hear there's cholera down at the Lye.'

'She had cholera, certainly. I don't think she was delirious.'

Jeremy turned back and stared at her. 'She had cholera? And you stayed there and talked to her? Christina, are you mad? Do you want to bring it here and kill us all? And after what happened to your own brother too?'

'Not everyone catches the disease. If I do – so be it. But I judged it important to hear what she had to say.'

'And what was that?' Jeremy sneered.

Flatly, Christina said, 'She told me that you killed Jean-Paul by pushing him into the furnace.'

There was complete silence. Jeremy was as white as marble. He glanced quickly at the door, as if looking for escape. Christina moved so that she barred his way. His eyes glanced at her, briefly, and shifted rapidly away.

'Is it true?' she asked, although she hardly needed to hear the answer.

'True?' His voice was high, nervous. 'Of course it's not true! It's a damned lie – it's spite, that's all, the venom of a slut of the streets. You saw her that day, Christina, you saw what kind of a woman she is. She wants money, money to get her out of the cesspit she's made for herself down there. What's she threatening – to spread the story around Stourbridge if she's not paid off? Something like that, I'll be bound!'

'She's not threatening anything,' Christina said quietly. 'She died as soon as she had told me.'

He stared at her, then laughed again. 'Died! Then there's nothing to worry about! Provided she's told no one else, the story can die with her. The whole thing can be forgotten.'

480

'*Forgotten*? You seem to forget yourself that Jean-Paul was the man I loved – the man I planned to marry! I shall never be able to forget his death.' Christina's voice rang through the room. 'Neither shall I forget what Maggie Haden told me. Jeremy, I ask you again – *is it true*?'

'And I tell you again, it's not!' he snapped. He looked at her and his expression changed, the anger dying out of it to be replaced by a softer look that she eyed with mistrust. 'Christina, let's stop quarrelling. What are we talking about after all – the word of a common whore against mine. How can you believe what she said when you've seen the kind of life she led? All right, I treated her a little unkindly, perhaps, but it was no worse than a girl like that deserves. And I had to stop her fastening her claws into you, for that's what she would have done. You'd have had her at the door every week, begging for food and money, if I hadn't intervened that day –'

'And threatened her with the same fate as you dealt Jean-Paul,' Christina interposed.

'I *didn't*, I tell you. Oh, I might have told *her* something like that, but it was only to frighten her off, it wasn't true. Jean-Paul's death was an accident, nobody was at fault –'

'So why did you tell me Joe did it?' she asked, and saw him stop short.

'I tell you that?' he said at last. 'No, you're mistaken there – I would never point the finger at another man. It was an accident, Christina, nothing more. You were over-wrought, your memory deceives you.'

'My memory is very clear. You told me, oh, very reluctantly, that Joe pushed Jean-Paul into the furnace. You whipped up my grief and anger, and when I said I never wanted to see Joe again, that I'd like him to starve in the gutter, you undertook to remove him from my sight. And sent him to Newcastle, to be of benefit to Cousin Alfred and the rest of you.'

Jeremy looked at her and then shrugged. 'You have it all worked out very neatly in your head. Obviously you will not listen to reason. But Christina, my dear –' He came towards her, hands outstretched, a boyish appeal on his handsome face. 'Why torture yourself with all this now? I told you before, I was jealous of Compson. He had such a hold on you, and I admit I wanted you for myself. I believed you had some feeling for me – with him out of the way, there would have been a chance for me. Can you really blame me for what I did?' He was close to her now, looking down, head tipped sideways, a charming, half-rueful smile on his face and one eyebrow quirked. 'You know, there really was something between us once,' he said softly, and lifted one hand to stroke her cheek, gently, sensuously. 'There was a response when you looked at me; when I touched you. I think it's still there now . . . isn't it? Christina?'

Christina watched, mesmerised, as he bent closer. His lips were almost on hers; she could feel the soft brush of them, teasing and tantalising. His breath was warm. 'I know it's still there,' he murmured, and slid his arms around her body.

With a movement that was as quick as the spring of a leopard, Christina leapt away. She twisted herself from his encircling arms, hitting out blindly with her own, and felt a satisfying crack as her hand caught him across the cheekbone. With an exclamation, he reached for her again, his fingers cruel this time on her arms, and again she twisted away, using her nails like talons to maintain her freedom. Startled and bleeding, he let go of her and she backed against a chair and stood watching him, breathing hard.

'You little hussy! Why, you're no better than a street-girl yourself.'

His eyes hardened. He moved towards her again and Christina backed further. Suddenly afraid, she glanced towards the door, but he was now barring her way as she had barred his. The bell, too, was out of reach. Jeremy read her glance and laughed harshly.

482

'There's no help there, sweet cousin. And didn't I hear you tell Rose that you wouldn't be wanting her again? So no one's likely to walk in on us, are they?' His face changed, the smile disappearing, a deliberate cruelty replacing the handsome little-boy look that had ensnared Aunt Susan and almost deceived Christina herself. 'All right,' he said slowly. 'So we've come to a showdown. There's nothing worse you'll think of me now.' He came close and laid his hands on her shoulders, while Christina stared up at him, her heart beating with slow, heavy terror. 'I might as well take what you've denied me all these years,' he said thickly. 'Yes – denied me. Held it out like a prize to be awarded for good behaviour, then snatched it away when I was almost at the winning-post. Have you any idea what that did to me, you stubborn little trollop? Do you know how it made me feel, the way you flaunted yourself at me and then withdrew – and what it was like, not only to suffer that but to be castigated for it by my father and my uncles? You humiliated me, made me look a fool; you made me a laughing-stock. I've never forgiven you for that.'

'And does being a laughing-stock matter more than being a murderer?' she demanded. 'Take your hands off me, Jeremy, and leave this house. I want no more of you.'

'You want no more of me?' Again, the harsh, frightening laughter. 'Then I'm afraid you are going to get something you don't want, little cousin. You're going to get as much of me as I can give.' His hands were wrenching at her dress now, ripping the soft material from her body. Christina cried out and pulled at his hands, twisting and turning to escape, but Jeremy was using all his strength now and she was helpless. She fought, scratched, punched, kicked at any part she could reach – but it was like fighting an octopus. He was never still, twisting and evading as she struggled, and all the time he was tearing her clothes, so that her dress fell in tatters around her and her breasts spilled from her broken stays.

483

'Marry a common workman, would you!' he growled as his teeth nipped cruelly at her ears and shoulders, moving down to bite into the softness of her breasts so that she cried out again, weeping with pain and fury. 'Give him what you refused me – you, so proud you'd bear a bastard from a Frenchman! I've wanted to do this for a long time, Christina, I've wanted over and over again to teach you a lesson, to tame your wildness and beat your obstinacy into submission. If you'd been my wife . . . Why, you vixen!'

Christina, now half-naked, was fighting harder than ever, using her feet and knees now to strike wherever she could. But her disadvantage was too great; Jeremy was twice her size, with all the strength of bone and muscle of a slim but sinewy man. He had both her wrists in one hand now, held above her head, and he was forcing her to the floor, lying heavily on top of her while with his other hand he fumbled with his own clothes. And with his mouth he was stopping any screams that might have penetrated to the kitchen two floors below.

'Now,' he muttered, and she could feel his naked thighs against hers, the rigid muscle ready to make its final violent assault. 'Now we'll see who calls the tune . . .'

With a moan of fear and rage, Christina lay powerless beneath him. It was as good as over. She felt the bitter nausea rise in her throat and closed her eyes. Let it be quick, she prayed, just let it be quick.

What in God's name is going on here?

The voice, accustomed to bellowing across the clamour of a glasshouse, thundered through the air.

Unbelievingly, Jeremy turned his head and froze. She felt the madness die out of him. And then he was jerked away from her, lifted bodily into the air and thrown like a doll to the floor, several yards away.

'What the hell's he done to you? Are you hurt? Christina, my love . . .'

'Joe!' she whispered, and tried to struggle to her feet. But her legs were weak and she fell back again to the floor, looking up with beseeching eyes. Joe bent and lifted her, with the utmost tenderness, into his arms.

'The bastard,' he muttered, looking down into her bruised face. 'I'll kill him . . .' He laid her on the sofa and turned back to where Jeremy, his fingers shaking as he tried to gather his clothes together, was just getting to his feet.

'You filthy swine,' he said between his teeth. 'You low, crawling, slimy reptile. You're not fit to live.' He dragged Jeremy to his feet and knocked him down with a massive, bunched fist. 'Not fit to live . . .' He lifted him, knocked him back to the floor and then stood looking down with contempt, slowly rubbing his knuckles. 'Well? Aren't you going to fight?'

Jeremy touched his bleeding lip and stared up with an attempt at his old condescension. 'Fight *you*? I've better things to do.'

'So I saw,' Joe said grimly. 'In that case, I'll simply thrash you.' And he proceeded to do just that, knocking Jeremy systematically around the drawing room that was Susan Henzel's pride and joy until there was scarcely an ornament left whole or a piece of furniture left standing.

Christina, shivering on the sofa around which the battle raged – for Jeremy was forced now to try to defend himself – watched with appalled fascination. More than once, she tried to intervene, afraid that Joe really would kill her devious cousin. But her pleas went unheard and she could do nothing but crouch there, the tears running down her cheeks, shuddering with shocked reaction.

At last Joe tired of his game. He took Jeremy by the collar and thrust him bodily from the room. He slammed the door and turned to survey the wreckage.

'I've wanted to do that for a long time,' he said, unconsciously echoing Jeremy's words.

'Oh, *Joe*,' Christina whispered, and he came quickly

across the room and took her in his arms. 'Joe, thank goodness you came. I thought – I thought he was going to –'

'He bloody well *was* going to,' Joe said shortly. 'And if he had, I'd have killed him for certain, and no playing about. Christina, my love, are you all right? Did he hurt you? You're all bruised, look, here on your face and neck. And your shoulders. And –' His eyes moved to her breasts, covered now with the purple marks of Jeremy's teeth, and he swore. 'Dammit, I wish I *had* killed him! What in hell was it all about?'

'I told him about Maggie,' she whispered. 'I told him she'd sent for me – and I told him what Maggie told me.'

'What Maggie told you?' His brows came together. 'I didn't know she'd told you anything. I thought she'd just asked you to take Emily.'

Christina shook her head. 'No. She didn't ask that. I did that because I wanted to. She sent for me because there was something important that she knew, and thought I should know too.' She looked up into his dark brown eyes, her own a clear green in spite of her pain. 'She told me that Jeremy killed Jean-Paul. He pushed him into the furnace and then put the blame on you. And I – God forgive me, Joe – I half believed him. I never knew –' she began to weep '– even after we were married, I never really knew whether it was true or not.'

He stared at her. His eyes darkened and then grew lighter. A look of pure relief spread over his lean, brown face.

'*He* pushed the Frenchman in? He *meant* to do it? Christina, I've never known for sure what happened that day. I swear I never meant Thietry that sort of harm, bitter though I felt, but I've always had a sort of fear that I might have pushed him, that it might have been me. I could never remember just where I was, or where he was – we were all in a huddle, it could have been any of us . . . But it was *him*, after all.' Forgetting her bruises, he clasped her against him in a great hug of relief. 'And I was always afeared, somehow, that you did still blame me.'

'I know,' she said. 'It's been between us all this time. It's been like a blemish on our marriage – on our love.'

'But not any more,' Joe said, loosening his arms and bending to kiss her with infinite gentleness. 'We'll be all right from now on, my love. There's nobody else to come between us.'

He carried her upstairs and laid her in the big bed they shared. And although her body was sore and aching, she would not let him go but clung to him and begged him to make love to her, and when he resisted, for fear of hurting her, she stroked him and caressed him, using all her skills, inborn and learned, to make it impossible for him to refuse.

And when he finally gave in and they came together, it was in the gentlest, most tender union they had ever experienced. And the most complete.

1851

Chapter Twenty-Three

The Crystal Palace, they called it.

Christina and Joe went to see it in July, taking Harry and Ruth with them. It stood in the middle of Hyde Park; a shining canopy that glittered in the sun like a creation from a fairy tale.

Christina and Joe, walking arm in arm, strolled slowly around the outside of the tremendous structure, marvelling at the sheer size. 'Nearly three times the size of St Paul's,' Harry told them, 'and almost three hundred thousand panes of sheet glass!' He had also known the exact weight of the iron used ('Forty-five thousand tons'), the length of the guttering ('Twenty-four *miles*') and the number of men employed to build it ('Over two thousand at one stage alone'). These figures, and many others which he quoted to anyone who would listen, were of absorbing interest to Harry, for he was now working with his idol Brunel on the plans for the construction of Paddington Railway Station, designed by the same Joseph Paxton who had designed the Crystal Palace itself.

'There are trees in there,' Joe remarked as they approached the entrance. 'Great elms. And birds, flying about amongst the branches. You'd think they'd be frightened away by it all.'

'Frightened? How could anyone be frightened by this?' Christina stared up as they passed through the doors. 'Look at the sky, so blue through the roof. And the flowers and plants – why, it's like a huge garden. There *ought* to be birds. And surely I can hear organ music and – oh, *Joe*! The fountain!'

The great main avenue was before them, thronged

with a coloured mass of people. On either side stretched rows of stands and exhibits, overhung with flags and banners which added yet more colour to the basic design of red, yellow, blue and white. The galleries along each side were of wrought-iron and lattice, and above all soared the massive filigree of iron and glass that seemed to fill the great spaces with a glowing light, an airy stillness that echoed to the chatter of human voices and the clatter of machines.

But Christina had eyes only for the great fountain, the centre-piece of the whole exhibition. Tall and graceful, it was difficult to believe that its weight (Harry again!) was four tons. It looked as if it must weigh nothing, as if it were spun from the silk of spiders' webs; as transparently dazzling as the water which sprang from its different levels and flung sparkling droplets around its shimmering sides. It was made entirely from crystal, cut and polished to the purity of ice. Together with its sister exhibits, the Alhambra chandelier which was twenty-four feet high and the floor chandelier which stood at eight feet, it drew all eyes. And Christina would have remained in front of it all day, lost in wonder at its ethereal beauty, had not Joe pulled her away at last, complaining that he wanted to see something else besides an oversized ornament. 'Nothing but a damned great frigger,' he remarked caustically, and Christina smiled.

Slowly, they walked around the great glass halls and galleries. There was far too much to see in one visit: as well as the British exhibits, there were sections for Russia, France, Turkey, China, India, Switzerland – the list went on and on. They would come back tomorrow, and the next day, for they were staying a week in London and intended to visit the Great Exhibition several times, as well as seeing the other sights. But today, they were primarily interested in the glass, and in their own stand.

All the same, it took some time to reach it. There was

492

so much else of interest to pass along the way. Christina could not help stopping to exclaim at the elaborate furniture: the '*tête-à-tête*' made by Hilton of Canada, the great bedstead from Austria which looked more like a bishop's tomb, the table from Ireland which was held aloft by the statue of a gladiator. And the diamonds drew her like magnets – the great Koh-i-noor, or Mountain of Light, brought especially from Bombay, and the Hope Diamond, looking like pieces of cut crystal, yet flashing with colours that no crystal had ever yet achieved.

Joe was good-humouredly impatient at her constant digressions, but he was just as bad, as Christina pointed out when he showed a distinct tendency to linger in front of the machinery that was on view, particularly the new express locomotive brought by the South Eastern Railway Company.

'You're as bad as Harry!' she exclaimed, dragging at his sleeve. 'Come back with him tomorrow, and I'll go round with Ruth. But now – do let's go and see the glass.'

And there, at last, it was in glittering display. Vases and jars in every style – Grecian, Etruscan, Egyptian, cut glass, enamelled glass, glass that glowed with the rich colours of ruby, turquoise, and blue, glass that was gilded, glass that was so prickled with decoration that it needed gloved hands to touch it. Glass that shimmered and flashed and shone; glass, glass, glass.

Christina caught her breath. Never had she seen such a vast array of the substance she loved most. Never had she dreamed of such a rich variety of shape and colour, nor known such magic enchantment as that of the glass world which encompassed her at that moment.

How Papa would have loved it, she thought with a sudden pang. And for a few brief, spinning moments, time turned on its head and memories showered around her: her father's death and the reading of his will, with the first signs of his cousins' hostility which later grew and deepened to evil, culminating in a violent and horrible death which, even now, she could not be sure was murder; Jeremy's approaches, and her own trust in him so cruelly destroyed; Jean-Paul, who had introduced her to the delicacies of making love; a skill which she had later been able to bring to her own marriage, enhancing the robust passion she shared with Joe and which showed no signs yet of diminishing.

And Joe: her husband, big and magnetic, secure now in his position, confident enough to let his whole gigantic personality flow freely. Joe, who had won over Aunt Susan and Harry and even Alice and Adela, and who had brought to her life a fulfilment she had never dared dream of.

Occasionally, just occasionally, Christina wondered what her life would have been like, had Jean-Paul lived. And she had finally admitted, not without a certain sadness, that their love was too delicate to survive the rough storms that would certainly have beset them. Christina's nature was too tempestuous, too headstrong for Jean-Paul's sensitivity; she would have come slowly to dominate him and so done them both harm. She needed someone stronger than herself, someone who could go with her and then call halt; someone powerful without being a tyrant, earthy where she was passionate. She needed Joe.

She gazed absently at the shimmering glass and let her mind come forward, to the years since their marriage. It hadn't been an easy time; there had been many difficult moments. Moments like the time when she had risked cholera to bring Emily home and found Susan and Joe, for once, aligned against her and equally furious. And when Adela, refusing to come from Alice's, had said, bitterly, that her life was now ruined. But Adela was married now, to a young relative of Alice's John, in Warwickshire. And, like Aunt Susan, she had finally come to accept Joe, even to like him, though she could never quite forget his origins; but after all, weren't many of the great men today

– including the one-time gardener Paxton, who had designed this beautiful palace of glass – from humble beginnings?

And the rest of the family seemed happy enough too. Alice and John now had three children, a daughter and two sons. Harry was doing well in his chosen career. Ruth was still with Christina, apparently happy enough to be her closest friend and companion. And Aunt Susan was the same as ever; a little more content, perhaps, with a man once more in place as head of the family, but still inclined to throw up her hands and exclaim with disapproval. It wouldn't have seemed the same if she didn't.

As for Christina, she smiled as she thought of her own family. Paul, her first-born who carried the Henzel name yet was unmistakably a Thietry; Emily, who was Joe through and through, five years old now and unmistakably in charge of the nursery; and the two little ones, Roger, conceived, she was sure, on that day when she and Joe had finally come together in true understanding, and Sarah, named for Joe's mother, a rolling, chuckling year-old bundle of mischief and enchantment.

The future generation. She spared a sad thought for Tommy, who had died quite suddenly a year ago, outliving Mrs Jenner's prophecy by several years. His life had been short but she believed it had been happy. Happier than most, for Tommy was rarely seen without a smile on his flattened face and even in death he had worn an aura of peace. They missed him badly, she and Harry and Ruth; none of them had fully realised just what a haven his quiet nursery had made.

Slowly, she and Joe moved around the displays until they came at last to their own. She looked at it critically; the table glass, the epergnes, the chandeliers that they had been making ever since the Exhibition was first announced a year or more ago. All their best designs were there, many of them blown by Joe himself and the other glassmakers he was training to his own exact standards.

They had been carefully packed and transported, polished until they shone with a lambency that almost hurt the eyes. Their colours were rich, their decoration exquisite.

In the centre of the display stood a small raised platform, covered with deep blue velvet, the colour of the midnight sky itself. And on it stood a large glass, gracefully shaped with a line that flowed from foot to lip, its stem twisted and airy yet strong enough to support the heaviness of the thick crystal bowl.

Before it was the inscribed card which announced that Henzel Glass had been awarded one of the Prize Medals for 'excellence in production and workmanship'. Christina felt her hand tighten involuntarily around Joe's. She looked up into his face and smiled.

The Chalice. The symbol of Henzel Glass. Christina felt the tears sting her eyes, remembering the day it had been made. Maggie Haden had been there; it was before she had known Jean-Paul. And none of them had known the future.

She looked at the engraving which Jean-Paul had done without her knowledge. The entwined initials, C and J. Christina and Jean-Paul.

She had thought once that they might be Christina and Jeremy. But now, holding her husband's strong hand, she knew what they stood for and would stand for as long as she lived.

Christina and Joe.